Jarad Henry

than ten years, and is currently a strategic advisor with Victoria Police. He has a degree in criminology and regularly speaks about crime trends at conferences and seminars. Jarad's debut crime novel, *Head Shot*, was shortlisted for the Victorian Premier's Liter y Awards, and for the Ned Kelly Awards Best First Crime Nov( . *Blood Sunset* won the Fellowship of Australian Writers' Jim Iamilton Award, and was shortlisted for *The Australian/Voge* Literary Award.

# JARAD HENRY

# BLOOD SUNSET

ARENA

ALLEN&UNWIN

First published in 2008

Arena Books, an imprint of
Allen & Unwin
83 Alexander Street
Crows Nest NSW 2065
Australia
Phone:    (61 2) 8425 0100
Fax:      (61 2) 9906 2218
Email:    info@allenandunwin.com
Web:      www.allenandunwin.com

National Library of Australia
Cataloguing-in-Publication entry:

Henry, Jarad.
Blood sunset

ISBN 978 1 74175 420 9 (pbk.)

A823.4

Type design by Kirby Stalgis
Set in 12/15 pt Fairfield Light by Midland Typesetters, Australia

**FSC**
**Mixed Sources**
Product group from well-managed forests and other controlled sources

Cert no. SGS-COC-3047
www.fsc.org
© 1996 Forest Stewardship Council

The paper this book is printed on is certified by the © 1996 Forest Stewardship Council A.C. (FSC). SOS holds FSC chain of custody SGS-COC-3047. The FSC promotes environmentally responsible, socially beneficial and economically viable management of the world's forests.

Printed and bound in Australia by The SOS Print + Media Group.

10 9 8 7 6 5 4 3 2

*For the detectives. Nobody sees what you see.*

# 1

*TO GET WHAT YOU WANT, you need to know what you want.* My mother first told me this when I was a young boy. Think hard about what you want, she said, for knowing what you want is more difficult than actually getting it.

It wasn't until a few weeks before my fortieth birthday that I fully understood what she'd meant. I was sitting in an unmarked squad car, tired and hungry and thinking about bed, when a call came over the dispatch that would change the direction of my life forever. Of course, I didn't know that then. If I had, I wouldn't have been nearly so blasé about answering the call.

'VKC to any unit in the vicinity of Luna Park.'

I stifled a yawn, clicked the transmit button and replied with my call sign: 'St Kilda 511.'

'You've got a deceased male, possible drug overdose. Location is at the rear of Café Vit, adjacent to Luna Park. The café owner found the body and is waiting for police. What's your status?'

I groaned. Fatal drug overdoses were always dispatched to detectives in the divisional Criminal Investigation Units. Usually they were straightforward and you were done with them within a couple of hours, but sometimes – especially late at night – you could be stuck forever waiting for the undertakers. I was scheduled to knock off at 7 a.m., and I wasn't interested in overtime that the boss wasn't interested in paying for.

I wished my partner, Cassie Withers, was with me. She'd received a call from the hospital saying her father was crook again and for the past half-hour I'd been filling in the night's running sheet. It was something Cassie normally did and it showed in my handwriting.

'What's your status, 511?'

I clicked the mike. 'Still one up, but I'll handle it. Have the undertakers been dispatched?'

It was a stupid question, more a protest than anything. The dispatcher never called the undertakers unless they were requested to by the investigating officer; in this case, me.

There was a period of silence while the dispatcher thought of a polite answer.

'We'll wait for your instruction, detective,' she said eventually.

'Fine. ETA two minutes.'

Warm coffee sloshed in the foam cup between my legs as I pulled away from the kerb. Fitzroy Street, the main thoroughfare through St Kilda, was calmer than it had been all night. The pubs and restaurants lining the strip were now closed. Only a few nightclubs and convenience stores were still open.

Tall palm trees were silhouetted against the glow of streetlights as I coasted along the Esplanade towards Luna Park. With the window half-down, even in the pre-dawn I could tell tomorrow would be another hot one.

Soon I was at the Acland Street junction where the only signs of life were a row of taxis idling outside the strip clubs and a group of leftover disco-heads munching burgers and fries at McDonald's. Scanning the side of Café Vit, I spotted a loading bay at the northern end of an empty car park. I parked and activated the covert blue and red lights on the dashboard, then gathered my clipboard and daybook, opened the boot and took a torch and a handful of gloves from a dispenser. Almost as an afterthought, I slid my digital camera into my pocket, then walked towards the loading bay. A chubby man in a white shirt stepped out from a doorway at the rear of the café and hurried over, his stumpy legs moving quickly beneath a round belly, like a penguin. Another overweight restaurant owner, I mused. All that food can't go to waste.

'Morning, sir,' I said. 'I'm Detective Sergeant Rubens McCauley. You called the police?'

'Yes, yes, thank God,' the man said, wiping a hand across his meaty face. 'I have dead body in back. Come see.'

A European accent; Dutch or possibly German I thought. We walked to the rear of the café and I noted the loading bay was fenced in at the sides but there was no gate, meaning a person could easily access it. I stopped the man from going any further.

'Where's the body, sir?'

'He is in back, against bin.'

'Just wait here, please. What's your name?'

'I am Karl. Karl Vitazul.'

He held out his hand for me to shake but I was busy opening my daybook. It wasn't the place for handshakes anyway.

'Would you mind spelling that for me, please, sir?' I asked.

He did and I wrote it down. 'Thank you. Do you know the person?'

'I recognise him, but I do not know him.'

'You recognise him? Is he a customer?'

Vitazul frowned, shook his head. 'No, but he visit the park often.'

I stared over at the O'Donnell Gardens, a patch of parkland that backed onto the rear of the café. Black, still mounds lay beneath the palm trees. On warm February nights the homeless didn't need the shelters.

'Is he a vagrant?'

Vitazul shrugged.

3

Deciding not to ask any more questions at this stage, I waited as a police divisional van pulled up next to my car. Our combined flashing lights made the loading bay look like a Vegas show. I watched as Kim Pendlebury stepped out of the van. We'd worked several cases together over the years, including one where her partner had been executed during an underworld war. Kim was a tough cop and a competent investigator, but the case had taken its toll and she'd subsequently transferred out of the detective bureau back into uniform.

'Okay, Mr Vitazul,' I said, 'here's my card. We may need to talk in a minute. For now, this is Sergeant Kim Pendlebury. She's going to ask you some more questions.'

As Kim took Vitazul away, I snapped on a pair of rubber gloves and followed Kim's partner, a younger cop named Mark Finetti, towards the loading bay. Finetti was another story. We'd butted heads on more than a few occasions, mostly because he'd once had a fling with my partner, Cassie, and couldn't get over her promotion to the detective unit, but we'd come to an unspoken understanding since my return to work and now managed to get along. He was a cocky, arrogant bastard, and about as subtle as a flying brick, but there was a place for blokes like him in the job. In joints like St Kilda, you needed the brawn as much as the brain sometimes.

'Another druggie croaks himself on my shift, third since Christmas,' Finetti said, sweeping the torch beam back and forth. 'Why do I always get the shit work?'

'Probably do it because they know you're on duty,' I joked. 'All that muscle you got terrifies them, makes them more nervous than a turkey at Christmas time.'

'Yeah, righto.'

'I'm serious. Soon as word gets out Big Bad Finetti's on the prowl, they all whack up whatever they've got.'

We stepped through the gates to the smell of stale alcohol and food scraps. I used my torch to navigate alongside a rubbish bin so as not to dirty my shirt.

'Got one a while back in his car,' Finetti said. 'Last year. Prick didn't even make it a hundred metres down the street after he scored. Carked it right outside the rehab on Grey Street. Reckon they add that to the road toll?'

'Nah, just the Finetti toll.' I poked him in the back as we squeezed between a row of boxes and crates stacked waist high. 'Still order your uniforms a size too small, show off those pecs?'

'Piss off. Haven't seen you in the weights room lately, McCauley. What's up, getting too old? Got a hernia? Or wait, maybe you just wanna go when nobody's –'

Finetti stopped mid-speech and an uncomfortable silence ensued. It had been a month since my return to work and everyone was pretty used to me being back. It didn't help that I showed no obvious signs of physical injury from the shooting. I half-expected Finetti to apologise but was glad he didn't.

We stopped at a small pile of glass on the ground, which looked like it was from a light bulb. I shone my torch beam at the roof and, sure enough, a globe had been smashed.

'Finetti, get your pen out.'

'Already have. Let me guess, you want me to ask Vitazul about the globe?'

'Just make a note about it. We'll ask him later.'

A row of wheelie bins abutted the rear wall and a set of stairs rose to the back door. I saw the feet first, two runners illuminated in the torch beam. As I approached, I tucked my tie inside my shirt so it wouldn't drape over the body, a trick I'd learnt several years back when I'd ruined a new tie at a crime scene, almost doing the same to the evidence. That sorted, I rolled my sleeves up and ran the torch beam from the feet to the head, realising with a start that the deceased was a teenage boy, maybe fourteen or fifteen. I'd expected him to be older, but I kept that to myself and proceeded to assess the scene. The boy was slumped against one of the bins. A belt was wrapped around his left bicep, a syringe protruded from the crook of his arm and a trickle of dried blood ran down to his wrist. His head sagged, eyes closed, mouth loose and drooping. Strands of brown hair hung from beneath a red baseball cap.

Finetti checked his pulse and said, 'Nada! Cold as leftovers, too. Probably checked out sometime last night.'

I squatted beside Finetti and peered under the boy's cap. The pale face jolted me with the memory of my best mate from high school, Tommy Jackson, who'd gone the same way. The similarity in build and facial structure were remarkable. At the age of eighteen, Jacko had left our childhood town of Benalla and moved to Melbourne, after which I'd never seen him again.

I stepped back from the body and breathed out long and low. It had been almost twenty years since Jacko's death and I didn't want to think about it now.

'What's the matter?' Finetti asked. 'You know him?'

'No.'

'Then what?'

'Never mind.'

He gave me a questioning look, then said, 'Mate, if you want to sit this one out, that's no biggie. Maybe you should take the statement and let Kim work the body?'

I rolled my left shoulder and tried to loosen muscles and ligaments that gripped my joints like an octopus. A familiar metallic taste washed around my mouth.

'Want me to get Kim?' he prodded.

'I said *never mind*.'

Finetti rested the clipboard on his knee. 'Don't get defensive, Rubes. I'm just saying I understand. You've only been back on deck a month and this is your first stiff.'

'Since I've been back,' I corrected. 'Not my first.'

Finetti raised his palms. 'All right, fine. What now?'

'Tell me what you see.'

'Expensive runners, for a start. Seiko watch, probably stolen. New jeans and T-shirt too. Ditto for that.' Finetti lifted the boy's T-shirt and patted the front pockets of his jeans. 'Feels like a wallet in here. Let me get it out, see who he is.'

'Careful,' I said. 'Watch for needles. Better double up.'

He pulled on a second pair of gloves and gingerly removed a canvas wallet, handing it to me. The contents, or lack of, reflected the boy's adolescence. No driver's licence. No credit cards. Only a debit card.

'Dallas James Boyd,' I read out. 'There's a Medicare card in here too. Same name.'

'A Medicare card of his own?' Finetti repeated. 'Clearly didn't live with his parents.'

I emptied the remaining contents, counted out a few dollars in coins, unfolded a piece of paper and held it under the torch beam. It was a receipt from the 7-Eleven on Fitzroy Street.

'Looks like he bought a twenty-dollar mobile phone recharge card,' I said. 'Dated yesterday, er, last night, 10 p.m. Make a note to confirm it matches his mobile phone.'

I also found a business card behind the debit card for a youth worker named Will Novak. I knew Novak, he ran a hostel up on Carlisle Street and had been in St Kilda for as long as I could remember. The kid must have been a client.

I handed the wallet back to Finetti, who placed it in an evidence bag before checking the other pocket.

'Beer bottle lid,' he said, turning it in his hands. 'Amstel, boutique beer, not the sort you'd expect a teenage junkie to drink.'

I shrugged, unsure what to make of it, if anything, and told Finetti to document the item and bag it. Next I studied the boy's arm and the belt around his bicep, dictating my observations and taking photographs.

'Deceased doesn't appear to have any recent track marks. There's a leather belt around his arm, makeshift tourniquet. Needle is a Terumo brand, normally associated with injecting drug use. It appears new.'

Shining the torch around the base of the body, I found a wrapper for the syringe alongside a spoon and cigarette lighter. I asked Finetti to chart the location of each item in his notes then shone the torch around the area. Squatting down again, I checked inside the boy's mouth and looked under his T-shirt but still couldn't find what I was looking for.

'Where's the lid?' I said.

'Lid?'

I pointed to the wrapper next to the body. 'This syringe is brand new, so where's the orange lid?'

Finetti swept his torch from side to side, but couldn't find it either. 'Could be anywhere, maybe it's under the body. Let's take a look.'

He set his torch down and gripped the boy under his armpits, ready to hoist him up, but I put a hand on his wrist before he had the chance.

'Gentle, mate. He's a kid.'

'So what, he's dead.'

'Just preserve the scene. Evidence, remember?'

Finetti stared at me a long moment. Even in the dim light I could see what he was thinking.

'Sometimes things are just what they seem, McCauley. This is just a pissy overdose, that's it. An *accident*. We had one last week, two the week before, this is no different. Junkies at large, mate.'

'Yep, righto. Lift him and I'll have a look.'

Without much effort, Finetti propped the boy up and I shone my torch on the ground beneath his body, but still no lid.

'So where is it then?' I said when Finetti put the boy down.

'Shit, I don't know. Could be under one of these bins, could've fallen into a crack or down a drain.' He shone his torch on the boy's face. 'He could've swallowed it for all you know. Either way, who gives a shit?'

Maybe Finetti was right. The kid could have put the lid in his mouth while whacking up and accidentally swallowed it as the effects of the heroin took hold.

'Look, man, no offence,' Finetti continued. 'Don't make an issue out of this. I know you're keen to get back in the groove, but you don't need to prove anything to me. You don't need to prove anything to anyone.'

'What's that supposed to mean?'

'Three little words,' he said, holding up three fingers. 'Nil suspicious circumstances. All you gotta do is write that on the inquest sheet and we're done.'

I stared down at the dead kid and tried not to think about my old mate Jacko or the pain in my shoulder. Instead I got on with the task of photographing the body from several different angles.

'I don't know,' I said after a while. 'Maybe we need to get the techs down here. Work the scene properly. Then they can write it up as NSC.'

'Get your hand off it, Rubes. What are they gonna do that we can't – come in here and take some pictures? You're already taking pictures.' Finetti got down low next to the body, poked his tongue out and made a face to the camera. 'Quick, get a photo of me and the dead kid, maybe we'll hang it in the female locker room. Reckon Cassie and Kim'd like that?'

I rolled my eyes and told him to get up.

'I just think he's a bit young, that's all. They're normally older.'

'Oh, turn it up. They're all shitheads. Matter of fact, I'll bet my next two rest days that this kid's record is longer than my dick.'

'That wouldn't be hard.'

'Gets pretty hard when your missus comes around, tell you that much.'

We both laughed.

'So what's it gonna be?' Finetti prodded. 'You write this up as NSC, we'll get the undertakers down here and be home before eight. If you wanna muck about with the whole stage show, we're looking at lunchtime. An hour's unpaid overtime is better than five. Come on, man. I know you love your beauty sleep.'

Feeling suddenly deflated, I laced my hands behind my head and looked up at the sky. A haze of pink and purple spread from the east as dawn approached. On the other side of the fence I heard the first tram of the day rattle by.

'Okay,' I said. 'NSC it is. I'll get Kim to finish up in here and call the body snatchers. Then we can all knock off.'

'You're the man, Rubes,' said Finetti, a cheeky grin on his face. 'What d'ya say about having brekkie at Greasy Joe's? I'm so hungry I could eat a shit sandwich.'

'Don't start drooling, mate. We need to keep the body clean. And don't go stealing anything out of the kid's pockets either. I know what you're like.'

Finetti's rebuttal echoed through the loading bay as I headed back to the car park.

'Let me guess,' said Kim, who had cordoned off the entrance with crime scene tape. 'Dispatch got it wrong? The guy didn't OD. He drowned or got hit by a truck?'

'Nope. Think he came out the back door of the restaurant looking for the toilet, slipped on the back step and landed on a syringe.'

'For real?' she said, stowing the roll of tape in a tackle box.

'Nah, they got it right. Accidental overdose.'

'Nil suspicious?'

'Yeah, think so.'

'Nice one, we can get home on time,' she said, checking her watch.

I was silent, unsure.

'What's the matter? You all right?' she said, looking up and reading my face.

'Yeah, I'm fine.'

'You don't look fine.'

'He's just a kid, that's all. Probably from one of the hostels. What's Vitazul's story?'

'Ah, pretty standard, really. Says he came to work early to clean up after the previous night. He was taking out the rubbish and found the body. Seems pretty freaked out.'

'Did he touch anything?'

10

'Nope. Said he didn't want to.' She glanced over her shoulder. 'Said he was too scared.'

Following her gaze, I saw Vitazul slumped against a palm tree, staring up at the scenic railway. Within a few hours the park would be filled with kids, tourists and thrill seekers. How ironic that so many children came here to play, I thought. So many idyllic memories forged in a suburb that for others symbolised only pain and sorrow. But that was St Kilda, the home of extremes. Children played in Luna Park while paedophiles preyed on runaways in the surrounding gardens. The homeless begged for change in streets lined with luxury cars and trendy nightclubs. Drug addicts bought and sold their wares less than a stone's throw from tourists in chic restaurants. Cheap hostels provided accommodation to ex-felons and prostitutes alongside homes priced in the millions. And every morning large machines ploughed the beach, removing broken bottles and syringes hiding in the sand like urban landmines. The coexistence of danger and pleasure, risk and excitement. That's the St Kilda I knew.

'Why did Vitazul call the police?' I asked Kim. 'Why not an ambulance?'

'I asked him that. He just looked at me and said, "Young lady, the boy is grey like the ghost. He is dead, so I call police."'

'Believe him?' I asked.

'S'pose. Why, what's going on in there?'

'Never mind. Just go in and assist Finetti. I'll finish up with Vitazul and call the undertakers. It's going to be another hot one today so I want the body out of there before it starts to reek.'

When Kim was gone, I leant against a lamp post and rubbed my shoulder, welcoming the distraction of physical discomfort and pain. It was better than thinking about my old mate from Benalla or wondering what had happened to the kid in the loading bay. And it helped block out my doubts about there being nil suspicious circumstances.

# 2

GENTLE MOVEMENT WOKE ME. Footsteps crept up my chest, then soft purring vibrated in my ear. Prince licked me on the cheek and let out a pleading meow. I opened my eyes and looked blearily at the clock on the bedside table: 12.43 p.m. Finetti had been right on the money. We'd finished at the death scene around 8 a.m. and I'd slept just over four hours. Not bad for a night shift.

I ran a hand over Prince's black coat then headed to the kitchen at the far side of my single-bedroom apartment. It was seven years since I'd moved into what was initially a marital investment property that my ex and I had purchased in the glory days of our relationship. Back when Ella and I were first together, Albert Park was a suburb of run-down miners' cottages and seedy corner pubs. Now even the smallest houses cost into the millions. Because we'd got in early, I had what the bank called 'top-end equity', meaning my apartment was worth far more than what I owed on it. Even so, the mortgage still zapped most of my pay every month.

Prince ran ahead and sat by his bowl. The insulin was running low. I'd need to go by the vet later and buy some – something else that chewed into my cash flow. I peeled the plastic wrapper off the syringe and an image of the syringe sticking out of the boy's arm that morning flashed in my mind. Psychologists had an explanation for this: *pictures of the subconscious.* Cops call them flashbacks. Many years ago, I'd learnt to accept them as little more than an annoying intrusion. A bullet in the shoulder and twelve months of physical rehabilitation had changed all that. Nowadays, an innocent syringe for a diabetic cat became a dead kid in an alley; an old lady with a jaunty perm at the bus stop became the elderly rape victim of similar appearance I'd interviewed years ago; the backfiring of a car became a gunshot.

After filling his bowl, I stood and watched Prince demolish his food. My kitchen was original art deco and my favourite room in the apartment. Even if I could have afforded to, I wouldn't have updated to a modern look. The old-fashioned character and warmth far outweighed any fancy stainless steel.

As always, the left side of my torso had stiffened during sleep, leaving my muscles and ligaments surrounding the small circular scar tight and rigid. I went into the bathroom and ran the water a while before stepping into the shower to begin my daily routine of exercises. After several minutes and a series of stretches, movement became easier and I was able to wash myself properly.

I shaved and dressed, then downed some toast and took a glass of orange juice to the lounge window. Even before I opened the door to the balcony, I could feel the sun burning through the glass. When I did open it, the heat hit me like a furnace. It radiated off the bitumen, off the concrete walls of the nearby warehouse, and off the metallic snakes of cars traversing three storeys below. Some of the cars were caked in dirt and road grime, courtesy of water restrictions. Today would be another total fire ban, the fifth consecutive day in a row, and the city was feeling it. Immediately my eyes began to water and a familiar itch worked its way through my sinuses. I sneezed loudly, took a tissue from my pocket and blew my nose. How long before a cool change would come?

'Got a cold, mate?' The voice came from the balcony on the left. It was my neighbour, Edgar Burns, leaning on his walking stick, emptying water from a bucket into a pot plant. No doubt the water came from his shower, a water-saving practice Edgar employed religiously.

'Not a cold, Ed. Just hayfever. Driving me nuts this season. Too hot and dry.'

'The weather, my arse,' Edgar said, slopping water over the edge. 'Bloody pollution, that's what it is. Look at all these cars, for God's sake, smoking up the place. When I was a boy we all took the tram wherever we wanted to go. These days everyone needs a car just to go to the bloody milk bar. Lazy as a lizard drinkin'.'

I'd known Edgar for as long as I'd lived in the apartment block and somehow he always managed to give me an opinion.

'Not too many milk bars around here, Ed. Rare as rockin' horse shit.'

'You know what I mean. Look at that over there.'

He pointed towards the city skyscrapers, enveloped in a thick brown layer of smoke that had blown down from bushfires in central Victoria.

'You could be right. Pollution.'

'Too right. Won't catch me out here on days like this. It's about as dry as a nun's nasty. No wonder you're sick.'

As Edgar waved goodbye and hobbled back into his apartment, I decided to make more of an effort with him this year, maybe take him to the footy when the season began. We'd watched the Poms go down 7 for 311, chasing a total of 407, at the previous year's Boxing Day test. Vaughan had managed 144 from just 12 overs but the batting order fell over after he was dismissed and in the end they were no match for the Aussies. Edgar had damn near copped a heart attack when Ponting put three in the crowd off one over. We'd had a right old time.

With the heat getting more oppressive, I got down on my haunches and checked the soil in the rose pot next to the door and decided it was damp enough to survive another day. There were a few thrips I was able to kill with my fingers, but I knew from experience this wouldn't get them all. My mother had given me the Silver Jubilee as a cutting and it had taken well. Even in full sun it seemed to be the only plant around surviving the heat. I repositioned it and tried not to think about the day Mum had given it to me. Instead I stood up and looked out over the edge of my balcony, my eyes taking in the palm trees of Albert Park, the glittering lake and the territory all the way towards St Kilda. Edgar often described it as a million-dollar view. On a figurative level at least, he was dead right. It was what had sold me on the place all those years ago. Today, though, it also reminded me about the dead kid, Dallas Boyd. By now his family would have been notified, word would have hit the street, and the obligatory bunches of flowers would have turned up and begun to wilt and die in the loading bay. Just like the kid.

After almost twenty years in the job – five in the former Drug Squad – I'd learnt that in most cases of teenage drug abuse there was usually something important missing from the kid's life. Love, discipline, guidance, self-esteem. Something. I'd seen it on a personal level too. Jacko had been a good bloke, a victim of circumstance, and I wondered whether the same could be said for the kid in the loading bay. What kind of life had Dallas Boyd lived?

Draining my orange juice, I stepped back into the relative cool of the lounge room, where I removed an old photo album from the television cabinet. At the kitchen bench, I wiped dust off the cover and opened it to the photos of my family. In one shot, my mother and father stood beside an HT Holden on their wedding day, proud as punch, with the family home in the background. It had been too long since I'd seen my mum. My father too, for that matter. In another photo my older brother, Anthony, and I stood like burnt lobsters, waving to the camera from the edge of the local swimming pool. The photos brought a smile to my face but they weren't what I was looking for. I flipped through the album, past pictures of myself and Anthony getting older, until I came to a series of shots taken during a camping trip on the Murray River. I scanned the shots until I found the one I was looking for: three boys and two men beside a boat with the river in the background. Like a lot of the other photos in the album, it was heavily faded and yellowed at the sides.

I studied Jacko's face, remembering the cheeky gap between his front teeth, how his baseball cap was always lopsided, strands of hair covering his ears. And I thought again about why he'd decided to leave Benalla in the first place. *Something missing.*

Closing the album, I noticed the red light on my answering machine flashing. I'd turned the ringer off before bed, which was why I'd missed the calls. I clicked the play button.

'Yeah, McCauley, it's Ben Eckles. Just thought I'd check in. Heard you were a bit off with the OD this morning. Listen, I've got you down for the morning shift tomorrow. Anyhow, you're probably asleep now, so just give us a buzz when you get up to confirm the roster can stay as it is.'

I held my finger on the pause button, thinking. Finetti must have said something to Eckles, the senior sergeant temporarily in charge of the St Kilda Criminal Investigation Unit. The counsellors had warned me about this: that some of them would want to babysit me and ease me back into the casework. They'd even advised me not to return to the CIU. Take a less active role, they'd said. Something with less pressure. The primary school liaison team, perhaps. Yeah, right. The initial forecast was eighteen months, yet I'd passed the medical and psychological assessments in just over twelve. I drummed my fingers on the bench, unsure how to take my boss's message. I wanted respect, not sympathy.

I smiled at the next message, from my brother. 'Wakey-wakey, hands off snakey. Mate, Anthony here, s'pose you're still asleep, slacker. Anyway, just confirming this arvo's appointment. Don't forget, three o'clock at the usual. And do your stretches. *Real* stretches, too. Fifteen seconds each grouping. I don't want you suing me. See ya.'

The 'usual'. He made it sound like a drink in a pub.

The third message was from Ella. 'Hey spunksta, it's me. Still on for tonight, I hope? I finish at six, probably be at your place about seven. Give me a call, let me know what to bring. If you can't get hold of me, leave a message with the triage nurse, she'll pass it on. Ciao!'

I dialled the Alfred Hospital switch but missed Ella on a lunch break, so I left a message and thought about our plans for the night. Nothing special, she'd said, just a DVD and a bottle of red. I was still adjusting to the kind of date you had with your wife post-separation-possible-reconciliation. What was the word she'd used last time? *Rebuilding, reconnecting?* A DVD was a safe option, I supposed. Maybe she just thought I was too much of a tight-arse to take her to the movies.

I double-checked my daybook and saw a notation reminding me to see Anthony at three and be home for Ella at seven. Inside the diary were loose photocopies of the notes Finetti had made at the death scene that morning. Something about the missing syringe lid still bothered me. If the kid had prepared his fit like any other junkie, he'd have injected himself in the same location he was found in. As such, all the paraphernalia should have been located near the body. Yet we hadn't found the lid, even after the body was removed. What did that mean? I tried to tell myself it was nothing. Like Finetti had said, the kid could've swallowed it accidentally, or it could've simply fallen down a drain or into a crack or under a bin. At the end of the day, what did it matter? The kid had injected himself and overdosed. Simple. It happened all the time.

I began a cursory tidy-up of the apartment, stacking the dishwasher and putting on a load of washing. But doing house-work wasn't going to remove the image of Dallas Boyd slumped against the wheelie bin. Nor would it remove the doubt that

17

squirmed in my gut or the possibility that I'd ignored my own instincts, instincts that had lain dormant for over twelve months.

I sat at the bench and reread Finetti's notes, wondering if it would've been any different had I scribed and Finetti dictated. Then it hit me. Something *was* missing. I opened the daybook to a fresh page as the threads of a theory began to form, welcoming the feeling as I listed an anomaly I believed needed further investigating: *Mobile recharge receipt – no phone?*

The receipt we'd found in Dallas Boyd's wallet indicated a mobile recharge card had been purchased at 10 p.m. the night he died, yet no mobile phone had been located on or near the body. These days, everyone had a mobile phone. So where was the dead kid's?

That made at least two anomalies, but there was something about the tourniquet that wasn't quite gelling either. I went over Finetti's notes again but nothing jumped out, so I connected my digital camera to the television and began scrolling through the pictures I'd taken. Zooming in on the leather belt, I tried to make my theory take shape, but all the image did was frustrate me. I needed to see the belt again. I needed to hold it in my hands. There was only one place to do that.

# 3

THE VICTORIAN CORONER'S OFFICE was located in Southbank, less than three kilometres from my apartment. A low-level facility made of steel and glass, the complex spread across half a city block and was divided into three joined buildings: the coronial court, a forensic pathology centre and an area specifically designed for the identification of bodies.

The allocated police bays outside the complex weren't for the private vehicles of police members, but my Falcon was only two years old and always passed for an unmarked car, so I parked and followed the main walkway to the building in the middle. Inside the foyer, I approached a circular reception desk for the Victorian Institute of Forensic Medicine. The morgue.

Behind the desk a grey-haired woman sat chewing on a pencil as she stared into a computer screen, Paul Kelly's 'Dumb Things' playing on a radio behind her. Clearing my throat, I asked to speak with Matthew Briggs.

'And you are?' she asked.

'Police,' I replied, flipping open my badge case.

'What's it in relation to?' She sounded like a suspicious

mother guarding her precious child against the neighbourhood riffraff.

'A case I'm working on. The undertakers said Mr Briggs signed in a body this morning. I need to ask him some questions about it.'

She punched a few digits into a phone, waited a brief moment, then put down the handset and said he wasn't available before going back to reading whatever it was on her screen.

'Ah, what does that mean?' I asked. 'Has he gone home for the day, or is he just away from his desk?'

She shrugged. 'Could be in the toilet for all I know. Maybe you could call his mobile.'

'Good idea. Are you able to tell me what the number is or should I speak to someone more senior – your manager perhaps?'

The woman faced me angrily. 'I'm getting it for you now, if you can be patient.'

After a moment she was back on the phone. When she hung up, she spoke without looking at me.

'Take a seat by the window. He's on his way down.'

Matthew Briggs arrived shortly after, tall and thin, dark eyes set deeply into a pale face, like a skeleton. A green medical gown hung loosely over his hunched shoulders, as though he'd spent too long bending over bodies. We shook hands but Briggs made no attempt to invite me anywhere else.

'Thanks for your time,' I said. 'I just have a few questions about the overdose brought in this morning. Has anyone come by to see the body?'

'Yep, someone made an ID an hour or so ago,' he said.

'Who?'

'Some guy in a summer suit. I don't think it was his father.'

'Then who?'

Briggs shrugged and looked at his watch.

'I also wanted to ask when there'll be an autopsy,' I said, getting to the point.

'I thought that's what it might be about. I'm used to working with police.'

He didn't continue because he didn't need to. With cops, especially detectives, everything was urgent. Me showing up to put a rush on the post-mortem was about as original as butter on a sandwich.

'The PM's scheduled for Monday morning,' Briggs read off a clipboard. 'The pathologist is Dr Julie Wong. Why?'

I knew Dr Wong and felt sure she would listen to me. Monday was too long to wait.

'Tell Julie she needs to change the booking to tomorrow morning,' I said.

'Excuse me?' Briggs said. 'Detective, I just explained to you that the body is scheduled for Monday. That's the best we can do.'

'Well, it's not good enough. There are things that need to be confirmed before the death is ruled accidental.'

'You don't need to tell me that. That's what we do here. And we do it in our own time, in accordance with key performance indicators.'

'Spare me the induction spiel, Briggs. Just tell Julie to trust my judgement and book the boy for a preliminary exam tomorrow morning. If she doesn't find anything in the prelim, you can do it next month for all I care. Just check it in for tomorrow.'

'You've got some nerve, detective. Last night we get three guys brought in from a car crash on the Westgate Freeway. Uni students, heading down the beach for a holiday. For some reason the car flips and, bang, just like that they're all dead.'

I'd heard about the accident and knew what was coming.

'The families are having a group funeral on Monday, so we're putting these guys up front. On top of that, we've got a guy who ended up in a fight at a pub last night. He copped one in the jaw, cracked his head open on the pavement. A *homicide*.'

I understood the predicament of having to prioritise human

21

bodies, but if what I was now thinking was true, Dallas Boyd deserved immediate attention.

'Listen, there are anomalies with the Boyd case, things that don't add up,' I said, handing Briggs the list I'd made earlier. 'Look!'

He took the list, studied it and pointed to the last line on the page. 'What do you mean by this? *Leather belt – teeth marks?*'

'That's why I'm here. I need to see the belt, to check if there are any teeth marks on it. You've still got it, I presume?'

Briggs shot me a questioning look. 'Of course we still have it. Things don't just go missing around here.'

'Yeah, righto. Can I see it or not?'

'Why?'

'Let me see it and I'll explain. What's the big deal? I don't need to touch it.' I realised I was standing over him and stepped back. 'Look, it can stay in the audit bag. Just let me see it.'

'Only if it stays in the bag.'

'Fine.'

'Come with me.'

I followed him through a door into a hallway. Long familiar with the layout of the building, I knew he was taking me to a storage room where personal belongings of the deceased were kept, but was glad he left me at the door. I often found it worse to be surrounded by the clothes and personal belongings of dead people than the actual bodies.

When Briggs came back he closed the door and handed me a clear plastic bag with a thin leather belt inside. It seemed somehow smaller and more innocent than it had around the boy's arm.

'The belt was used as a tourniquet,' I explained, turning it in my hands. 'As you'd know, junkies keep the tension in the belt by pulling it tight with their teeth, so they can use their other arm to inject the syringe. They pretty much have to when they're alone, but look here.' I pointed at the surface of the leather. 'This doesn't have any teeth marks on it.'

Briggs nodded, thoughtful, as I gave him back the belt. He was probably wondering why I hadn't noticed this, along with the missing phone and syringe lid, earlier, or why the incident had been classified by the police as accidental.

'As individual anomalies they mean very little,' I said, following Briggs out to the foyer. 'But now I'm putting them all together it starts to look like the kid may not have whacked up in the loading bay.'

'I don't understand,' Briggs said. 'Coagulation and lividity are consistent with the position he was found in.'

I lowered my voice as two doctors walked in front of us. 'I'm not saying he didn't *die* in the loading bay. I'm saying he might have *injected* himself elsewhere. If that's the case, then we have to ask how he got there.'

'Okay, I see your point, but it doesn't change the fact that you green-carded this as accidental. You can't just come in here and change your mind, then expect us to juggle bodies like tables in a restaurant.'

'I realise that,' I said, 'but if it turns out someone else may have been involved, we can't leave it until Monday. I don't even have a TOD.'

'That I can help you with,' Briggs said. 'We had stable temperatures most of last night, so calculations were made on body movement at the scene. I shouldn't be telling you this, because they're only estimates, but based on rigor mortis you're looking at time of death around midnight last night.'

I nodded my appreciation. All I needed now was the final step.

'Listen, just give Julie Wong this list and tell her I'll be here tomorrow morning. If she can't do the preliminary exam, then so be it, but she needs to see this list.'

Briggs sighed, his face exhausted.

'Just give her the list,' I said gently. 'It's not your decision to make, Matthew. It's hers.'

•

I went back to my car and sat in the driver's seat with the door open. Heat radiated off the concrete and the bushfire smoke irritated my eyes and throat. The missing syringe lid was one thing, but the absence of a mobile phone and now the confirmation of no teeth marks on the tourniquet smacked of another person's involvement. What that involvement translated to, I wasn't sure. There was one thing I *was* sure of: I'd made a mistake in writing the overdose off so quickly and that needed to be rectified.

How to achieve it was going to be a problem. What was I going to do, walk into the squad room and tell Eckles I'd fucked up? Admit that the psychologists were right all along, that I shouldn't have come back so soon. That I wasn't ready for desk duties, let alone dead bodies.

I looked around for a tissue to blow my nose but didn't have any. I was angry with myself, and the heat and the hayfever were only making it worse. I drove to a service station, bought a pack of tissues and a bottle of water. At the counter, I guzzled the water and noticed the front-page headline of the *Herald Sun*: FREEWAY HORROR. I knew it referred to the accident Briggs had mentioned. It reminded me that Dallas Boyd had died a silent death and I knew that if I kept quiet, no one would ask questions. My reputation would remain intact and the overdose would remain an accident, just like the hundreds of others each year.

As much as I hated the idea of admitting fault, I wondered whether somebody out there had been counting on Dallas Boyd dying silently, that we would rush the job, write it off as another overdose and simply wipe our hands of it. The very idea of this struck a nerve, because I'd always been alert to such attempts. People tried to trick the police every day and most of the time they failed. Or did they? How many other kids had died an accidental death that wasn't an accident?

Being a good investigator meant being in tune with your instincts; instincts that let you know when something wasn't right. During my rehabilitation I'd allowed those skills to gather

24

dust, to go blunt. Worse still, early this morning I'd allowed a junior officer to cloud my judgement. As I drove out of the service station, I made a decision. It was time to face the smirks of my colleagues, the whispering behind my back and the rumours that I'd lost the touch. And it was time to prove them wrong.

# 4

THE SMALL ROOM LOOKED over the main floor of the YMCA gymnasium, a row of treadmills and exercise machines facing a wall lined with televisions and mirrors. I stood in the doorway watching two men spotting for each other over a bench press. The stronger of the two was pressing eighty kilos. If you counted the bar, it put it up to ninety. There'd been a time when I could max that. Not now. Not yet anyway.

I closed the door, unbuttoned my shirt, stripped down to my underwear and studied a poster of a male body depicting core muscle groups. Another showed nerve points, ligaments and skeletal structure. I flexed my biceps, and decided I'd need to live in the gym and do nothing else but lift weights if I ever wanted to look like the men in the posters. I put my pants and shirt on a coat hanger and hung it from the door handle. Relaxation music played from a stereo in the corner. The room was warm and humid and filled with the smell of lavender and baby oil. I could hear the faint pounding from the squash courts next door and felt better already, even if I could no longer participate in any of the activities going on around me. Just being here was therapy. That and the massages.

'Early,' Anthony said as he entered the room. 'Good form.'

I shook my older brother's hand and sat on the padded table.

'Stretched, warmed up?'

'Of course,' I lied.

Anthony unzipped his gym bag, removed a towel and a bottle of oil.

'Don't lie, Rubes. This'll hurt if you don't stretch.' He tossed the towel over. 'Do some now. Back in a sec.'

I stood in front of the mirror and rolled my shoulders, neck and arms, then gripped my elbow and held it behind my head, stretching the lateral muscles in my back and my triceps. After a minute I grabbed a handful of fat on my stomach in frustration and tugged at it. Not a big handful. Not a sixpack either. Used to be.

'Worried about the gut, Rubes?' Anthony said, coming back into the room. 'Don't stress too much. You wanna see some of the slobs that come in here with their New Year's resolutions that last all of two sessions. Mate, I've seen better bodies in a scrapyard.'

'How do I get rid of it?'

'You need to sweat it out.'

'Sit-ups?'

'Useless.'

I stood still while he examined the scar on my shoulder. Anthony was taller than me, thinner, fit as a butcher's dog. Lighter hair too. The golden boy. Our father's genes.

'How's it been? Stiff in the mornings?'

I smirked and Anthony pushed me playfully. 'So stiff you could hang a towel off it, right? You know how many times I've heard that one?'

'How many?'

'Lost count. What about this, a guy comes in the other day with a sprained ankle. I asked how he got it and you know what he says?'

'No, but I assume you're going to tell me.'

'Smart arse. Maybe now I won't. How's your shoulder?'

'Tight. Tell me.'

He lifted my arm, moved it in an arc and listened with a stethoscope to my ligaments clicking. 'Still swimming regularly?'

'Three times a week. Tell me about the ankle guy.'

'No weights, I hope. Told you about that, remember?'

'Just the swimming,' I said. 'Come on, now I wanna know about this guy.'

He put the stethoscope down and rolled his own shoulders, like a boxer before a fight. 'Okay, he was riding his bike along the Esplanade, checking out all the chicks, and bang! He goes over the edge and falls three feet down to the sand, comes off the bike in front of the whole bloody beach and twists his ankle.'

Anthony was laughing and so was I. I'd once seen a man do the same thing on roller blades, except he went into a palm tree. St Kilda was full of dangers.

'Okay, let's get going,' Anthony said. 'You're not running yet, are you?'

'That's why I've developed a gut. How long before I can?'

'I said soon. On the bed. I'll do your back first.'

I lay on my stomach, closed my eyes while he ran oily hands up and down my back. Good pain, they called it. The hands moved up to my neck.

'Geez, you're tight as a frog's arse.'

'That's what Ella used to say.'

I heard him chuckle. 'Been a bit tense lately?'

I nodded.

'Stressed?'

'A little.'

'Dangerous job, police. Bad for you.'

'A plumber died in a ditch last week,' I countered. 'He didn't retain it properly and got buried alive. All jobs are dangerous.'

'Not this one. Brace.'

I closed my eyes as Anthony ran an elbow down my back. I didn't come here to be lectured.

'How's the family?' I asked in between elbows.

'Going away next week, actually. Echuca. Mate's got a team in the Southern 80. You should come.'

A ski race on the Murray River. Lots of drinking and fast boats. A couple of deaths every year. Car accidents, boat accidents, all sorts of mishaps and drownings. And he thought my life was dangerous.

'Can't,' I said. 'I'm working.'

'Righto. On your side. Arms relaxed.'

I rolled over and he kneaded his hands up and down my biceps and triceps. This was the worst part, the most painful.

'Shoulder's starting to loosen. Might be able to get on some light dumbbells soon. Nothing too heavy. Been to see Mum lately?'

The question caught me off guard, just as it was meant to.

'Ah, not since Christmas.'

'Since Chrissy?' Anthony whistled. 'Been four times this year, I have. It's only a two-hour drive, mate. It wouldn't kill you to visit occasionally.'

'I'm going on Sunday,' I said.

'You should. She misses you.'

'How d'you know that? She can't even talk.'

Anthony pushed me back down on the bed, face first. I didn't resist because I deserved it.

'She's our mother. Of course she misses you. It's a stroke, Rubes. Shit, it's not Alzheimer's. She knows what's going on.'

I said nothing. He was right.

'She was there for you, remember? All of us were. Lot of time waiting in the hospital. It's not right if you don't go. Disrespectful.'

I let my body go limp and welcomed the pain. Mum's stroke had happened last spring and I could probably count on one hand the number of times I'd visited since. My beautiful mother, the matriarch of our family, reduced to a vegetable.

'Roll over. On your back.'

I did as instructed and stared at a framed photo of my brother's family on a desk in the corner. Son, daughter, wife. Perfect nuclear family. It reminded me of the photo I'd looked at in my lounge earlier in the day. Perfect camping trip.

'Don't forget Jonathan's birthday tomorrow,' Anthony said. 'Spit roast. DJ in the garage, the works. You're still coming, I assume?'

I had the invitation on my fridge, but had forgotten all about it and suddenly hoped I hadn't double-booked.

'I've put in for a night off. Hopefully I'll be there.'

'Come on, Rubes. He's turning eighteen, mate.' Fingers pressed painfully into my left shoulder. 'Wouldn't be the same without you. He loves you, you know?'

'I'll be there, Andy,' I said, using the name we'd all called him since childhood. It didn't really match, but he liked it better than Tony.

'Is it all right if I bring Ella?' I asked.

'Sure.'

'Thanks.'

Anthony continued working, unsure how to follow up.

'How's it all going?' he asked.

'Okay, I think. I'll be seeing her tonight as well. Nothing fancy, just a DVD and a few bevvies.'

'Sounds nice.'

'Yeah.'

We were silent then and I wondered what lay ahead. My separation had affected the entire family and I knew everyone wanted us to rekindle our relationship. It was a difficult topic.

'How's Chloe – halfway through uni and loving life?' I said, changing the subject.

The hand pressure released.

'Yeah, uni starts up again next month. Summer comes to an end, thank Christ. Her social life's getting out of hand. She goes out to nightclubs and parties and God knows what else. She came home at seven the other morning. Gabrielle nearly had a fit. Can you believe it, *seven* in the morning?'

'That's pretty normal, Andy. She's still a good kid.'

'A good kid, right,' he repeated, and there was a long silence before he said, 'Caught up with Dad lately?'

'Jesus, what is this, the Spanish Inquisition?' I said, pushing his hand away and rolling off the bed. 'I haven't seen him since Christmas either. Just over a month ago. You gonna earbash me about that as well?'

Anthony wiped his hands on the towel, screwed the lid on the oil and tossed it in his bag.

'You can be pretty selfish sometimes, you know that?'

'Oh, piss off.' I snatched up my wallet, peeled out a fifty and flicked it on the desk. 'I come here for physio, Andy. Not to be accused of neglect. I'm trying to make something positive happen with El and get back in the harness at work. That takes time and a lot of emotional energy.'

'Fair enough, but don't forget being a cop made you like this.' He pointed at the scar on my shoulder. 'That's just the flesh. Your shit goes all the way to the bone.'

I slid into my pants, yanked on my shirt and started doing up the buttons. Any benefit from the massage was gone. I was tenser now than I'd been all week.

'Think I'll find another masseur.'

'That'd be right. Push away everyone who cares about you. Keep going, pretty soon you'll be all alone. Then you'll be happy. You gotta know what you want to get what you want.'

I didn't bother with the last few buttons or my shoelaces, just jerked the door open.

'Wait,' he said.

I stopped.

'I'm sorry. I'm a prick, I know.'

I wanted to agree, but couldn't. I was a prick too.

Anthony let out a long breath, then said, 'I shouldn't take it out on you. I've just got my own shit to deal with now, that's all.

I can't handle Mum's and Dad's as well. I just . . . I'm sorry, I need help.'

I stood in the doorway as Anthony zipped up the gym bag, sprayed disinfectant on the massage bed and wiped it down in angry swipes.

'What is it?' I asked, suddenly ashamed of my behaviour and looking at my brother in what seemed like the first time in ages. Really looking at him.

'Remember when we were kids, Rubes?' he said. 'We had that storm come through town, after the Ash Wednesday fires finally ended? Mum and Dad were out. We sat on the roof, watched the storm brewing on the hills. Remember?'

I nodded and came back in the room. For sure I remembered. It was February 1983, we were teenagers, and our farmhouse had survived the worst bushfires in living memory. Then there were the clouds. They were dark and angry, a mixture of black and orange, and they marched down from the hills as though God had sent them to earth to extinguish the blaze. I'll never forget running back inside, stealing a sixpack of Dad's beer, climbing onto the roof and smoking a joint with Anthony as the lightning started.

'We hadn't seen decent rain in years,' I said. 'When it eventually came, we just sat up there and let it soak us.'

Anthony sat on his desk.

'Mum and Dad came home early. We shit ourselves, tried to hide the beer and the hooch, remember that?'

Yeah, I remembered that too. I'd climbed off the roof, soaking wet. Anthony had tossed down empty beer bottles and I'd bloody dropped one but the rain on the roof shielded the noise. Afterwards, we lied to Mum and Dad, said we'd been at Jacko's place.

'The lie was never gonna work,' I said, remembering Mum's fierce reaction and her handy use of the wooden spoon. 'Dad smelt the beer on us a mile off, told Mum to deal with us. I suppose one look in the fridge he would've seen 'em missing too.'

Anthony laughed wryly. 'Didn't get done for the hooch though, did we?'

'No. Not the hooch.'

Anthony went silent then and I felt an internal panic.

'Andy, what's going on?'

'It's Chloe,' he said at last. 'I found these in her bedroom.'

He handed me a bag with three pink tablets in it, each stamped with the Mercedes symbol.

'Ecstasy,' I said.

Anthony nodded gravely. Nuclear family nightmare.

'You found these in her bedroom?'

'In one of her drawers.'

I put the pills on the desk and leant against the wall with the muscle man on it.

'Searching her room, Andy?'

'No.'

'Right.' I waited.

'Well, just as bloody well I did. What if it goes on? She could end up in hospital, or worse.' Anthony rubbed his face. 'I should've seen it, I s'pose. All the late nights and weird music. Whatever happened to seeing a band at the local pub?'

I often wondered the same thing.

'No bands worth seeing any more,' I said. 'Too many popstar shows.'

'Fuckin' joke. I haven't told Gabrielle yet, don't know if I should. Not sure how she'll handle it. Would you talk to her for me, Rubes?'

'Who, Gabrielle?'

'No, Chloe.'

'Shit,' I said, letting out a low whistle. '*You* should talk to her, Andy. You're her father.'

'Oh, come on! You know kids don't listen to their parents. You're a cop, for Christ's sake. You've worked in the Drug Squad. She'll listen to *you*.' He handed the fifty-dollar note back. 'Come on, you owe me that much. Keep your money, just help me out.'

I stared at the money, realising I had no choice. He needed my help.

'She's still a good kid, Andy. It's probably just a phase. All kids go through it. Even we did.'

'What, a bit of hooch? We never took this shit.'

'It could be worse, you know? A lot worse.'

'I envy you, Rubes,' Anthony said, staring at the photo on his desk. 'No kids to worry about. Sometimes I wonder if life would be easier like that, if I only had to care about myself.'

I said again that I'd talk to her.

'Thank you. I appreciate it.' Anthony picked up the bag of pills. 'What do I do with these?'

'Put them back or she'll know you've been snooping.'

Anthony scoffed at me, said there was no way he'd give them back.

'Well, if you want my advice, tell her you found them in the laundry or she'll never trust you again. She'll just get better at hiding it, maybe even move out. Go live with druggies, do all the rave parties, scoff pills every weekend. Next thing you know, she'll come back when you're not home and piss off with the DVD player. Imagine that.'

Anthony emptied the pills into his rubbish bin. 'She'll never trust *me*. Hell, I'll never trust *her*.'

'That's the spirit.'

I picked up the picture on the desk and stared at it. On the surface they were a happy family. What about beneath the surface? As far as I knew they had always been happy. Sure, there were normal tantrums and fights, but the kids attended good schools and they never went without anything. Then again, you'd be surprised at the sort of homes we got called to after a domestic blue. And I couldn't tell you how many smashed picture frames I'd seen. Sometimes bigger houses just hid bigger problems.

I put the picture down and thought about Anthony's recount of the storm in 1983. We'd been busted for drinking the beer, but Anthony had taken the rap and said it was his idea. In truth it was the other way around. I'd stolen the beer from the fridge. I'd even rolled the joint. But being the eldest, Anthony accepted responsibility and Mum's wrath with the wooden spoon. And it wasn't the only time he'd taken the rap for me. There was the car accident. Not serious, but again I avoided accountability. Then there were the dope plants among the tomatoes, parties when our folks went away and the girls from down the street in our bedroom late at night. Bringing the memory up was clever manipulation on Anthony's behalf. A cunning reminder of how many times he'd been there for me.

'Andy, if you don't want to take my advice, why did you even ask me to talk to Chloe? I mean, obviously I don't know anything about kids. Like you said, I don't have any of my own to worry about. So what the hell would I know?'

Anthony stared up at me with a pained expression.

'I'm sorry,' he said, rummaging in the bin for the pills. 'I shouldn't have said it like that, but I'm not giving them back. I'll tell her I found them in the bathroom. Just like you say, okay?'

'Laundry.'

'Whatever. Just talk to her, will you?'

'Okay, I'll do it, but not at the party tomorrow night. I'll do it in my own time.'

'Sure, whenever. Thanks, bro.'

I put a hand on his shoulder. 'It's going to be okay, mate. A lot of kids go through this and they come out the other end in one piece.'

He just nodded, eyes fixed on the picture. 'What about Mum and Dad?' he said after a moment. 'You can't forget about them either.'

'I haven't.'

Even as I said it I knew I wasn't being honest. Why was it that I had time and energy to spend with my elderly neighbour, Edgar, but was avoiding contact with my parents? I left Anthony then, knowing something had to change.

# 5

THE DRIVE BACK TO ST KILDA took me through Albert Park where the Formula One race would be held in less than a month's time. The normally lush lawn that surrounded the lake was brown and patchy. Even the lake itself looked like a dam on a barren farm left to dry out and die.

I plugged the earpiece into my mobile phone and dialled the St Kilda watch-house, asking to be put through to Cassie Withers. Because she'd left early last night, she'd agreed to pull the quick changeover, meaning today she would be back on duty for the afternoon shift. I slowed for a red light as she came on the line.

'Cass, it's Rubes. How'd you go at the hospital?'

'Imagine spending six hours in a cheap plastic chair, then you've got it.'

She left it at that and I figured she didn't want to talk about it over the phone. Eckles was probably somewhere in the squad room watching her. A Salvation Army volunteer approached my window shaking a donation can but I let him walk by.

'What's up?' Cassie asked.

'I need a favour. Can you check who made the ID this morning on the overdose and let me know if we've got a current address? Kid's name was Dallas Boyd. I also need a date of birth.'

'Ah, okay. Why?'

'Never mind, I'm just filling in the boxes.'

I heard keys tapping and figured she was checking the system. The light went green but the car in front didn't move. I blew the horn until it did.

'The kid was sixteen,' she said. 'Born 1 November 1992.'

I looked around for somewhere to write it down but my daybook was on the back seat, so instead I scribbled it on the back of my hand.

'Still there?' Cassie asked.

'Yeah, sorry. The ID. Can you check the incident fact sheet and tell me who made the ID?'

'I don't need an IFS to tell you that. Eckles took someone down to make the ID after lunch. Let me check his name.'

I changed lanes at the St Kilda junction and headed south towards the beach. Two hookers stood on the corner of Alma Road, hands on hips, gaunt faces hidden behind oversized sunglasses. Recognising one of them, I flashed my headlights. She lifted her skirt and flashed her leg back in sarcasm as Cassie picked up the phone.

'A social worker,' she said. 'Works at the crisis centre on Carlisle.'

'Will Novak?' I asked.

'Good memory.'

'I'm still a detective, Cass,' I said, then wondered aloud why the kid's parents hadn't made the ID.

'Nobody's saying any different,' she replied, adding, 'The address I have for the parents is a commission flat in Collingwood. The high-rise complex on Hoddle Street.'

'Yep, I know it.'

'What are you playing at, Rubes?' Cassie prodded. 'We're

done on this. I've got your inquest brief in front me. Nil suspicious circs, it says, right here in your own handwriting. Why all the questions?'

'I'm back on deck tomorrow morning. I'll fill you in then. Thanks.'

I ended the call before she had a chance to ask anything else and an uneasy feeling settled on me. She was my partner and friend and I'd broken the pact: *in us we trust*. But then for all I knew, she probably didn't think I was ready to be back at work either.

I parked outside a corner property bordered by a six-foot-high brick fence. A sign on a gate read 'Carlisle Accommodation & Recovery Service'. CARS operated out of an old mansion donated by its late owner, an elderly woman whose children had drowned in a boating accident in the 1950s. Her bequest had caused a shitfight among the remaining family members when she passed away in 1982, but her wish held up and CARS had been providing support to the street people of St Kilda ever since. As far as I knew, Will Novak had worked there since the organisation first opened its doors.

I walked through the front gate with my daybook under my arm, up a gravel path to a front porch that stretched the entire length of the three-storey house. Beautiful bay windows with ornate leadlight lined either side of a double-fronted door wide enough to fit a car through. A teenager in a striped tracksuit sat on the steps leading to the porch, rolling a cigarette. He made me as a cop even before I walked past.

'How are ya, sarge?' he drawled.

'Not bad,' I replied, noting the deep shadows under the boy's eyes and the shrunken cheekbones that were the telltale signs of addiction. His eyes were mere slits, he hadn't shaved in a few days and his hair needed a wash. Probably only fifteen or sixteen, but he looked so much older. Heroin does that. It beats the kids down, steals their youth.

'Will Novak in?'

'Dunno. What's it to you?' he said, not even looking up from his cigarette.

'Just want to talk to him.'

I opened the front door but stopped as the boy mumbled something.

'What's that?'

'Said he's out back,' the kid said. 'Last I seen he was pretty upset. We all are.'

'Upset?'

'About Dall. That's why you're here, isn't it?'

'You knew Dallas Boyd?'

'Yeah, course.'

'I'm sorry.'

'Right.'

'May I help you?' a voice said from the doorway.

The first thing I noticed about Will Novak was that he'd shaved his head and grown a neat goatee beard. Last time I'd seen him, more than a year ago, he'd had long hair and was dressed in a T-shirt and boardies, standard youth-worker attire. Now he wore a white business shirt tucked into a pair of beige slacks with brown boat shoes. I wondered if he'd worn the outfit to look professional at the ID or if this was now his usual get-up. I was about to produce my badge when he recognised me.

'Rubens? Rubens McCauley?'

'Yeah, hello, Will.'

We shook hands and I saw that his eyes were bloodshot, his face pale and drained.

'This is . . .' he stammered. 'I'm sorry, it's been a bad day.'

'Yeah, I know. Is there somewhere we can talk?'

'Sure, follow me.'

He led me down a hall towards the rear of the building, past a reception desk and another hallway. Posters advertising different welfare services hung on the walls. The building was old and musty, and eerily quiet. Floorboards creaked under our feet. Stopping, Novak gestured for me to enter an office that overlooked a courtyard surrounded by bench seats and a garden with people standing in the shade, smoking cigarettes.

He eased into a chair behind a desk stained with coffee and old age and offered me a seat in a chair opposite.

'What a day,' he said, staring out the window, looking slightly dazed. 'Good to see you again. Shame it's not a happier occasion.'

I nodded. I'd first met Will Novak while working a case in which a parolee was wanted for the rape of a local prostitute. Novak knew where the offender was hiding and tipped me off, and we arrested the guy without much delay. Around the same time I'd moved into my flat and was in the process of pulling down a wall between the entrance and the lounge. I ended up hiring Will's brother – a carpenter – to do the job. The wall turned out to be load bearing and required a few hands on deck, so Novak – who was himself quite handy and often laboured for his brother – helped. A year or so later Ella hired them both to remodel the ensuite in her own apartment.

'How're you holding up?' I asked him.

'Well, as I'm sure you'll appreciate, I've been through this several times over the years, but never with somebody like Dallas.'

'He was a client of yours, I take it?'

A weary nod. 'I guess there's no harm in discussing him now, is there? I mean, it's different when they're . . . when they're still with us.'

'Wanna tell me about him?'

Novak nodded and clasped his hands together. 'Dallas was one of my success stories. I first began seeing him when he was eight. He came to live here at the age of ten. For the first few years he was a great example of what can be achieved with positive care and the right support structures. I made some genuine inroads, but it wasn't easy. We tried placing him with foster parents a few times, but he rebelled. Later on, he went through bouts of early drug use, including heroin at the age of fourteen, before ending up in Malmsbury for an armed rob.'

I made a note to contact Juvenile Justice about Dallas Boyd's stint in kiddie prison.

'What happened when he got out?' I asked.

'He was referred back to me by one of the outreach programs we're affiliated with in the juvenile centres. Anyway, he came back here and got clean. I helped him find his own accommodation and, as far as I knew, things were going well for him. He hadn't used in over a year and . . .' Novak tore a tissue from a box on his desk and wiped his eyes. 'I'm sorry. It's just you work so hard to help these kids, and just when you think they're in the clear, they relapse and in a second it's all over. It's a bloody tragedy.'

I looked out the window, giving him time to compose himself. Outside, a young woman squashed a cigarette in an ashtray and walked towards a doorway on the other side of the courtyard. She wore pyjamas so I figured she was a live-in client and the doorway led to the accommodation rooms.

'Why were you asked to formally identify the body?' I said when Novak was finished with the tissue. 'Why not his family?'

'Family?'

'His parents live in Collingwood. In the commission flats.'

'Well, Dallas might have had a biological mother and a step-father, but I wouldn't call it a *family*.'

I waited, suspecting there was more.

'Like most of my clients, Dallas was also a client of the Department of Human Services, you understand? Child Protection, to be precise. I can still remember the first time I saw him, just a little kid covered in bruises. He could hardly walk.'

'Did he have any recent contact with his parents? Visiting arrangements?'

Novak let out a long breath, fished through a file on his desk and handed me a folded-up piece of paper. I unfolded the page and recognised it as a pathology report on a urine specimen. The patient's name was Rachel Boyd.

'Dallas was worried about his little sister,' Novak explained.

41

'Rachel was crying every time she went to the toilet, said it hurt to pee. So just last December, we brought her in here and had a nurse take a urine sample.' He took the pathology report back and folded it into the file. 'Rachel had chlamydia. As far as I'm concerned, there's only one reason why a five-year-old girl gets chlamydia.'

My stomach tensed.

'Who was it?'

'The stepfather. Complete scum of the earth.' Novak clenched his jaw. 'Being a social worker, I don't say that about many people.'

'Does the girl still live with them?'

He eased back in his chair, shooting me a look of suspicion. 'Pardon my cynicism, but like I said before, I've been through this with other clients who've passed away in similar circumstances. I don't recall there being this level of depth in the investigation.'

'Depth?'

'The questions you're asking. I mean, don't get me wrong, I appreciate the interest. I'm just not used to seeing this level of inquiry from cops regarding a heroin overdose. You wanna level with me here?'

He was right to be curious. Mostly ODs *were* written off quickly, so it was no wonder he found my questions peculiar.

'Call it the new face of community policing.'

'Hey, I've never held out on you, man. I've always played ball.'

'I know that, Will. I'm just being thorough. You said you helped Dallas find his own accommodation. Was that through the Ministry of Housing?'

'No. Part of my role is to source government grants for my clients. The grants pay for all sorts of things like accommodation, food, travel, study, even gym membership. With Dallas, I was able to help him rent and furnish a one-bedroom unit off Barkly Street. Nothing flash, but he was learning to survive on his own.'

'What's the address?'

'Of Dall's apartment?'

'Yeah, I'd like to have a look. Help polish off my report.'

Novak leant across his desk. 'Hey, if something's going on here, I have a right to know. I basically raised that kid as if he were my own.'

I felt the human element of Boyd's death weigh heavily upon me. Workers like Novak weren't unlike many of the dedicated detectives I'd met on the job. They worked long hours for little pay and were relentless in supporting their clients. That the clients were often the scourge of society was inconsequential to them. They saw beyond that and dedicated their lives to helping these people. And I admired that.

'There's some things that don't add up, that's all. But don't go shooting your mouth off. I'm keeping it close to my chest until I get a better picture.'

'You think he was murdered?' he said.

I looked over my shoulder, as if the office had ears. I wasn't expecting the question, and wasn't sure I knew the answer.

'Like I said, there are some anomalies. I can't go into it yet, but if it turns out something untoward did happen, I'll let you know as soon as I can. How does that sound?'

He gave me a conspiratorial nod. 'Sure, and I'll do what I can to help.'

'Can you tell me the address?' I asked.

'I can do better than that.' Opening a drawer in his desk, he searched around and fished out a key with a yellow tag on it. 'As part of my agreement with the government, I go on the record for these kids when I get them a place to live,' he explained, tossing the key over. 'The government requires that I have a key to access the property if need be. More often than not, they're just useful for when they lock themselves out.'

Novak read out the address and I wrote it down. On the page I saw a notation about the mobile phone and it reminded me to ask whether he could confirm if Dallas Boyd had one.

43

'Sure. Everyone has a mobile these days, don't they?' he said.

'You have the number?'

'Of course.' He got up and opened a drawer in a filing cabinet, then removed a folder. 'Forgive my inquisitiveness,' he said, looking genuinely puzzled, 'but what benefit will having his number be?'

I looked up from my notes and considered the question.

'Well, he didn't have a phone on him when he . . . when we found him. He probably left it in his flat. I'm sure it'll turn up.'

'Fair enough.'

He opened the folder, read out the number and I copied it down next to the address.

'One final thing,' I said. 'I'm trying to trace Boyd's final steps. When did you last see him?'

'A couple of days ago. We had lunch, actually.'

'And how was he?'

'Fine. I mean, he was a bit worked up.'

'How do you mean?' I asked.

'Well, he was in contact with Child Protection again, trying to have his sister removed so that she could live with him. The Child Protection Unit assigned to the case had been out to the flat. They were investigating the stepfather, but, as I'm sure you're aware, the removal of a child from the family unit is a last resort. They don't make those decisions lightly and the wait was causing him a bit of stress.'

'Okay, so that was the last time you spoke to him?'

'Yes.'

I thought about how removing the girl might have resulted in charges against the stepfather, possibly even prison time. It would be enough to make anyone angry.

'The stepfather, what's his name?'

'Vincent Rowe. Look him up on your system. I'm sure he'll have a thousand hits.'

I scrawled the name down and underlined it as Novak slid two business cards across the desk, one his own and the other belonging to a woman named Sarah Harrigan from the Department of Human Services.

'It's past five on a Friday,' Novak said, 'so you won't get any joy at DHS now, but she's the Child Protection Unit manager for the southern metro region. I'll tell her you're a good guy, get her to call you.'

I thanked him and passed my own card over. 'Just for the record, where were you around midnight last night?'

'Ah, you're asking me for an alibi?'

'For elimination.'

Novak looked out the window and exhaled slowly. 'I was helping out at the soup kitchen on Fitzroy Street.'

'At midnight?'

'Yes,' he said. 'Shit, I went into the 7-Eleven on the corner of Grey Street at one point and bought a packet of smokes to give out to the homeless. That's the only time I was away from the van.'

Glad the awkward moment was out of the way, I held out my hand. 'Sorry, Will. Part of the process.'

'Just let me know if you hear anything,' he said as we shook hands. 'Dall was a popular kid. If something happened to him, you'll have a lot of angry people around here. Could get ugly.'

I thought of the boy I'd seen outside and knew Novak wasn't exaggerating. Street kids were a tight bunch.

'Thanks, Will,' I said, sliding the keys to Dallas Boyd's apartment into my pocket. 'I'll be in touch.'

# 6

MAJESTIC VIEWS WAS THE NAME of the apartment block where Dallas Boyd had lived. It was squashed between two near-identical 1960s blocks on a narrow cul-de-sac and I wondered if it had been named as such because it had once been possible to glimpse water from the upper floors. If so, the growth of trees and urban development had put a stop to that. I drove past Majestic Views and parked a hundred metres down, watching the street through my rear-view mirror.

A prostitute leant against a telephone pole in the shade of a nearby tree. She was dressed in a pink bikini top and hotpants. I'd never seen her before and figured she was new to the stroll. She wasn't scrawny and undernourished like most of the girls I knew in St Kilda. Looking around for her spotter, I found him hidden behind a sun visor in a nearby Valiant.

Within minutes, a white HiAce van slowed and the girl bent to the driver-side window. A quick glance over her shoulder, a flash of headlights from her eyes in the Valiant, and she was gone. Before I started working St Kilda I'd never understood the male desire to pick up street girls, risking arrest, robbery or disease when you could easily go to any legal brothel and get a better service with virtually no risk. I'd since come to suspect it was the risk itself, as much as the sex, that was the attraction for many men.

From the back seat I grabbed the white polo T-shirt I'd been wearing earlier and changed into it. It was too hot for a shirt and tie, and I didn't want to look like a cop for what I was about to do. I tore a blank page from my daybook and folded it into my pocket, then walked back to the apartment block, ignoring the suspicious glance from the spotter, still slouched in the Valiant. Just as I reached the entrance to the apartment block a loud bang reverberated down the street. I dropped to a squat, my shoulder tense and blood pounding in my ears. A few seconds went by before I realised it was just a car backfiring. I leant against a brick letterbox and drew a breath.

The spotter in the Valiant was laughing at me. I snarled abuse at him before going through a gate and walking up to the third floor. Finding Boyd's apartment, I slid on a pair of gloves and used the key Novak had given me to open the door.

A carpeted entranceway intersected with a door on the right and another ahead. I opened the door on the right – the bedroom. It was warm and musty, the blinds closed, double bed unmade. Posters of black American rappers plastered the walls. I continued up the short passage into the living room. It was also badly in need of airing. An old sofa faced a television and there was a stereo in the corner. Other than an ashtray on a glass coffee table and a few dishes near the sink, there was no mess.

Through the kitchenette, a sliding door led into a bathroom and laundry. This room wasn't so clean, old flecks of toothpaste and shave bristles around the basin and vanity. I found a packet of OxyContin in the cabinet and remembered fondly the floating relief the same pills had given me during my initial rehabilitation. I also remembered the constipation, stomach pains and flu-like withdrawal when I finally decided to give them up. I closed the cabinet and caught a glimpse of myself in the mirror.

The grey etchings and stress lines around my eyes betrayed my age. I was only thirty-nine but looked ten years older. Women used to say I was handsome. While I still had the chiselled jaw Ella had once fallen for, my skin now looked moist and pasty, like the junkies I saw roaming the streets every day.

Back in the kitchen, I opened the fridge and found it stocked with leftover takeaway cartons, soft drink and VB beer. No Amstel. Next I opened the cupboard beneath the sink and found the bin, but it was empty. Above it on the bench was an answering machine, digital and more expensive than my own at home. Both this and the designer clothes Boyd was wearing when we found him seemed at odds with his status as a welfare recipient and ward of the state. I pushed play on the machine, a flashing light indicating he hadn't heard the message.

*'Yeah, Dall, Sparks here, mate. I've got what you wanted me to get. I went to the park last night like we said, but you weren't there, man. I've been ringing ya moby all night but no answer. What the fuck, man? Hanging on to this thing's freakin' me out, you better come get it soon or I'm gonna ditch it. That's it, man, I gotta run.'*

A mechanical voice stated the call had come through at nine fifteen that morning. I played the message again. The caller sounded agitated, his desire to see Boyd urgent. I checked the machine for other messages but there weren't any. I wrote the name 'Sparks' and the time of the call on the page I'd torn from my daybook and began a methodical search of the kitchen, starting in the corner, working my way through all the drawers, checking the oven and above each cupboard. I found little of value beyond a small stash of marijuana and ecstasy tablets in the freezer. The ecstasy pills had a different branding from what Anthony had shown me earlier and revived my unease about my brother's request. What was I supposed to do? Show Chloe pictures of dead people, tell her horror stories?

I left the drugs in place and moved back into the bedroom, where again I had the impression Boyd wasn't your average state ward. There were five pairs of runners in the wardrobe and maybe a hundred CDs in a vertical display stand. This kid had money. Pondering how, I noticed a Nokia phone charger plugged into a power socket and again wondered about the missing phone. Even Sparks, whoever he was, had said in his message that he'd been trying to call Dallas on his mobile phone. Had somebody removed the phone from his body? Wouldn't be the first time a deceased junkie was robbed by his own kind. But why not take his wallet and watch, even his runners?

I squatted down to search the bedside table. In a drawer with socks and underpants was a reminder letter from the YMCA in Prahran advising Boyd that his gym membership was due to expire. The letter was dated 1 December the previous year, less than three months ago. Clipped to the letter was a map of Surfers Paradise. I spread the map out on the bed and saw that someone had highlighted several streets in orange felt pen. Ella had family in Queensland and I'd been to the Gold Coast a number of times, so I immediately recognised the streets as popular tourist precincts. Cavill Avenue. Tedder Avenue. Orchard Avenue. In the top corner of the map was a name and address, obviously written by somebody with poor literacy skills: *Derek Jardine, 4/678 Sunset Cresant, Mermade Worters.*

Who was Derek Jardine? And why was the map clipped to the YMCA reminder letter? Anthony worked at the Docklands YMCA and would have access to client names. I made a note to call him, then searched the rest of the room but still failed to find a mobile phone. There was a shoebox under the bed with a collection of blank DVDs inside. The title *Die Hard With A Vengeance* was scribbled on one of the cases. Underneath it were others like *Goodfellas* and *Scarface*. I slid the box of pirated movies back and noticed a photo on a stand by the door. It was Dallas Boyd and a girl about the same age posing at St Kilda beach, white sand contrasting against the blue water and a burning red sunset behind them. The photo appeared recent, possibly taken this summer. Boyd even had on the same red baseball cap he'd been wearing when he died.

Who had taken the picture? I hadn't found a camera in the apartment anywhere. Maybe the camera belonged to the girl and they'd asked somebody to take it for them. But the photo looked so professional this was unlikely; nor was it likely that the picture had been taken with Dallas Boyd's missing phone, or any phone for that matter. While I was in rehab I'd bought myself a digital camera and done what I could to learn how to use it properly. It hadn't been nearly as easy as I'd expected. Whoever took this shot had experience. If taken by an amateur with a mobile phone or with a camera by somebody simply strolling past, the sunset in the background would leave the picture washed out with too much light. Instead the couple had been brought to the foreground by a keen eye and technical know-how.

I let some ideas roll around but nothing jogged. I focused on the girl. She was familiar, attractive but trashy, with a pink bikini top and a Celtic tattoo around her navel. Suddenly I recognised her. Replacing the picture, I locked the front door and ran down the concrete walkway to find the Valiant turning into Barkly Street. I chased after it, but was too late. As the Valiant took the corner, the hooker stared back at me from the passenger seat. The girl in the picture.

# 7

WHEN I GOT HOME THE PHONE was ringing. I fumbled with the keys, trying to balance my briefcase in one hand and a bag of groceries in the other. Inside, I tripped over Prince and damn near fell over as I snapped up the handset.

'Yes.'

'What kind of way is that to answer the phone?'

I smiled. It was Ella.

'Ah, sorry, just got in and had to rush for it.'

'Right. Are you decent?'

'Indeed I am,' I said. 'Every week I make a donation of ten dollars to the tips jar at the Stokehouse. They have university students working there. My tips help pay for their study. I'd call that decent.'

'I'd call it bribery. You're just paying for quick service on busy nights. No long waits at the bar.'

'Oh, ye of little faith. You'll ruin my image, you pessimist.'

'Realist, more like it. And I won't ruin your image at all. You do a good enough job of that yourself. I bet at least one item of your clothing has a food or drink stain on it.'

I looked down at my clothes and felt embarrassed. Sweat had soaked through my polo shirt and for a second I thought about stripping off just to prove her wrong.

'Am I right?' she prodded.

'Possibly.'

She laughed. 'Well, fair enough. Before we crap on any longer, I'm standing out the front. We agreed to meet at seven o'clock. It's now seven. Should I come up or stay out here looking like a desperate woman?'

'I like the sound of desperate.'

'Not funny, Rubens. It's bloody hot out here.'

'Well, get up here then!'

Ideally I would've preferred time to prepare for her arrival, but the massage and the search of Boyd's apartment had drained my afternoon. I stored the beer and groceries in the fridge, turned on the cooler and opened the blinds. In the bathroom, I wiped the toilet seat, washed my hands and sprayed on cologne.

Opening the front door, I saw Ella had dyed her hair a deep maroon since the last time we'd met, taking at least five years off her. I wanted to tell her she looked beautiful but decided against it.

'I like the hair,' I said instead. 'Come in.'

She stepped over the threshold, leaning in to kiss my cheek. 'Like the top,' she said cheekily, noticing my soiled shirt. 'Get that from the Salvo's on Grey Street?'

'Oh, lay off.'

She laughed, circled around the bench and put her handbag down on one of the stools. 'So, what's a girl gotta do to get a drink around here?'

I opened the fridge, snapped out two bottles from the sixpack and slid one over. One of the things I loved about Ella was her appreciation of beer. While she only drank it in the summer, there'd been a number of times when she'd matched me round for round.

We clinked bottles. 'So where's the little one?' she said, looking around for Prince.

'Outside killing birds, hunting native wildlife, searching for a mate.'

'Stop it. You shouldn't let him out. It's dangerous.'

'He's a cat, El. He has needs.'

'Sounds like a typical male,' she said, dangling her arms and speaking like a caveman. 'Man like animal. Must search for food, mate women and sleep often.'

We both laughed.

'Look, here he is,' I said, pointing at the door.

Prince breezed through the cat flap and rubbed against her leg. She picked him up and cooed at him while I opened a bottle of pinot to let it breathe while we finished our beers.

'Still on for tomorrow night?' she asked, nodding towards my nephew's eighteenth-birthday invitation on the fridge.

'Sure, but only if you want to. I know it's going to be strange with all my family there. I mean, I spoke to Andy today, and it's fine if you don't want to go, but I kinda feel like I should. Haven't seen my folks since Christmas and I think I –'

'It's okay,' she said. 'I'm looking forward to it.'

'Really?'

'Yeah, they're good kids. How are they, by the way?'

I didn't want to tell her about Chloe and the drugs, or my brother's request that I speak to her about it. I still wasn't sure how to approach it.

'Fine, I guess. Johnno's started year twelve and Chloe's back to uni next month. Everyone's growing up.'

She shook her head and I wondered whether she'd read the lie or was simply picturing the kids becoming adults.

'Time flies,' I said. 'Soon there'll be weddings and babies.'

'Oh, hold up, will you. Let them have fun for a while.'

I made a high-pitched wail like a baby crying and Ella shuddered. The thought of having children had never particularly appealed to her. Maybe if she had a steady partner. A committed husband.

'So what's on the menu?' she asked, putting Prince down and

sliding onto the sofa. 'What's the sultan of South Melbourne got on the cards tonight?'

'Well, it's Albert Park, actually.'

'Whatever. You sound like a Snoburb.'

'A what?'

'You know, one of those wankers who gets all snobby about what suburb they live in.' She put on a high voice and added, 'It's not South Melbourne, darling, it's Albert Park.'

I took a swig on my beer and tried to think of a comeback but couldn't.

'Anyway, I was going to do a rogan josh but it kind of loses grunt without the meat. So tonight I'll do a warm tuna and chilli salad. You still eat fish, don't you?'

'Yep.'

On a platter I arranged piles of mushrooms, ham and sun-dried tomatoes around a chunk of camembert, which I then carried to the lounge and set down on the coffee table. Ella helped herself to the platter, then stood in front of the stereo cabinet examining my CD collection.

'You got the new INXS album,' she said, selecting it from the rack. 'Good one.'

'Not exactly new,' I corrected. 'It's a tribute album. Lots of duets and reworking of the originals. Put it on if you like.'

'Sure will, but I'm just not sure I like the idea of someone trying to copy the almighty Michael Hutchence.'

I nodded. There wasn't a true INXS fan who wasn't insanely protective of the band's classic anthems. Michael Hutchence had a voice and a presence that could never be replaced.

'It's respectful,' I said. 'And they don't try to copy him. Trust me, I wouldn't even have it in my collection if they did.'

The track she selected was about as good as it got. 'Never Tear Us Apart' was probably the best recognised and most moving song released by INXS. Some people said it was simply a story of love at first sight and the passion that followed, but I disagreed. For me there was a real sadness in there, a knowing that the love wouldn't last. Sure, there was nothing in the lyrics specifically saying that; it was more in the way it was delivered. The version Ella selected featured a duet between Tom Jones and Natalie Imbruglia who, perhaps deliberately, sang with more optimism than the original. It was a beautiful recreation, but they could never touch Michael Hutchence's haunting vocals.

I tied on an old apron and Ella smirked at me from across the lounge.

'What?'

'Isn't that the one I bought you?' she asked. 'Like, five years ago?'

'Indeed it is,' I said, looking down at how faded and torn it was.

'Looks like you need a new one.'

'I tried to give it to the Salvo's but they wouldn't take it. Apparently they have enough troubles of their own. You know you're in strife when even the charities don't want your belongings.'

I went back to the fridge, took out the ingredients for the salad and began chopping it all into piles.

'You know something,' Ella said, 'you'd be quite a catch if you weren't so focused on work.'

'What's that supposed to mean?'

She rolled onto her stomach, facing me on the sofa. 'Well, you're intelligent, funny, and you like to cook. That's rare for a man.'

'Too focused on work?'

'Don't take it the wrong way. I just mean you shouldn't be so worried about being an ace detective any more. You've done your time for the police. Maybe you should think about yourself and do something else.'

'I need to work, El. I have bills and a mortgage.'

'I don't mean quit the police; I just mean do something easier. You know, plenty of cops go back to work but don't go back on the street.'

I put the knife down and considered her comments. It seemed everyone these days was telling me the same thing. Move on, McCauley, time to step aside and let another soldier take your place. Even Cassie had been hinting at it and, even though I would never admit it to anyone, I knew it wasn't such a bad idea. I could spend more time with Ella, and visit Mum and Dad more often. That would keep Anthony happy. And I might even get to go to the cricket again with Edgar. I filled a salad bowl with the beans and chilli, and tossed them with the tuna as I thought about how a new life could take shape.

The CD player was on shuffle mode and the band's new front man, J.D. Fortune, was working his way through a rendition of 'Suicide Blonde' when Ella suddenly screamed and dropped her beer bottle on the floor.

'Jesus Christ,' she shrieked. 'What the hell is that?'

'What?' I said, watching Prince dart away from the sofa.

She pointed at the television. 'That!'

Looking over, I realised I'd left the camera plugged into the AV port. Dallas Boyd's ghost-white body filled the screen, the needle hanging from his arm. I'd turned the television off but not the camera.

'You weren't meant to see that.'

'Weren't meant to see it?' She tossed the remote control on the coffee table. 'I just bumped the bloody thing and it's right there on the screen! What the hell is it anyway?'

Instead of answering, I unplugged the camera and stepped into the bathroom, ran the cold water and rinsed my face. I was embarrassed and knew it only validated her point. I wasn't on the ball.

'Get with it,' I said to myself in the mirror. 'Lift your game.'

When I opened the door Ella was there, a glass of wine in each hand. She handed me one. A peace offering.

'Maybe we both need a drink?' she said.

I took the glass but didn't move from the doorway.

'Tell me about him,' she said.

'Who?'

'The boy in the picture.'

Genuine concern filled her face and my sense was that she didn't want to judge me. She wanted to understand me. Right then I realised this was necessary for our future, and I made a choice. I would tell her.

By the time I'd told her about the case, it was almost dark outside. We'd drunk two-thirds of the wine and eaten all of the cheese and biscuits, but hadn't touched the tuna salad. Sitting beside her on the sofa, I stared at my reflection in the window, glad she had listened.

After a long moment she walked to the balcony. 'I need a smoke.'

I opened the door for her and followed her out. The city was alive with the sound of traffic, techno music pumping from a party nearby. The north wind had settled, leaving the smoky air still and warm, like a bonfire left to cool. I leant against the balustrade and lit Ella's cigarette first, then my own. She blew out a cloud of smoke and stared at the city skyscrapers.

'Sad about the fires,' she said. 'Apparently some of them have been deliberately lit. I don't know how those people live with themselves.'

I didn't know the answer either, but I did know she was trying to talk about anything other than what was really on her mind.

She was halfway through the cigarette before she spoke again. 'You know, that's the first time you've ever told me about one of your cases.'

I nodded.

'I know it's not easy, but I appreciate it. It helps me understand what you do, Rubens.' She took my hand, her skin warm and comforting. 'I want you to know you can tell me anything.'

'I know,' I said, looking into her eyes.

'No, I don't think you do. When you were in the hospital and they . . .' She cupped a hand over her mouth and I thought she was going to cry but she held it together. 'When they didn't know what was going to happen with you, whether you were going to live or not, I realised why you were in so much trouble. It wasn't just because those men were out to get you. It was because I blamed you for everything that happened to us, and I refused to understand what was happening in your life because I didn't want to know.'

She was referring to a case I'd worked more than a year before, when I'd been set up for the murder of an underworld figure and subsequently shot during the arrest of the killer. It was at a time when our marriage was at the point of no return. There were nights away from home, sometimes weeks at a time. We'd picked fights with each other over money, over stupid things. Meanwhile, there were corruption allegations, the disbanding of entire police squads. Some of my colleagues were involved in underworld killings and drug trafficking. Some were murdered, others went to prison. Some even committed suicide. Prior to all that, I'd spent two whole years on trial after a bikie gang member accused me of accepting bribes. Sure, I was eventually acquitted but I lost my wife in the process. The counselling sessions helped, but not enough. In the end it wasn't her fault and it wasn't mine. At least, that's what I told myself.

'I never want to go there again,' she said.

'I'm not going back to hospital, Ella. I don't work cases like that any more.'

'I don't mean that. I mean I never want to be confused again.' She frowned, struggling with her thoughts. 'What I'm saying, I guess, is that I want to understand you, Rubens. Because if I can't understand you, then I can't . . .' Again her voice trailed off and she looked away.

'What?' I prodded. 'If you can't understand me, then what?'

'Then I can't get to *know* you again.'

Squashing her cigarette in the ashtray, she set her glass on the outside table then buried her face against my chest. I held her, not wanting to move.

'I want you to find him,' she said.

'Who?'

'Whoever killed that boy.'

I pressed my nose into her hair and inhaled. Her smell was intoxicating and something uncurled in me. I looked out across the palm trees towards St Kilda. A glow of light rose from behind the ferris wheel at Luna Park, as though it too was on fire. I squeezed her tighter, knowing this was more than just a physical embrace. Without even knowing, she'd reminded me of why I'd fallen in love with her all those years ago. Ella had been the only person to ever truly believe in me and I suddenly realised, for the first time perhaps, that she may never have really stopped. I cupped her face in my hands and kissed her forehead, wondering how I'd ever got it so wrong.

'Will you stay?' I asked.

She eased out of my arms and, just like that, I knew I'd asked too soon. The moment was over.

'Not tonight.'

# 8

EVEN WITH THE AIR CONDITIONER ON, I slept rest-
lessly after Ella left, finally waking at 5 a.m., unable to get her
out of my thoughts. Despite her declining my offer to spend the
night, it hadn't spoilt the evening or undone any of the positives.
There seemed to be a glowing ember of hope now and I couldn't
wait to see her again, but I needed to be patient. I'd once read
somewhere – possibly in a trashy magazine at the doctor's clinic
– that a woman's heart was delicate, and that distance and space
were sometimes more important than flowers and phone calls.
It was all in the timing, apparently. I wanted to call or at least
send a text message, but it was too soon. I needed to blow on
the ember gently, fuel it gradually and pray that it would catch.

I quickly showered and made my way outside. It was going
to be another scorcher. Driving through St Kilda before dawn,
I noticed the strip was busier than it had been twenty-four hours
earlier. Groups of clubbers gathered outside nightclubs, hailing
taxis and staggering across the street.

Outside the Prince of Wales Hotel, an ambulance had pulled
into the kerb, its lights flashing. Two paramedics squatted over

a patient on the sidewalk, the fluorescent strips on their jump-suits glowing like beacons. In front of the ambulance, a divisional van had its blue lights going too. Must've been a brawl some-where. Another drunk bites the dust.

I slowed down, recognising the two uniforms questioning the victim's friends, one of whom held a bloodied tissue to his face. The other's shirt had either gone missing or had been used post-battle as a makeshift bandage. I wound the window down and asked the cops if they needed help. One of them quipped that if I could make it rain, they could use me. I nodded at the familiar complaint. The hotter it got, the more people drank and the more we were called upon to break up brawls and shitfights.

At the Acland Street junction, near where Dallas Boyd had died, I went over what I hoped to achieve today. Top of the list was to let Ben Eckles know I no longer believed the death to be accidental. It was a conversation I wasn't looking forward to, but I didn't care. I was in the hunt again and felt the clarity of my judgement and intuition returning.

At the police station on Chapel Street, I parked in the side car park, using the window reflection to adjust my tie. I took the concrete staircase to the third floor where the detective squad rooms were located. In the mess room the television was on but no one was watching. No one in the squad room either. Checking the whiteboard, I saw the night-shift detectives had signed out a car to attend a crime scene. In the notations column next to their names were the letters 'DD'. A domestic dispute.

The open-plan squad room stretched the length of the building and accommodated a team of fourteen detectives. My desk was in the back corner, wedged between a concrete wall and a row of filing cabinets. As I made my way between the desks, the domestic dispute notation reminded me that Dallas Boyd's stepfather needed attention. If, as Will Novak had said, Dallas had organ-ised for the Department of Human Services to check on his sister, there was a very real chance the girl could be removed from the home. Though it sounded like genuine motive, thinking about it now, the killing seemed too slick for a domestic homicide. Still, I couldn't rule it out without a thorough check.

Eckles' office overlooked the squad room, but the door was closed and the blinds drawn. It was just after six and I figured I had about thirty minutes before he arrived. I dumped my briefcase at my desk and took my daybook to a computer by the window. Soon after his assignment as senior sergeant for the CIU, Eckles had rearranged the room so that all four computers were lined up facing the window. His official claim was that it enabled detectives to look out the window every so often, thus reducing eye strain, but everyone knew the real reason was so Eckles could see what was on each screen from his office, which we had nicknamed 'the observation post'. In response, detectives who wanted a little privacy simply raised their chairs so their shoulders blocked the screen.

I did this now, even though Eckles wasn't in, and logged onto the Law Enforcement Assistance Program. While the LEAP database booted, I opened my daybook to my notes from yesterday and started on the list of names I needed to check.

*Sparks – nickname?*

*Derek Jardine – friend?*

*Vincent Rowe – stepfather*

First I ran a check on Dallas Boyd. Skim reading, I learnt Boyd had an extensive criminal history that had culminated in an armed robbery two years before. There were no other offences since then. As Will Novak had said, Boyd had stayed clear of the police after his release from Malmsbury. I wasn't sure what to make of this. I wasn't a big believer in the virtues of criminal rehabilitation, in either kiddie or adult prisons.

Reading on, I answered my second question when I saw the name 'Derek Jardine' in the case narrative. Jardine and Boyd had been arrested for the robbery of a Chinese takeaway store. I used the incident number to bring up the relevant information on Jardine. A year older than Boyd, he had a similar story, with numerous petty offences prior to the armed robbery. Nothing since. No fixed place of abode. However, there was an extra paragraph that wasn't in Boyd's narrative.

> Offender Derek JARDINE (DOB 10/10/1991) and co-offender Dallas BOYD (DOB 01/11/1992) are well known to each other through foster care and have committed numerous offences in tandem. Third offender Stuart PARKS (DOB 14/02/1993) is also well known to both males, both through the commission of crimes and the DHS Child Protection Unit. All three are accomplices in this matter, although it appears PARKS was unaware of the plans to carry out the robbery.

I wrote the name Stuart Parks next to the nickname 'Sparks' in my daybook, printed the entire file and returned to the main menu, then ran a name search on him. This was more like it. Parks had dozens of convictions, most recently for a residential burglary dated a week after Christmas. His address was registered as the Carlisle Accommodation & Recovery Service. I didn't get excited about that: a lot of the street people in St Kilda used hostels for an address even if they didn't actually live there. An address was necessary to receive welfare payments and these places were the closest they had to a home. Still, it meant Will Novak would probably know the kid.

I glanced at the clock on the wall: 6.30 a.m. Eckles would be in soon. I printed the page then opened my email inbox and typed a message to the Divisional Intelligence Unit requesting copies of both Stuart Parks' and Derek Jardine's mug shots. Using the number Novak had given me, I also filled out a request for a call charge record on Dallas Boyd's mobile phone, hoping the calls coming to and from the phone in the hours before his death might help ID a suspect. Finally I switched back to LEAP and printed everything I could find on the stepfather, Vincent Rowe. Gathering the pages off the printer, I hid them in my daybook as the door opened at the end of the squad room and Ben Eckles walked in.

'McCauley, you're in early,' he said. 'Wasn't sure if you were going to make it. I left a message on your machine but you never called.'

He walked through the room, suit faded and too big for his lean body. His red hair was slick and wet and combed back over a dome-shaped head. The haze of sunspots covering his face, responsible for his nickname, Freckles, had increased over summer.

'You don't need to remind me to show up for work,' I said.

He grunted as he unlocked his office, hit the light and dumped his briefcase on the desk. Following him in, I told him I needed a chat.

'Can it wait? I've just got here.'

'It's important.'

He tilted his long face, as if my simple explanation held all the answers. 'Just give me a few minutes.'

I walked into the mess room to check the TV for a weather update. Sure enough, thirty-seven degrees and no relief for the firemen. Even a brand-new fleet of water-bombers brought in from America wasn't helping much. I soaked a paper towel and was dabbing it against my eyes when Eckles walked in.

'What's the matter with your eyes?' he asked, a hint of sarcasm in his tone. 'Been out on the piss again?'

'No. Hayfever.'

'Hayfever? That's what my seventeen-year-old son tells me when he's been smoking dope. He thinks I'm stupid. Thinks I don't know why his eyes are bloodshot.' He leant into my face. 'Are you a pothead as well, McCauley?'

I smiled at his lame attempt at humour. Prior to my shooting, Eckles had been the boss of the uniform section downstairs. Back then, he had assisted the Ethical Standards Department by enlisting one of his rookies, Cassie Withers, to spy on me. At the time they'd all believed I was responsible for, or at least involved in, the murder of an acquitted cop killer. But Cassie, to her credit, had gone in with open eyes and we were both eventually able to prove them all wrong and find the real killer. Most cops saw her efforts, and mine, particularly after the shooting, as heroic and staunch. We had taken on the under-world and the ESD, and lived to fight another day. Eckles, on the other hand, didn't fare so well. Despite being promoted to run the St Kilda CIU, a lot of coppers were suspicious of him and I knew he quietly blamed me for that.

'A lot of people think I'm stupid,' he said, pouring a cup of coffee from an urn on the wall. 'You don't think I'm stupid, do you?'

'I think your son does more than just smoke dope,' I joked, trying to lighten his mood. 'Saw him down on Fitzroy Street last night, tight hotpants, lace T-shirt, outside one of the gay clubs. I think some of the boys downstairs got pictures.'

Eckles frowned at me, unimpressed. 'Yeah, righto. What's the problem with the OD?'

'Ah, well, I'm not sure any more that it was accidental.'

'What?'

'There were anomalies with the scene.' I was about to elabor-ate when we heard voices from outside. Two detectives walked by, said hello and continued on to the squad room. 'I don't think we should discuss it here. Day shift's about to start. Maybe we could go —'

'Speaking of which,' Eckles interrupted. 'Where's Cassie? Finetti said she bailed out early Thursday and left you with the OD. I'm not happy about that.'

Annoyance and frustration clouded my thoughts. Finetti and Cassie had worked together in the uniform section for almost five years, forming a strong friendship that had become intimate on at least one occasion. Now that he wasn't getting into her pants any more, things weren't as rosy between them.

'Seems Finetti said a lot, huh?' I said to Eckles.

Eckles checked his watch theatrically. 'Well, where is she, McCauley? I mean, I know her old man's sick, but she either works here or she doesn't. You basically sponsored her entry into the CI, and I can't run this joint properly if I don't even know who's going to show up.'

'Her father's not just sick, Ben. He has *leukaemia*. Jesus, Cassie paid for him and her mother to fly here to get the treatment he needs.'

'I know that. I just think . . .'

His words faded as Cassie walked into the mess room.

'Think what?' she said innocently.

Cassie was short and stocky, but incredibly athletic, with short blonde hair she'd recently had cut and styled into a spike. It was a rough and grungy look, and there'd been mumblings about dykes when she first had it cut, but I absolutely loved it about her. No bullshit. Sexy without the make-up or fancy fingernails.

'Heard my name,' she said. 'What's the go, boss?'

'Sarge was just saying he wishes he could help you out a bit,' I said. 'I'm suggesting he put you on permanent day shift. What do ya say, boss?'

'Ah, yeah,' he said, giving me a curt smile and walking away. 'I'll have a look at the roster and see who I can juggle.'

I winked at Cassie and followed Eckles back to his office. He closed the door and nodded towards the chair facing his desk.

'Nice one,' he said. 'Now I've gotta come good on that or she'll bitch to the lezzos over in Equal Opportunity. That's all I bloody need, the hairy armpit brigade marching through here with their women's rights.' He slumped in his chair and shook his head. 'That's what's wrong with the job these days. We used to be a *police* force, now we're just a *pussy* force.'

I waited, silent, letting him rant.

'Don't tell me you agree with affirmative action?' He pointed out the window. 'Let me tell you something, McCauley. This isn't a fucking university; this is the real world. Having fancy pussy like Cassie fluffing around only makes it harder for blokes like you and me to get the job done. I don't care what anyone says, females just get in the way. I mean, can you really see her out there wrestling with drunks or brawling with some shithead off his face on meth?'

I didn't bother replying. I could name numerous occasions when female cops even smaller than Cassie had dealt effectively with the mad, the bad and the sad.

'You wanna hear this or not?' I said.

'Sure, go.'

I explained the anomalies at the crime scene, starting with the missing syringe cap and moving through to the lack of teeth marks on the leather belt. I told him about the missing mobile phone and the CCR I was requesting, and ended by detailing the expensive clothes the victim had been wearing and how he hadn't had a single criminal conviction over the past year. I didn't mention anything about my visit to the morgue, the conversation with Will Novak or my search of Boyd's apartment.

When I'd finished, Eckles rubbed his jaw, swivelled away from the desk and looked out the window.

'So you're saying somebody else injected him?'

'I'm saying I think he was murdered.'

'Whoa, hold up a second.' He fished a report from a tray on his desk. 'That's your eighty-three from yesterday morning.'

Eighty-three was code for an official police report to the coroner.

'Now let's read from the summary,' he continued. ' "Nil signs of violence. Nil suspicious circumstances. Most likely cause of death is accidental overdose." '

I remained silent while he put the report back in his pile.

'Let me get this right,' he said. 'What you're telling me is that you think you might have green-carded a homicide, wrote it off as accidental?'

'I wouldn't put it that way.'

'Then how would you put it?'

'I'm telling you there are anomalies that need investigating; anomalies that weren't apparent at the initial crime scene.'

'What do you mean they weren't *apparent* at the crime scene? Everything you've just described was *at* the crime scene.'

I closed my eyes, knowing it was true.

'What I mean is, I didn't realise the significance of it all until I got home and thought about it.'

'So you wrote it off as accidental because you either ignored or missed the anomalies at first. Now you've had a change of mind.'

'Well, not exactly. I guess everyone on the scene concurred that it looked like a standard OD.'

'Everyone else? You mean Finetti?'

I nodded, the shame of it weighing on me.

'Since when do you let a cowboy like Finetti dictate a crime scene? This was your scene, McCauley. *You* wrote it off, so don't go blaming anyone else. *You* accept this fuck-up and own it —'

'All right,' I said, a little too forcefully, anger curling inside me like a fist. I needed solutions, not condemnation. 'What are we going to do?'

'We?'

'Well, you countersigned that report, boss. Like you said, it goes up the line.'

He stared at me a long moment. 'We wait and see what happens with the coroner. If they pick up suspicious circs then we don't look like dickheads calling in Homicide after the horse has bolted.'

'And what if the coroner doesn't pick up any other anomalies and all we've got to go on is what we know about the crime scene?'

'Then it's not a homicide.'

'Excuse me?'

Eckles let out a sigh. 'Look, we can't afford to be chasing so-called anomalies for every single death we come across. That's what the coroner's for. Besides, this department has suffered enough embarrassment over recent years, and so have you. I don't want you to pursue this any further and be thrown into the public laundry again. We've done our part.'

My gut churned. I saw right through him. It had nothing to do with saving the reputation of the Force or balancing resources or, indeed, my welfare.

'It's your job you're worried about, isn't it?' I said. 'You're the officer in charge here, the *acting* OIC, but you don't want a check against your name when it comes time to appoint a permanent. So you'd prefer to write this off as accidental rather than lose face by accepting we made a mistake.'

Eckles pressed his hands down on the desk and took a breath, measuring his words. 'I wouldn't say *we* made the mistake. I think the only mistake *I* made was letting you back on the team in the first place.'

'Really?'

'Well, I can't afford to have detectives on my team who make these kinds of mistakes. This is St Kilda, the busiest CIU in the country. Surely you understand this sort of thing makes me question your judgement.'

My left shoulder tensed and I rubbed it with my hand.

'What I understand is that you're still pissed off I proved my own innocence in the Varilla case. And if I was betting, I'd say that's why you put so much shit on Cassie, because your plan to pit her against me backfired. You were wrong about me and you were wrong about her. What does that say about your judgement?'

'That's ridiculous. I wanted to believe you were clean on that. I *knew* you were clean. We just needed to prove it, so I used Cassie to do it.'

I scoffed at that. It was complete bullshit and I was offended that he thought I was stupid enough to believe it.

'No, you see, setting Cassie against me and taking sides with ESD showed everyone what side you were on. Now you wonder why nobody trusts you. It's not that everyone thinks you're stupid, they just know you've got ambitions.'

'There's nothing wrong with that.'

'There is if you're prepared to sell out your own crew to climb the mountain.'

He breathed out long and low, as though attempting to calm an inner rage.

'You know what your problem is, McCauley? You don't respect your superiors. That's always been your problem – you're recalcitrant and you have an ego the size of a Jamaican's dick.'

I wanted to argue back on that one, but instead I got to the point.

'Look, let's move on. It's in the past and we need to be a team. I mean, we're all on the same side, right?'

He didn't answer that.

'Come on, boss. I'm here now and I'm not going anywhere. You might wish I wasn't here, but I am, and in the end you don't get to choose who stays on the CI. My rep goes higher up the line than this office, so let's just work together on this and find a solution.'

Eckles walked around his desk, leant over me. The smell of coffee wafted from his breath as he spoke, his voice a coarse whisper.

'Maybe I agree with all that, but you're missing the point. You've just come in here and admitted to me that you made a mistake. A big mistake, so this *is* my choice. You're on a return-to-work pass. All I have to do is dish you up an unsatisfactory performance report and you're back at home watching *Days of Our Lives*.'

'Maybe you need your ears checked, Freckles. Your signature is on that inquest sheet too. So we're in this together. How do you think it'll look if a genuine homicide gets written off as accidental on your watch?'

He stepped back and pursed his lips, making his face look like a squashed tea bag.

'Fine, do what you want, McCauley, but I'm warning you, I won't go down for this. See, I have friends too. I didn't just bend over for ESD without getting something in return. They owe me, mate, and they've made it perfectly clear that careers in this organisation are built on the scalps of rogues like you. So don't screw me on this or I'll serve you up quicker than shit off a shovel. You got that?'

Yeah, I got it, all right. The Police Force is like a huge carnivorous machine, completely unforgiving. Everybody knows you don't get even by trying to fight it, so what I did next probably wasn't the wisest of moves, but sometimes you can't help yourself.

'You know something, Ben,' I said from the doorway, loud enough for everyone in the squad room to hear, 'you talk about my lack of respect. The truth is, I *used* to respect you, back when you were a cop.'

'What's that supposed to mean?'

'You're not a cop any more. You're a fucking bureaucrat.'

# 9

AT MY DESK, I PACKED MY daybook and the LEAP reports I'd printed into my briefcase. All eyes in the squad room were on me. I'd disrupted their routine, and although many of them would be silently agreeing with me, any overt signs of support would almost certainly see the offending member on the boss's shit list.

In the end only Cassie had the front to approach me. 'Took a message for you, from Dr Julie Wong at the morgue,' she said, handing over a Post-it note. 'She'll be ready to see you in about an hour. Got women all over town, haven't we?'

I managed a smile as Cassie checked over her shoulder, concern and intrigue meshed across her face.

'So what's going on? You and Freckles sounded worse than the two Paddy and Zoff copped last night.'

Paddy and Zoff were the night detectives who'd been called out to the domestic dispute.

'Why, what happened?' I asked.

'Guy comes home pissed from the pokies, hears girl on the phone. He unplugs the phone. Girl hits guy, guy hits back. Girl hits head on coffee table. Kaput.'

'Dead?'

'Not yet. Popped her head right open. They've got her on a brain bleeder at the Alfred. Homicide are on standby.'

'Shit. Speaking of hospitals, how's your dad?'

'Not so bad, for the moment,' she said, lowering her voice again. 'He's still in remission but they're keeping him in for a few more days.'

The strain was etched into her skin, like a pigment. It was the waiting that did it more than anything. Waiting for results, news, miracles. Long, incessant waiting.

'So why are you here then?'

'I can't go again, Rubes. I heard what was said in the mess room. Freckles is a first-class prick.'

'Hear, hear,' I muttered.

'How was I to know we'd land a dead kid after I left?'

'You weren't, so don't worry. It was my call to send you off and I stand by it.'

She nodded uneasily. 'I know, but I don't want everyone thinking my head's not in the right place. I like this job and I want to keep it.'

We were silent then. I wanted to tell her to take my advice, not to put the job first. That family was more important, you could always get another job. Learn from me, my mistakes. That's what I should have told her. But there were some things even friends didn't want to hear. Who was I to give advice anyway?

'Thanks for what you said to him,' she said finally. 'I've been putting in for permanent day shift since we got the news on Dad.'

I shrugged. At least I was good for something.

'No, I really appreciate you forcing his hand like that. Just tell me what's going on here, will ya? Last I heard it was a clean-cut OD. Now you're in there sounding like Tina and Ike.' She nudged me playfully with her hip. 'You wanna fill me in before your date this morning?'

'It's not a date.'

'The morgue, huh? Classy stuff, Rubes. All that cold stainless steel. You bring sexiness back into the office. I like it.'

I knew she was trying to cheer me up, so I tried to satisfy her with a smile. Behind her, Eckles had the phone cradled between his ear and shoulder, scribbling on a pad.

'Let's get out of here,' I said. 'I feel about as welcome as a fart in a phone box.'

We headed down the St Kilda Esplanade and followed it towards the city. I used the time to tell Cassie everything I knew so far. By the time I'd finished we were outside the coronial complex in Southbank. I leant over and rummaged through the glove box for a packet of antihistamine.

'Headache?' she asked.

'Nah, hayfever. Bloody bushfires,' I said, popping out a tablet and washing it down with the water I'd bought earlier. 'Now, if you don't want to come in, that's fine. This could be a bad one. Everything up until now suggests the kid was abused. I'm not expecting to hear any different once I go inside.'

'Hey, I worked a six-month secondment in the Rape Squad before I landed this gig, remember?'

I was about to ask what she was worried about, when I realised. 'It's Eckles, isn't it? You're worried if you help me, you'll be tarred with my brush.'

Cassie looked embarrassed.

'Don't worry, I won't let that happen. *I* made the mistake, not you. If the shit rolls downhill, it'll stop at my desk. It won't go any further.'

After a long moment, she got out of the car, defiant. 'Eckles can go to hell. Let's do this.'


At the entrance, I had to speak into a voice panel before the door clicked open. Inside, the foyer was dark and silent, reception desk empty. At half-past eight on a Saturday morning I figured cranky-pants was probably home in bed.

'This way, officers,' a voice called from behind us.

We swivelled around to see Matthew Briggs, the forensic technician, standing at the end of the foyer, beckoning us to a doorway. An overhead light silhouetted his lean frame against the dark hallway behind. He wore a green medical gown and white gumboots and his pasty face glowed in the light, like a ghost.

I thanked him for his help in having Boyd's autopsy rescheduled, but he walked ahead without reply, probably still annoyed. We went past the coronial library, down another hall and through a set of sliding doors, where a harsh smell of disinfectant filled the air. At the end of the corridor Briggs opened a door and gestured for us to enter.

The room was carpeted, with a table and chairs in the centre and two viewing windows on each wall. Through the glass was an autopsy suite similar to a hospital operating theatre. On the other side of the window, Dr Julie Wong, wearing a green hospital gown and white gumboots like Briggs, held an X-ray slide up to a viewing box. Wong was a gentle woman of Singaporean descent; I'd known her since my time in the former Drug Squad when several criminals – and some cops – had ended up on this very table. Her accent had an American hint to it, a product of an affluent upbringing and education in the US.

Behind her, a body lay on a stainless steel table, covered in a blue sheet. I tapped on the glass and nodded when she turned around.

'Morning, officers,' she said, her voice robotic through the intercom. Setting the X-ray down on a counter, she lifted her facemask. 'You know the drill. Take a seat at the table and watch, or grab yourselves a gown and boots if you want to come inside.'

I looked at Cassie and raised my eyebrows. She shrugged indifference, so I leant into the microphone and told Dr Wong we'd come in. After we'd gowned up, Briggs ushered us into the autopsy room. The musty smell of cold flesh, formaldehyde and disinfectant assailed us. I took slow breaths, getting used to it.

'I've just finished the prelim on your boy,' Wong said, then looked at Cassie. 'I'm sorry, I don't think we've met.'

I introduced Cassie, and there was a brief moment of confusion when she went to shake Wong's hand but stopped when she saw the blue gloves. Instead they just nodded to each other.

'Will that be all, doctor?' Briggs asked from the doorway.

'Oh, yes. Thank you, Matthew.'

When Briggs was gone I asked what his problem was.

'He's been here all night working on this,' said Wong. 'We've *both* worked hard to get the prelim done by today. Shall we get on with it?'

Cassie opened her notepad, and so did I. 'Thank you, doctor. We appreciate it.'

'Well, as you know, overdoses like this rarely raise any eyebrows, but your list of anomalies intrigued me and I cancelled two social appointments. I don't normally do that.' She waited a beat to emphasise her point. 'Tox screens normally take up to three weeks. Lucky for you, my husband is the chief pathologist here. He had them put through blood samples late last night. No urine, but I had initial results waiting on my desk when I arrived at five this morning. I'll get to those in a moment.'

Again she paused. This was the game. They fed you pieces at a time, keeping you interested, making you hang on every word.

'After seeing as many ODs as I have, you tend to get an idea about the typical victim. This boy doesn't quite fit.'

'How do you mean?' Cassie asked. 'He was a street kid.'

Dr Wong gestured to the body. 'Not all of them end up in here, detective. Those that do are generally of a specific profile. Above the age of twenty-five, mostly hard-core users with all the physical signs of addiction and the lifestyle it carries. I'm not saying this boy didn't die of a drug overdose. There are indications of haemorrhaging around both the left and right ventricles, indicating cardiac arrest.'

I nodded.

'Heroin, like any opiate, is a depressant, in that it slows the central nervous system. This boy's slowed down so much he eventually ceased breathing and his heart literally stopped beating. This is consistent with most of the overdose cases I see. However, let me refer to my notes.'

We followed her to a counter in the corner and waited while she flipped through a notepad.

'Ah, yes, here we go. This one had a full meal in his stomach. No analysis on the contents yet but it looks to me like a souvlaki. Secondly, I only found one needle mark. No other abscesses. Maybe we're looking at a relapse, which is common after a period of abstinence. Tolerance goes down, risk of overdose goes up. Was he incarcerated recently?'

I knew why she was asking. Prison was often the only time these people abstained from drug use. I told her Boyd hadn't been inside for more than a year and that all indications were that he was clean, of his own volition.

'Well then, perhaps that's something else to add to your anomalies,' she said.

I nodded. 'What else, doctor?'

'The liver. I've sent it off for testing but it appeared healthy to me. Even in kids this young, a lifestyle of drug and alcohol abuse can cause damage to the liver that is immediately recognisable to the naked eye.'

I wrote it all down then asked about the toxicology report.

'It's only the initial findings,' Wong said, 'but very interesting. The report's on my desk. I'll go get it. Back in a minute.'

While she was gone I walked over to the X-ray viewing box and studied a slide of what I recognised to be a human arm. The second slide depicted a rib cage and the third, a leg. Something about the third image intrigued me and reminded me of what I wanted to ask. I turned the light off as I heard Wong's footsteps.

She came back into the room carrying a single page in her hand.

'I have percentage breakdowns of different substances here, detectives. They are in the usual denominations of blood concentration,' she said, putting on a pair of rimless glasses to decipher her notes. 'I'll start with blood alcohol concentration. You said you found a beer bottle lid in his trousers?'

I nodded.

'That fits here. Results indicate a BAC of 0.01, meaning he only drank a little, or he finished drinking some time before he died.'

I made a notation in my daybook. *Last drink – where?*

'There were also moderately high levels of opiates in his blood,' Wong continued. 'This is where it gets odd. Normally when I see these cases, tox screens indicate a level of morphine of around 0.02 milligrams per litre of blood or higher. In this case the blood concentration is less than half that.'

'So what are you saying, doctor?' Cassie asked. 'The heroin didn't kill him?'

'I guess you could say he had a little help from an old friend,' said Wong, looking grim. 'Gamma hydroxy butyrate.'

Cassie and I both nodded. GHB was popular in the party scene and probably responsible for more overdoses than any other drug besides heroin.

'It's a strong anaesthetic,' Wong went on. 'High levels here too: 0.3 mil per litre. I read some medical literature before you came in this morning and I'm starting to think this may be the best indicator of how this boy died. The general consensus is that anyone with this level of GHB in his or her blood would lose consciousness very soon. If not revived, and their airways were obstructed, they would die.'

I wrote while she spoke, not fully absorbing the meaning of her words until she finished. When I realised what she was implying, a large piece of the puzzle fell into place.

'You're saying he was incapacitated,' I said. 'With this much

GHB in his system he wouldn't be able to walk or talk, much less get a fit ready and shoot up.'

'Somebody juiced him up then made it look like a heroin overdose,' Cassie agreed.

'That's one assumption,' Dr Wong said as she folded the report away. 'GHB is a strong depressant. Mix it with another depressant like alcohol or heroin and it multiplies the effect on the central nervous system.'

Again I thought about the beer lid and a series of images played in my mind. Boyd meeting up with the killer, accepting a beer, possibly in a private residence or somewhere away from prying eyes. The killer squirting GHB into the beer, waiting for Boyd to lose consciousness, before taking him out to a waiting car, driving him to the loading bay at the rear of Café Vit, injecting him with heroin and leaving him to die. It was a stretch, but possible.

'This kid didn't stand a chance,' I said, looking down at the body of Dallas Boyd. 'Whoever did this knew what they were doing.'

'Quite right, detective. I'd say he would've been dead within half an hour of ingesting the GHB and five minutes after the heroin.'

'Would the GHB have killed him anyway?' asked Cassie.

'Good question. My answer is yes, unless he received medical attention or was left in a recovery position to maintain airways. Why?'

'Says something about the killer, I s'pose.'

Cassie left it at that but I was intrigued. I'd first met Cassie while she was a constable in the uniform section. Even back then I'd admired her ability to think objectively, ask the right questions. Her promotion to the CIU had only sharpened this skill.

Moving on, I asked Dr Wong if the X-rays on the viewing box were Boyd's.

'Yes, they're from the deceased. Do any of your inquiries thus far lead you to believe this boy was abused?'

I nodded.

'X-rays offer vital information in these instances,' Wong explained, turning the viewing box on. 'Even if they offer no insight into the way a person has died, they can usually tell us a lot about how a person lived.'

We all stared at the three images in silence.

'I want to start by saying I've consulted your department on hundreds of cases over many years where there were multiple bone fractures. A classic example is road trauma. As you would know, victims of road fatalities often have extensive injuries, but they are invariably fresh and don't show signs of healing.' Wong screwed up her nose in frustration, as though she was having difficulty explaining herself. 'Look, I'm not sure about you two, but I have children, which only makes this one harder. Let me just show you what I mean.'

I looked over at Cassie, who'd folded her arms against her chest, as if bracing herself for what was coming.

'I'm not a radiologist, but I don't need to be to see what's going on here. These are just three slides that tell the story of what this boy endured in his short life. I've taken many more images, and you'll get it all in my report, but basically what you have here is a pattern of tremendous skeletal trauma and prolonged physical abuse spanning many years.'

A sharp pain stretched from my shoulder to my chest, as though I knew all along it would lead to this. That a story of horror would emerge.

'Bones heal themselves, provided they're set properly,' Wong continued. 'But like skin burns, bones that have been broken or fractured will often leave behind lesions that look like this.' She used a pen to point to the ribs on the second slide. 'Ribs are difficult to set, so are often left to heal on their own.' Running the pen around the rim of each rib, she indicated faint lines crossing the ribs. 'These are old fractures that have healed imperfectly. There are literally dozens of them on the ribs. More can be seen on the extremities. Look at this one, for instance.'

She moved back to the first slide, the right arm, and ran the pen down the humerus bone. 'This one here looks like a longitudinal spiral break. You can see the lesion is faint, but there just the same.'

I edged in next to Cassie for a closer look. A faint white line wrapped around the bone in a jagged spiral pattern.

'These injuries are sometimes seen in serious sporting mishaps,' Wong explained. 'Like when a footballer is heavily tackled and lands on his arm.'

'This isn't a sporting injury though, is it?' Cassie said.

'Well, the answer to that depends on what version you want: the courtroom or the gut?'

'The gut will do, doctor.'

'Remember Jason Tarper?'

We both nodded. Jason Tarper was a two-year-old boy who'd been found dead in his mother's car in Shepparton, about six years before. It was a hot day and the boy had been left in the back seat. Word from detectives investigating the case was that the mother had left him in there deliberately because she was sick of his crying, a theory they were never able to prove. There were allegations of physical abuse, also unproven. As far as I knew, the parents were still alive and had had three more children in the years since the trial.

'I worked the autopsy on that case,' Wong said, nodding to the X-ray on the light box. 'And this spiral fracture is a dead ringer. Back then we had a team of radiologists examine it and they theorised on a twisting motion. Let me demonstrate.'

She took my arm and stretched it behind my back, twisting it until the pain registered and I pulled away.

'Imagine dragging a child down a hallway like that,' she said slowly. 'No wonder the boy wouldn't stop crying.'

She frowned and I knew she was thinking about the toddler in Shepparton as much as she was Dallas Boyd. I had my own demons, cases I'd never forget. Cases where evil had prevailed. Clearly it was the same for Wong.

'It's a similar story with your boy here,' she said, snapping out of the trance. 'The bone literally shatters. As you can imagine, an injury like that would have caused tremendous pain and taken months to heal.'

Cassie had turned away from the slides. I wanted to ask if she was all right but thought it might embarrass her. Instead I studied the third slide of Boyd's leg.

'Have a look at this one,' Wong said, stepping in beside me. 'This is the femur, the largest bone in the body and the hardest to break.'

I stared at a blister-like lesion in the centre of the upper thigh. 'What would cause an injury like this?'

She shrugged. 'Something hard and blunt, probably a single blow.'

'Like a bat?'

'Again, I couldn't go up in court for it, but I'd say that's a good possibility.'

I turned to the outline of Boyd's body under the sheet. The GHB might've stopped his heart beating, but I knew his dying had started many years before.

'This is what I'm telling you,' Wong concluded. She stepped over to the autopsy table and held her hands over Dallas Boyd's body like a priest giving the last rites. 'This boy lived in constant pain for many of his early years. Most people break only one or two bones, if any, in their entire lifetime. I haven't finished yet, and already I've counted more than thirty-five separate fracture lesions.'

'Jesus,' Cassie said from behind me.

I thought of the pain I'd lived with since the shooting, and tried to imagine this boy living in pain every day of his life.

'Is this recent?' I asked, pointing at the femur bone. 'I mean, how long since these have all healed?'

'You're asking all the right questions, detective, but they're not easy to answer, not without appropriate time.'

'A guess?'

'I'd say well over six years since the last break, which may suggest the abuse ceased some time ago, but I'll be keeping the body for further analysis. I'll also bring in a radiologist for this.'

That fitted with Dallas Boyd having been in state care since he was ten. I wrote it all down. 'Anything else?'

Dr Wong walked back to the counter and went over her notes again. I stayed by the body, lifted the sheet and stared at the pale face of the boy I'd found dead against the bin. Dallas Boyd was at peace now and no longer in pain.

'That's all for now,' said Wong, closing her notebook. 'From a forensic point of view, I hope I've been able to help.'

'You have,' I said, 'and thank you for the trouble you went to. And please thank Matthew Briggs for us also.'

She nodded. 'I just hope you find whoever did this.'

'The abuse or the murder?' Cassie asked.

'Both,' Wong said. 'No one deserves any of this.'

I looked down again at the body beneath the sheet and thought about the LEAP reports I'd printed out on the step-father. Though I was yet to study them, I knew there would be answers in there. I imagined breaking down the door and dishing up my own style of blunt-force trauma. If only it were that easy.

'One more thing,' Dr Wong called out as we walked to the door. 'Will you call the Homicide Squad or should I?'

# 10

OUTSIDE THE WATCH-HOUSE, I left the car in gear while I waited for Cassie to get out.

'You're not coming in?' she asked.

'Nope. Eckles made his thoughts clear enough.'

'So did you.'

I wasn't going to argue. 'Look, I'm going home to read through the LEAP reports on the stepfather. Can you get a status on my CCR request on Boyd's mobile phone and see if the mug shots on Parks and Jardine have come through?'

'They the mates you mentioned?'

'Yeah, I need to talk to them, especially Parks. He left a message on Boyd's answering machine, said they were supposed to meet up the night he was killed. Sounded like he was hanging on to something for him. We need to know what that was all about.'

'You don't think the stepfather's good for it?' she said.

I was silent a moment, pondering if I was dismissing him too quickly. If I hadn't heard the message from Sparks, and if Boyd's beer hadn't been laced with GHB, I probably would've thought the same thing.

'Like the doc just said, this guy beat the crap out of the kid for years,' Cassie prompted. 'The kid finally gets on his own two feet, then goes about trying to get his little sister removed from the family home. Sounds good to me.'

'You're probably right,' I said, just to keep her happy. 'But check on the mugs and the CCR anyway, will you?'

Heat flooded the interior as Cassie got out, then leant in through the door.

'No offence, Rubes, but what are you doing with this? Whether it turns out to be a domestic shitfight or something else, this is officially a Homicide job now. All we have to do is type up a handover brief. That's it, we're done.'

'I'm not ready to put this to bed yet, Cass.' I hoped that would do it but she didn't move. 'Don't worry about me. Just tell Freckles I'm typing up my job application for the primary school liaison team.'

As she disappeared inside, I sped away with no intention of going home. There was something I needed to do, something somebody should have done many years ago.

I drove on autopilot, the Saturday morning congestion on Punt Road passing in a blur as I crossed the Yarra River and headed north towards Collingwood. When the square blocks of commission flats appeared on the horizon, my heart rate quickened. I wondered which unit the man I wanted to see lived in. Up high in the building a woman stepped through a sliding door and I watched her drape towels over the walkway rail. Distracted, I almost ran into a car in front. I hit the brakes and skidded to a halt centimetres from the rear of an Audi. A horn sounded from behind and the driver of the Audi shook his head in the rear-view mirror. I let out my breath, loosened my tie and reminded myself to stay focused. An older colleague had once told me to always play the ball, not the man. It was a rule I tried to follow in life and work. I repeated it to myself until I was calm and back on track.

The traffic moved forward and soon I pulled into the car park at the front of the towers, parking in one of the allocated police bays. From under the seat I retrieved a can of capsicum spray I'd stolen from the academy and always kept in the car, just in case. After sliding the can into my hip pocket, I walked to the entrance. An overweight man with a ruddy complexion sat behind the security counter. A bottle of Coke and a half-eaten sausage roll covered his copy of the day's *Herald Sun*, which was open at the sports section. Funny how unfit people always loved sports. A name tag on his white shirt read 'George Pappa'.

'Morning, George,' I said, sliding my ID under the security grille. 'Police.'

'Guessed that,' he said. 'What can I do you for?'

'I need to talk to a resident here, Vincent Rowe. I think he lives up on –'

'Level ten, apartment four,' Pappa said. 'Don't think he'll be awake now though. Prick doesn't usually get up till two or three.'

As he passed the ID back, I detected a familiar smell. A closer look at his eyes confirmed my suspicions. Seemed hayfever was doing the rounds.

'What's he like, this bloke?' I asked.

'Typical shithead who likes to beat up on the missus. Cute little girl though. Rachel, I think her name is.'

'Does he smack the girl around?'

'Wouldn't surprise me. Tell you what does surprise me: we don't have a car space out there especially for his visitors.'

'Is he a dealer?'

'You should know more than me.' Pappa shrugged. 'Cops are always here to see him. Speaking of which, where's your partner? You blokes normally come in pairs.'

'Only on TV.'

Pappa stuffed the last of the sausage roll in his mouth. 'Not just on TV. Been here ten years, never seen a copper go up there alone.'

I looked up at the enormous tower and realised he was right. You could probably die in there and they'd only call for someone to collect your body when it started to stink.

'That's why you're going to come with me, George.'

'Huh? Not me, boss. I don't go up there. Just stay here and patrol the grounds. I don't visit the tenants.'

'You do today. Come on, up you get.'

Pappa crossed his meaty arms and leant back in his chair. 'Tell you what, I can call him up and tell him to come down or you can go up there on your own. Either way, I'm not going up.'

'Not good enough, George. I need your help.'

'Hey, you get to go home after this. I have to work with these people.'

'Is that marijuana I smell on you, George?'

'Huh? Not me, boss.'

I pressed my face close to the glass.

'Sure? What about those bloodshot eyes? Maybe you want some chips with your munchies.'

'Eyes aren't bloodshot. Just hayfever.'

'What about that car out there, the old Mazda I saw in the security bay? Looks like a blind man tried to park it.' I held up my mobile phone. 'Might get the boys from the station to come down, run a drug test on you. Sure your supervisor would be happy to know you're stoned on the job?'

'All I have to do is come up, right?' he said.

'And stay with me while I talk to this guy,' I replied, holding his stare.

A heavy sheen of sweat lacquered the fat man's forehead and he gulped. 'Okay.'

We rode a lift scarred with cigarette burns and graffiti to the tenth floor. Somebody had altered a 'No Smoking' sign to read 'No Smacking'. I wondered if it referred to heroin or the discipline of children. The elevator crawled up slowly and groaned to a stop. When we stepped out, the acrid smell of curry and spices stung my sinuses but Pappa didn't seem to notice. Maybe it was one of those things you got used to. Overhead a fluorescent light flickered as Pappa led me towards the end of the hall. Along the way he picked up a syringe with his bare hands and dropped it in a yellow canister he carried in his pocket. Another thing you probably got used to in the commission flats.

'Filthy things are everywhere,' he said. 'Reckon I collect two hundred of them every week.'

I said nothing, thinking of Dallas Boyd's apartment in St Kilda and how luxurious it must have seemed in comparison to this shithole. At the end of the hall we stopped at an orange door covered by a mesh security grille.

'This is it,' Pappa said. 'Do your thing, boss.'

I knocked on the grille and the twang of metal echoed down the hall. No answer. I leant closer to the door, heard a TV inside, knocked again. This time there were footsteps and a little girl's voice called, 'Who is it?'

I nudged Pappa. 'You work here. She'll know you. Tell her to open the door.'

'Ah, hi Rachel,' he said. 'It's George from downstairs. Is your daddy home?'

'He's asleep.'

I nudged him again.

'Can I talk to you for a second, please?'

There was silence and I thought she might've been scared off. I was about to ask Pappa to try again when the door opened and the girl stood on the threshold, security mesh shading her in darkness. The sound of cartoons and the blue glow of a television came from behind her.

'Hi, George,' she said. 'Are you here to watch *The Lion King*?'

'No, sweetie. We're here to see your daddy.'

'Okay. Who's that with you?'

The kid was smart, I quickly realised. And cautious. A natural survival instinct in the flats. I squatted and talked to her at eye level.

'Hello, Rachel, my name's Rubens. Can I speak to you for a second?'

'Mummy says I'm not supposed to talk to strangers.'

'That's right, you're not.'

The capsicum spray dug into my thigh as I crouched. I contemplated telling her I was a cop but figured that would only backfire. To these kids, cops were the enemy. They arrested your parents and older siblings. They crashed through your front door and took you away from your family.

'Tell you what, Rachel,' I said, hiding my daybook behind my back and putting on a smile in case she could see through the grille. 'Why don't you wake Daddy up, tell him a friend wants to talk to him. Do you think you could do that?'

Rachel's face changed to a mask of fear as an adult shadow appeared behind her. 'I'm awake,' said a nasal voice. 'What do ya's want?'

Standing up, I realised I was significantly taller than the man on the other side of the door, but I wasn't sure whether this would play in my favour or not.

'Vincent Rowe?' I asked.

'Who wants to know?'

I pressed my badge against the grille. 'I'm here with some more information on your stepson, Dallas Boyd. Can I come in?'

Rowe turned back to check the lounge, hesitation in his voice. 'I'm not really dressed properly.'

'I don't care if you've got a syringe on the coffee table, Mr Rowe. I just need to clarify who should receive your stepson's possessions.'

'Possessions?'

That was the hook. Greed. It got them every time.

'Dallas had a number of items in his apartment and we need to finalise where it will all go. It'll only take a minute. Then you can go back to bed.'

'All right.'

The door clicked open and we stepped into a dimly lit room, sunlight framing the curtains. The smell of cigarettes and stale beer hung thick in the warm apartment, turning it into a putrid incubator. Rowe was a thin man, face gaunt and unshaven. Bare-chested, tracksuit pants hanging loose off his bony hips, wiry arms covered in tattoos and pus-infected abscesses.

'Don't mind the mess,' he drawled. 'Bit of a rough time, ya know?'

I held my breath as I followed him through a lounge crowded with empty beer bottles, overflowing ashtrays, dirty dishes and piles of soiled laundry. No Amstel anywhere. My eyes were drawn to the television and the sofa, where the little girl had curled up against a pillow and teddy bear. She looked cleaner than anything else in the room.

To the left was the kitchen.

'Come in 'ere,' Rowe said, taking a cigarette from a pack on the cluttered bench. He lit the smoke using the gas stove, making no attempt to open a window.

Pappa hung back, leaning against the doorway, as I followed Rowe into the kitchen. In the sink I noticed an orange syringe cap.

'So what's the go with Dall's possessions?' Rowe asked, blowing smoke towards a ceiling stained yellow in the corners. 'Probably best it all comes here, yeah?'

Watching for needles, I pushed aside several beer bottles on the bench to make room for my daybook. I had no intention of filling in any reports. It was all for show.

'Probably,' I said. 'When did Dallas move out of home?'

'Shit, years ago, mate. He was a survivor, ya know? Didn't matter what happened, he always bounced back.'

*Did he bounce back from all those broken ribs?* I thought. *What about the shattered arm, you bastard?*

'He was only sixteen, Mr Rowe. Most kids these days stay at home well into their twenties. Why'd he move out so young?'

Rowe took a deep drag and tapped ash in the sink. 'S'pose I best be honest, hey?'

'Appreciate that,' I said.

'Me and Dall didn't always get along so well. He's not me

kid, so he was always against the discipline, me bein' the step-father and all.'

'When was the last time you saw him, sir?'

'Christmas Day, mate. Came over to give Rachel her pressie. Didn't stay long though. What kind of possessions are we talkin' about? Last I heard he was living in some hostel in St Kilda.'

'We'll get to that. He had a mate named Sparks. Know him?'

Rowe twisted his lips, blew smoke out his nostrils. 'Nup. What kinda name is that anyway, Sparks? Did Dall have a stereo or one of them iPods? What about a plasma telly? Always wanted one of them.'

I guessed Rowe had handled a few plasma televisions in his time; just never kept any. They'd all gone up his arm.

'What d'ya reckon, Rach?' he called into the lounge. 'Maybe we could get a new telly and DVD player. That'd be all right, hey?'

The girl didn't respond and I looked back at Rowe and waited.

'What?'

'Mr Rowe, just for our records, where were you at midnight last Thursday?'

He took another long drag on his cigarette, then threw the butt in the sink.

'There aren't any possessions, are there?' he said. 'Ya just here to size me up.'

'Just answer the question and we can move on, please.'

'Nup. This is my house, and it's me son who's dead, even if he was only me stepson. Fuckin' pigs all full of shit. Let ya in on good faith and all the while ya lookin' to work me over. When am I supposed to get me time to grief?'

'Grieve,' I spat. 'And you never treated Dallas like a son.'

'Fuck off, copper. I know me rights. Ya wanna stay here then let me see ya warrant.'

'I don't need one. We were invited in, weren't we, George?'

I turned to Pappa, whose face had paled.

'Leave me out of this, boss,' he said, raising his hands submissively to Rowe. 'I just walked him up, that's all.'

'Yeah, we'll see about that,' Rowe snarled. 'Slimy fat fuck, sell me out to the jacks. Fix you.'

He launched across the room but I pushed him back against the sink and held him there, then brought my hands up to his throat, pushing his face against a cupboard.

'I know about you, Vincent,' I said, the muscles under my shirt flexing tight as I whispered in his ear. 'I know you beat the shit out of Dallas every chance you got. I know about all the broken bones you covered up, and I know he was working with Child Protection to have Rachel taken out of here. Dallas didn't leave out of choice. He left for a better life. That's what he wanted for Rachel.'

'Better life?' Rowe grunted. 'Look what happened to him.'

I pressed my fingers into his neck, releasing pressure only when he moaned.

'This place is no better. Look around you. The joint's a pigsty, syringes and shit in the sink. Tell me something, how many times has Rachel watched you shoot up?'

'Piss off.'

'How do you discipline *her*? Do you put smack in her Coco Pops to make her go to sleep? I bet you sneak into her bedroom late at night too.'

He snorted and thrashed under my grip, saliva spilling from his mouth as he fought to wriggle free. 'You're a low dog,' he snarled. 'She's me little angel and I'd never fuckin' touch her.'

'Sure.'

He hawked a mouthful and spat at me, but I dodged it and hit him hard across the face. I wanted to lay into him about the chlamydia and the sexual abuse, but I couldn't risk it for Rachel's sake.

'You're finished, copper,' Rowe drawled. 'Be on the phone to the ESD the minute ya gone.'

I registered the threat and it occurred to me that I'd lost the plot. If this went through to the Ethical Standards Department there would be no escaping. Having the security guard to witness it all only made it worse. Not only that, I could already see Rowe was not capable of planning and executing a murder as slick as Dallas Boyd's. Even if he was, Boyd would never have trusted him, so there was no way he could've spiked his drink. I released my grip as a woman in a soiled nightgown appeared at the kitchen door.

'What the fuck's goin' on?' she said.

I recognised the familiar-shaped jawline, thin brown hair and slanted eyes. Dallas Boyd's mother. Once upon a time she might have been attractive. Now her hair was dishevelled, her wrists covered in track marks. A heavily rounded stomach was visible beneath the nightgown. She was pregnant.

'Oh, this just gets better,' I spat, pushing Rowe to the floor. 'You've got another one on the way. I'm going to finish what Dall started. DHS will be paying you both a visit soon. Might wanna clean up this shithole, cover up those track marks.'

I glanced at the girl on the sofa; her eyes were wide and unreadable. She clutched the teddy tight to her chest, trying to protect it. Or was it to protect her?

'Let's go, boss,' Pappa said. 'This isn't right.'

I looked back at the girl just before the door slammed behind us, echoing in the hall like a prison gate.

In the lift, I felt empty of emotion, as if it had all been used up. Ignoring the 'No Smacking' sign, I lit a cigarette though I really needed a drink. For a moment I thought about spending the day at one of my locals, but decided it was still too early. Instead I drove back down Punt Road and over the river, finding a park near the Fawkner Gardens where I waited for my anger to subside.

# 11

THE EMERGENCY DEPARTMENT at the Alfred Hospital, where Ella worked, was located at the western end of a huge complex in Prahran. I decided to cut through Fawkner Gardens to get there. In the cooler seasons the gardens were a pristine spread of lush lawns and sports fields, tennis courts and picnic benches, all canopied by rows of elm and maple trees. After three months of water restrictions that prohibited watering lawns, the park had become a barren wasteland. No joggers or cyclists. No picnics and no tennis.

Dry leaves tumbled across my path as another northerly gusted through the city, bringing with it more dust and smoke from the bushfires in the north-east. Emerging from the park, I crossed Commercial Road just as a chopper landed on the helipad overpass. Within minutes a medical crew lifted a stretcher out of the cabin and wheeled the patient towards the trauma unit. The sight aroused memories of my own stay here more than a year ago, when the shooting had almost cost me my life. Fortunately I had no memory of either the frantic attempts to resuscitate me or the early treatment of my injuries. All I recalled was being holed up in a bed on the fourth floor.

I looked up at the enormous building and pinpointed the window that had been my only connection to the outside world for what had seemed like a lifetime, though in reality had been little more than three weeks. Walking up the path towards the main sliding doors, I passed the smokers' huts, then entered the emergency department where I was immediately overcome by the sense of unease that gripped me any time I was in a hospital.

Even before the shooting, I'd always hated hospitals. To me they were depressing places, worse than prisons sometimes. Today was no different. People were slumped in the waiting room, some watching outdated sitcoms on a television in the corner, others asleep. The smell was not unlike the morgue, a smell I always associated with sickness and human anguish. Then there was the sound of the machines: the PA system, the generators, the never-ending hum of the fluorescent lights. It was like being trapped in a bunker.

At the triage desk, a tradesman with his hand wrapped in a bloody towel demanded to know why it was taking so long to see a doctor.

'Sir, our team is stretched to the limit,' said a nurse I recognised, a friend of Ella's. 'Your injury isn't life threatening and we need to –'

'Not life threatening?' said the tradesman, unwrapping the towel and causing a thick pool of blood to run down his elbow and spill on the desk. 'I could bleed to death out here.'

'If you keep pressure on it, like I told you to, you won't lose any more blood. *Please* be patient. We've just had three more firemen brought in from the bushfires. Their injuries are much more serious than yours.'

'That'd be right. Take care of your own.' The tradey leant over the counter and kicked the panelling. 'I've waited three fuckin' hours out here and all you've done is stand there yakkin' to ya bloody friends.'

'There's no need to swear or get aggro. Security!'

A hulking security guard with a face like a cane toad stalked over and the tradey got the message, grumbling to himself as he sat back down. Having been married to a nurse, I knew the tradey had just cost himself at least another hour in the waiting room. I waited while the nurse slid on gloves and wiped up the blood from the desk. After tossing the waste in a medical bin, she looked up, probably expecting another angry patient.

'Now what can I do for . . . *Rubens*, hi!'

'Hey Jen, expecting someone else?'

'Rough one today,' she said, lowering her voice. 'The fires have thrown the whole place right off. My partner's up there with them on relief duty. I feel like I've sent him off to war.'

I nodded, sympathetic.

'I take it you're looking for El?'

'Yeah, I know it's crazy in there today, but if you could just see if she can pop her head out. I'll only take a few minutes.'

'Few minutes, huh?' She smiled wryly. 'That's all men ever need.'

I laughed as Jen swept through the doors into the emergency department. Drama in real emergency departments was never as chaotic as depicted on television. Ella often said you could be lying in a bed and a person in the next cubicle could die and you probably wouldn't even know. In her experience, there was rarely any yelling or screaming, and it wasn't often you saw patients being rushed through the room on gurneys. You sure as shit didn't see doctors or nurses break down when a life was lost.

Ella came out carrying a clipboard, a stethoscope around her neck. Pinned to her uniform pocket was her ID, photo looking nothing like her. She walked to the side of the triage counter and I followed.

'You're a tad early,' she whispered, smiling but flustered. 'We're not supposed to meet until seven.'

'Yeah, I was passing by the hospital and thought I'd see if you had time for a quick lunch.'

Truth was I simply wanted to see her and it was just lucky I had a workable excuse.

'You'll need to do better than that, mister,' she jeered, seeing through my lame effort. 'Can't do lunch today. The fires are getting worse. We just had three more CFA guys brought in.'

'I know. Jen just told me, said you're busier than a one-armed paper boy. What's going on in there?'

'I think three of the fires have merged to create one big superfire. It's rolling down from the Alpine forest and they can't stop it.' She gave a pained expression. 'All up, we've got five in there already with all sorts of trouble. Heat exhaustion, smoke inhalation, a broken leg. Even a cardiac arrest.'

'Shit.'

'That's on top of our everyday regulars,' she said, nodding to the waiting room. 'Plus they're evacuating all the country hospitals in the vicinity of the fires, transferring patients to city beds, just in case. What the hell's happening to the world anyway? There's no water, the city's surrounded by fire and everything's covered in smoke. It's like an apocalypse.'

Alarm hit me as I thought about my father, who lived in Benalla, about a hundred kilometres north-west of the danger zone. My mother's nursing home in Kyneton wasn't far off either. I needed to call the emergency hotline for information.

'Look, I can't really just stand here and chat,' Ella said. 'Is something wrong?'

'Ah, no, nothing's up. I just need some advice. I haven't got a present for Jonathan yet and don't know what to get.'

'Is that it?' she said, face disbelieving.

I shrugged.

'How old is he turning, eighteen?'

'Right.'

'Well, that's easy. Just buy him something for his car. He'll love driving for the next few years so it's a sure thing. Just go down to –'

She stopped as one of the patients climbed up on a seat in the waiting area and began yelling about treatment delays, trying to encourage everyone else in the room to rise up. The cane toad security guard eventually put a stop to the commotion by waving a set of handcuffs in the man's face.

'I don't want to buy him something for his car,' I said. 'That's something his family and friends will do.'

'But you *are* his family.'

'You know what I mean.'

She frowned before offering another suggestion. 'I know! Get him a French shirt and cufflinks. Bet his mates won't buy him that.'

I nodded, liking the idea. There would be plenty of formal occasions where my nephew would need a good shirt and tie.

'That'll work. Where should I go?'

'There's a sale on at BCM down on Chapel Street.'

'A sale? You mean shirts discounted from three hundred dollars to two. I can't afford that.'

Ella poked me in the stomach. 'That's right. You're not in the Drug Squad any more, are you?'

'That joke's getting old.'

'Works every time though. Another option is Guy Wire. I drove past the other day. It's still there.'

Now I smiled at her. Guy Wire was a more reasonably priced men's clothing store down the Windsor end of Chapel Street. When Ella and I lived together, we went there a lot. Even now many of the clothes in my wardrobe had been purchased at Guy Wire with Ella by my side.

'You don't think that's too lowbrow for him?'

'Well, he's not gonna expect Armani or anything, is he?'

'You mean from a low-paid cop?'

Ella didn't answer and I knew I was reading too much into it. 'I'm kidding. It's a good suggestion.'

She looked at her watch. It was time to go.

'I do have one other thing,' I said. 'A favour.'

'Ah, I knew there was an angle.' She pursed her lips. 'What is it?'

'The kid I was telling you about last night, Dallas Boyd.'

'What about him?'

I waited for the security guard to wander past before I continued. 'I've just seen the coroner this morning. Turns out he was abused for many years. Lots of broken bones, some not healed properly.'

'No wonder he turned to drugs.'

'Well, he's got a younger sister who still lives with the abuser,' I said, then looked around. 'You sure we can't go somewhere else to talk?'

'No. I have to get back in there. What's up?'

I lowered my voice. 'I want to help DHS get her out of there. I saw her this morning. It's a cesspit, no place for a child to grow up.'

'So what do you want from me?'

I slid a piece of paper across the counter. 'Her name's Rachel Boyd. I've written it down. I want to know if she's been brought in here for treatment.'

'Rubens, what are you talking about?'

'I don't have a birth date, but she's six years old so it shouldn't be hard to isolate her details from any other patients who might have the same name.'

'Are you crazy? I can't just check up on a patient's medical history.'

'Sure you can. On that computer over there. It'll give you her whole medical history.'

Ella leant across the counter, her voice a sharp whisper. 'No, you're missing the point. What you're asking me to do is *illegal*. And you can't use it anyway, not without a subpoena.'

'I don't care about court rules. I just need to know.'

'Right, you don't care about court rules. Of course you don't.' She stared at me, hoping I'd budge, but then realised I was serious. 'And we only have our own data anyway. What if she's been to another hospital?'

'That's fine. I just want something I can use to convince her Child Protection officer she needs to be removed, or at least boosted up the priority list. If I can give them any indication something might be going on, they'll watch things more closely and eventually get enough on him to move in.'

'Yeah, I get that, but if something was going on, and we suspected it, we're mandated to report it. We're all trained to look out for it. DHS would have it already because we would've given it to them.'

I shook my head, not willing to accept that.

'You're trained to look for bruises and to report it when a kid says "Mummy bashes me". How many kids do you think dob on their parents? These people are *scum*, Ella. They teach their kids to lie. By the time somebody steps in it's too late. We end up finding them dead in a laneway with a syringe stuck in their arm. Come on, El. This is a bad one.'

'So what's your solution – the foster system? I mean, she might end up with an elderly couple and the old man likes to touch her up at night. How do you know you won't be making it worse for her?'

'Look, all I know is if she stays in that place she'll end up with chlamydia again, or worse.'

Ella's face contorted with horror. 'You mean, she was . . . ?'

'Yeah, *that* kind of bad.'

She let out a breath and looked over my shoulder. After a long moment she looked back at me. 'All right. I'll check it out this afternoon when I put in my time log. But I can't promise any results. Like I said, we only have our own records.'

'That's fine. Thank you. I'll let you go now.'

I was wondering about the appropriate way to say goodbye when I remembered something. 'Hey, do you know the emergency hotline for the fires? I want to check on Mum.'

'Check in reception. There's a poster on the wall.'

I thanked her again and went to touch her arm but she was already hurrying away.

'Let me know how you go with your mum,' she called back over her shoulder.

'Sure, I'll see you at seven.'

I watched her disappear through the doors into the emergency room, knowing I'd broken my earlier commitment not to contact her today. I just hoped she could see my reasoning.

# 12

I DIDN'T WASTE ANY TIME buying my nephew's present, pulling together a shirt, tie and cufflinks in less than ten minutes. There was a pair of jeans I would've liked for myself but they'd have to wait until next month. It was no use getting them until the heatwave ended anyhow.

Back home, the apartment was relatively cool. Prince wanted out, so I let him go but I knew it'd only be a few minutes. I reckoned cats must be allergic to discomfort or extreme temperatures. After pouring a glass of water, I checked the answering machine but there were no messages. Next I sent Ella a text saying my parents were safe. Seeing my father at the party tonight was preying on my mind but I tried not to think about it, deciding instead to do something I hadn't done in a long time.

In the kitchen I laid out four slices of rye bread, spread avocado on each, then added shredded chicken, sundried tomato and spinach leaves. Prince came in while I was arranging the sandwiches on a plate. He leapt up to the bench but I read the move and caught him mid-flight.

'Not yours, mate. At least another five hours for you,' I said, carrying him to the scratch pole in the lounge and patting him for a while. Picking up the sandwiches and some orange juice, I headed over to Edgar's apartment. The door was around the walkway even though his place was directly next to mine. He normally had lawn bowls on Saturdays but given the heat I figured he'd be home. I knocked and heard the familiar sound of his dog barking.

'Who's there?' Edgar called through the door.

'Police! We have a search warrant. Open up, Burnsey!'

The door cracked open an inch and an eye peered out. 'Bloody coppers, can't trust you lot. Show me the warrant.'

I held up the plate of sandwiches. 'Will this do?'

Edgar opened the door and his silky terrier rushed out and began sniffing my ankle. 'Get him, Tank. Chew his leg off!'

'You had lunch yet, old fella?'

'Old, my bloody arse.'

I handed him the plate. 'Chicken and avocado, mate. Got the cricket on in there?'

'You bet. Sri Lanka are four for one-fifty. Taking them to the bloody cleaners. Come in and have a seat.'

I followed him through the entranceway into the lounge. The apartment was much the same setup as mine though the furniture was about as old as Ed. And it had that musty smell typical of many elderly people's homes. It reminded me of my dad's house and again I felt guilt and shame gnaw at me for having avoided my parents lately.

'What kind of bread is this?' Edgar asked, studying the sandwiches.

'Rye. I know it's probably not what you normally have but it's very good for you. And it's very similar to –'

'I know what white bread is. This is brown. Sometimes you don't make any sense at all, you know that?'

'That's because I like confusing you. Got a glass?'

'Juice again? When are we gonna have a beer together?'

'You can't drink beer, Ed. Your doctor told you –'

'I don't give a shit what the bloody quack says. I've drunk beer all me life, never done me any harm.'

'I know, but your liver . . .'

Edgar took the orange juice with a disgusted look and poured out two glasses, shuffling around the kitchen bench. As usual, he'd shaved and ironed his slacks and polo shirt. He'd also polished his leather loafers recently. Despite having nowhere to go, he still dressed himself with pride. It was a dignity and self-respect that seemed unique to men who had served in the defence force.

'Come sit,' he said, gesturing to the lounge. 'Look like a shag on a rock standing there.'

Setting the plate on the coffee table, I eased into a sofa. The old TV was on but the sound was muted, ABC radio coverage playing instead. Tank sat in front of us, looking at the sandwiches.

'Cheers,' I said, raising my orange juice to Ed's.

Ed nodded approvingly after taking a bite of his sandwich. 'This is bloody good, Rubens. Must be the fancy bread. Did that young Ella teach you how to make this?'

'No, I taught her.'

He laughed. 'Well, good to have you over.'

'Good to be here,' I said.

I noticed there was a news update on and I asked if he could turn the sound up. On the screen a reporter scurried across a street as a convoy of fire trucks roared past. Burning embers blew through the air as the reporter scrambled into a waiting SUV, the cameraman obviously labouring to keep up. Once the SUV got going, the camera refocused and the reporter relayed his update.

'Fire authorities are saying Victoria is officially suffering the worst bushfire crisis since the infamous 1983 Ash Wednesday disaster. More than twelve people have died, as many as thirty have been taken to hospital for treatment, and almost fifty homes have been wiped out overnight.'

The screen cut to footage of the fires from a helicopter. The Alpine ranges looked like a row of erupting volcanos, giant plumes of smoke wafting into the air.

'More than half a million hectares of national forest have been destroyed,' the reporter went on. 'Three of the major fires have joined together, and firefighters are still battling the inferno. In a further blow for already exhausted firefighters, local water supplies are down to less than twenty per cent.'

A map of the state appeared, with red fireballs indicating the affected areas. They began north of Melbourne and headed all the way around down to the south-eastern coastline. It looked as though the fires were surrounding the city and moving in. I remembered Ella's comment about the apocalypse. She hadn't been far off.

'In a positive break for police, a man in his twenties has been arrested and charged with three counts of arson and aggravated vandalism,' said the reporter. 'It's believed the man may be responsible for up to seven separate outbreaks across the Alpine region. He's expected to face an out-of-sessions hearing tomorrow, where more charges may follow.'

The reporter signed off and Edgar muted the volume.

'Filthy little rodent,' he snarled. 'You know what they should do to him?'

'What's that, Ed?'

'Slice off his old fella, sizzle it up in a frying pan and make him eat the bastard. That'd bloody learn him.'

'Sounds like you wanna be the chef.'

'My oath I'd do it. Be my pleasure. In fact, you know what I'd bloody well do?' He leant forward on his chair, waving a finger. 'I'd sew up his arsehole and just keep feeding him until he burst. How d'ya reckon he'd cop that?'

I smiled at the image.

'I'm serious, Rubens. That's what's wrong with this bloody generation. They haven't been smacked on the arse hard enough.

None of my lot ever ran amok like the kids do these days. We did what we were told and we respected our parents.'

I wondered whether Edgar was referring to kids like Dallas Boyd, and whether parents like Vincent Rowe deserved respect.

'I hope he goes to prison for a long time,' he continued. 'But I doubt it. He'll just get a bloody slap on the wrist. Courts are so piss-weak these days. Don't get me started on that! One of my RSL mates got beaten up and robbed last year. Your lot caught the mongrel and guess what happened?'

I shrugged, trying to recall any assault on an elderly victim in St Kilda before my return to duty.

'Suspended sentence.'

Now I remembered. It was an ATM job. The victim had been knocked to the ground by an offender who tried to snatch his money as it dispensed from the machine, not realising that the victim had just been checking his account. During the struggle the victim cracked a hip bone. He'd spent two weeks in hospital and would probably never walk again without severe pain. For us it had been an easy one. A detective had viewed the CCTV footage from the bank and identified the crook as a local shithead. He was charged and bailed, but in the end the court decided jail time wasn't necessary. No wonder so many elderly people were angry and bitter. No wonder men like Edgar opted to stay home most of the time.

'Howard told me you lot did a sterling job, looked after him nice and proper,' said Edgar, his walking stick gripped tight, like a flagpole.

I figured Howard was the victim.

'We need people like you, Rubens. With all this drug stuff, we can't even go to the bank without some mongrel knocking us over the head.' He thrust the stick towards the television and Tank scrambled to the side. 'And now they're burning the place down, killing people and wrecking their houses. I don't even want to go out on my balcony any more the air's so bad.'

His lower jaw trembled and I saw the fear and loneliness that was the beginning of the end for many elderly people. I'd seen it before in victims of burglaries and assaults. A loss of hope. When the negatives overtook the positives. If it kept up, pretty soon Edgar would stop ironing his shirts and polishing his shoes. He might even give up altogether.

'You know, statistically older citizens have a less than two per cent chance of ever being the victim of an assault,' I said, trying to reassure him. 'And most burglars don't want to break into a house when someone's home. You're at home most of the time so it's very unlikely anything will ever happen to you.'

'I don't care about any of that rubbish. I saw what that mongrel did to Howard.' Edgar used his walking stick to brace himself as he stood. I went to help him but he waved me away. 'I'm fine. I just want to show you something.'

He hobbled over to a buffet by the balcony window and handed me a silver frame with a black and white photo of two men in uniform, rifles braced across their chests.

'That's me and Howie in England,' he explained, his hand shaking as he pointed to the man on the left. 'We served in the infantry together. Six years in total.'

I studied the picture, once again reminded of my father's home where similar photos lined the mantelpiece. A different war perhaps, different people and a different generation, but the faces were the same: young and keen, with a hint of fear behind the bravado.

'Howie took a piece of shrapnel in the shoulder,' Edgar continued. 'He could've gone home, but he stayed on. Got himself fixed up and served out the rest of his tour in the rations regiment, keeping us all fed. He was a real patriot. He loved this country.'

He took the picture back and replaced it. I wasn't sure why he'd used past tense, whether Howard was dead or if he'd simply given up loving Australia.

'He would've died for this country,' Edgar said. 'And this is how we repay him. It's a fuckin' disgrace.'

I winced, not at Edgar's swearing, but at the feeling of betrayal and loss that so many of the older generation felt. I knew what he was saying. His cynicism wasn't dissimilar to that of many police after years in the job. Too much emphasis was placed on supporting the villains, not enough on the victims.

'You're right, Ed. It is a disgrace,' I said, putting a hand on his elbow and helping him back to the lounge. This time he didn't resist.

'I like having you next door,' he said, handing his dog the last of his sandwich then staring at the floor as he spoke. 'It makes me feel safe. But you know what? As much as I enjoy your company, it'd make me feel much safer if you weren't here.'

I sipped my juice uneasily. 'I don't understand.'

'Go to work, Rubens,' he said, his eyes welling. 'Get out there and stop these mongrel dogs. I served this country for more than twenty years. Now it's your turn. There may not be any bombs or trenches, but we're at war all right.'

I didn't know what to say.

'You do a good enough job,' he went on, 'then maybe when you're my age you'll still feel proud enough to call this country your own. Maybe there'll still be a place for you.'

'But Ed, I *am* working. I'm just on a day –'

My phone started ringing and I cursed the interruption. I wanted to tell Ed I was back on the job, that it was simply a rest day. I wanted him to understand, but he turned away and I knew it wouldn't matter what I said. I snatched up my phone and checked the caller ID. It was Cassie.

'You're not home, are you?' she said after I answered.

'Nope.'

'I just called your house, since you said you were going home. No answer. Where have you been?'

I looked at Edgar and made a face like I was annoyed.

'Ah, out and about. What, has Eckles got you working a GPS on me?'

'Just tell me where you are.'

'Academy. Primary school liaison course.'

'Okay, smart arse. I just hope you didn't do what I think you did.' She lowered her voice to a whisper. 'The hommies are in the office with Freckles.'

I stood up and moved into Edgar's kitchen, trying to compute what Cassie had just said. Maybe Dr Wong had phoned the Homicide Squad after we'd left the morgue and they'd sent in a response crew. Cassie was silent and I knew there was more.

'What else?' I said.

'Ah, ESD's in there as well. They're all talking to Mark Finetti.'

'Finetti? What's going on?'

'I don't know. I've heard your name being mentioned a bit. Just get back here.'

# 13

IT TOOK ME OVER HALF AN HOUR to get to St Kilda. Ordinarily I would've been cursing the drivers and trams but Cassie's phone call had left me hollow and uneasy. What the fuck was ESD doing asking about me? Why were they talking to the Homicide Squad? And what about Finetti? Surely they didn't know about my visit to the commission flats.

By the time I pulled into the watch-house car park it was after 1 p.m. Inside, the blinds in Eckles' office were down but I could see the investigators crowded around the table in the adjacent conference room. Cassie rolled over in a chair as I dumped my briefcase and daybook at my desk.

'Eckles wanted the handover brief,' she said. 'I told him to wait until you'd signed it but he wouldn't cop it. They let Finetti out a few minutes ago.'

Before I could say anything the door clicked open and Eckles appeared, a tall man with receding white hair and a starched uniform beside him. The red crowns on his epaulettes identified him as the divisional superintendent, the highest-ranking cop in the southern metro area.

'That's him,' Eckles said. 'In the corner.'

'Very well,' the superintendent said. 'Let me know how you go.'

'Yes, sir.' Eckles clicked his fingers. 'McCauley, in here, let's go!'

Three men and two women sat at the conference table, sleeves rolled up, daybooks and notepads open in front of them. A guy I knew, Nik Stello, stood at the head, adding notations to a whiteboard. I recognised the two short-haired women as detectives from the Sexual Offences and Child Abuse Unit and nodded to them. Eckles directed me to a seat at the end and introduced the two men as Detectives Gurt and Quinlan.

'They're with Ethical Standards,' Eckles said, closing the door. 'And you know Nik from Homicide. His crew's been assigned the Boyd case.'

I nodded at Stello, a younger Italian detective I'd worked with many years before when he'd been a police prosecutor. Far as I knew, Stello was a skilled legal craftsman, able to shape evidence like a brilliant sculptor. How this translated to running an actual murder investigation was another matter. I'd heard he'd recently been appointed to the Homicide Squad and figured he was still finding his legs. Was this a case of prioritisation, of giving a no-count case to the new guy, or simply luck of the draw?

'Let me make this quick,' said Eckles, 'since we don't have much time. Stello will take over the investigation into the death of Dallas Boyd as of today. Dr Wong has briefed his crew and they're awaiting orders to effect an arrest. You're to submit all reports thus far to him and be forthcoming with any information you've yet to document. Is that clear?'

This puzzled me. Less than three hours before, Eckles had instructed me not to pursue the matter, to let it go down as accidental unless the forensic pathologist ruled otherwise. Now Wong said it was homicide and suddenly he wanted full cooperation. Something wasn't right.

'Is that clear, detective?' Eckles repeated.

'Whatever.'

'Good. Nik, your show.'

I looked at Stello, waiting for his questions. His skin still had the polished look I remembered, like glazed terracotta. Neatly styled black hair swept back over his head, a gold cufflink sparkled at his wrist. He looked more like a model than a homicide investigator and I wondered if people still called him Stiletto.

'Right, er, we're especially interested in your thoughts on suspects,' he said, and glanced at a report in his hands. 'I've got your partner's handover brief here and it seems the most logical place to start is with Vincent Rowe, the stepfather. Is that your view?'

I looked around the table, trying to establish the meaning behind the question. All eyes were on me. Did they know I'd just been to visit the stepfather? Was that why ESD were here? Logic told me otherwise. Even if Rowe had called ESD after I'd left, this was too soon. There had to be something else.

'I think he's good for a child abuse case, but I doubt he killed Dallas Boyd.'

'What makes you say that?'

'Because whoever killed Boyd had finesse.'

'How do you know Rowe doesn't?' Eckles cut in, shuffling through papers in front of him. 'I've read this guy's sheet. Genuine scrote. Lady basher, history with little girls too.'

Not having seen Rowe in his family environment, those at the table were right to assume he was good for the murder, but I'd looked into his eyes. Though I'd seen a man capable of murder, it wouldn't be one of this calibre. Crash and bash was more Rowe's style. Also, whoever killed Dallas Boyd had his trust.

'Do you know something we don't, McCauley?' Eckles prodded.

'Whoever it was slipped GHB into his drink,' I said quickly. 'That means Boyd dropped his guard and the killer took advantage of it.' I looked at the female cops from the SOCA unit. 'As you know, Boyd was working with the Department of Human Services to get his little sister removed from the unit. He hated his stepfather. There's no way he'd drop his guard around Rowe. He was probably terrified of him.'

The two SOCA cops turned to Eckles. The recognition was subtle but there just the same.

'What aren't you telling me?' I asked.

'Turns out your mate downstairs knew the kid,' Eckles said.

'Mate?'

'Finetti,' said Stello, sliding a page across the table. 'This is dated just prior to Christmas. Finetti took a statement from Boyd about his stepfather. Have a read.'

At above date and time I took a statement from Dallas BOYD (DOB 01/11/1992) about an assault committed on his younger sister, Rachel BOYD (DOB 07/05/2002). BOYD stated he believes his stepfather, Vincent ROWE (DOB 03/04/1971), was responsible for both sexual and physical abuse of his sister over a prolonged period of time. He wishes for police to intervene. Contact with SOCA and the Department of Human Services has been made.

Sarah HARRIGAN of DHS Child Protection Unit assisting. Advised that BOYD's family is of interest to DHS.

BOYD stated he is fearful of stepfather avenging complaint and is concerned ROWE will harm him or his sister to prevent removal from home. Also stated stepfather has made threats through third parties that he will kill BOYD if sister is removed from home. ROWE has violent history and is known to police. BOYD advised to take due care and avoid all contact with stepfather.

Intervention order pending.

Handing the report back, I wondered why Finetti hadn't mentioned any of this at the crime scene. Relief washed over me as I realised this was why the ESD were involved. I wasn't the focus of attention after all.

113

'Finetti was covering his arse,' I said. 'He knew the kid was in danger and he did nothing about it. Then the kid turns up dead. No wonder he kept quiet at the crime scene. He *wanted* it to be accidental.'

'Don't worry about Finetti,' Gurt said. 'We'll discuss that in a moment.'

I went to reply but Eckles cut me off. 'You're missing the point. Finetti's report indicates a direct threat against this boy. Less than six weeks later he's dead. The stepfather is our most logical starting point. Is there anything else Stello and his men need to know about before they arrest him?'

*Stello and his men*, I thought. Sounded like a B-grade action flick. I wanted to tell them I'd seen the stepfather and that Rowe wasn't slick enough to pull it off, but I knew how that would end.

'You're right,' I said instead. 'Rowe is the best starting point. There's nothing else from me.'

Eckles nodded to Stello and the SOCA cops, who stood, packed up their notes and walked out. I went to follow but was called back.

'Not you,' said Gurt. 'We're not done yet.'

Quinlan adjusted his tie, as though shaping up for a fight. The two ESD men wore near-identical grey suits, white shirts and blue ties, and both had sandy brown hair. They could've been brothers, though Gurt carried more weight than the other; like a before and after ad for a weight loss program. Feeling suddenly uneasy, I realised something wasn't right. Eckles had been too confident earlier, which didn't fit with the dilemma we shared for having initially ruled Boyd's death accidental.

'What have you done?' I said to Eckles, easing back into my chair. 'What have you told them?'

He said nothing.

'You were quick to shoot down Finetti before,' Gurt said. 'I must say, I'm impressed with your loyalty. Quite courageous, really.'

'Hey, if Finetti knew this kid and didn't say anything at the scene, then he needs to answer for it.'

Gurt shuffled through his daybook, found the page he wanted. Quinlan opened his book too, as did Eckles, and they all wrote the date and time on a fresh page. When they were ready Gurt cleared his throat.

'Detective, we wish to discuss your decision to state the death of Dallas Boyd as an accident despite believing otherwise. Are you happy to answer some preliminary questions about this or would you prefer we proceed straight to a formal interview?'

My mind went into a spin dive. A formal interview? Didn't they just say Finetti was the one who'd mishandled himself? And why was Eckles so cocky? Why wasn't he in the shit too? He'd countersigned the bloody incident report.

'Detective?'

'Yes, go!'

'Okay, for the record, I'd like to know why you actively pushed to have this death ruled accidental, even though there were signs that clearly indicated the contrary.'

'I didn't. At first the scene appeared typical of a normal OD. There were no suspicious circs I'd usually expect when somebody stages a murder.'

'Usually expect?' Quinlan said.

'Yes. I go out of my way to look for suspicious circumstances at a scene like this,' I said, shooting an angry look at Eckles. 'I don't do it because I want to impress people. I do it because that's how I operate. If you expect anomalies, then you won't miss anything.'

'So what happened this time?' Gurt asked.

'There were no obvious anomalies with this one. No bruises, no signs of a struggle. Nothing.'

'That's not what Mark Finetti tells us.'

'What does he have to say?'

'Finetti informs us that he noticed several anomalies that he brought to your attention.'

Suddenly it all fell into place. Finetti had been interviewed over his information report on Dallas Boyd and the missed anomalies at the crime scene. He'd obviously taken the easy way out. I shook my head in disgust.

'He also states that you specifically instructed him not to question your judgement,' Quinlan added.

'What?' I snapped. 'That's bullshit. I absolutely refute that.'

Gurt looked at his partner and together they leant over the table, a pair of hyenas stalking injured prey. 'Detective, your colleague alleges you deliberately covered this up. What do you have to say in response to that?'

I wanted to find Finetti and put his head through the floor. He'd recognised the victim and chosen not to say anything. He'd known Dallas Boyd was in fear of his life and had done nothing except write a half-arsed information report. And now everyone was covering their own arse. Maybe it was time I did the same, admit I felt pressured into calling it an accident. Maybe report right then and there that Eckles had ordered me to leave it up to the pathologist to find forensic anomalies, to ignore the missing syringe lid and the other evidence at the scene. But what would any of this achieve? Eckles would deny it and the ESD would believe him. And blaming Finetti held no weight. It would only cement everyone's view that I shouldn't be on the team.

In the end there was only one card left.

'It's total bullshit. Like I said, the scene looked clean to me. There were no obvious anomalies. As far as I knew it was just another OD.'

Gurt let a false smile play across his face. 'What about your list?' He unfolded a page from inside his daybook. 'The list you gave the pathologist?'

I swallowed. They had me.

'Ah, well, none of that was clear until later in the investigation,' I said. 'Jesus, I wrote that when I got home. But what's the point anyway? You've obviously made up your mind. Why don't you just hit me with a PJ now and we can all get on with it?'

'Relax, McCauley,' Quinlan said. 'We're not interested in charging you with perverting the course of justice. Right now I'm just curious about what you want me to believe. Either you knew this was something other than a simple overdose and deliberately ignored your suspicions, or you missed what I regard as telltale signs of foul play.'

They were all silent then, waiting for me to acknowledge I was in a corner. The punches would land no matter which way I turned.

'In other words, even if you didn't *cover* this up,' Gurt finally said, 'you still *fucked* it up. That leaves us with only one conclusion, McCauley. You're not fit for duty.'

'That's not your call to make.'

Gurt just nodded. There was no need for him to add anything. He and Quinlan would put their report in, together with the allegation from Finetti. Add to that a vote of no confidence from Eckles and I was down for the count. I'd be lucky even to land a slot in the primary school liaison team.

I closed my eyes, ashamed it had come to this. Like Dallas Boyd, I'd dropped my guard and allowed my opponent to land a deadly blow. I was falling, the canvas fast approaching, the referee calling the round a knockout.

'Let's go, McCauley,' Eckles said. 'It's time you went home.'

'What, you're suspending me?'

Eckles took a moment while Gurt and Quinlan packed up their folders.

'I wouldn't call it suspension,' he said when they were gone.

'What then?'

'You have a sick mother, don't you? Alzheimer's or something?'

'Stroke,' I said, knowing what was coming.

'Well, maybe you need some time off. Maybe her condition is affecting your judgement, which is understandable. Family matters like this are important. I've checked your leave balance and I think it'd be wise for you to take some carer's leave to look after her, sort things out a bit.'

117

I stared out the window, not really seeing anything. It was an old trick, an underhanded one. Suspending someone meant inquiries and due process, union involvement and all sorts of headaches for everyone. For an acting OIC, it wasn't ideal to have a suspended detective on your list. Better to do it quietly, find a convenient excuse to shuffle someone off.

I looked at Eckles. 'And if I don't want to go on leave?'

'We both know you don't have a choice.'

'Righto. So how long then?'

He shrugged.

'What, you want me off indefinitely?'

'Let's call it three weeks to start with. We'll see how you're travelling after that.'

I stood up and pushed my chair hard into the table. 'This isn't about my welfare,' I said. 'And it's not about my mum either, so don't insult me. You're pissed because I backed you into a corner.'

'Don't push me, McCauley. This is a gift.'

'It's a fucking farce, that's what it is.'

I went to walk by him but he stopped me at the door. 'Remember, I've got friends,' he said, nodding to where Gurt and Quinlan had been sitting. 'Today was just a warning, McCauley. You only get one. So do yourself a favour – go back to your desk, pack up your shit and leave quietly.'

As I held his stare, his words from this morning replayed in my mind. *Careers in this organisation are built on the scalps of rogues like you.* To men like Eckles, ambition was everything. The only thing better than flushing someone else's career down the shitter for a promotion was to stand back and watch them do it to themselves. No way was I that foolish.

'Fair enough, boss,' I said. 'Thank you for your understanding. I'll just clear a few things from my desk before I go.'

# 14

DESPITE WHAT I'D SAID TO ECKLES, I had no intention of clearing my desk. Everything of value was in my daybook and briefcase. The only thing I wanted to take was a photo of me on crutches, cuddling Prince at the welcome home dinner my parents threw for me when I came out of hospital. They'd made the trip to Melbourne to take me home and I remembered being helped up the stairs to the apartment, my shoulder heavily bandaged, body thin and weak. When they opened the door, Ella was there, holding Prince. It was the turning point in my recovery and in our relationship.

Mum had given me the picture later on, told me to keep it as a reminder of what I'd overcome. Throughout my rehabilitation it had stayed with me. Any time I felt the odds piling up, I looked at the photo.

I looked at it now as I put it into my briefcase, questioning my ability to forge ahead. For a Saturday the squad room was busy, everyone preparing for the St Kilda Festival tomorrow. All four computers were occupied, detectives two-finger-typing briefs and operation plans. Cassie leant back in her chair, ear held to a telephone, a pained look on her face. More news about her father, I wondered. As usual, Eckles had his door closed and the printer whined, spewing out endless LEAP reports. Another burglary. Stick-up at the TAB. Rapist prowling the parks. Dealers selling pills out of a hotel room. Like a finely tuned theatre production, the whole crazy show would go on without me.

Glancing at my in-tray, I saw that the Divisional Intelligence Unit had left an envelope for me. Inside were the two mug shots I'd requested of Stuart Parks and Derek Jardine, Dallas Boyd's co-accused in the 2004 armed robbery case. There was also the call charge record on Dallas Boyd's phone, which listed all calls made to and from his mobile in the hours prior to and after his death. For the moment, I focused on the mug shots, which included details about the offenders alongside each picture. The first shot, of Jardine, had been taken more than two years before. It depicted a pimple-faced adolescent. Fourteen years old. I sat back down and studied the face but nothing jolted. Jardine had the innocent look of a schoolboy, his hair styled into a spike. But the eyes told a different story. Like Boyd's little sister in the flat, they projected fear and hopelessness. It was a look I knew would be replaced by one of defiance and anger in years to come.

The shot of Stuart Parks was more recent, and I immediately recognised the gaunt face and stringy hair. Even the tracksuit was the same. Stuart Parks was the kid I'd spoken to outside the youth service yesterday. I stowed the pictures in my briefcase and locked it.

My mobile phone rang. The ID screen read 'private number'.

'Ah, I'm looking for Detective Sergeant Rubens McCauley,' said a female voice.

'Speaking.'

'Right. This is Sarah Harrigan from the Department of Human Services.'

It took me a second before I remembered she was Dallas Boyd's contact at the Child Protection Unit.

'Yes, I've been expecting your call. Thank you.'

'Well, this is most unusual,' she said. 'Will Novak from the Carlisle Accommodation & Recovery Service told me you're looking into the death of one of our clients, and that I should call you.'

'Yes. Dallas Boyd. I was told he was liaising with you regarding his stepfather, Vincent Rowe. Is that true?'

'Well, I'm not sure what Mr Novak thought I might be able to tell you. As I'm sure you're aware, it's strictly against the policy of DHS to give out information on our clients informally. There are privacy principles and interdepartmental guidelines I'm required to follow. If you wish, I can email you a coversheet requesting a transfer of information and we can proceed from there.'

'How long will that take?' I asked.

She made a clicking sound with her tongue that forced me to hold the phone away. 'Maybe a week.'

'A week? Can't you just talk to me over the phone? I don't want any files or anything, just a few pointers. I mean, the kid's dead, so what difference does it make now?'

'He's still a client, detective, dead or alive. We can't just discuss details of our work without formal arrangements. It would be like us asking you to tell us the ins and outs of a case you're working on. Surely you understand that.'

*No, all I understand is that you're a typical bureaucrat,* I thought.

'Look, if you're prepared to wait until Monday, I might be able to meet with you.'

'Meet me?'

She lowered her voice and now I needed to block my other ear. 'I can't give you anything specific, no reports or anything, but I'm happy to meet with you in person.'

'On Monday?' I said, puzzled.

'It's the best I can do. I need to pull the files and read up on them. Will said you'd be discreet with the information.'

'Of course.'

'Then I'll get back to you.'

Looking down at the pictures of Dallas Boyd's two co-offenders, I realised this was as much help as I would get without a subpoena. I sensed she was about to end the call so I stopped her.

'Can you also check if you've got any information on two boys named Derek Jardine and Stuart Parks?'

'Ah, now you're pushing it. What I'm doing is highly –'

'Just check your info on Boyd then,' I said, short-circuiting the chance of another lecture. 'I think the three of them were friends. It would help if I could talk to them. If you just check in Boyd's file, maybe there'll be something in it.'

I spent the next hour photocopying the reports I had on the Boyd case, then arranged a courier to have it all delivered to the Homicide Squad. When I was done, I waved goodbye to Cassie – who was still on the phone – and took the stairs down to the men's change room. A clock above the door read 3.15 p.m. Changeover time. I stood by the lockers and listened to the male voices and laughter echoing from the shower room.

When the taps turned off and Finetti came out, I walked up behind him and slammed his head against the locker, crashing it against the wall. He let out a grunt of pain, one hand clutching my elbow, the other struggling to keep the towel around his waist.

'You sold me out,' I hissed in his ear. 'You told them I covered up the OD, wrote it off as accidental. Why?'

Finetti's skin was wet and slippery and he managed to twist his head around though I maintained pressure on his windpipe. Two cops looked around from the end of the lockers, both in underwear.

'What the hell's going on?' one of them said. 'Let him go!'

'Not until he admits it.'

122

'Admits what?'

I turned back to Finetti. 'What did they offer you? A slot on the CI? A rush through on the next board?'

'What is this, McCauley?' said the other cop, stepping close to me.

'Between me and Finetti,' I snarled. 'Get out of here.'

'Get out of here?' he repeated. 'This is *our* locker room, McCauley. *You* get out.'

I looked at Finetti. 'Tell them to disappear, mate, or they hear it all.'

'Hear what?'

'All right,' Finetti spluttered. 'Guys, give us a minute here, will ya?' When they didn't move he shouted, 'Just go!'

'Okay, man, you got it.'

When they were gone, I let go of Finetti, who collapsed on a wooden bench, gasping for breath. I pushed a pile of towels out of the way and sat on the bench opposite him. 'Why'd you do it?'

He wouldn't look up, and when he sniffed I wondered if he was trying not to cry. The job is like that sometimes. It takes away your armour, makes you weak and brittle.

'You and I both know how it went down,' I persisted. 'Sure, I was off the mark. I let the kid's age put me off. I let *you* put me off. In the end I called it an accidental OD, like you wanted, but none of that gives you the right to stitch me up.'

'I know,' he said. 'I'm sorry.'

'Don't fuck with me, Finetti. Why did you do it?'

'Because I knew they'd go me for neglecting duty of care,' he said, finally looking at me. 'Jesus, I took a statement from the kid just after Christmas. He told me his old man was gonna kill him and all I did was write a fucking report. Six weeks later he's dead with a needle hanging out his arm. Of course I wanted it to be accidental.'

I shook my head, unhappy with the explanation. 'That's not what I want to know. Why did you tell them I pressured you into agreeing it was accidental? You were the one pressuring *me*. Why did you turn it around? Why did you tell them I covered it up?'

His mouth dropped open but no words came out. He pressed his fingers into his eye sockets. 'I can't,' he finally said.

'What do you mean, you *can't*?'

I raised my fist, wanting to punch him. Violent charges of adrenaline pulsed through my system and my arms tensed, muscles stiff and rigid, like wet rope.

When Finetti finally looked up at me, fear glinted in his eyes and immediately I knew.

'Eckles, wasn't it?' I said.

He didn't answer, didn't have to.

'Eckles pressured you into making the allegation, didn't he?'

He covered his face. 'I had no choice. Shit, Freckles said to go along with it or I could take a holiday with you.'

It figured. The ingeniousness of the scam lay in its simplicity. By urging Finetti to say I'd pressured him into going along with an accidental ruling, Eckles effectively created a smokescreen and cleared himself of any wrongdoing. Even if the cover-up scenario wasn't believable, two cops apparently agreed the death wasn't suspicious. Eckles had no reason not to sign the incident report and so couldn't be held accountable for doing so. No matter which way it went, everyone would blame me.

Finetti stared up at the ceiling. 'I'm sorry, Rubes.'

'Sorry doesn't help me, Finetti. You put me in the ring and I wore a lot of punches up there. I need you to fix this.'

'I can't. I mean, I can't tangle with these guys like you can. There's nothing I can do now. ESD are running with it. I'm sorry.'

I slapped him. 'Not good enough. I fucked up at the crime scene but I never covered anything up. That was *your* move. So don't sit there saying you can't help me. Either you make good on this or I go out there and let your little dance with Eckles go public. Every cop in Melbourne will know your form.'

'What was I supposed to do, man? Freckles had the clamps on and I had to fold. You should go and speak to *him*.'

'Fuck that. I took a fall for you, pal. Now you owe me.'

I could see him doing the maths, weighing the options. It was a decision every one of us feared: either follow an unethical order or watch your own career go down the drain. Finetti had taken the easy way out to save his own skin and he'd been caught out. Whatever choice he made now would define him, not only as a cop but also as a man. The emotional strain of it was alive and crushing. It left his cheeks slick wet, his lower lip trembling. I could almost hear the blocks falling into place as he realised he didn't have a choice at all.

After a long moment he blew out his breath and let his head fall back against the locker. 'Okay, McCauley. You win. What do you want me to do?'

# 15

THE WATER WAS MURKY, a mixture of green and brown.
I could only see a few feet ahead, but the taste of salt and the
rhythmic movements kept my mind off Eckles, Finetti and the
ESD. Nice even strokes, a breath after every third. At the southern
end, I turned and began the return leg. Today there were about
twenty others with me, a steady stream of bodies gliding through
the water. I knew people who swam every day, even in the winter.
Brighton Beach Icebergs. Some were aged in their eighties, even
older. As much as the exercise, I reckoned it was the isolation
and mental escape of it all that was the real secret.

After fifteen laps, I climbed out and towelled off on the
boardwalk. By the time I dressed it was past five and a crowd
had gathered on the balcony looking over the baths. I contemplated heading up and ordering a beer, but needed to get home
and feed Prince before meeting Ella at seven.

Taking Beach Road to the Esplanade, I drove with my
window down. The sun sat high over the bay on the left, breeze
flooding the car with warm and salty air. A dozen or so kite
boarders skated across the glassy water beyond the marina.

Diesel's 'Fifteen Feet of Snow' came on the radio and I turned up the volume to catch the end of the opening riffs, singing along with the lyrics. I once saw Diesel perform to a small crowd with nothing but an acoustic guitar and a voice that could literally tear your rib cage open. It was his raw energy and grunt that got me every time.

As the vocals faded, I killed the volume and rolled my shoulders, pleased I'd made the trip to the baths. The swimming had loosened my back and shoulder, though it hadn't cleared my head as much as I'd hoped. The events of the day and the details of the case floated through my mind as I passed Luna Park and took Beaconsfield Parade towards home. Pulling into the car park beside my apartment block, I made a conscious effort to push it all away, to focus instead on Ella, my family and the night ahead.

The afternoon heat had left the apartment like a kiln. I turned the air conditioner on high, then dumped my towel and swim bag in the laundry. Prince heard the cupboard open and rushed to his food bowl. I topped it with a tuna sachet. By five thirty I'd showered and was dressed in a linen shirt, beige cargo shorts and leather sandals. At the mirror, for once I was pleased with what I saw. The afternoon sun had left my face tanned and the bags under my eyes almost unnoticeable. My skin had a healthy sheen, cleansed by a dose of salt water. I ran a comb through my hair, slapped on some cologne and decided to leave the day's stubble intact. After gathering my wallet and phone, I selected a bottle of wine from a box in the pantry and stowed it in a carry bag with the wrapped present. Now I was ready.

The Stokehouse Restaurant on St Kilda's Lower Esplanade is a Melbourne institution. Situated on prime beachfront, there isn't a better place in the city for a drink on a sunny afternoon. Upstairs is pure swank. Tuxedos and business suits. Trendy meals at not-so-trendy prices. Downstairs is more my flavour, especially in the beachside courtyard, where the only barriers between you and the water are a walking track and a few metres of sand.

At the bar I nodded and smiled at Logan, who'd worked at the Stokehouse for as long as I could remember, as much a part of the atmosphere as the view. He was preparing a row of screwdrivers in tall tumblers. While I waited I picked up a copy of *Inpress*, a free newspaper promoting the Melbourne band scene. Wolfmother were on the front cover. After snatching a Grammy Award from big American acts like Nine Inch Nails and Tool, the Sydney trio were still going gangbusters. They'd recently headlined the Big Day Out rock festival and were backing it up with a nationwide tour. Looking more closely, I realised the picture had been taken on a rooftop just across the Esplanade, the Palais Theatre and Luna Park in the background.

After serving the screwdrivers, Logan sidled over. 'Hey, big fella, put it here,' he said, holding his hand out across the bar. 'Can't stay away, can ya?'

'Not when the beer's cold and the sun's shining,' I replied, smiling and shaking his hand.

'Mate, the sun's shining too much this summer. Check that out.'

He pointed to a TV on the wall. The seven o'clock news had just started and the bushfires were the lead story yet again. On the screen, traffic on a highway was queued for miles as people fled another town under threat.

'I see it on TV and it doesn't seem real,' Logan said. 'It's like one of those American doomsday movies. Then I look outside and it's right there in front of us, in *Melbourne*. Look!'

I followed his line of sight, out to the beach. Suspended behind a blanket of smoke, the sun was crimson red and looked like a ball of fire over the water. It happened only at certain times of the year, and only when it was stinking hot. I knew cops who called it the blood sunset. It was beautiful yet threatening at the same time, because you knew that as soon as the sun extinguished itself in the bay and darkness fell on the city, people would lose the plot. Fights in the pubs, rapes in the hostels, brawls outside the nightclubs and stabbings on the foreshore were all par for the course when the heat was up. I looked back at Logan, who twisted his earring nervously.

'I'm telling you, man. Armageddon's coming. You better be ready.'

'Then you better get me a beer,' I said. 'A Heineken, nice and cold. And a glass of Chandon too.'

Logan raised his eyebrows. 'On a date, stud?'

'Ah, sort of. It's Ella, remember her?'

'No shit. *The* Ella?'

I nodded. Many years ago I'd proposed to Ella in the restaurant upstairs, and during our marriage we'd come back every year to celebrate our anniversary.

'She's not here yet, but we've got my nephew's eighteenth birthday party tonight, so we're having a quick drink here before we go.'

Logan nodded approvingly and poured my beer. 'I'll keep the Chandon on ice until she arrives.'

I paid for the drinks and dropped a two-dollar coin in the tips jar. Outside in the courtyard I selected a table by the grass and watched the teams of kite boarders slice white wakes across the water. Further out, a lone windsurfer sped across the surface.

I sipped gratefully and thumbed through *Inpress* to the gigs section, looking for the listings at the Esplanade Hotel. The Espy, as we locals called it, was a musical icon. As the name suggested, it looked out over the walkway along the bay, with an almost uninterrupted view of the water. But it wasn't the view it was famous for, it was the music. For more than a hundred years the Espy had been regarded as one of the nation's premier live music venues. Everyone, from legends like Jimmy Barnes and John Farnham right through to more recent rockers like Paul Kelly and Jet, had performed there. In an average week the Espy played host to over fifty bands across three stages, and the best part was that a lot of it was free. I'd lost count of how many acts I'd seen there.

But even more than that, the Espy was one of the last remaining places in St Kilda to resist the lure of developers and dance scene promoters, many of whom would chop off their arms to take over the venue and convert it into apartments or some freakshow of a nightclub. Even the Prince of Wales Hotel, just a block up the road and previously a similar venue to the Espy, was now known more for its swanky restaurant and disc jockeys than the rock bands that occasionally played there. Pubs like the Espy offered more than just entertainment; they were a modern-day David fighting an endless battle with the Goliath of inner-city progress.

I was writing down a couple of Wolfmother's tour dates when my mobile phone beeped. Looking down, I saw it was a text message from Ella: *Sorry, won't be able to make it. Explain later. Xo.*

I was dialling her number when a hand tapped my shoulder. It was Ella, mobile phone in hand. She leant in to kiss my cheek.

'Sorry, just wanted to see your reaction.'

'What the . . . ?' I cancelled the call. 'You're pranking me?'

She winked and I realised it was her off sense of humour.

'That's low, El.'

'How low?'

'Lower than a snake's arse.'

She laughed and slid into a chair, summer dress riding high on her thighs, hair tied back, revealing a patch of pink around her neck and shoulders.

'Been sunbaking, have we? Hard day at the office?'

'Ever the detective,' she said, sliding on her sunglasses. 'No, my bloody tram broke down so I had to walk three blocks. Got blisters to boot. That's why I'm late.'

'Want to go inside, out of the sun?'

'No, I want to smoke,' she replied, dragging her chair into the shade of a palm tree and nodding to the newspaper on the table. 'Checking the gig guide, huh? Who's playing?'

'Wolfmother,' I said. 'They're doing a night at the Espy next week.'

'The Espy? God, is that place still going? Thought they would've converted it into apartments or something by now.'

'Yeah, right. I think the locals would rather burn it down than see that happen. I'd bloody help them.'

She waved me off in indifference.

'Anyway, I'm on the members list,' I said. 'I can get tickets if you wanna come.'

'Why not something like Bennetts Lane?' she said. 'I hear Missy Higgins is doing a members set there. Now *that's* something I'd like to see.'

'Fair enough,' I said. 'You get us tickets and I'll come, then you can come to Wolfmother.'

'Yeah, as if. Aren't you a bit old for Wolfmother?'

'Hey, who're you calling old? I'm not even forty yet. Can't a bloke my age still enjoy a decent gig? Besides, you could be my strapping young rock chick. What do you say?'

'Yeah, right.'

'Is that a yes?'

'I don't even really like Wolfmother. They're just a cheap imitation of Led Zeppelin.'

'I thought you *liked* Led Zeppelin.'

'I do.'

'Then you'll like this. Come on, it'll be fun. I'll even shout dinner beforehand. We can go to Leo's and grab a big plate of marinara, maybe a bottle of –'

Ella raised her palms and started laughing. 'All right, I'll think about it. Can I just enjoy a drink here first?'

As if on cue, Logan appeared with the Chandon.

'Chandon, ma'am? On the house.'

'Ah, sure. Thank you!'

'My pleasure. You're always welcome here, Ella.'

'How do you know my name?' she asked, surprised.

'How could I ever forget?'

When Logan was gone she shot me a look of suspicion. 'Very clever, mister. What's the occasion?'

'Does there have to be one?'

'Well, no. It's just that . . . I don't know.' She slid her sunglasses down her nose. 'Are you trying to impress me?'

'Me?' I said, innocently.

'Well, I am impressed.' She took a sip, held her glass towards me. 'What a day, huh? Look at the sun. I've never seen anything like this before. Thank God we didn't get any more CFA brought in.'

'So the rest of the day was slower?'

'Well, let's see.' She counted fingers. 'Two cardiacs in one hour, *before* I had lunch. A PFO during lunch, then a tradey fell off his ladder, broke both legs and fractured his skull – brought in by chopper, no less.'

'What's a PFO?' I asked.

'Pissed and fell over.'

I laughed.

'Got three old ladies with food poisoning too. Note to self: never eat pork rolls from cheap bakeries. Then to top it all off, some poor kid knocks a pot off the stove and spills boiling water all over his face.'

I wondered how she'd gone getting the information on Rachel Boyd, but didn't want to ask. 'I got Johnno's present,' I said instead. 'A bargain too. Shirt, tie and cufflinks for under one-fifty. Like you suggested: the Windsor end of Chapel.'

'Nice one!' She removed a package wrapped in silver paper from her handbag. 'As it happens, I bought you a present too.'

'Me? It's not my birthday.'

'Just open it.'

I recognised the familiar blue and white striped cloth before I'd finished unwrapping it. 'A new apron,' I said. 'Good one!'

'I figure if you're going to cook for me, you can at least look good while you do it,' she said, nudging me, a huge smile on her face.

'I don't know what to say, El. Thank you.'

'Don't say anything. Just make sure you throw the old one out. And keep the dinner invites coming.'

'I will. Matter of fact, I'm thinking of starting my own cooking show. See if I can teach some of the slobs of the male species how to lift their game. Call it something like *Cop These Apples*. Maybe improve the image for male cops across the country. We get a bad rep, you know?'

She laughed. 'You deserve a bad rep.'

We clinked glasses and went back to watching the beach. The north wind blew sand about in swirly gusts. It wasn't very pleasant and I decided to watch my ex-wife instead. I liked the way her sunglasses perched atop her nose, the way she smoked her cigarette almost thoughtfully. I liked the way her lips delicately sipped the champagne, the sun reflecting off the glass.

'So how was your day?' she asked, breaking the silence. 'Shoot any scrotes?'

'Any *what*?'

'Scrotes. That's what you call them, isn't it?'

I chuckled. 'Only the nice ones. And no, I didn't shoot any today. We don't do that any more. They've all been shooting each other lately.'

She smiled, waiting, but I didn't know whether to go on about my afternoon. Ella was a tough woman, used to seeing the ugly side of life. Accidents. Illness. Trauma. Things most people ran from. But a cop's world was different. There were things even emergency department nurses weren't meant to know about. Things only police should see. Then again, I reminded myself, it was keeping these things from her that had driven us apart in the first place.

'I had a blue with the boss today,' I finally said. 'I called him a bureaucrat.'

'Bet he liked that.'

'Yeah, not as much as he liked it when one of my colleagues stitched me with ESD and had me kicked off the squad.'

Ella set her glass down on the table, then blew out cigarette smoke in an angry puff. 'Whoa, hold up a second. You lost your job?'

'Well, not as such.'

I spent the next ten minutes telling her about my work that morning on LEAP, the fight with Eckles and my visit to the morgue, leaving out graphic details of the abuse. I outlined my meeting with Boyd's stepfather at the commission flats and how Eckles had pressured Finetti into making the false allegation. I ended by saying I intended to keep an eye on the case, but didn't tell her about my side deal with Finetti because I still didn't know how it would work out.

'So as of now, I'm officially on carer's leave,' I said in conclusion. 'Eckles is in the clear and the Homicide Squad have got the case, even though they're chasing the wrong bloke.'

'God, I thought I'd had a big day.'

I nodded and looked out at the bay, towards the sunset. I could see the windsurfer now heading in the opposite direction.

'What are you going to do?' she asked me.

'Well, I'm not going to take it lying down.'

'So you're still working the case?'

'You bet I am.'

She squeezed my hand and removed a folded page from her handbag. 'In that case, I suppose you'll still need this.'

I unfolded the page and saw that it was a printed list of Rachel Boyd's attendances at the Alfred Hospital.

'Thank you,' I said.

'Don't thank me yet. Read it first.'

Rachel Boyd had had three attendances in total, the most recent in October the previous year. Less than six months prior. When Ella shuffled forward to explain it all, her knee rested against mine. I made no attempt to move and nor did she.

'The first two are a couple of years old,' she said. 'The initial one was for an operation to remove her tonsils. I read the file notes and the op was due to a referral.'

I recognised Ella's handwritten notations under the computer records and waited for her to go on.

'The second record was in late 2006 for a car accident,' she said, running her finger along the middle row. Again she had scribbled some coded notations underneath. 'Nothing serious. Just whiplash and minor bruises.'

'Who was driving?'

'Don't know. I thought about that. There's a date and time here if you want to cross check with police records.'

I doubted it would lead anywhere. DHS weren't interested in car accidents.

'The third one is interesting,' she continued. 'Less than a year later she came back for an infection.'

'Infection?'

'Yeah, that's all it said on the preliminary diagnostic chart, so I looked further into the record and it looks like she was treated for a urinary tract infection. Now at first there's nothing unusual about that. UTIs are very common in kids, especially young girls.'

I swigged the last of my beer and looked around for Logan, hoping to get his attention. 'So what was so unusual?' I asked, unable to spot him.

'Well, that she was brought to us for one thing. A urinary tract infection isn't normally the type of thing you come to a hospital ER for. You go to a chemist or a GP. That's not to say we turn you down, especially when the little girl has no parent present.'

'So who brought her in?'

'Her brother, Dallas.'

'Right, that figures. So did you treat her for it?'

'That's the thing. See, she was diagnosed with a urinary tract infection and prescribed antibiotics. I checked on the type of antibiotic and found this.' She ran her finger down the page and pointed to a highlighted word: *Zithromax*.

'It's a very strong antibiotic,' she explained. 'I remembered what you said at the hospital this morning, so my alarm bells went off when I saw the name of the medication.'

Now I understood where she was headed. 'What's it normally used for?'

'Well, lots of things, but it's often used to treat sexually transmitted diseases. I tried to track down the doctor but she's moved on. Gone overseas, I think.'

'Great. I thought you said you guys are trained to identify this sort of thing.'

'We are.'

'So let me get this right: the doctor prescribed a strong antibiotic for a urinary tract infection that was probably something more serious but didn't tell anyone or try to investigate further. Why didn't she at least order some tests?'

Ella just shrugged, which annoyed me. Couldn't she see where this was leading?

'Well, it seems pretty obvious what's happened here,' I said. 'Dallas Boyd brings his sister in for a check-up, probably not knowing what's wrong with her except that it hurts her to pee. The little girl's probably too embarrassed to say anything about the stepfather, so nobody knows the truth. Sure, she gets treatment and the sore peeing goes away, but nobody reports it, even though the doctor must've smelt a rat. So the little girl goes home, takes her medication and it all goes away. Until the next time Daddy gets into bed with her and the chlamydia comes back.'

'You don't know that, Rubens. It might've been a bad urinary tract infection that hadn't been treated and the Zithromax could've been prescribed to flush it out. We could be completely wrong about all this.'

I knew that was unlikely and so did Ella. I'd seen it too many times before and so had she. People unsure of a difficult path and instead taking an easier one. A path with many cracks in it. How many other cases were there like this, I wondered. How many other kids had fallen through those cracks? How many villains were hiding in them?

'This isn't my fault, Rubens.'

'I know. It's nobody's fault. It's the system.' She went to reply but I cut her off. 'But you know what: the system is made up of people, El. People like you and me and that doctor. The system should've stopped it the first time. Instead, we ignored the warning signs and allowed it to happen again.'

I got up and walked to the bar for another beer. I was annoyed that the night had started out like this and wished I hadn't got Ella involved in the first place.

'Everything all right out there, bro?' Logan asked as he poured the beer. 'Want me to send out some oysters or something? You guys look like you need it.'

'No, thanks. Rough day, that's all.'

'Well, that's why they call it happy hour, you know?' he said, handing the beer over and pouring Ella another glass of champagne. 'Everyone's supposed to be *happy*.'

I sipped the beer and decided to forget about the case while Ella was around. Back at the table, she'd folded the paper away and lit another cigarette out of my packet.

I put a hand on her shoulder as I sat back down. 'I'm sorry about all this. Let's just try and enjoy ourselves. I'll deal with this later. I just get frustrated by it all. I shouldn't have got you involved.'

'No,' she said. 'I'm glad you did. You're right. We did fail this kid. Makes me wonder how many other times it's happened.'

'What, at the hospital?'

'No, just in general.'

'Well, that's why I want to take this one to the end. We can't change the system, Ella. All we can do is play our part. That's what I want to do.'

She stubbed out the cigarette and raised her glass again.

'Then let's do it.'

# 16

ANTHONY AND HIS FAMILY lived almost directly opposite the Caulfield Racetrack. Thankfully we weren't tourists, because the taxi driver was about as familiar with Melbourne's leafy eastern suburbs as a desert camel. Finally we arrived at the house, which was almost a hundred years old and midway through a complete renovation.

Music thudded from behind the garage door and an arrow pointed to a side gate where a bunch of balloons had been tied. First mistake, I thought. Eighteenth birthday bashes were notorious for attracting gatecrashers, especially in the suburbs. Inviting guests to simply enter via the side pathway was asking for trouble.

The path led to a paved courtyard over which a pergola had been constructed. Dozens of red and black balloons and streamers hung from the rafters and a sign over the rear of the garage read 'Happy Birthday Johnno!'

About fifty guests were already there, the majority looking barely eighteen in frayed jeans, bright T-shirts and sunglasses. There was a brief lull as they stopped to see who'd arrived. Not recognising us, they quickly went back to talking, laughing and drinking. I looked around for my nephew but couldn't find him. After a few minutes Anthony's wife, Gabrielle, came through the back door with what looked like a tray of potatoes wrapped in foil. She carried them over to a spit roast by the fence, the delicious-smelling smoke reminding me that I hadn't eaten since lunch with Edgar Burns.

Gabrielle set the tray on a table beside the spit machine, then made her way over and said hello. She was a tall woman, with jet black hair and pale skin. Ella says she's beautiful but I reckon she looks unhealthy.

'I'm so glad you could make it,' she said, smiling at the two of us. 'Come inside and let me get you a drink.'

I followed the two women through the door, watching Ella's hips move freely beneath her summer dress. No doubt about it for me: she had the jump on Gabrielle any day. At the kitchen bench I wanted to put my arm around her, but instead slid the wine out of the carry bag and handed it to Gabrielle.

'No need for this,' she said, opening the fridge. 'We bought plenty of wine. Plus there's beer in the laundry fridge – real beer – and champagne in here. Rubens, if you want red, speak to Anthony; he's got some special ones put aside.'

What she really meant, I knew, was that my chosen bottle wasn't good enough. She was probably worried one of her social club friends would see it and assume she was only a few steps off drinking cleanskin labels.

'I'll leave you girls to it then,' I said, and went into the laundry where Anthony was packing beers into a tub full of ice. I shook his hand and accepted a Corona. It was ice cold and tasted sweet as ever, even without the lime.

'Place looks good,' I said, nodding to the backyard. 'Where's Johnno and Chloe?'

'Ah, they should be out there somewhere. Last I saw they were in the garage talking to the DJ. Chloe's new boyfriend.'

'Boyfriend, huh?'

'Yeah, been together a few months now.' Anthony lowered his voice. 'I reckon he's the one selling her the drugs.'

I frowned, not wanting to talk about it here. 'You don't know that.'

'Maybe, but just after she hooked up with him, all of a sudden she started listening to that bullshit music. A month later I found the pills in her room.'

'What have you done with them?' I asked.

He looked away. 'Nothing yet. I'm waiting.'

'Waiting for what?'

'Never mind.'

He opened the back door and the sound of a repetitive bass line filled the room, throbbing from inside the garage. I watched as he went over and told the DJ to turn the sound down. The DJ did as instructed and a number of the kids inside the garage made a face at Anthony as he walked out.

I was about to follow him onto the patio when I heard a familiar cough from along the hall. I walked down to the guest bedroom and saw my father by the bed, apparently looking at something on the dressing table.

'Dad,' I said.

He turned around quickly, startled. 'Hey, Ruboy. Good to see ya.'

'Good to see you too,' I said, smiling at the nickname he'd used my whole life. We shook hands and I pulled him into a hug. He was leaner than he'd been at Christmas, and his grey hair seemed thinner. He wasn't yet sixty-five but looked much older, almost as though he'd aged a year for every month since Mum's stroke. When he pulled away, I saw he'd been looking at a picture of Mum in her garden. It was one of my favourite shots of her, taken about ten years ago. I had the same photo in my apartment, above the television. She was a strong woman back then, able to spend a whole summer's day in the yard, digging and churning mulch and soil, only to come inside and work magic in the kitchen. God I missed her.

'So you're staying here tonight,' I said, trying to sound chipper. 'No need to drive so no worries, huh?'

'Yeah, no worries at all.'

He blew his nose into a handkerchief and I wondered if the weather was giving him hayfever too. I didn't want to think that maybe my father had been crying before I walked into the room.

'I don't know how I'm supposed to sleep with all that bloody racket out there,' he said. 'What kind of music is that anyway?'

'You'll be right, Dad. Just turn your hearing aid down. You won't hear a thing.'

'What was that?'

We both laughed at the old joke even though Dad didn't wear a hearing aid.

'Let me get you a drink,' I said. 'You want beer or wine?'

'Neither,' he said, standing in front of the dressing table mirror and straightening his tie. 'I want a scotch. Crisp and on the rocks.'

'A scotch?'

'Bloody oath, and I want to drink one with my grandson. He's eighteen now, so he's allowed a man's drink. None of this lolly water they all drink these days.'

I followed him into the hall and swigged from my Corona, wondering if it constituted lolly water in my dad's eyes. Out in the garage, I found Jonathan and Chloe helping themselves to a chest filled with ice and an array of different drinks, mostly pink, green and yellow in colour. I wished Johnno a happy birthday and gave him a hug. His hair was spiked like a mohawk with bleached tips and coloured prongs at the back. It probably cost more to maintain a haircut like that than to run the Falcon.

'Hey fellas,' Johnno called to his mates in the garage. 'This is my uncle, the one I was telling you about.'

I turned around and held up my beer. Some of them returned the salute and I figured Jonathan had told them I was a cop. *Hey fellas, watch what you say because my uncle's a detective who worked in the Drug Squad.* The way the squad had been disbanded so publicly, I wouldn't have been surprised if some of them came over and tried to score off me.

'Come outside, Johnno,' I said. 'Your Pa wants to have a drink with you.'

'Yeah, sweet. Where is he?'

'Making you a drink. Scotch, I believe.'

'Cool,' he said, bravado mixed with a hint of uncertainty.

'Can I come too?' Chloe asked, swigging from a bottle with pink liquid in it. 'Or is this some kind of macho initiation crap?'

I laughed. 'Sure. You want some scotch too?'

'Ah, do I look like a scotch girl?'

'I wouldn't know what a scotch girl looks like, Chloe. Although going by that lolly water you've got, I'd say you're more of a Ribena girl.'

'Ribena? This is a Bacardi Breezer, thanks very much.'

'Yeah, give me a taste of it.'

She handed it over and I took a swig. It was sweet and revolting and I handed it straight back, then put a hand on Jonathan's shoulder.

'Right then, let's go watch your little brother gag on a man's drink.'

'I won't gag,' he protested.

'We'll see.'

We joined Anthony and Dad at a table under the pergola that was set with four tumblers, a bucket of ice and a bottle of Johnnie Walker Blue. It was my father's favourite drink but I liked the double meaning for my nephew.

I saw that Ella was helping out with the salads inside the house. I called her to see if she wanted to join us but she said she'd come out when it was all ready.

'So, to Johnno,' my father said, raising his tumbler. 'You're a man now. You can vote, drink and smoke if you want.'

'Dad!' Anthony scolded. 'He will not smoke, not as long as he lives here.'

Chloe and I smirked at each other, then I took a sip of the scotch. It was cold and it burnt my throat like dry ice. You could tell it was good by the way it settled in the glass and around the ice in the bottom, something my father had taught us as boys. Yet it was an acquired taste, and going by the grimace on Jonathan's face, I doubted it was one he would acquire tonight.

'You know, I remember when I was eighteen,' Dad said to Jonathan. 'I was getting ready for life on the farm, then my numbers came up.'

I nodded and so did Anthony. We'd heard the story a hundred times.

'I was on the first ride over there,' Dad went on. 'Stayed the full four years and made it out in one piece. A whole other country, that's what they said.'

'You talking about Vietnam?' Chloe asked.

'That's not what I call it. You don't want to know what I call it.' Dad looked again at Jonathan; the story was definitely aimed at him. 'And it *was* a whole other place. A God-awful place. Hot and full of no one you could trust. You know what got us through it?'

Knowing what I did now about many Vietnam vets, I could've said heroin, but instead let my nephew answer.

'Drinking?'

'Not just any drinking, son,' said Dad, holding up his glass. 'Scotch. Only the good stuff too. We used to knock it off from the Yanks. They'd have it shipped in from back home, and we'd sneak off with the bottles while they were sleeping.'

We all took a sip and I felt a sadness unravel in me as I watched the spark in my father's eyes burn out. Normally he ended this story by saying how returning home and getting married was when the real war started. There was no way he would say that now, not with his beloved wife of almost forty years stroke-afflicted and bedridden in a nursing home. I looked at Anthony and saw that he had seen it too.

'So, Johnno, wanna tell me what you got for your birthday?' I said, changing the subject.

'Didn't Dad tell ya?'

'Nope.'

'He's giving me the Land Rover.'

I was momentarily stunned. I'd noticed the P-plates on the four-wheel-drive out the front but hadn't thought anything of it. Anthony leased the car through his physio business and often let his kids drive it, but it wasn't more than five years old. I shouldn't have been surprised. Gabrielle had been the only child of wealthy fabric importers and the family home had been left to her in their will. For Anthony, it meant he'd entered his forties with a million-dollar-plus property to his name, completely mortgage free. No wonder they could afford to give their son a four-wheel-drive. The money was on tap.

'That's awesome, mate,' I said. 'Do me a favour though and tell me when you're planning to drive it so I know to stay off the road.'

Jonathan looked at his dad, unsure how to react.

'I'm just kidding, Johnno. That's shit hot, mate. Congratulations!'

We all drank our tumblers and Anthony poured another round, excluding Jonathan, who wanted to go back on the lolly water.

'So what about you, Chloe?' I said. 'Enjoying your holidays?'

Suddenly a sharp pain exploded in my shin and I realised Anthony had kicked me under the table. He obviously assumed I was about to embarrass everyone by taking Chloe on about the pills. I was so incensed by this that I didn't hear Chloe's answer and had to think of something else to say.

'So how long have you got left?'

'Of the holidays? I just told you that.'

'No, sorry, I mean university. How long until you finish?'

'Oh, two more years. It can't go quick enough, I tell you what.'

I smiled uneasily, unsure if she knew something was going on. 'Well, enjoy it while it lasts. You don't get holidays like that in the workforce.'

'Only in the police force, huh?' Anthony said. 'I don't know anyone who takes as much time off as you, Rubes.' He laughed at his own joke but soon realised he was out of line. 'I'm sorry, I didn't mean it like that. I know it wasn't a holiday.'

I brushed off the insult and lit up a cigarette. I felt like offering one to Jonathan and Chloe just to spite my brother, but didn't. When Dad said he was going to the bathroom, both kids took the opportunity to escape back into the garage with their friends, leaving just me and Anthony at the table.

'I'm sorry, Rubes. It just slipped out.'

'Mate, I wasn't going to say anything *here*. Jesus, I know it's sensitive.'

Anthony lowered his head. 'I know, mate. Shit, I'm just a bit jumpy.'

'No shit. How's everything else going, aside from that?'

'Fine – that's the thing.' He drained his scotch and nodded towards the garage. 'Look at them. Christ, you'd never know. They look like normal kids.'

I looked over. Two of Johnno's mates appeared to be arm wrestling, Chloe and her girlfriends cheering them on.

'They *are* normal kids, Andy.'

'Yeah, maybe. Have you checked out the DJ yet?'

'No. Why should I?'

'Because like I said, that's her boyfriend and he's probably the one selling her the pills. The way I see it, you just go in there, let him know who you are and what you do. Let him know you're on to him and get him to back off. Christ, it'll scare the shit out of him. Simple.'

'Well, for a start, if he is her boyfriend, I doubt he's selling her anything. He's probably just giving it to her.'

'What, like some kind of sugar daddy?'

'I'm not saying that.'

Anthony's eyes flared wide with rage. He pointed a shaky finger, like a broken spear. 'Don't go there, Rubens. I don't want to hear about that. She's still my little girl.'

'Relax. You're getting ahead of your –'

'Relax? My daughter's on drugs and you don't even give a shit. Jesus, how can you tell me to relax? I knew I shouldn't have asked you.'

Anthony seemed aggressive, in the mood for a scrap. He'd always been like that when he got into the grog. I sipped my scotch and let it settle in my stomach before I decided to give him some home truths.

'Listen, Andy, you're not going to like this, but you need to try and understand something that it's taken me more than ten years to figure out. Something many of my colleagues, and most of the population, still don't get and probably never will.'

He leant forward, interested.

'We're fighting an impossible battle. And it's not just the drugs. A multi-billion-dollar music and entertainment industry has sprung up in the past decade. We're talking about record sales that rival The Beatles. There are nightclubs in Europe that have become multinational corporations and are listed on the world stock exchange. They send their DJs on worldwide tours, fly them in on private jets and helicopters, like bloody movie stars. And walking hand in hand with it all are the drugs.'

Anthony stared into his glass, absorbing it all. 'So you're saying the music is a front?'

'No, I'm saying they're co-dependent. One's spawned the other, like the chicken and the egg. And the music is fashionable, it's everywhere. On the radio, in the clothing stores, in the movies. Mate, they even play it on the sports channels.'

'Right, I get it. The more popular the music becomes, the more popular the drugs are?'

'Right, and vice versa.'

Anthony gestured towards the garage where Johnno's and Chloe's friends were now dancing to a style of music I recognised but would never appreciate.

'You mean music just like this? What that guy's playing in there?'

I nodded, then immediately regretted it as he pushed back his chair.

'I knew it. I'm not having it in my house,' he said, storming around the table.

'Let it go,' I said, stopping him. 'You don't want to make a fool of yourself. Not here. Not tonight. Johnno would never forgive you.'

The resistance didn't last. He was unsteady on his feet and I realised he was drunk. He eased away and pointed at the garage angrily. 'It's fuckin' bullshit, Rubens. What kind of noise is that anyway?'

'What do you want them to listen to, Andy? Cold Chisel?'

'What's wrong with that? This is just synthesised crap.'

I stayed where I was in case he made another go for the garage.

'I agree, but what would you do if the DJ played "Khe Sanh" and they all got in a circle and sang about wanting more speed and novocaine?'

Anthony screwed up his face, as though he'd only just realised the meaning behind the iconic lyrics.

'Suppose you'd want to hear "Run to Paradise", too,' I added.

'That's what I'm talking about. The Choirboys, classic Aussie rock. Real music.'

'And another song about drugs.'

Anthony pushed my arm away and sat heavily in a chair, still looking at the garage with the same angry stare. I wondered if I ever got that look on my face when I was drunk.

'How big is it, Rubens? I mean, I've read the newspapers but how do I know what's rubbish and what's real? I want you to tell me the truth.'

'Andy, it doesn't matter. Let's just enjoy Johnno's birthday. You don't need to worry about –'

'No!' He laid his hands flat on the table. 'I want to know. I want you to tell me. I wouldn't have a clue about any of this.'

Before I could say anything, he got going about morals and

how you couldn't just condone something simply because it was popular.

'I try to set good standards,' he went on. 'I sent the kids to private schools. We get them involved in sports and give them plenty of support. We even talk to them about sex. But all these new drugs . . . I don't have a clue. Sure, we smoked hooch when we were kids. Big deal. I told Johnno about that one day, that we'd smoked a joint or two as kids. He just laughed. Apparently everybody smokes dope these days, even the girls.'

His head dropped into his hands. Some of Jonathan's mates were looking over at us, wondering what was going on. I tapped Anthony on the leg and he looked up.

'Sometimes I feel like I live in a hot air balloon,' he said slowly. 'Everything looks fresh and beautiful from up here. Soon as I get near the ground, I see the details and I don't like it. I want to put more gas in the balloon and go back up.'

I nodded, because I agreed with him and because I liked the analogy.

'God, I don't even know what it's like to have a bloody mortgage.'

'Lucky you,' I said.

'You think living in the shadow of your dead parents-in-law is lucky? I can't even take a piss without Gabrielle asking how much money I've spent.'

I didn't reply to that.

'The point is, I'm ignorant, Ruby, and I want you to tell me the truth. How big is it, mate?'

I drank the last of my scotch but didn't top my glass up. 'When I first saw pills in Melbourne, they were selling for fifty bucks each in the clubs,' I began. 'That was about ten years ago. Now they're going for half that. What does that tell you?'

A frown creased my brother's forehead as he did the maths. It was a simple explanation but in many ways it defied the common rules of economics: that something illegal could go down in price, despite massive attempts to stamp it out.

'A lot more people are into it?' he said.

'There's an insatiable demand, Andy. Worldwide, we're talking hundreds of millions of pills consumed each year. In Australia, Melbourne is the epicentre. We get more seizures per capita than anywhere else in the world. In one operation alone, we seized over five million tablets. That's enough to get the whole city high.'

'Jesus.'

'Not even Jesus could stop it, mate. I don't even think we can slow it down. Not any more. It's too big.'

'Oh, come on. That's a bit defeatist, isn't it? Surely we can teach them how dangerous it is. Surely we can tell Chloe?'

Anthony's look was almost pleading – *searching* – for something that wasn't there. An answer. His face was only about a foot away from mine, and I was beginning to regret trying to explain something even I couldn't understand. The truth was, nobody knew how dangerous it was. Governments the world over had tried to scare people into saying 'no' by overdramatising the risks and dangers. The problem, of course, was that when those risks and dangers didn't eventuate, when people took the drugs and nothing bad happened, they simply assumed they'd been lied to by the government. That meant any important messages – any truths – got flushed along with all the hype.

'I don't know, Andy. You'll need to leave it with me. I'm not saying anything to her tonight, but I will talk to her. I want to help you.'

'What will you say?'

'I don't know. I need to really think about it.'

For a moment it looked like he might try another angle, but then he gave up. He went to pour himself another drink but I snatched the bottle.

'You don't need any more. Drink some water and sober up a bit. We've still got all night and you need to enjoy yourself with Johnno.'

He nodded and I put my arm over his shoulder, feeling almost sorry for him. My brother was a good man and he didn't deserve this sort of stress. I promised myself I would do what I could to help him.

'Okay, mate, I'm going inside to help with the food,' I said. 'Sitting next to this spit makes me feel like eating the arse end out of a dead rhino.'

That triggered a smile. I slapped him on the back as he headed towards the garage. 'Now you go in there and have fun with your kids.'

# 17

BY MIDNIGHT THE PARTY was on its way into the messiness that only alcohol can cause and only large amounts of sleep can cure. Not long after, Ella and I were in a cab. Fortunately this driver knew his way around town and neither of us had to give directions.

As it happened, the DJ had gone on to play 'Khe Sanh' and 'Run to Paradise' and many other classic rock anthems, and, sure enough, everyone sang and cheered in a circle, just as drunken teenagers had done for many years and would no doubt continue to do for many more. It just went to show that no matter how fashionable electronic music became, Australians always reverted to type when it came to a backyard shindig. In the end I regretted having the debate with Anthony about the drugs. Though he sang and carried on with everyone else, there was something missing. An innocence, perhaps. Maybe he would've been better off staying in his hot air balloon.

Along St Kilda Road, a canopy of maple trees entwined with green nightlights arched over the boulevard, giving it the feel of a space-age tunnel. Warm air blew in through the windows as we skirted the buildings of downtown and headed into Carlton. When the cab pulled up outside the building where we'd shared an apartment for more than five years, Ella kissed me on the cheek and whispered in my ear, 'I want you to come upstairs.'

Following her into the foyer, I watched her hips again as they swayed beneath her dress. She moved with more vigour this time and I knew she was putting it on. At the elevator she looked back over her shoulder and caught me watching her.

'What are you doing?' she said, smiling.

'Stalking you.'

The look she gave me told me she was both scared and excited at the same time. I wondered whether she could see the same in me. When the elevator opened I followed her in and she kissed me, first gently, then with more force. I pulled her back against the wall, not wanting it to end. Soon we were staggering through the front door of her apartment. As we reached the bedroom, she unbuckled my belt with awkward hands and I lifted her dress up and over her shoulders. I sat back on the bed and she straddled me, my hands trembling as I guided her onto me. We kissed deeply and she ground herself against me with slow but deliberate thrusts. I was engrossed in her taste and the faint smell of sweat and perfume as she moaned in my ear. I resisted the urge to tell her how long I'd wanted this and how I'd missed her. Instead I just held her as she shuddered and squeezed my head tight against her shoulder.

When she was finished, I pulled her down onto my chest and stroked her back, staring at the ceiling. How long had it been since I'd held her like this? How long since I'd been in this bed, in this apartment? For a moment I wondered how many other men she had been with like this, how many others had stared up at this ceiling. The room was dark now, but the streetlights from outside pierced the window and bathed her figure in shades of soft blue, like a dream. It was a long moment before I realised I was holding my breath.

'Is there something wrong?' she asked, her voice muffled against me.

'Ah, no, it just . . . it just doesn't seem real, that's all.'

'It doesn't seem real to me either,' she said, rolling off me. 'Do you wish it wasn't real?'

Beneath the sweat and frazzled hair I saw a person lost in uncertainty and in need of stability. In that moment I knew it didn't matter how many other men had been with her. For them, it would never be like this. For her, and for me, there was only one lover.

'No. I'm glad it's real,' I said.

She squeezed my hand as I slid off the bed and walked to the kitchen for a glass of water. At the sink I paused, looking around the dark room. A freshly pressed hospital uniform hung from a cupboard door handle, dry-cleaning bag draped over it. The blinds in the lounge and dining area were open, the city sky-scrapers rising high above. I'd expected the place to feel more familiar, but it didn't, and I had the sense that this was a good thing. We'd bought the two-bedroom apartment off the plan before the real estate boom in the late nineties and lived in it until our separation.

With two glasses in hand, I walked to the window. About fifty metres east I could see Lygon Street – Melbourne's Little Italy – winding up after another hot Saturday night. Back in the bedroom, I slid in beside her and pulled the sheet over us. Ella took a sip of water and hugged the sheets as I rested my head on her chest, listening to her heartbeat.

'I want to tell you a story,' I said after a while. 'When I was a kid, my best mate was Tommy Jackson. Jacko, we used to call him. Our dads used to work together on the building sites. We all took holidays together and –'

'Wait. I think you told me about him. Is he the one you lost touch with, the one who moved to Melbourne?'

'Yeah, but I never told you why he moved.'

I pictured the events and tried to arrange them into words.

'I guess I'd sensed a problem with Jacko, but it wasn't till this one camping trip that I began to understand what was going on. Me, Jacko, Anthony and our dads spent a week on the Murray. Towards the end Anthony caught a cod, over two feet long. Dad and Jacko's old man were real proud. It was the highlight of the trip and we were going to cook it up for dinner. When it was cooked, Dad flayed the fish on a platter and handed it to Jacko.' I took a breath, trying to control my emotions. 'Jacko was clumsy, always falling over, hurting himself. When he got close to the table, he tripped on a stick and the fish went everywhere. We tried to salvage as much as possible, but it was useless and we ended up eating canned soup. Everyone was mad at Jacko, even me. His dad went right off, told him to go to his tent and not come out.'

'Poor kid,' Ella said.

I ground my teeth as I recalled what happened next. 'I don't know why, maybe because we were all watching, or maybe because he'd had enough, but Jacko didn't budge, just stood there, shaking. I can't remember exactly what he said, but he gave his dad some attitude and that was it. His old man threw a full beer can across the campsite. It hit Jacko right in the face, dropped him like a wet towel.'

Ella tensed beside me.

'He beat the absolute shit out of him, Ella. Right in front of us. Anthony and I tried to stop it but he was too strong. He just kept hitting him and hitting him until Jacko was unconscious and covered in blood.'

'Jesus. What did your dad do?'

'Nothing. That's the point. He just sat there, the gutless bastard. He carries on about how tough he was to go to Vietnam, but he couldn't stop his own mate from beating up a *kid*.'

I rolled off her and stared up at the dark ceiling, feeling queasy from the acids mixing with the alcohol and dinner in my stomach.

'We ended up going home the next day and Jacko had to go into hospital. I don't know what happened between my dad and

Jacko's dad, but we never went on any more camping trips together after that. Jacko's family moved out of town and I'd only see him every so often. Even when we did catch up, we never spoke about that day.'

'He leave to escape his dad?' asked Ella.

'S'pose. Left town as soon as he turned eighteen. By then I was old enough to know what happened on the camping trip wasn't a one-off event. I was also old enough to know that all the bruises and scratches Jacko'd had over the years weren't from falling over.'

We lay there for a while then and I listened to her breathing over the top of the traffic on Lygon Street. Somewhere in the distance a siren wailed across the city. Another emergency; somebody else's this time.

'One day I decided I was going to come down to Melbourne to find him and I made Dad come with me. We hit St Kilda and asked around but nobody wanted to help. Even the coppers weren't interested. Back then St Kilda was wild. It scared the shit out of me. How was a kid from the country going to survive in a jungle like that? Anyhow, we spent a full week looking for him, but we were never going to find him. For the next two years I worked with Dad on the building sites and life carried on. Just after I turned twenty we heard Jacko had died of a drug overdose. About a year later I joined the police.'

Ella ran her hand through the hair on my chest. It was a sensual touch that felt out of place and I wanted her to stop, but I didn't tell her.

'And you blame Jacko's father for that?' she said after a while.

'Course I do.'

'What about your own dad? Did you ever speak about it later?'

'No.'

'Maybe you should've.'

'I didn't know how he'd take it.'

'Well, it's not too late, you know?'

'Yeah, I know.'

We were silent again, and I remembered one of the nights Dad and I spent trying to find Jacko. For hours we stood at the entrance to Luna Park, just hoping he might happen by. But he never did, and Dad and I never spoke about it. By then I'd worked out that Dad had known about the abuse for many years but had chosen to do nothing about it because he was mates with Jacko's father. Since then I'd accepted – through my own silence – that Dad's guilty conscience was punishment enough. But it wasn't. Dad needed to know that his failure to act or intervene made him culpable, that he was part of the problem. Part of the *system*. Just like anyone who chose to ignore something in the hope that someone else would deal with it. It wouldn't be a pleasant conversation, but Ella was right. I had to tell him. Things would never be right between us until I did.

'I guess I just feel a bit weird, that's all,' I said. 'I mean, these last few days have been full on, and tonight with Johnno turning eighteen and all. That's how old Jacko was when he left Benalla.'

Ella seemed to consider this, then rolled over and faced me. 'I saw you with Anthony tonight. You looked like you were arguing. Do you want to tell me about it?'

I hadn't considered telling Ella about Anthony's request for me to talk to Chloe because I wasn't sure what angle to take, and I wasn't even sure what Ella would make of it.

'He was drunk and he wanted the music changed, that's all. Do you want to go out on the balcony and have a smoke?'

It was an obvious lie and I knew what was coming. She shrugged me aside and sat up.

'No, I don't want to smoke. If something's going on, I want you to talk to me. I know he's your brother but I'm your –'

She caught herself mid-speech and stared at the window. I put my hand on her naked back.

'What are we doing, El?'

156

'I don't know,' she said, reaching over for the water and drinking the last of it.

I slid out of bed and took the glass back to the kitchen. At the sink I splashed cold water on my face and was struck by a moment of clarity. Why didn't I trust her? I'd let her in on my movements at work, so why not the family? Just then I realised there was no other way. *To get what you want, you have to know what you want.* If I wanted her back, if I wanted our old life back, I needed to treat her like a wife instead of an ex-wife. I needed to trust her again.

I turned around with the glass, but stopped when she came out of the bedroom in a bathrobe, a cigarette in hand.

'You still want that smoke?' she asked.

'No.' I handed her the glass of water. 'Anthony found drugs in Chloe's room. Ecstasy tablets. That's what we were arguing about.'

'Oh no.'

'He wants my help but he doesn't want to hear what I've got to say.'

'What's there to say? She needs to stop. You know how many drug overdoses we see in emergency every weekend?'

I nodded. 'I know that, but it's complicated. He wants me to talk her out of it. I think he wants me to scare her.'

'So what are you going to do?'

'I don't know.'

'You want me to talk to her? I could tell her about all the kids we see on the weekends. That's scary, just the number of them coming in.'

'And so could I, El. I could also tell her about all the brawls, assaults, rapes and car accidents we get because people can't handle their drinking. Do you think that'll turn her off alcohol?'

'You can't make that comparison. Alcohol is legal. Ecstasy isn't.'

'Doesn't automatically make one more dangerous than the other though.'

'Right.' Ella finished the glass of water in one gulp and picked up a bottle of wine off the bench. She held it in the air like a trophy. 'This is alcohol, Rubens. It's been around for centuries. Jesus Christ even drank it, so we know exactly what it does to us over time, and we know exactly what's in it. Look, it says it right here on the label.'

She swayed on her feet, trying to read the alcohol percentage information. She'd obviously drunk more than I thought, and I knew there was no point doing this now.

'Look, I know all that,' I said. 'Let's not talk about it now. I *am* worried about it. I mean, it could just be a phase and she'll grow out of it, or it could get worse. But I need to think it through before I speak to her. I want to make things better, not worse.'

She put the wine down and raised her palms to the air, feigning indifference. 'Fine. Let's go back to bed then.'

# 18

*WE WERE IN THE DRIVEWAY OF a vacant office complex, the car creeping over smooth bitumen. Tyres sloshed in puddles. It was dark and cold and I knew how it would end. The concrete and glass surrounds were as familiar as my bedroom. The door was unlocked but I didn't open it. Could've but didn't. Don't know why. Headlights framed a rusty skip bin.*

*The car stopped and the driver said nothing as I slid out, silent, floating. Sirens in the distance. Why were they taking so long? I wanted to scream but nothing came. The driver stalked around the bonnet, gun trained on me. His hand tightened, squeezed. The gun exploded and I felt the bullet pierce my shoulder but I didn't fall. Hadn't then, didn't now. The driver came towards me, head-lights catching his face. It was Anthony this time.*

I started awake, panicked, drew a breath. One, two, *where the fuck am I?* Something exploded again. *Crash!* I looked about the room. Someone beside me, in the bed. Ella. I took another breath. *Bang!* Something outside. Bottles smashed and tumbled. A garbage truck. What was it they said about dreams? And why was Anthony the shooter?

I sat up, sheets damp with sweat, mouth dry as a ditch. The clock read 5 a.m. I rolled off the bed, muscles stiff and rigid. The window was bare, blinds left open from the night before. Light piercing the window slats brought back memories of when we first moved into the apartment and couldn't afford blinds. The east window had always woken me at sunrise. I sat down again and stroked Ella's forehead but she didn't move. A throbbing in my head reminded me I'd consumed too much alcohol and probably needed more sleep, but I was awake now and wanted to make the most of the day.

In the bathroom, I searched for painkillers, feeling like a burglar ransacking the drawers, not knowing where anything was any more. Eventually I found a packet of aspirin and swallowed two tablets before showering and dressing in the same clothes I'd worn the previous night.

'Are you leaving?' Ella croaked, eyes barely open.

I smiled and sat down beside her. 'Just going to make breakfast.'

'Can't wait to use the new apron, huh?'

In the kitchen, the fridge was near empty, save for a few vegetables, margarine and juice. I figured Ella probably ate out a lot these days. Hopefully that would change soon. I headed downstairs, a cheeky smile stretching my face as I recalled staggering into the elevator last night.

Outside, I stopped on the pavement and almost had to remind myself where I was. Ordinarily the city skyscrapers – less than two kilometres away – rose high over the rows of terraces that lined the children's playground opposite the apartment building. But not today. Today I couldn't even see through the park. In winter there were days like this, when clouds of fog settled on the city and dropped visibility to less than a hundred metres, closing airports, constipating the main arterials and making everyone late for work. But this wasn't fog, it was smoke, and I'd never seen it this bad.

Then there was the smell; the rich, pungent scent of burnt

timber. Unlike the sour odour of exhaust pollution, it wasn't offensive, but its origin was equally ominous. A giant monster was raging. Last I'd heard it had killed fifteen people, destroyed more than fifty homes and almost a million hectares of forest. Countless livestock and wildlife had been lost too. Walking to the convenience store on Lygon Street, I wondered how long my folks would be safe. After loading up a basket with eggs, bananas, bread and milk, I stood at the counter and noticed the headline on the morning *Herald Sun*: LOOTERS.

'Ah, don't tell me . . .'

Scooping it up, I read the caption underneath: *Heartless thugs raid empty stores as town flees and more homes burn.* There was a photo of a man running down an empty street with what looked like a DVD player in his hands.

'Can you believe this bullshit?' the cashier said angrily, pointing at the photo. 'The firemen are up there trying to save the joint and this cocksucker's helping himself to the TV shops.'

The story outraged me too, just as the editor had no doubt intended. It was bad enough that some of the fires had been deliberately lit. Now they were looting the shops. What next, people's homes? I wondered what Edgar Burns would say about it.

'They're not just *trying* to save these towns,' I said. 'They're *dying* to save them. Just yesterday five firefighters were brought into the Alfred Hospital for burns and smoke inhalation. One of them had burns all over his face. He'll never look the same again.'

The cashier shook his head in disgust. 'They oughta line those scumbags up and let the whole town throw rocks at them, then send them off into the bush with no clothes on. See how long they last in the wild with all the hungry animals.'

I liked the idea but Edgar's was better. 'No, you know what they need to do? They should chop off his old fella, fry it up in a pan and make him eat the bastard.'

'Bloody oath, man,' the cashier laughed. 'That's brilliant.'

I handed over the money and carried the groceries back to the apartment, where we ate breakfast, then went out onto the balcony, trying to make out the buildings through the smoke. At one point the peak of the Eureka Tower – currently the tallest apartment building in the southern hemisphere – was just visible. Other than that, we might as well have been staring at a dirty bed sheet. It wasn't long before I had my first sneezing fit for the day. Ella laughed at me and said she was all out of sympathy for sick people, but agreed to find me a Zyrtec on the condition that I do the washing up.

I thought about sneaking in with her while she took a shower, but didn't want to push it, unsure how much alcohol had played a part in her decisions last night. The ember had caught and a flame had flared. All I needed to do was shelter it and keep it going. In lieu of this, I considered asking Ella if she wanted to come with me today to visit Mum then decided it was too soon. There were some things I needed to do on my own. By the time she'd dressed I needed to get going. She drove me home and we agreed to meet again that night at eight for dinner, this time at an Italian restaurant on Lygon Street.

I fed Prince and changed into a pair of trousers, white summer shirt and black leather loafers. On my way out of Albert Park I stopped at the village and bought a bunch of flowers from the florist and a vanilla slice from the bakery, one of Mum's favourite treats. By nine I was on the Calder Highway, pushing one-ten as the city traffic cleared, driving through acres of dry and barren farmland, a channel of grey smoke plumed on the horizon. It looked like a giant mushroom cloud rising up beyond the Macedon Ranges. All around it the sky was dirty orange, and I lowered the window and let the hot smoky air slipstream over my face, sparing a thought for the fire crews and the thousands of people who lived in its path and couldn't just close their doors or turn off their televisions when they were over it.

When the pine plantations took over and I could no longer see the smoke clouds, I began sorting through my CDs, looking for something to listen to. Though I kept all my original albums in my lounge room, I had copies of all my favourites in the car. Among them were Jet's *Shine On*, Cold Chisel's *Breakfast at Sweethearts* and even a few AC/DC classics like *Back In Black* and *Hells Bells*. There were also a few mixed compilations Anthony had downloaded for me from the internet. I was usually happy to put these on shuffle and let the machine decide what I listened to, but today there was no question about it. I knew what I wanted to hear and found it towards the bottom of the console. Crowded House's *Recurring Dream*.

Skipping to track 16, 'Something So Strong', I listened to Neil Finn sing a beautiful story about the power of love, how it could let you soar as high as the clouds, or just as easily spit you out and crush you to the core. Hearing the lyrics now, after spending the night with Ella, I understood what Finn meant when he spoke about bringing life to frozen ground. But the sad irony was not lost on me either. The band's drummer, Paul Hester, had hung himself from a melaleuca tree in Elsternwick Park, near Brighton Beach, a few years back. I remembered stepping out of the shower the day it happened and hearing it on the news. Couldn't believe it. But how many suicide jobs had I been called to over the years? Had to be at least a hundred, maybe more. Dr Wong had told me once that over two thousand Australian men killed themselves every year. Relationship break-downs were among the most common reasons. Love and jealousy. Something so strong.

I muted the stereo when the track ended and rang Anthony.

'How's your head?' I asked when he picked up.

'It's still in the toilet. Been there since about 3 a.m. when I finished praying to the big white god.'

I almost asked what he meant, then realised he was talking about vomiting. There was a double standard in there some-where, I was sure. A father wondering why his kids experimented with drugs, then getting so drunk in front of them that he finished the night puking in the toilet.

'Must've been the food,' I joked. 'I think the meat on the spit was a bit off.'

Anthony croaked out a laugh. 'Could've been the gravy, had plenty of that.'

'You mean the kind that comes in a bottle with a blue label on it?'

'That'd be the one. What's up, Rubes?'

'Been thinking about Chloe,' I said. 'I'm going to talk to her this week. Any ideas where to catch her? Don't really fancy doing it at your joint. Maybe somewhere else.'

'Good point.'

I overtook a semitrailer, eased back into the left lane. I could hear Anthony emptying bottles into a rubbish bin. 'If it's not a good time maybe I'll call back?'

'No, sorry, just cleaning up. Go on.'

'Your daughter, Andy. Where do I find her?'

'Ah, right, her work's probably best.'

'Where?'

'Service station in Brighton. New Street, near North Road. If you drive down –'

'I know where it is. Time? Day?'

'Okay, ah, Tuesdays and Thursdays. Morning shift. Six till two. Best time's in the arvo, I reckon.'

'Consider it done, mate. You never asked me to do this, okay?'

'Okay.'

'I mean it. Far as she's concerned, I'm doing this off my own bat. It's gotta be that way or else it won't work. It could backfire and I'd never hear the end of it. Agreed?'

'Fine. Thanks again for this, Rubes. I appreciate it.'

When I passed a 'Welcome to Kyneton' sign, I got to the point. 'Look, I need a favour from you, actually. You have clients at your gym paid for by DHS? Young kids? Teenage screw-ups.'

'Like Chloe, you mean?'

'I won't even dignify that, Andy. This is serious. I'm talking about state wards. Hard-case junkies.'

'Ah, sure. Youthies, we call them. Youth workers line it up and get the funding. The kids come in a few times, lose interest, never come back. Course we're happy to keep receiving the money.'

'You have access to names?'

'I might. What I do with the names is another matter though.'

'Don't shit me, Andy. Important case, this one. Get a pen.'

'All right. Let me go inside.' I heard him opening and closing doors before he came back on the line. 'Go on. Shoot.'

'Dallas Boyd and Derek Jardine.'

'Done. What are you going to say to Chloe? I reckon you just –'

'Don't worry about Chloe. Just worry about the names. I need to know if they're clients of the YMCA – anything you give me might help. Write the names down, Andy. Use the pen.'

'I have.'

'How soon can you get back to me?' I said, hoping he could do it right away.

'System's not automated yet. I'll need to check the files. What sort of case? Rape, murder?'

I said nothing.

'Come on, man, if I'm gonna help I wanna know. Shit, what if they come after me?'

I turned off the highway into the main town centre. At the roundabout I went right, into a residential street.

'Gotta go, Andy. Find me the names, call me soon as you can.'

'All right. You're no fun at all, you know that?'

'Catch ya.'

I switched off the phone and stopped outside the nursing home. An ambulance blocked the entrance and paramedics were pushing a stretcher towards it. There was an elderly woman under a white blanket with people fussing over her. My heart skipped a beat. It was my mum.

# 19

MUM LAY ON HER SIDE, eyes closed. Her face was distorted, a permanent frown etched on her forehead.

'She had a fall,' one of the paramedics said, ushering me to her side. 'Landed badly. Nurse found her on the floor.'

'Mum,' I said, touching her shoulder. 'It's okay. These people are taking you to hospital.'

'She knows that. Do it every fortnight,' said the medic, moving around to the front of the ambulance while his colleague got the gurney ready for loading. I turned to the nurse, a thin woman about my own age, gaunt face. I'd met her when we'd first moved Mum into the nursing home but I couldn't recall her name.

'What does that mean, every fortnight?'

'Check-ups. Hospital rehab. Rotating tests, sometimes X-rays, sometimes MRIs or cat scans. Your brother, Anthony, often comes up for them. Of course this one wasn't scheduled. How'd you know to come so soon?'

'I didn't. I was just visiting,' I said, watching the medics load the gurney into the back. One of them followed Mum in. 'Where are you taking her?'

'The usual.'

I looked at the nurse, embarrassed at not knowing what 'the usual' was.

'Kyneton Private,' she said.

'Mind if I ride in the back?'

The medic on the inside clipped an oxygen mask to Mum and said, 'You can ride up front. Not in the back.'

'What about you?' I asked the nurse as I opened the passenger door. 'Are you coming?'

'I've got forty-three other people to look after, plus there's a whole swag coming in from Bright in case the bushfires hit there. Sorry.'

'I keep odd hours,' I called after her as she walked away. 'Shiftwork makes it hard to visit.'

She nodded, sympathetic.

'I've been off work a long time too. Only been back a month,' I added, feeling stupid. Who was I justifying myself to? Her or me?

After I climbed in, the driver radioed through a status call to the hospital and we drove out of the nursing home.

'A fall?' I quizzed him. 'What happened?'

'Don't know. Nurse says she must've fallen out of bed. Hurt her hip.'

I winced. 'How bad?'

'Don't know that either. She's not able to communicate that to us, so we'll have to wait for the X-rays. Hopefully she's just bruised.'

An overwhelming sadness hit me as I thought about Mum's fragility, how old and defenceless she'd become. Driving along the town perimeter, we passed teenagers riding BMX bikes on a dirt path. As kids, Anthony and I had had bikes. I'd fallen once, leaving my arm lacerated and swollen. I remembered the pain and the shock, and my mother's firm but caring hands washing the gravel and dirt out of the wound. I remembered her telling me to breathe slowly, ignore the sting of the Betadine.

I remembered her patience, but most of all I remembered her always *being* there.

'How could she have fallen out of bed?' I asked.

'Happens all the time. They get up, go to the toilet, slip. Sometimes they have nightmares, roll right out of bed. Sometimes they do it deliberately, like they want to hurt themselves. You know, for attention.'

'Attention?'

'They get lonely in there. We get a few at Christmas time, sometimes Easter.'

'You mean when they miss out on important occasions?'

The driver nodded. 'Wedding anniversaries and birthdays are big ones too.'

The light turned green and we drove the last few kilometres in silence. Mum had missed Christmas, and now Jonathan's eighteenth birthday. But surely she wouldn't do that to herself . . .

'She'll be okay,' the driver said as we pulled into the hospital. 'A fall's never good for the elderly, but your mum's a real fighter. They say she can't speak, but I don't believe that. She just looked at me, told me all I needed.'

I held Mum's hand as they wheeled her into the hospital. The nurses were ready, but they waited patiently while I leant over her, looking into her slanted face. Her left eye drooped, and drool slithered from her lips. I wiped it away with a tissue. Her right eye twitched, looked up at me and her breathing began to stagger. Was this a reaction to my presence? I squeezed her hand and kissed her forehead, inhaling the aroma of soap and musty linen.

'You're in the wars again, Mum. Beds are for sleeping in, not surfing.' I waited for a reaction but there was none. 'They're just going to do some tests, make sure you haven't gone and broken anything. I told them that was impossible with bones like yours. They're like steel, all that milk you drink.'

I smiled, but again there was no reaction. Her right eye closed, opened slowly. Not looking at me. After a few moments,

I nodded to the nurses and they wheeled her away. I knew then why I'd avoided coming to see her and it had nothing to do with my job.

An hour later I was led to a room with two beds either side of a window that overlooked a courtyard. Mum was in one bed, 'Mrs Isabella McCauley' already written on the slot above. The other was empty. I pulled a curtain across for privacy and stood next to her. She wasn't asleep, but the painkillers had left her drowsy.

'Brought you some flowers,' I said, arranging them on the bedside table. In my haste, I'd left the other flowers and the vanilla slice back in the Falcon and had to buy another bunch. 'Got the results too. No breaks. Just like I said, bones of steel.'

Looking down at the mound beneath the sheets, I wondered how extensive the bruising was. The nurses said she'd been lucky, that she'd fallen the right way. What was the wrong way?

'Dad's on his way back up from Melbourne. Gonna stay the night here with you. Nurses even found a room with a spare bed in it. How good's that?' I said, sitting down and taking her hand. It was cold, so I rubbed it, trying to warm her skin. It was her left side and I wondered if she could actually feel me. The stroke had knocked out the entire right hemisphere of her brain. Left hemiplegia, the neurologists called it. Ischemic clot. For Mum it meant a near total loss of motor skills on the left-hand side of her body and acute aphasia. Speech paralysis.

'Do you want something? Drink of water maybe?'

She pointed her right arm towards the bedside table, hand curled into a ball.

'The roses; you want to see the roses?' I said, following the line of her arm.

She mumbled what seemed like a yes. I carried the flowers to the bed and held them close to her face. She breathed, closed her eyes and for a second the frown disappeared.

'Nice, huh? They're Alexanders. Your favourite. Could've got you anything though. Everything's in season these days. Even tulips. Guess they just grow everything indoors. Doesn't matter about the weather. That's plain cheating, if you ask me.'

Watching her with the flowers reminded me of the many times she'd led me through her garden, pointing out her new roses. In spring the previous year, I'd watched her churn the soil and add mulch to a dry garden bed. Her hands were muddy and she'd looked clumsy with the shovel, knee pads strapped around her overalls. But it was a beautiful garden, lush with colour and fragrance. Somehow she always managed to plant species that survived the drought. There were Alexanders and Icebergs and Blue Moons, even a Penny Lane that climbed an archway.

'Grown this one from a cutting,' she'd said proudly, handing me a pot with a stem protruding. 'It's a Silver Jubilee. It'll look good on your balcony, but don't let the pot get too hot. And don't water at night, only in the morning.'

'Or what? Will it turn into a Gremlin?' I'd said, smiling.

She'd laughed. 'It'll get black spot, silly. Lovely to see you, Ruby. Bring Ella up next time?'

'Sure thing, Mum.' I hugged her. 'Next time.'

That was two days before the stroke.

I put the flowers back, sat down and held her hand again. This time she faced me.

'My shoulder's getting better,' I said. 'Anthony's working miracles. Says I'll be lifting weights again soon. Soon as he's finished with me, we'll get him to go to work on you. You'll be out in the rose garden again in no time.'

I squeezed her hand but she looked away. She was beyond bullshit, and I no longer knew what to say. I didn't want to talk about the birthday party and she probably didn't want to hear about it either.

'Want to hear a joke, Mum?'

She groaned a yes.

'The Prime Minister is on the election trail and he needs to increase the senior vote, so he goes to a nursing home to make friends with the residents.' She gave a weak smile, even though

I was certain I'd told her the joke before. 'Anyway, the PM walks up to a little old lady and says to her, "Good morning, ma'am, do you know who I am?" To which the little old lady replies, "No, dear, but if you ask the young chap at the reception desk, he'll be able to tell you."'

I laughed at my own joke and was sure Mum did too. I felt the sadness rise up inside me and had to draw a deep breath to keep myself from losing it in front of her.

'I spent the night with Ella,' I said after a long break. 'At the flat in Carlton. Things are going well between us, I think.'

Her right hand came up, touched my arm and squeezed. She groaned and the right side of her lips pulled to a smile. I hugged her then and almost lost it again, choked with pain and guilt.

'I love you,' I whispered in her ear. 'I'm sorry I haven't been around for you lately. That's going to change.'

A tear slid down her cheek. As I wiped it away, I decided I didn't want to be here when Dad and Anthony arrived. I was ashamed and angry and couldn't face them. What was I going to do – tell them I was sorry? Tell them I'd do more, visit every chance I got? It would mean nothing, not without action.

For a long while I sat beside her, stroking her cheek and waiting for the painkillers and sedatives to take effect. Soon her breathing slowed and I had the strange sensation that this was what it would be like to euthanise a person. I shook off the morbid thought and remembered a question Mum had asked me not long after my return from hospital. *Why do you do it?* It was about a month before the stroke, and the only time she'd ever questioned my career direction. Sometimes I thought she knew something was on the horizon; that her body was preparing to shut down.

A marriage counsellor had once asked me the exact same question – albeit for different reasons – and instructed me to list my responses, a task I failed to accomplish. Even now, I still couldn't articulate it. Some detectives I knew – Cassie, for example – described it as a calling, but I wasn't sure about that. I only knew that if you had a skill, something you were naturally good at doing, then that was a gift, and if you didn't pursue it then your skill was wasted and so was the gift. To me, that transformed skill into purpose. It was like an ecosystem, in that if everyone ignored their skill, their gift, the world would be worse off. People who depended on you would suffer. People like Dallas Boyd and his sister, Rachel. People like my elderly neighbour, Edgar Burns. People like Chloe. And people like Jacko.

Yet even as I thought all this, I knew I wasn't being honest. Ella had depended on me too, and I'd let that world fall apart. I'd let her down. What about the rest of my family? Mum was in a nursing home, Dad was a shadow of his former self, and now Anthony needed me. Surely our *purpose* in life extended well beyond our careers.

I squeezed Mum's hand and wished I could ask her advice. What would she say to me, I wondered. Give up and go home? Quit and spend all day on the couch? Tell Edgar Burns you're too tired for it? Tell Anthony you can't help him? Forget about Dallas Boyd and his little sister? No, I knew what she would say. I knew because she had said it all her life. *To get what you want, you have to know what you want.*

Right then I made a choice. I would go back to Melbourne and hunt down whoever had killed Dallas Boyd and see to it that both he and Rachel received the justice they deserved. I would embrace my purpose and I would follow it to the end.

# 20

THE DRIVE BACK TO MELBOURNE took almost an hour less than the drive up. I kept the speedo on one-thirty all the way and the stereo muted. I wasn't in the mood for love songs or any other music. I just wanted to get back to Melbourne and go to work. I arrived in St Kilda to find most of it had been blocked off for the festival and I had to badge a team of council workers guarding the barricades before they'd let me through. Even then, I had to drive at snail's pace along the tram tracks.

Thousands of people walked the streets, like a parade without a cause. Tables and umbrellas covered the sidewalks, waiters flitting between them. Large banners hovered over the street, welcoming everyone to St Kilda. A concert was underway on the foreshore, a past *Australian Idol* personality headlining. All of it infuriated me. Didn't they realise what went on in this place? I wanted to blow my horn until they all moved along but had to sit patiently, wasting time.

Finally I pulled up outside the 7-Eleven, double-parked and waited for all the customers to leave before I walked in. Dallas Boyd had bought a recharge card for his mobile phone here at ten o'clock Thursday night, less than two hours before he was murdered. Yet we'd never found a phone on or near his body, and it still hadn't turned up. It was a loose end that needed to be tied.

The shop attendant, a man of Pakistani descent, crouched over a cardboard box, stocking the fridge. 'Excuse me,' I said, showing him my badge. 'I need to view your tapes for last Thursday, from about 9 p.m. onwards.'

'This could make a problem,' he said. 'Police have already taken the disk.'

I thought about this; the only likely explanation was that Stello had come for it.

'When?'

'I am thinking late yesterday. I was not here.'

I cursed myself for neglecting to swing by the day before; instead, I'd gone for a swim.

'Hang on. You said they came by to collect the disk?'

'This is correct. The disk.'

'So your system is digital. Not on tape,' I said, looking up at the camera above the console.

'Correct. No tape.'

'Okay, so why is there a problem? Can't you make me a copy?'

'It will take a long time and I am the only person here,' he said, looking around nervously. 'I am thinking it is easier to get the copy from your colleague, yes?'

'Sir, I really need you to copy me the disk. This is important, and I'm happy to pay you for a blank disk if that's what you're worried about.'

The man hesitated, then led me through to an office at the back of the store where a computer sat atop a desk cluttered with folders, boxes and empty takeaway containers.

'I must be quick,' he said, clicking on the computer screen. 'Customers can steal as they please if I am not in the store.'

'Sure,' I said. 'If you show me what to do, you can get back to stocking your fridge.'

'No, I will do it myself,' he said, typing a series of commands. An image of the shop appeared on the monitor, the date and time counting forward in the bottom right-hand corner. It was still cued up for 9 p.m. on the Thursday, probably saved from Stello's copy.

'It is Thursday, yes?' he asked.

'Yes, from nine onwards.'

'I can only give you three hours per disk.'

'Fine. Give me from nine-thirty onwards.'

The man went to work. The image disappeared and a measuring scale appeared on screen, showing the progress of the burning. A minute later the disk tray opened.

'All finish,' he said, handing me the DVD.

'Can I watch it quickly?' I asked. 'You know, just to make sure it worked?'

'I am promising you, it will work.'

'I believe you, but it would be great if I could watch it here.'

Taking the disk, he put it in the tray and pointed the cursor arrow to a control box at the bottom of the screen. I recognised buttons similar to those on my DVD player at home.

'Fast forward with this button,' he said. 'When you are finished, press stop and eject. I must be going back to the store.'

When he was gone, I pressed fast forward and watched dozens of customers walk in and out of the store as the clock counter skipped towards 10 p.m. A few minutes before ten, Dallas Boyd entered. I pressed play and the movement slowed to natural speed. The volume was muted and I tried to find a dial but couldn't. Deciding it wasn't necessary, I watched as Boyd moved around the store, from the fridge to the confectionery aisle, eventually stepping towards the counter. At this stage he asked for something, and the attendant turned and pulled out a recharge card. Meanwhile, Boyd quickly snatched a chocolate bar off the console and slid it in his pocket.

'Cheeky little bugger,' I said.

As the attendant handed Boyd the receipt and recharge card, a girl in a miniskirt entered the store and came into view. It was the girl I'd seen in the picture in Dallas Boyd's bedroom, the hooker outside the apartment block. She sidled up to Boyd and put an arm around him. I paused the image and called out to the shop attendant for help.

'I need a printout of this girl,' I said when he came in. 'Can you do that?'

He muttered something in another language as he leant over me and punched in the keyboard commands. When the page was printed, he snatched it up, removed the disk and handed them both to me.

'Will that be all?'

'Yes, thank you.'

I took Grey Street into the red-light district, looking for the green Valiant or the girl in the picture. Despite the heat, or perhaps because of it, the street seemed devoid of prostitution. I turned down Greeves Street, a favourite on the hooker circuit, but still failed to see a single girl. This wasn't right. Normally there were at least twenty girls out during the day, more at night. I drove around again and finally spotted a transvestite who went by the working name of Dixie Normas.

Dixie, aka David Castleton, had a story similar to many others: absent father, sexual molestation as a young boy, a runaway at first. There was big money for young boys on the block. Big risks too. He'd been raped and assaulted at least twice, busted for drugs and solicitation more than once. Puberty blues and the rock spiders were no longer interested in him, but there were plenty who were. At age twenty-five, he was one of the hardest-working girls on the block.

I parked across the street and walked towards him. He must have read the determination in my face because he started walking away.

'Hey!' I yelled. 'Stop, I wanna talk to you.' He kept walking and I jogged to catch up, grabbed him by the arm and turned him around. 'I told you to stop.'

He yanked his arm free and stared at me. Up close I saw that he no longer took as much pride and patience with the make-up. Maybe his clientele liked it that way, or maybe he was just worn out.

'I'm not talking to you, not now,' he said, taking a step back. His heel caught in the sidewalk and he grimaced as he stumbled.

Catching his elbow, I helped him upright. 'I'm looking for someone,' I said, showing him the picture I'd printed at the 7-Eleven. 'She's a new girl. Who is she and where can I find her?'

He turned his head away, and in profile he looked like a man. Like many trannies around St Kilda, he'd had the implants but not the tackle chop. Whenever we locked up a trannie, we had to put them in a cell on their own because they didn't belong in the women's or the men's.

'Just look at the picture,' I said. 'This is important.'

'And so am I. I'm not doing this, not today.'

A late model BMW slowed on the other side of the road. Despite not being able to see through the tinted windows, I knew the driver was watching us. He was probably a pervert angling for a blow job and was unable to find anyone out today. I stared at the dark windows until the car drove off.

'What's your problem?' I snapped at Dixie. 'I just want a name. She's not in a blue; I just need to speak to her.'

He handed the picture back and turned to walk off but I grabbed his wrist and held it firm.

'You know the rules, Big Dick. You respect me and I'll do the same for you. If I need help, you don't get to choose when it suits. I decide when it's important. You don't walk away and you don't give me attitude. You just answer my questions and give me what I need. That way, when you need my help there's some left over.'

He knew exactly what I was saying. Pretty soon every hooker becomes a victim and they need us just as much as we need them.

'Look, today's not a good day for us, that's all I'm saying.'

'What do you mean? I don't care about the festival.'

'I'm not talking about the festival,' he hissed. 'Why do you reckon the streets are empty?'

'What are you talking about? Where is everyone?'

'Like you don't know.'

Suddenly a cold dread washed through me. 'What's going on, Dave?'

'You really don't know, do you?'

'No. What is it?'

He stepped under the shade of an elm tree and leant against a brick fence. Another car drove past, slowed and tooted its horn. Neither of us acknowledged it.

'I've never bullshitted you, Dave. I've always played fair. Just look at the picture and tell me what's going on around here.'

His eyes shunted back and forth, searching the street, before finally he looked at the picture. It wasn't a long look.

'You're right. She is new to the stroll. Her name's Tammy, I think. That's all I know.'

'Surname? Address?'

He shook his head and handed the picture back.

'Did you know her boyfriend, Dallas Boyd?'

He looked up at me sharply then. 'Yeah, I knew Dall. Everyone did. He was a cool guy, young but smart.'

'Sad,' I said. 'From what I gather he was cleaning himself up.'

'If that's what you call it.'

'What's that supposed to mean?'

'Nothing. He knew the risks. We all do.'

I wanted to ask whether he thought the death was accidental and what the word on the street was, but I had the sense that it didn't matter. The street had killed Dallas Boyd no matter which way you saw it.

'Okay, so where the hell is everyone?'

He broke away from me then and yelled 'Talbot Reserve' over his shoulder as he scurried around the corner. There was no

179

point going after him. I went back to my car and drove down to Barkly Street, turned left and stopped when I saw the crime scene tape and a squadron of police cars barricading Talbot Reserve.

# 21

TWO NEWS HELICOPTERS hovered above the park like vultures and numerous journos had already gathered. Parked across the street, I counted six police cars and fifteen cops. All eyes were on the mouth of a narrow alley at the rear of the park where a crew of crime scene examiners were taking photographs of something behind a large blue tarpaulin. I angled for a better look and saw another tarpaulin stretched above the pack, tied from one tree to another, blocking any chance of helicopter footage. I recognised most of the cops at the scene, including the district response inspector and three detectives from the Homicide Squad. Further down the street was the familiar white van, waiting for the body.

I bit my lower lip. Was it Dallas Boyd's girlfriend in there? Wishing I had a police radio, I thought about ringing the watch-house to ask what was happening but then I saw Cassie speaking to a crime scene examiner. I typed a text message asking her to call, then saw her check her phone, excuse herself and step aside.

'Don't look over,' I said when she rang. 'I'm parked across the road.'

She looked over.

'I said don't look!'

'Bollocks, Rubes. No one can hear. What're you doing?'

'Driving past. Saw the cars. What's going on?'

'Ah, this is a bad one. Looks like some kind of shitfight gone really wrong.'

'Is it Tammy?' I asked.

'Who?'

'The girl, is her name Tammy?'

'Nah, his name's Justin Quinn. About sixteen. Know him?'

I scanned my memory for the names I'd crossed over the past few days but drew a blank. A sense of relief settled on me. 'No,' I said. 'Stabbing?'

'Sort of. Somebody slit his throat. The pathologist says the guy cut him so deep it almost severed his spinal cord.'

Instinctively I touched my throat, feeling guilty for having been relieved. I was glad to be in the car, not over there.

'Are you okay?' I said.

'Sure.' She attempted a smile but even from this distance I could see she wasn't good. 'Humans are the worst animals, you know?'

I nodded. 'You don't look so flash.'

'The heat's killing me, 'scuse the pun. Call me a sook, but I don't know how much more I can hack. Did you see the blood sunset last night?'

'Yeah.'

'Probably be another one tonight,' she said. 'Everyone's going troppo, know what I mean?'

She was right. The city was losing it.

'How's it looking with witnesses?' I asked.

'Same old story. Plenty of people around but nobody saw a thing.' Cassie ran a hand through her hair. 'Strange thing is, the pathologist thinks the kid's been dead since late last night, but it wasn't called in until this morning when two hookers tripped over the body. I questioned them and I don't think they saw anything.'

That explained the absence of hookers and junkies on the street. They were probably either being interviewed back at the station or were holed up somewhere, scared shitless.

'Maybe this time they're telling the truth,' I said.

'Well, whoever did this was quick and quiet.'

'And vicious. What about motive?'

'We're thinking drug related; a rip-off or payback. Kid's wallet was emptied, pockets turned out. Known meth-head and the hookers said he sold dodgy gear every other day. Not exactly a protected species.'

Her explanation made sense, but there were gaps. I wished I had a picture of the boy; anything to rule out a link with Dallas Boyd.

'Look, I gotta go,' she said, blocking an ear against the noise of the helicopters. 'I'm supposed to be meeting Mark down at the foreshore.'

'Finetti?'

'Yeah, he's on foot patrol for the festival. Wants to talk to me – about *you* no less. What's the story, Rubes?'

This concerned me. What did Finetti have to say to Cassie? We'd made a deal but it hadn't included anyone else.

'There's no story. Just stay out of whatever Finetti's got planned. This is between him and me, not you.'

'What kind of shit is that, McCauley? You really piss me off sometimes. It's all right for you to expect everyone to be open and transparent, but when the shoe's on the other foot it's a different story. What the hell's going on with you and Mark?'

'Look, I'll tell you when the time's –' I stopped when I saw Ben Eckles pull up across the road in an unmarked sedan, blocking her from my view.

'Now I've really gotta go,' Cassie said, her tone flat and tired. 'Here's the boss.'

I punched Will Novak's number into my mobile phone. I needed to find Tammy, and Novak would know where to start. The phone nearly rang out before he answered.

'Afternoon, Will. Rubens McCauley here,' I said. 'Did I wake you up?'

'Very funny. Nah, I was outside with a client when I heard the phone ringing and had to run inside. What's up?'

'I need to find Dallas Boyd's girlfriend.'

'Girlfriend?'

'Her name's Tammy, I think. Blonde, maybe eighteen years old. Cute but rough, if you get my drift. She works the stroll, maybe up on Barkly.'

'So go up to Barkly,' he said. 'She'll definitely be working today. The festival's in full swing – there'll be thousands of perverts instead of hundreds.'

'She's not working today. Nobody is.'

'What's that supposed to mean?' he said.

'Well, that's why I'm calling. I need an address.'

'Excuse me?'

'I need her address. Surely you know where she lives.'

'Well, actually I don't. She's not a client of mine.'

'Not yet.'

Novak breathed out heavily into the phone. 'Look, I don't know where she lives.'

'I think you're going to want to know what's going on. And it's not something I want to discuss on the phone.'

Novak hesitated before replying. 'Ah, sure, give me about five minutes.'

I drove to the hostel, double-parked and waited a few minutes before Novak came out. He was dressed in a pair of sandals, board shorts and a pink polo shirt, a day's worth of stubble surrounding his neatly trimmed goatee.

'What's happening?' he said.

'If you can get me an address for Dallas Boyd's girlfriend, I'll fill you in.'

'I told you, I don't know where she lives.'

I pointed at the hostel. 'Ask your clients. Someone will know.'

Novak nodded uneasily and hurried off. I wound the window up and turned on the air conditioner. A tram rolled by, full of passengers on their way to the festival. I wondered how many had seen the crime scene at Talbot Reserve. What a welcome party.

A few minutes later Novak appeared with a Post-it note in his hand. 'Got an address,' he said when I wound down the window. 'Not as easy as you might think though. Whatever's going on around here has them all spooked. I had to bullshit one of the kids about Tammy and tell him I had a cheque for her. You wanna fill me in?'

I told him to jump in and waited for a tram to ease forward, then made a U-turn. Before we reached the Barkly Street intersection I explained that despite some initial dead ends the investigation was moving quickly and that there were a number of important leads, Tammy being one of them.

'Hold up a second,' Novak said. 'Last I heard you were still trying to confirm that Dall was actually murdered. I take it you've done that and this is now officially a homicide investigation. Is that the case?'

'Yes.'

'What about Dall's stepfather? Did you speak to him?'

'Yes, and he's clean.'

'What! That sicko beat the living shit out of Dall for almost ten years. He even threatened to –'

'I know,' I cut in. 'I didn't say he wasn't a scumbag. I just said he didn't kill Dallas.'

Novak appeared to consider this while we waited to turn off Carlisle Street.

'So where am I going?' I asked. 'What's the address?'

'Three-sixty Barkly. Three blocks up. We could've walked.'

'Not in this heat. Besides, I don't think you wanna walk past this,' I said, turning the car and driving slowly by the crime scene.

'My God, is that what I think it is?' Novak asked.

'Yeah, somebody was killed last night.'

185

'A lot of my clients frequent that park. Do you know what happened?'

I nodded. 'Stabbing.'

'Who?'

'Can't tell you that, Will. You'll have to wait until an official identification's been made.'

'What kind of shit is that? Here I am, on a *Sunday*, helping you get close to a witness. Don't tell me to wait. You know how I feel about my clients. Losing Dall was bad enough. If there's another one I have to bury, I wanna know about it,' he said.

I pulled up outside the apartment block Tammy lived in and looked at Novak. There was only one right way to do this. 'Will, if I tell you the victim's name, it didn't come from me, okay?'

He nodded.

'It was a boy named Justin Quinn,' I said, watching for any sign of recognition.

His eyes narrowed in thought. Then he shook his head. 'I don't know him. Not one of mine, thank God.'

I stared over at the apartment building. It was of the same era as Dallas Boyd's, made of grey besser block with a faded mission brown trim and an internal staircase. Unlike Boyd's building, the name of this one had fallen off. I hoped I hadn't made a mistake in telling Novak the name of the victim. I thanked him for his help and asked him to wait in the car. But he shook his head.

'You know what this means?' he said.

'What?'

'There's no way Tammy's going to talk to you now. She's new, so she'll be too scared. She'll just clam up.'

'So what are you saying?'

'I need to come with you, help you explain things to her.'

'You can't be serious.'

'I am. She'll trust me. She definitely won't trust you.'

'Will, this is a police investigation. You're not a cop. You can't be involved.'

186

'Ah, hello.' Novak waved the Post-it note. 'I already *am* involved.'

'Not like this you're not. I can't have you questioning a potential witness.'

'Fair enough, but she won't talk to you unless I'm there to ease her anxiety.'

I swiped at sweat on my forehead and stared at Novak, realising he was probably right.

'Hey, be my guest,' he said calmly. 'You go up there and see how far you get. My guess is she won't even answer the door.'

I hesitated. This wasn't my usual approach. I was old school and I respected the old-school code of mutual understanding between police and crooks. Most of the hookers upheld the code, but if Tammy was young and new to the game she wouldn't know the rules. And she definitely wouldn't trust me.

'All right, but you leave it to *me* to do the questioning. Got it?'

'Fine.'

'I'm serious.'


We crossed the street to the apartment building. As we climbed the internal staircase to the second floor I heard a baby crying and wondered how many other hookers lived in the complex and how many had children living with them.

'This is it,' said Novak, reading from the note in his hand.

I knocked, waited. Nothing. Knocking again, I remembered the security guard at the commission housing estate telling me I was too early, that these people were nocturnal.

Novak went to speak but I cut him off. 'I know,' I said. 'I don't care if she's asleep. I'll keep knocking until somebody answers.'

'I was going to say I've got her mobile number,' said Novak. 'The kid I bullshitted, he gave it to me as well as the address.'

He handed me the note. I dialled the number and heard it

ring inside. The first time it rang out. On the second try, footsteps followed. Novak smiled as I hung up and knocked again.

'Jesus Christ!' shouted a male voice. 'Who the fuck is it?'

I looked at Novak. 'Who's that?'

He shrugged, leaving me to speak through the door.

'Police! I need to speak to Tammy.'

'She's asleep. Come back later.'

I almost laughed. The nerve of these people. 'No, mate, that's not how it works. Wake her up.'

'What's it about?'

'Don't worry about that, and don't worry about trying to clean up the mess inside either. We're not going to come in. I just want to talk to her.'

'Fuckin' bullshit. How do I know you're not here to arrest her or somethin'?'

Novak stepped forward. 'We have some information about Dallas Boyd, but we need to confirm this with Tammy. We're not interested in seeing what you've got inside. We just need to talk to her.'

A moment of silence went by, then a shadow moved beneath the door.

'How do I know youse are even cops?' asked a different voice. A female voice.

I held my badge up to the eyepiece and eventually the door opened. Tammy was shorter than I recalled and seemed thinner than in the picture in Dallas's flat, the remnants of last night's make-up smudged across a face that had probably endured more years than birthdays.

As she hugged a satin dressing gown close to her chest, I noticed sores on her wrist and a large bruise around her neck, as though somebody had strangled her. Her hair looked like a bird's nest, dark roots replacing bleached blonde. Still, she was an attractive girl and could remain so if she took care of herself. But I knew she wouldn't.

'So ya got some news on Dall?' she said, her voice coarse and shaky.

'I'd like to ask you some questions first,' I said. 'Is that okay?'

She shrugged. 'Ask away. Maybe then you can answer some for me.'

'Like what?'

'Like how he overdosed even though he wasn't usin'.'

Novak turned away. 'Right.'

'What?' Tammy said, her lower lip beginning to tremble. 'Think I'm making it up? Think all of us are junkies, don't ya?'

'I didn't say that,' said Novak.

'Then what, ya think he knocked himself?'

Tammy glared at him, angry. I shot him a look also, annoyed he'd jumped into the conversation.

'Perhaps I need to introduce Will Novak,' I said. 'He's not actually a detective. He's a social worker.'

Tammy's eyes grew wide with recognition. 'You're from the hostel down on Carlisle Street,' she said. 'Dall told me about you. Said you were helping him.'

Novak nodded. 'He was one of my clients. Lived at the centre for about two years. I helped him overcome many of his problems, including heroin. Even helped him get his apartment.'

'Then you'd *know* he wasn't a junkie.'

'Just because he'd been clean for some time doesn't mean he didn't relapse and start using again.'

Tammy made to snap at him again, then turned away. She brushed a hand over her eyes.

'We're investigating all possibilities,' I said. 'When was the last time you saw Dallas?'

'The day he died,' she said, still facing away. 'He spotted for me, then we went down to Lambs for a souvlaki.'

I opened my daybook, wrote *Tammy* and *Fitzroy Street* at the top of a fresh page. I wanted to ask for her surname and other details but that would have to wait.

'Okay, where else?'

She turned to face me, revealing a line of mascara streaked down her cheek like a scar. 'Like I said, we got chips and a souvlaki, then we went to the 7-Eleven. He needed a recharge card for his phone.'

I wrote this down and asked what happened next.

'Ah, we hung out a while,' she said, her eyes dropping. 'Then we went down the beach for a walk.'

I looked over at Novak, who nodded. He'd seen it too. A lie.

'You went to score, didn't you?' Novak said, putting a hand on her arm. 'It's all right. We're not interested in that. We just want to know what happened, who you saw. Who you spoke to.'

Tammy sniffed, stared at the ground. Her legs appeared to be shaking under the dressing gown and I wondered whether it was grief or if she was hanging out.

'Okay,' she said. 'We scored some gear and went down to McDonald's to meet Fletch.'

'Who's Fletch?' I asked.

Tammy nodded to the door. The guy inside.

'Your boyfriend?'

'No way! Like I said, me and Dallas had been together since last year. Fletch just lives here, spots for me sometimes when I'm on the block.'

The man in the green Valiant I'd seen the other day. I wrote the name in my daybook.

'Tell me about that bruise around your neck,' I said.

Her hand shot up to her neck and covered the bruise protectively. 'What do you care?'

'I care because I'm a policeman.'

'Are you trying to be a smart arse?' she scoffed.

'Sort of. I care because I like to know what goes on around here,' I said, pulling my cigarettes out of my pocket and offering one to Tammy. The last thing I felt like was a smoke but they were often the best way to break the ice. Novak took one too and we all lit up.

190

'You didn't grow up around here, did you, Tammy?'

'No,' she said, giving me a curious look.

'Where did you come from? Is Tammy even your real name?'

'What difference does it make?'

'A lot, actually. See, I'm not sure if Dallas or Fletch in there explained this to you, but this is how it works. If you want to play up around here, then I need to know who you are and where you're from so I know who to contact if I ever have to identify your body.'

I let that sink in, ignoring Novak shifting on his feet. Tammy drew on the cigarette and blew out smoke in cool defiance. I wasn't worried. I'd had this conversation before and I assumed Novak had too, albeit with a different intention.

'Tammy, if you work around here, then sooner rather than later you're going to need the police,' Novak said. 'It works best if you establish a rapport with them. It's a very simple under-standing: you help them and they'll cut you some slack. Some bogan drives past and hurls a beer can at you, maybe they'll let it slide; but if you get robbed or raped, they'll show good form. I've worked here for twenty years and I've met some real arsehole cops. Sometimes the only difference between them and the crims are the badges.'

She remained silent, thoughtful.

'But things are different now,' Novak went on. 'Very different. These days I vouch for the local cops, especially the detectives. They're hard but fair. They might rub you the wrong way, maybe even disrespect you, but they'll never go lazy on you.'

'Yeah, righto. What do ya want from me?'

I squashed my half-finished cigarette and made sure it was completely out, but still didn't risk flicking it into the garden bed below.

'Well, you can start by telling me your full name,' I said. 'Where you come from, where your parents live, how old you are, what sort of tricks you turn, who your regular clients are. All the usual stuff.'

191

'And whether I come here often?'

I didn't smile and eventually she got the hint and told me her story. Tamara York had grown up in Tasmania in a family of loggers. A high school dropout, she'd stolen cash and got a one-way ferry across the ditch to Melbourne in 2007. She tried to tell me she'd had no idea about St Kilda and had simply arrived here by chance, but I knew that was bullshit. I'd heard the story so many times before I could write the script. Like most of her kind, she was running from her past. A deviant uncle perhaps, maybe a mother who took the uncle's side. Either way, it didn't matter. The drugs and the street gave her a family, a daily mission, a purpose. That was the commonality.

I knew there were gaps in her story but that was fine. I'd heard enough for now, and told her she could expect more chats with me in the future. If she lasted. Novak gave her a business card and said he'd also be available if ever she needed him.

'Thanks,' she said, nodding towards the cigarette pack in my pocket. I gave her another and studied the bruise on her neck as she lit it.

'You know, it's not right for him to do that to you,' I said.

'Who?'

'Fletch.'

Tammy screwed up her face. 'Fletch didn't do this. He saved me.'

'Saved you?'

'Yeah, some rich freak tried to strangle me the other night. Fletch got there just in time, belted the guy over the head and dragged me away.'

Yet again, I wondered why these girls persisted. A few hundred a night wasn't worth it. Surely there were other ways to fund a habit. Then something about her explanation caught my interest.

'Why do you say he was rich?'

'Easy, he was driving a Beamer.'

'Did you report it?' Novak asked.

Tammy shook her head, probably regretting not doing so now she knew we would follow it up.

'So what happened?'

'Doesn't matter. It's too late now, isn't it?'

'Tammy, I told you, I like to know what goes on around here. This is my patch, and whether you people like it or not, we're in charge. We control the street, not you or your feral clients or any other shithead who decides to come down here. So tell me what happened. If there's some nob rolling around touching up the girls, I want to stop him.'

She looked at Novak and I had the sense she was embarrassed about something.

'It's fine, Tammy,' he said. 'We've heard it all before. Nothing you say will offend us.'

'Suit yourself. I was down in Elwood the other night, near the beach – you get better crawlers down there – and this fat slob in a Beamer rolls up and asks how much for a smoke. I doubled my usual price once I saw the car. He nodded and I climbed in.'

I took a few notes but mostly listened. When she used the word 'smoke', I knew she was talking about oral sex.

'Anyway, we went around the block and parked outside the gardens on Dickens Street. I went to work on the guy but he couldn't get it up. He kept patting my head and telling me I'd been a good girl but now I was bad. He had this foreign accent, like Russian or something, I couldn't tell. That always creeps me out,' she said. 'When they talk. You can do whatever you like with your hands and face and your dick, but just don't talk to me.'

'So he wasn't a regular of yours?'

'Not of mine, but he is a regular in St Kilda. I've seen the car before. Navy blue, dark windows, big alloys. Personalised number plates. I'll know it if I see it again.'

'You remember the plates?' Novak asked.

She shook her head and finished the cigarette. 'I would've told you that straight up, wouldn't I?'

'Okay,' I said, annoyed again that Novak had interfered with my questioning. 'What else?'

'I couldn't get him hard and was about to say something when he just started to strangle me, like really tight. I almost choked right there. Lucky he had sweaty hands and I managed to twist away and start screaming. I think I might've scratched him, which isn't bad considering I chew all my nails.'

I looked at her fingers and considered the possibility of having them checked for skin, but figured it was too late and an assault wouldn't get priority anyway.

'I guess the guy didn't notice Fletch following us. He sure copped a shock when the door opened and a baseball bat came flying through.'

I nodded approval as did Novak. Some rich prick out there with a big old shiner on his face, making up a story to the wife about being done over in a road rage incident. I waited for more details but the story was finished and I decided to leave it for the moment. I might pass it on to Finetti or one of the others, but right now I wanted to focus on Dallas Boyd.

'So you say Fletch isn't your boyfriend, just a spotter?'

'Yeah. Like I keep telling you, Dall and I were *together*.'

'Sure?'

'Why would I lie about that?'

I didn't want to believe this could all boil down to a simple love triangle, but couldn't discount it completely. Men did all kinds of crazy things in the pursuit of the opposite sex. We were a pathetic species sometimes.

'Well, now that Dallas is gone, maybe you need someone to help you through the grief, someone to look out for you. Maybe you and Fletch can work something out.'

'Look, mate, Dall was my only boyfriend. Fletch might throw me some dice for a bit of play every now and then, but that's just business.' She let her dressing gown fall to the side, exposing her bruised shoulder. 'Nobody rides for free.'

I had to smile. Her boyfriend was dead, some fruitcake had

194

beaten the crap out of her and she was living in a cesspit with a guy who probably fed her smack every night just to keep her dependent. All this and she still had a whore's pride.

'Does Fletch see it that way?' I asked. 'Maybe he got sick of paying, wanted Dall to move on.'

'Bullshit!' she snapped. 'Fletch is just . . . he just looks after me.'

Novak pointed to an abscess at the crook of her elbow. 'Looks after you, does he?'

Tammy yanked her arm back. 'Dall and I were gonna go places. See, that's what I loved about him. Most of the people around here are too lazy to even go on proper welfare. Not Dall, he had goals, you know? He had *plans*. He was trying to get us outta this shithole.'

'What kind of plans?' Novak asked. 'Far as I knew, he was happy in his apartment.'

'Well, he never said nothing specific, but he kept talking about getting Rachel outta the flats and us all moving away, starting a new life and shit. All we had to do was stick together, and then . . .' She didn't finish, instead turning away and looking out over the dry garden below.

The man I recognised from the green Valiant stepped out of the flat in a pair of boxer shorts. A large tattoo of a dragon crawled up his lean torso.

'What's goin' on?' he said to Tammy.

'I'm fine, Fletch. We're just talking about Dall.'

Fletch put an arm around her, revealing a line of track marks up his wrist.

'Want me to stay here with ya?'

She straightened her dressing gown and turned around, composed. 'No. We're nearly done. I'll be in soon. Go back to bed.'

Fletch gave us both a cold look. When he'd gone, I decided to move things along.

'So you went to McDonald's with Dallas. Then what?'

'Well, I left with Fletch. Dall had to meet somebody. Somebody from the park.'

'The park?'

'Luna Park?' said Novak.

'Yeah, a perve, you know; a rock spider.'

I was confused, then suddenly I remembered Dixie's response when I'd said Dallas had cleaned up his act. *Clean, if that's what you want to call it.*

'Hang on. Dallas was meeting a paedophile?'

'S'pose so. That's what he did.'

Novak moved closer. 'What, are you saying he prostituted himself? I've never heard such –'

'Fuck no,' Tammy said. 'He was too much of a sook for that. He was just a scout, you know? He'd line up other kids to go in the movies they were making. Get a finder's fee and a percentage of the profits, plus he kept copies to flog on the side.'

'He was making kiddie porn?' I said, disbelieving.

She nodded. 'Not much I wouldn't do – done almost everything there is to be done. Some real sickos come down here. But Dall, he worked for a whole other type. I've seen some of the movies and they're real freaks, man. Make *me* look like a nun. He used to keep a whole box of them in his room. He'd go down to Luna Park and sell 'em like hot dogs. Some nights he'd have to come home and burn more copies.'

'Jesus,' Novak said, clasping his mouth. He looked as though he wanted to puke.

I wasn't usually surprised by the things I saw or heard in St Kilda, but this jolted me. Dallas Boyd selling child porn wasn't what I'd expected, especially given his concern about Rachel. Then again, everyone in St Kilda had a hustle. If you weren't hooking, stealing or selling drugs, you had to earn your money somehow.

'Who was he supposed to meet down there?' I asked.

'Dunno. Never told me any of that. Glad.'

'Don't lie to me, Tammy.'

'I dunno,' she insisted. 'Like I'd wanna. All I know is he left us at Macca's to go meet someone at Luna Park. Obviously felt safe enough to wait for whoever it was by himself. I mean, there were still a lot of people around.'

I pictured the Acland Street junction late at night. It was a busy intersection, about fifty metres from where Boyd's body was found. There were always people there after dark, usually drunks from the nearby nightclubs and gutter crawlers cruising for hookers.

'What time was this?'

She shrugged.

I waited for a guess but none came. I should've expected it. A lot of these people had no concept of time. They only knew whether it was day or night.

'Okay, how long was it after you went to the 7-Eleven?'

'Maybe an hour.'

That was good. I now had a timeline to work from. It looked like Tammy wasn't going to be able to assist much more and I wanted to finish, but there was one more loose end I needed to tie up.

'Dallas had his mobile phone on prepaid, correct?'

She smiled at me. Gapped teeth. Yellow from methadone. 'Ya know how it is, they're harder to trace.'

'What sort of phone was it?'

'Dunno. Nokia something. Annoys the shit out of me.' She looked past me then, towards the sky. 'Stupid bloody ringtone. "Hi Ho Silver".'

I wrote this down, along with the other notes I'd made, unsure of the significance. When I looked up I saw that Tammy's lips had stretched to an odd smile as she stared at the clouds. Maybe she could see Dallas up there, like a memory playing out in her mind.

'Do you know a kid named Stuart Parks?' I asked Novak. 'Calls himself Sparks.'

'Sure, he's a local,' he said. 'Everyone knows him.'

*Then I should know him too*, I thought. Just went to show how long I'd been off the ball.

'Where can I find him?'

He gestured towards the south. 'Maybe try the squat down on Clyde Street.'

I knew the place and decided to end it there. 'Thanks for your time,' I said to Tammy.

She didn't reply and we left her in the doorway, hugging herself as though it were cold. I looked back on the stairs and our eyes met. Hers were wild and alert now and the smile had gone. The cynic in me said she just needed another hit, but I saw genuine grief there too. This was the human element. Death didn't care about money. It hurt everyone, rich and poor. I just nodded to her. There was nothing else I could do.

# 22

IT WAS FOUR THIRTY BY NOW and the festival crowd was at full peak. The Acland Street intersection was packed with families and daytrippers either pounding the pavement or spilling out of the trams.

I stopped outside the hostel and waited for Novak to get out, then saw someone pull out and decided to leave my car there.

'You're going there now, aren't you?' said Novak. 'To the squat?'

I nodded. 'Sparks left a message on Dall's answering machine. I think he knows something.'

Tears welled in Novak's eyes. He wiped them with his hand and looked across the O'Donnell Gardens to the café Dallas Boyd had died behind.

'I had no idea Dall was into any of that . . . that *filth*. Just when you think you know someone, bang, out pops a secret that floors you.'

'Yeah, that came out of left field for me too,' I said. 'There was no way we could've seen that coming. Like Tammy said, he kept it quiet.'

'You know something?' said Novak. 'I've never let these kids fool me into thinking they're angels, because they're not. They lie, they cheat, they hurt people. But if you give them a chance you can build a rapport with them and eventually they trust you. If they trust you, then you can help them. I figured as long as I had that attitude, I'd never have the wool pulled over my eyes. But this has got me stumped. I thought Dall told me everything. I thought he trusted me.'

'Everyone has secrets,' I said, fishing the key to Dallas Boyd's apartment out of the glove box and handing it to him. 'Thank you, Will. It's not every day I get this kind of help.'

'Not every day a kid like Dall gets killed. Well, maybe that's not true any more, not with this other boy dead.' Novak let out a long sigh. 'What the hell's wrong with this place?'

'Sometimes I ask myself the same question.'

'Yeah, well, I hope you find the son of a bitch, nail his hands to the front of Luna Park, let every street kid in St Kilda come down and kick the shit out of him.'

'Hey,' I said, 'when all this is over, maybe we can catch up for a beer sometime.'

'Sure, I'd like that. Maybe I'll ask my brother to come along too. He always asks about you. How's the apartment going, by the way?'

'Ah, you know, same old story. Too small, but it's close to all the action. I don't think I'll ever get out of there.'

'And Ella, how's she? Still over in Carlton?'

'Yeah, she's doing well, mate. Listen, what say I give you a call tomorrow, let you know how it's going with the case? Maybe then we'll put a time together for a beer?'

'Sounds good, I'd appreciate that. Thanks again. You take it easy.'

I slid the capsicum spray in my pocket then pushed my way through the crowd, past McDonald's where herds of parents lined up to buy their children food. A cacophony of adults shouting and kids screaming meshed with the smell of frying fat. I made my way towards Clyde Street, a quiet lane shaded by elm trees and lined with European cars parked outside renovated homes that had made many of the local real estate agents filthy rich. In the middle of them all I found what I was looking for: a run-down cottage surrounded by overgrown weeds, with windows boarded over with plywood and corrugated iron. Across the front of the house somebody had spraypainted *The Apocalypse is Coming*. I wondered whether it had been written by somebody who lived there or by one of the developers who valued these properties as much as the homeless.

I crept up a gravel drive and stopped at a rock wall beside the house that had probably once been draped with azaleas or home to a fernery. All that was there now were a scattering of syringes, rubbish and an old sprinkler system. The thing I hated most about squats was that there were no clear entries. The doors and windows were always boarded up and the only way in was usually through a vent or a makeshift manhole that the residents had created. And you never knew what fruitcakes would be inside. Being on my own only made it worse.

I knocked hard on the side of the house and a dog barked on the other side of the wall.

'Sparks, you in there, mate?' I called out. The dog barked again and I heard it trot across the floorboards. 'Anyone home?'

'What ya want?' came a reply.

'Lookin' for Sparks,' I said, putting on my best junkie voice. 'Is that you, mate? I gotta fix ya up with some cash.'

I wasn't sure whether Sparks was the person yelling back at me, or if he was even inside, but whoever it was, I knew the offer of money would bring them out. I took out the capsicum spray and shook it, ready to dose the dog or any other feral that came for me. I heard the sliding of timber and a lean figure slid out of a lower window. It wasn't Sparks, but I recognised the stringy hair and rat-like face from the wall of pictures in the watch-house mess room. I hid behind a rotten fence and steadied myself with the pepper can as he shuffled down the drive.

'Boo,' I said, stepping out with my badge case open. 'Where's Sparks?'

His hooded eyes were heavily glazed but he quickly took in the badge and the spray in my other hand.

'Ah, ya prick. Tricked me.'

'Fell for the oldest one in the book, old son. No money today, I'm afraid, but there's a few smokes in it for you.' I put the badge away and opened my cigarette pack. 'Real smokes too. None of this roll-your-own shit.'

He made a grab for the pack but I pulled back. 'Where is he first? Inside?'

'Nup.'

'Then where?' I said, shaking the pack in front of him. 'No one else has to know.'

'At the beach,' he said curtly. 'Foreshore.'

I quickly computed this. Half a million people in St Kilda. Thirty-five degrees. Half of them at the beach. A needle in a haystack.

'*Where* at the beach? Does he have a mobile?'

The man shrugged, eyes still on the smokes. I gave him a handful and walked off. There was no way I could do this alone. I rang Cassie and arranged to meet her at the foreshore playground.

'I'll be with Mark,' she said. 'That okay with you?'

'Finetti? What's he still hanging around for?'

'He's on foot patrol, looking for someone. Apparently you guys cut a deal.'

I cursed under my breath. I'd asked Finetti to find Sparks for me and keep him under wraps so I could question him without anyone knowing. Naturally, part of the deal was that he didn't talk about it.

'You want to fill me in now?' she said.

'Not really.'

'Then I'm not meeting you. Whoever it is you want to find, you can do it yourself.'

'Wait,' I said, catching her before she ended the call. 'We did have a deal. I just wanted Finetti to find this kid for me but he obviously hasn't kept his end of the bargain.'

'Ruby, you know how many people are down here today?'

'Yeah, you're right. I'm sorry.'

'Sorry for what – keeping secrets or being unreasonable?'

'Look, just meet me and I'll explain. Ten minutes.'

'Fine.'

I ended the call, knowing I'd messed up. Once again I'd broken the cardinal rule between partners. I was rehearsing my explanation to Cassie when I noticed an overweight transvestite in a red dress watching me. Another newcomer. Sometimes it seemed there was one every week. I walked past him and headed back into the crowd, where it took over five minutes just to pass Luna Park. At the entrance, high-pitched laughter from a thousand children screamed out at me, as if the park itself were alive. It reminded me of the first time I'd ever been there as a child, when my family came to Melbourne and stayed with relatives. I remembered the ghost train and dodgem cars, how a girl threw up inside the spinning gravitron. I remembered my mother buying us fairy floss and ice cream. The only other time I'd visited Luna Park was with Dad, years later, when we travelled to Melbourne to look for Jacko.

As I waited at the traffic lights, I looked back at the O'Donnell Gardens and the rear of Café Vit where Dallas Boyd had been dumped. For the first time I considered the paedophile angle as a possibility. Tammy York had said Dallas was involved with a paedophile crew, helping them find kids for porn movies and selling copies on the side. It made sense on one level but not on another. Sure, he needed money and selling porn was one way to get it. The way he probably saw it, if he didn't make money out of it, then somebody else would. So why not?

*Rachel* was why not. Why would he get so involved with rock spiders when his own sister, someone he loved, had been molested? Maybe he didn't see the connection; or maybe he did and that was why he'd wanted to get her out of the commission flats. Then there was another possibility, one I didn't want to consider but had to. Maybe Dallas Boyd wanted to get custody of his little sister so he could put her to work and collect another finder's fee.

Whichever way I looked at it, I was completely at a loss with establishing a motive. Being part of a spider web would've left Boyd wide open to any number of people wanting him dead. A victim after revenge? An angry parent? A rival hustler? Aggrieved customer? I also considered the location. Did it mean something? Was it chosen for reasons other than the pragmatic? A warning to others? I let some ideas roll around but nothing surfaced. It was too hot, too crowded, and I needed more information.

At the foreshore, an outdoor stage rose into the air. A DJ stood above the crowd bent over a set of turntables. Electro music vibrated around me like an underground heartbeat. *Doof-doof, doof-doof.* Everywhere I looked, people were dancing – on the grass, on picnic tables, across the sand, on each other's shoulders, even in the water.

I spotted Cassie at the edge of the bike track. She was in a tank top and cargo shorts, a hand shielding her eyes from the sun.

She started when I tapped her on the shoulder, then spoke into a mike. 'He's here. Give us five.'

She turned to me. 'Are you going to keep doing this?' she said, unsmiling.

'What?'

'You know exactly what. You're running your own show and shutting me out. You need to start trusting me. I can't be your partner if you don't trust me.'

I looked away, embarrassed. We sounded like lovers having a fight.

'I do trust you.'

'Bollocks! First off, you lied to me yesterday when you told me you were going home after the morgue. You never went home. You went and roughed up Boyd's stepfather.'

'How did you –' I stopped when I realised. 'Eckles knows, doesn't he?'

'You bet he does. The hommies arrested Vincent Rowe and kept him in the box all night. Finally kicked him loose about four hours ago, but not before he'd told them all about your little visit, know what I mean?'

I laced my hands behind my head, pissed off they'd found out so quickly.

'Come six o'clock this morning, Eckles is hopping mad,' Cassie continued. 'Dragged me into his office, threatened me with suspension till he realised I wasn't there with you. Seems you made quite an impression. Good enough for this shithead to file a nine-eighteen on you.'

I looked up at the sky, let the sun sting my eyes. A nine-eighteen was the numerical code for an ESD complaint form.

'Why are you being so stupid?' she said. 'Next time you get backed into a corner, let me know about it. We're supposed to be a team. A partnership.'

'I know. I'm sorry.'

'What, that's it? You're *sorry*?'

'It won't happen again, Cass. I haven't included you because I don't want you in the shit with me. Finetti's fair game – he asked for this when he sold me out – but you're different. You've got a clean sheet and I'm not about to spoil that.'

'Screw that, McCauley. We're partners and that means more than just working together. It means we trust each other, rely on each other. So don't tell me to just sit back and watch you do all this on your own.'

'Okay, okay!' I said. 'Where the hell is Finetti?'

She pointed towards the marina. 'On foot, with Kim, heading that-a-way. We got a few calls from the car park. Thieves everywhere.'

I followed her line of sight and realised what she meant. All of St Kilda had been blockaded due to the festival and the closest car park was beyond the marina, a good kilometre away. It wouldn't take long for the local shitheads to work it out.

'Let's do it,' I said.

We headed off past the marina where the millionaires kept their Bertram Sunseekers and Moonrakers, one of which I was sure had never been out to sea.

'You guys out there?' chirped the radio. I recognised Finetti's voice.

'Two up,' Cassie said. 'The marina. What's up?'

'We got your man.'

I felt a charge of adrenaline.

'You got him?' Cassie repeated. 'Where?'

'Car park, like we figured. Coming equipped. Dickhead even had a jemmy on him.'

'Nice one! See you soon.'


We clattered down the stairs to the parking lot. Under a palm tree about thirty metres away, Kim Pendlebury held Stuart Parks with his hands cuffed in front of him. Built like a battleaxe, Kim had arms and hands that could crush the average man, let alone a skinny runt like Sparks.

'Wagging school today, Ruby?' Mark Finetti said, clearly nervous since our last encounter.

'Got a day pass from the couch,' I said. 'Dr Eckles can get rooted. So what's the go?'

'You tell me. We put the bracelets on this kid and he starts saying he's got something for you.'

'Me?'

'Yeah, says he'll only talk to *you*.'

Why would Sparks want to talk to me? In fact, how did he even know my name?

'Anyway, you've got about five minutes before the van arrives,' Finetti went on.

'Five minutes?' I edged closer to him and kept my voice low.

'We had a deal, mate. I needed him on ice. He's no good to me in the van or back at the station.'

'Hey, we're not babysitting the kid any longer than we have to. Not unless you cut us in.'

Cassie pushed between us. 'That's fair enough, Ruby. You can't keep us in the dark with this. What's going on?'

'He was mates with Dallas Boyd,' I said.

'No shit,' Finetti said. 'We saw that on LEAP. What I don't get is how you two know each other. I mean, you ask me to keep a lookout for this kid, and all the while he's looking for you too.'

'I don't know what he wants with me, but it shouldn't matter,' I said. 'I asked you to find him and keep him on ice. How am I supposed to talk to him back at the station?'

Cassie waved a radio in front of me. 'You want me to cancel the van, then let us ride the wave with you?'

'No way. I'm in enough shit over this already.'

She held up the radio again. 'Now you've got about three minutes.'

'I don't want you to go down for working out of school.'

'Oh, come off it. All we're doing is talking to a local scrote. We're not stepping on anyone's toes.'

A helicopter flew over and Cassie waited for the sound to clear before she asked Finetti to leave us alone. He screwed up his face but gave in and walked over to join Kim and Sparks beneath the tree.

'The stepfather was a no-go zone,' she said curtly. 'Even you should've known that, but this is different. As far as they're concerned, this kid doesn't even exist.'

'No, you don't understand. Everything is different now. There are things even the hommies don't know. Things I haven't told you.'

'So tell me.' Cassie shook the radio. 'Two minutes. Make a choice.'

I felt anger and annoyance in equal measure. I was painted

into a corner. She held the mike to her mouth. 'St Kilda 507 to VKC.'

'Go ahead 507,' said the dispatcher.

Cassie raised an eyebrow. One last chance. I reached out, grabbed her wrist. 'Okay. You win.'

She told the dispatcher the kid was clean and to cancel the van.

'Now you tell me everything,' she said to me. 'That's the deal.'

I nodded.

'Leave nothing out. I mean it.'

So I told her how I'd confirmed that Boyd had purchased the phone recharge card at around 10 p.m. in the company of his girlfriend. They'd walked down to McDonald's where they'd parted company and Boyd had met with somebody to exchange kiddie porn. Whoever this person was, they were critical to the case. If not the killer, at the very least they were the last person to have seen Boyd alive. I finished by explaining my visit to Tammy York and how Will Novak had helped out.

Cassie stared across to Sparks. 'Rock spiders, huh?'

'That's how it looks, but it doesn't sit well. Everything I've found so far suggests Boyd wanted to help his sister, who was being molested by the stepfather. Why would he get involved with rock spiders when she was a victim?'

'Maybe he just became part of the machine,' she said, shrugging. 'Prey becomes predator. We see it all the time, Rubes.'

'Yeah, I guess.' I still wasn't sure but let it go.

'And you reckon this Sparks kid knows what Dallas was up to before he died?' Cassie said.

'They were supposed to meet up that night,' I said. 'Sparks left a message on Boyd's voicemail saying he was hanging on to something for him. He sounded pretty freaked out, so he obviously knows something.'

Cassie slid the mike back on her kit belt. 'Well then, I guess we'd better see what the kid has to say.'

# 23

STUART PARKS WAS NO OIL PAINTING. He looked pale and unwell, his shoulders arched over a lean frame. The grubby singlet he was wearing did him no justice either, revealing bony arms, cheap tattoos and a series of abscesses on his wrists. Teenage stubble sprouted on a gaunt face dotted with acne.

'So what gives?' I said. 'My partner says you wanted to talk.'

'Not 'ere. Somewhere else.'

Looking back towards the crowded Esplanade, I didn't think it was a good idea to walk Sparks back to where my car was, so I waved Cassie over, handed her my keys and asked her to fetch the Falcon from the hostel and meet us at the marina.

'Take Barkly Street. You should get through the traffic.'

'What about them?' she said quietly, nodding towards Finetti and Pendlebury.

'They've done all they need to do.'

She headed over to tell them they could go, leaving me with Sparks, who fidgeted with the handcuffs.

'Bit tight?' I asked.

'What do you reckon?'

'Well, don't worry too much. It's because they're new. They'll stretch out a bit after a while.'

He gave me a death stare. I couldn't help but smile. 'Relax,' I said, checking the cuffs and ratcheting them down a notch. 'It's an old joke. Surprised you haven't heard it before.'

'I have and it's still not funny. Never has been.'

'Yeah, okay. What are you so edgy about?'

'Got me smokes in me pocket,' he said, ignoring my question. 'Reckon ya could get one for me?'

'How do I know you don't have a syringe in there?'

'How do I know you're not gonna do me for the jemmy bar?'

'Why shouldn't I?'

'Because you want what I've got. Bigger than any go-equipped bullshit.'

I nodded. The kid knew the rules. I carefully removed a crumpled pack of cigarettes from his pocket and lit one for him.

'Let's take a walk.'

We headed back through the car park towards the marina. Sparks was moving too quickly. I put a hand on his shoulder to slow him down.

'So, Sparks – that's what they call you, isn't it? Can I call you that?'

'Call me whatever ya like when we get to the car.' He held up his hands to take a drag on the smoke. 'Not sayin' nothin' till ya take these off. Make me feel like a leper. Everyone's starin' at me.'

'There's no one around, mate.'

'Yeah, what d'ya call that?' he said, nodding to the left where a family had just arrived back at their car. He was right; they were staring. I stepped in beside him to block their view and guided him up the stairs. We didn't speak again until we reached the marina where Cassie waited in the Falcon. She stayed in the driver seat while I sat Sparks in the back, removed the handcuffs and engaged the child lock. I got in the front and looked at him through the mirror on the sun visor. He seemed small and vulnerable now, arms wrapped around his bony frame, glancing back and forth like a cornered rat.

'You hungry?' I asked him.

'What?'

'Could murder a burger right now. Are you hungry, Cass?'

Cassie shrugged. 'Sure, but not one of those Macca's burgers. I want a *real* burger.'

'Exactly. What about a big fat burger with the lot from Smithy's?'

Smithy's was a fish and chip shop on Beach Road in Brighton. There were hundreds like it across the city, but it was my favourite spot for a burger. I often went there after swimming at the baths when the exercise left me famished and craving fast food.

I used my mobile to call ahead and soon we were in the car park facing the water, munching our burgers and slurping Cokes.

'So what did you want to tell me?' I asked after a few bites.

'First off, ya gotta know I ain't no dog, so I'm not gonna lag on no one.'

'No one's asking you to,' I said.

'Right, well, I'm just sayin' I'm no dog, that's all.'

This was normal. Nobody wanted to admit they were an informant. I took another bite of my burger and waited.

'Everyone's sayin' Dall knocked himself or that it was an accident,' Sparks said after a moment. 'But that's bullshit, isn't it?'

'What makes you say that?' Cassie asked.

'Mate, soon as I saw ya at the hostel I knew it was bullshit,' he said, looking at me in the rear-view mirror. 'When I asked Will what ya were doin' sniffin' around about Dall, he said ya was looking into it.'

I figured that was how the kid knew my name. I asked if Will had told him anything else.

'Didn't have to,' Sparks said. 'Jacks don't go sniffin' around for no suicide. Dall didn't knock himself, did he?'

'No, and it wasn't an accident either.'

211

Sparks rested the burger in his lap and let out a low sigh. 'Shit,' he said. 'I knew it.'

'You can trust us,' Cassie said. 'We need your help to catch whoever did it.'

He folded his arms and stared out the side window. 'I never said I'd fuckin' trust ya. Don't trust cops. Fuck that.'

'Must be a reason you asked for me though,' I said.

He didn't reply.

'Dallas was into something, wasn't he?' Cassie said. 'Is that why you asked for Rubens as soon as we arrested you? Because you knew he was looking into it and you knew what Dallas was into?'

Still nothing.

'What about the message you left on Dallas's answering machine?' I asked. 'You said you had something for him, something he asked you to get. But he didn't show up, did he?'

Again, silence.

'This is important, Sparks. I know Dallas was supposed to meet somebody at Luna Park about eleven the night he died, to sell some kiddie porn. I need to know who that person was. Do you know who it was?'

I turned to face the windscreen, hoping to depersonalise the conversation, like going to confession with an unseen priest.

'Look, if you don't want to tell us something specific, that's fine,' Cassie said. 'Just tell us about Dallas. Why don't you start with that? You were mates, did time together, didn't you?'

'*Were* mates,' Sparks said finally. 'Least till we landed in Malmsbury after the armed rob. After that we went our separate ways. Dall chased the money, and I fell in love.'

'You fell in love?' Cassie said.

'Yeah, with heroin.'

'Right, and Dallas wanted money,' she went on. 'What do you mean by that?'

'Exactly what I said. Dall wanted cash. Apart from saving his little sister, it was all he cared about, all he ever spoke about. That's what happens when you go away: you think about things.

Dall thought about money and his little sister. The only difference was, Dall sounded like he had a scam ready for when he got out. He wasn't a dreamer like all the other shitheads in there.'

A panel van pulled up next to us and two guys with ponytails got out, unloaded kite-surf bags and trekked off towards the beach. It now seemed apparent to me that Dallas Boyd had formed a plan to sell child porn while he was still in jail, but how? Had somebody approached him there? I wanted to open my daybook and scribe but couldn't risk spooking the kid. We had to keep it informal.

'What about Derek Jardine?' I asked. 'The other guy you did the armed rob with.'

'Ah shit, there's a name I haven't heard in a while. Last I heard he pissed off to Queensland, not long after we all got out. Dall and him were real tight. I was just a ring-in.'

That probably explained the map of Surfers Paradise I'd found in Dallas Boyd's apartment. Still, Sparks wasn't making total sense.

'So if you all went your separate ways after Malmsbury, why the phone message?' I asked. 'Didn't sound like the sort of message you'd leave for a bloke you weren't mates with any more. What happened?'

'We *weren't* mates,' he said quickly. 'I was just doin' a job for him. Like I said, I was just a ring-in. Was back then, still am now.'

'What sort of job?' Cassie prodded.

'Dunno if I should tell ya that now. Think I've made a mistake.'

I heard the shift in tone. Fear. It turned his voice sharp and high-pitched, like a child's. He grabbed the handle, tried to yank open the door, but the child lock kept it shut. 'What the fuck, man? Let me out!'

'It's all right, Sparks,' I said. 'You're safe here. Just tell us what Dallas asked you to do for him.'

'I can't,' he spluttered. 'I'm fuckin' scared, man.'

'Why?'

'Because I'm gonna be next. First they got Dall, then Jussie.'

Two tears slid down the boy's acne-scarred face. He looked pleadingly at Cassie, then at me.

'Justin Quinn,' Cassie muttered. 'The kid in Talbot Reserve last night.'

'You think the same person did both?' I asked Sparks.

'Makes sense,' he said, wiping snot on his wrist. 'Both into the same shit.'

'Sparks, I promise you, no one knows you're talking to us,' I said in a calm voice. 'Ask around about me, everyone'll vouch that I'm a straight player. I don't break promises and I don't bullshit anyone. So if you don't want to tell me what you and Dall were into, then fine. But I think you know something that'll help us nail whoever did it. And I think you *want* to help us, otherwise why would you ask for me?'

'We already know he was selling kiddie porn and you were holding on to something for him,' Cassie added. 'We think whatever that was got him killed. Am I close?'

Again Sparks kept quiet. There was nothing else we could say. If he didn't want to open up, we couldn't force him, so we just waited. After a long moment, he finally spoke.

'If I tell ya's, ya gotta promise to do somethin' about it,' he said. 'Too many times the jacks just sit on their arses and do nothin'.'

'You have my word we'll go after this one,' I said, turning to face him. 'Whoever knocked Dallas knew what they were doing; same too with what happened last night to Justin. So believe me, we want this bloke to pay.'

'All right, fuck it. Do ya have a DVD player?'

'Ah, yes. Why?'

'Because the kiddie porn's just the start of it. So take me back to St Kilda. I have to show ya somethin'.'

# 24

SPARKS DIRECTED US BACK to the squat on Clyde Street, the Falcon jolting over the bluestone roadway as we came alongside the house. I looked for the fat trannie in the red dress but couldn't see him anywhere. He'd probably found a client.

'Keep drivin',' Sparks said. 'Park at the end of the street.'

I did as instructed and he ran back to the house, disappeared into the drive. From this angle any view of the squat was blocked by a brand new double-storey townhouse with a 'For Sale' sign out the front. I was wondering idly if living next door to drug addicts was part of the real estate agent's sale pitch when Sparks reappeared with what looked like a black carry case for a laptop. But he wasn't alone. A brindle-coated dog leapt after him.

'No way, Sparks. No dogs in the car.'

'Huh? He's just a puppy, mate. Six months old.'

'I don't care. I'm not having a pit bull in my car. Take it back inside.'

'He's not a pit bull. He's a bull mastiff.'

'Whatever. Take him back.'

Sparks backed out of the car, put down the laptop case and dug out a DVD in a plastic sleeve.

'Look, man, you wanna see what I got here or not? This is some bad shit, but I'm not leavin' my little mate in there with those guys any longer than I have to. Either Hooch comes or I go back inside with him.'

I looked at the dog. He was dirty and underfed, his ribs clearly visible, the back half of his body wobbling, his tail whipping back and forth.

'All right. Get in, but make sure you hold on to him. I don't want any dog puke on my seats.'

Sparks hoisted the dog inside, but failed to keep him still and he leapt into the front. Cassie laughed, enticing the dog off me and onto her. Eventually Sparks took control of the animal, settling him on his knee.

'Where to now?' I said, frustrated. It was just after six and I was supposed to be meeting Ella in two hours. 'Why did you ask me if I had a DVD player when you've got that laptop? Can't we just watch it on that?'

Sparks explained that the laptop didn't belong to him and that he'd tried to use it but there were passwords blocking his access. When Cassie asked how he'd watched the DVD, he said he'd broken into his mum's house while she was at work and watched it there. It was a plausible enough story.

'So we need a DVD player,' said Cassie. 'Obviously the one in the watch-house mess room is out of the question.'

She was looking at me as she spoke and I wondered whether she meant the station was off limits for me or for Sparks. For a moment I contemplated suggesting we go to my apartment and watch it on my own telly, but there were lines even I didn't cross. Having crooks in my house was one of them.

'I've got a laptop,' Cassie said instead. 'On my desk. Fully charged too. Drop me off out the front, I'll run in and get it.'

I took the backstreets and double-parked across the road from the station. Just ahead of us, a group of local junkies gathered

216

around a phone box, probably waiting on a dealer. Sparks slouched in the back seat, muttering about not wanting to be seen.

'Right, where do you wanna go?' I asked him when Cassie was back in the car.

'Go to Anal Park,' he said. 'I'll tell you why when we get there.'

'Anal Park?' Cassie repeated.

'Alma Park,' I said. 'It's a gay beat at night.'

When we crossed into East St Kilda, Sparks instructed me to park just shy of the railway line, opposite a bicycle track that wound through the western section of the park. We followed him to a picnic table adjacent to the bike track, where he let his dog off the lead and set his laptop on the table next to Cassie's.

'Got another condition,' he said. 'If I give ya what I've got, ya gotta go blind for somethin'.'

Cassie rolled her eyes. 'Depends what you're talking about. If you mugged somebody, we can't turn a blind eye to that.'

'I didn't roll nobody!' he said, throwing a stick. The dog ran after it but didn't see it land and became confused, running in circles. 'Few days ago I hit a joint just down the road from here. One of them big old joints, like all the Jews live in. It was about two in the arvo during the week, so I figure I've got a good chance nobody's home.'

'Because you've done it before?' Cassie asked.

Sparks just looked at her.

'Well?' she said. 'Don't pretend it's your first time.'

'I'm not. Who cares anyway? I mean, all those rich mother-fuckers have insurance.'

Cassie went to reply but I cut her off.

'Come on, Sparks. Give us some credit. We're not going to arrest you for a pissy little burg. We'll just add it to the jemmy bar we found you with in the car park today. That's two points for us.'

'Yeah, righto. You want this or not?'

'Go on.'

He threw another stick for his dog. This time the dog found it and began to chew it.

'Dall asked me to do the burg,' he said when he came back to the table. 'I hadn't spoken to him since we got out. Like I said, we went our separate ways. Anyway, one night last week he finds me on the street, says he's got a job for me. I told him to get rooted since the last time I accepted a job from him I ended up in the can. But then he showed me the cash. Two large for a shitty burg, mate. Gave me a grand up-front and an address, said all I gotta do was slip in during the day when the rich-prick owner was at work. Said he'd give me the other grand on delivery.'

He shook his head in frustration and sat on the edge of the table.

'Delivery of the laptop?' I said, looking at the case in front of me. 'This is what your voicemail message was about?'

'Yeah. Sounds simple, right – do a burg and hoist a laptop?'

Cassie and I both nodded.

'No one pays two large to rip off a laptop unless they're plannin' somethin' with it,' he said. 'I knew I wasn't just doin' a burg, but an earn like that doesn't come along every day for a shitman like me, so I took the cash and said I'd do it.'

He paused and we waited for him to go on.

'Anyway, few days ago I door-knocked the joint and made sure no one was home. When no one answered I went around the back, climbed the veranda and went in through the bathroom window. No alarms upstairs in those joints.'

I nodded at the familiar method of entry. The kid was definitely no rookie.

'Went in the first room and found the laptop, exactly where Dall said it would be,' Sparks continued. 'Then all of a sudden I hear a car pull up out the front. I look out the window and see this Beamer in the bloody driveway. I'm high-tailing it when I see a set of keys on a table. So I swiped the fuckers and hauled arse out the window like a monkey.'

218

'Do you think he saw you?' Cassie asked.

'Nah, I was gone before he was even in the house.'

'You get a look at him?' I said.

'Mate, all I saw was this set of wheels in the fuckin' driveway and I was outta there.'

I considered all this as the dog came bounding back over, the stick covered in slobber. He dropped it at our feet and barked. Sparks picked it up, hurled it away and wiped his hands on his shorts.

'The laptop wasn't enough for you though, was it?' I said. 'You took the car as well.'

'I got the keys, all right. It was like the lottery, man. All I had to do was go back there and take it. Mate, I just pressed the button and she opened up. Just like that, a fuckin' gift.'

Cassie and I exchanged glances. The story was a familiar one. Whenever a burglary or break-in occurred, home owners always checked the obvious items like televisions, cash and jewellery. They rarely noticed the spare set of car keys missing. Not until it was too late. A home burglary with the lot.

'Drove it all the way down to Frankston and back, even went to the beach and pretended I was rich,' Sparks said. He shot a nervous glance at Cassie. 'Wouldn't believe how many chicks actually looked at me when I was in that car.'

'So where is it now?'

'Left it on the Esplanade.'

Cassie scoffed.

'I did! Shit, what am I gonna do with a Beamer, man?' he cried. 'I'm just a fuckin' junkie. Give me a video camera and I'll turn it into cash the same day, but a hundred-thousand-dollar set of wheels – I wouldn't know where to begin. Shit, check your records. Rich prick probably found it the next day and took it home without even reportin' it.'

Neither of us were convinced but I decided to push things along. 'Look, forget the car. Tell me about Thursday night. You were supposed to meet Dallas but he never showed, right?'

'Too right he never showed. He told me to meet him at midnight outside Luna Park. He was gonna give me the other grand for this bloody thing.' He nodded at the laptop. 'I got there on time, waited a whole hour. Even rang his phone about five times but got no answer. First I thought he might've just forgotten about it, but Dall wasn't like that. He was reliable and he wanted the laptop, so I knew something was up. The next morning I left a message on his voicemail, then went to CARS and found out he was dead. After that, I wanted to see what I was holdin' on to for him, so I tried to turn the bastard on but it's got a password. I was about to chuck it when I found this disk in the carry case. When I watched it, that's when I realised I was in trouble.'

He let out a deep breath and seemed to deflate.

'Hang on,' I said. 'If Dallas wanted this laptop so bad, why would he get you to do the burg? Why wouldn't he do it himself?'

'All day I've been askin' myself the same question,' Sparks said. 'First I figured he was too cool for it, like he wouldn't wanna get his own hands dirty for a shitty little burg. Ya know, just get old Sparks to do it, the fuckin' junkie ring-in, like he did with the armed rob. But now when I think about it, I reckon he knew the prick and didn't wanna risk gettin' seen. So he asked me to do it.'

It sounded plausible, though I suspected there was more to it. But we were getting to a critical point and I didn't want to lose him.

'Who are we talking about? This rich prick you robbed, what's his name?'

'Peter Parker.'

I went to write it down, then realised he was bullshitting me. 'As in *Spider-Man*?'

'Or in this case, *rock* spider man.'

'Come on, Sparks. We can't take him down if we don't know who he is. Give us a name.'

'Look, I don't know who he is, all right? Even if I did, I said I wasn't no dog. No names, remember?'

'Fair enough,' Cassie said. 'But you never wanted to know who you were robbing? Surely you asked.'

'Well, actually I did ask, but Dall said I didn't need to know. Said the money and the job was all I should worry about. Fuckin' typical, always keepin' the details to himself. Tell ya what though, now I'm glad he didn't tell me.'

Cassie's nose and forehead were beaded with sweat. I was the same and it wasn't just the heat. I swiped the sweat away and told Sparks to show us the DVD.

'Uh-uh, not me,' he said, standing up and whistling for the dog. 'This is as far as I'm gonna go. There's some filthy shit on there. I've seen a lot of crud in my time, but nothin' like that. You wanna look at it, be my guest, but I'm not watchin' it again. I'll be over here with Hooch. Call me when ya done.'

He led the dog across the park to a drinking fountain. Cassie moved around and sat next to me. I could feel her shoulder pressed against me and the scent of her perfume reminded me that I needed to call Ella and cancel dinner. It was the last thing I wanted to do but we were barrelling on the wave and we had to keep riding.

'Sure you want to do this?' Cassie asked. 'Maybe we should log it with the techs and get them to do it right. What if we lose a file or something?'

I shook my mind clear and focused on the case.

'I don't think so. Not yet. Dallas Boyd was killed because of this laptop. Whatever's on this disk has something to do with that.' I turned on Cassie's laptop. 'Let's see what we've got.'

When the computer finished booting I slid in the disk but nothing happened.

'You're hopeless,' Cassie teased, nudging me with her shoulder and turning the laptop towards her. 'Shove over.'

I watched her hands dance over the keyboard. 'Bingo!' she said within a minute. 'I've got pictures and movie files.'

I leant over her shoulder as she ran her finger across a list of files on the screen that appeared to be sorted by date.

'They're all recent,' she said. 'Created mid last week, all except one.'

She clicked the first file and a photo appeared, filling the screen. The picture wasn't pornographic but it still turned my stomach. Two naked toddlers – a boy and a girl – playing on a beach somewhere, neither more than about two years old. The picture had obviously been taken by a camera with a powerful zoom lens; the genitalia filled the centre of the shot. I wondered where the parents had been and how they hadn't noticed their children being photographed.

'Sick,' Cassie said.

The next three shots were of the same two children taken from different angles. In one shot I made out the blurred image of a man's leg next to the children. The father, I guessed. Behind his leg were a row of coloured beach boxes. I felt a charge of recognition and pointed at the screen.

'Those beach boxes. I know them.'

'Brighton Beach,' Cassie said.

'Right.'

The fourth photo nearly knocked me off the bench seat. It was of poorer quality than the others and depicted a teenage boy, maybe fourteen or fifteen, performing oral sex on an adult male. I forced myself to study the picture. The camera had been placed in such a way as to capture the image of the boy but not the older man, whose head and shoulders were outside the frame.

Cassie explained that the image was actually a movie file. She clicked the keypad and the boy's mouth began to move up and down the man's penis. The camera zoomed in on the boy; all we could see of the man was his hands and penis. It was repulsive.

'Holy shit,' Cassie said. 'That's Justin Quinn, the kid killed in Talbot Reserve last night.'

'You serious?'

'Serious as a heart attack. I was bloody well there today. I saw his face.' She put a hand to her mouth. 'That's fucking him. Jesus.'

She slid off the bench and walked away. For a second I thought she was going to vomit, but she just stood under a tree, facing the sky, hands laced around her head. I wanted to offer her something but there was nothing I could say. Instead I tried to absorb this new information. Justin Quinn being the kid in the movie changed things significantly. It meant Sparks had probably been right to assume his murder was connected to Dallas Boyd.

The movie was short, less than a minute in total. When Cassie came back she suggested it was probably a sample clip, like an advertisement or trailer to promote a full-length version.

'This looks like a hotel room,' I said, tapping the screen. 'There's a notepad or something on the bedside table. Can we enhance it, blow it up?'

She shook her head. 'Not without high-end software. Let's open the next one.'

The images that followed were still shots of the boy performing the same act, this time with the male offender on a bed. Despite my repulsion, I noticed something about the camera work. Like most men, I'd seen my fair share of pornography and to me this was an amateur job, but not in the 'mockumentary' sense. This was genuine amateur, as though a camera had been set up in the cupboard.

'It's like a hidden camera,' I said. 'But it zoomed in before so someone must be operating it. The kid must've known he was being filmed. Maybe they're trying to make it look like he didn't know?'

'There's another possibility,' said Cassie, grimacing. 'Somebody was operating the camera from another room. You know, via remote control.'

I considered the scenario. Some like-minded men hire two hotel rooms, side by side. The camera is set up in one room, hidden in a cupboard and linked to the recording equipment in the other. They test it out, check that it works. Then they hire someone like Dallas Boyd to find them a desperate street kid in need of fast cash. The kid gets paid, probably given drugs, and together they make themselves a little kiddie porn.

'Makes sense,' I said. 'Part of the appeal, I suppose. Give it an underground feel and you create demand.'

Cassie clicked the next file: another movie clip. It opened with a shot of the interior of a house. Polished boards, large white door, stained-glass entranceway. The front door opened and two high school kids in uniform rambled in, holding hands and giggling. They shut the door and began to kiss against the wall, school bags sliding to the floor. This time the lighting was better and it was more choreographed, but it still had the feel of an amateur production. The camera moved in as the kids fondled each other, tearing at each other's uniform.

'Dallas Boyd,' I said, recognising the boy.

I focused on the girl and recognised her as Tammy York, but her hair was styled in pigtails to make her look younger.

'That's his girlfriend,' I said, wondering why she'd not mentioned this.

'Didn't she say Dallas never did skin work?' Cassie asked.

'No, she said he never did kiddie porn. Said he just scouted for them and sold it on the side.'

'What the hell is this then?'

'I don't know.'

The two of them moved up the hall, past the camera and into an open-plan living area, where the curtains had conveniently been drawn and all the lights turned on. They proceeded to have sex on the sofa, the camera zooming in to capture the girl's shaved genitals. The film ended after a minute or so and I had to agree with Cassie: these were sample clips. I looked at the laptop Sparks had stolen and realised he was right to be scared. If this was an illegal porn racket, with paedophiles running the show, losing the laptop and disk would've caused a major panic. If they fell into the wrong hands, they could bring them all undone. But why kill Dallas? The only likely explanation was that they knew he was behind it. How they knew was another question. So too was the murder of Justin Quinn. Had he been involved in the theft as well, or was it to keep him from talking? Sparks hadn't mentioned anything about him.

Cassie clicked ahead and opened another series of photos. They were less offensive but the intent was just the same. In the first shot a group of children frolicked in a public swimming pool. The second depicted a young girl, perhaps five or six, standing on a diving board.

'That's the Albert Park Aquatic Centre,' said Cassie, clicking some buttons and leaning into the screen. 'It's less than a month ago. The oldest file was created January fifteen, the most recent last week. Even the movie clips are new.'

I thought about the sequence. It was all recent. Maybe the person who owned the disk had been in the throes of having the sample clips professionally edited, or added to a mailing list or website?

'Whoever made this disk knows their way around a camera,' Cassie said, scrolling back to the first few pictures of the children on Brighton Beach. In the background the sun was setting over the water, and I was suddenly reminded of the photo of Dallas and Tammy that I'd seen in the apartment. Had it been taken by the same man?

'I've tried to take sunset photos before,' Cassie was saying. 'It's not easy getting the lighting right. Maybe we're looking for a professional photographer?'

'A *local* photographer, Cass. First Brighton. Then Albert Park.' I pointed at the screen. 'That house with Dallas in it is Edwardian, and I bet it's somewhere close by. So we're looking for someone who's part of the community. Someone who blends in.'

Cassie turned away from the screen and stared at the park. In the distance, Sparks was wrestling with his dog.

'You know what I don't get,' she said. 'There's no password for any of this.'

'But Sparks said there was, said he couldn't get it started.'

'I don't mean the laptop. Even basic laptops have passwords. I mean this disk and these files. Why no password? If I had this disk, I sure as shit wouldn't keep it without some form of protection.'

I thought about the possibilities, then said, 'These files are all recent, right?'

'Right, some created last week. That means the files were loaded onto the disk then, not necessarily filmed. We don't know when the pictures were taken or the clips filmed.'

'Well, let's assume they're all recent. And let's also assume you're right about these files being promotional adverts for full-length productions. I think the disk is just a temporary storage device.'

She frowned and stared at the laptop.

'Think about it,' I said. 'You've just received a new collection that you need to disseminate safely or upload onto a website. But you have to store it temporarily somewhere, at least until the files can be encrypted or hidden.' I tapped the screen where the list of files was shown. 'The most recent of these was created last Tuesday. Sparks said he boosted the laptop on the Wednesday. What if they were just about to upload them, or in the process of doing so?'

Cassie's eyes widened as she sensed where I was going. 'Right, well that explains the disk, but what about this laptop? Dallas paid two grand for Sparks to boost it, and everything we've learnt so far tells us he was planning something, but we don't know what. To me, that's the real question. Why did he want this laptop?'

I rubbed my hands together as I thought about Cassie's question. I stood up and called out to Sparks. I wanted to make sure he wasn't playing us.

'Fuckin' gross, hey?' the kid said as he walked over, dog following. 'Didn't mind seeing Dall get it on with that school bitch though. That was pretty cool. But the other shit . . . can't believe he was into it.'

226

I ejected the disk, closed Cassie's laptop and stared at Sparks for a moment.

'What?' he said.

'You sure you don't know why Dallas wanted this laptop?'

'No, man. Like I said, he wouldn't tell me. But after seeing what's on that disk, isn't it obvious?'

'Enlighten me,' I said.

'Well, the dude was a player, a scammer. Maybe he was lookin' to do a number on them.'

Cassie and I exchanged a glance. She was thinking the same thing: blackmail.

'And you're not in on that?' I asked. 'Sure you and Dallas didn't scheme up some plot to make these perverts pay you off?'

Sparks stared at me with contempt. 'Hey, I've been straight up with ya both all along. If I was into any of that shit, why would I bring ya into it and risk me life talkin'? Why wouldn't I just ditch the laptop and bail out?'

Fear and anger glinted in his eyes and I knew he was telling the truth.

'All right, we believe you,' Cassie said, giving me a frustrated look. 'We're sorry, but we have to cover all bases. What about Justin Quinn, you think he was into it?'

'Well, that's another story. You ask me, I wouldn't put it past Dall to recruit someone like Jussie for a skin flick, just so they could put the pinch on 'em later.'

I nodded. It made sense. We now had a workable motive. And we also had a suspect.

'Okay, one last thing,' I said. 'You say you knocked off the car keys and the laptop from a house not far from here, right?'

'What I said.'

'Remember the house?'

He frowned in suspicion. 'Why?'

'Because you're going to show us. Let's go.'

# 25

WE DROVE TO A SHADED Elwood street lined with neat lawns and hundred-year-old maple trees. Most of the homes were old money, solid and secure, with intricate fretwork bordering full-length verandas.

'Halfway down,' said Sparks. 'Double-storey joint, big as a pub.'

I eased off the accelerator as a beautifully restored Tudor-style home appeared behind a picket fence.

'That's it,' said Sparks, sinking low in the back seat.

'No car in the drive,' said Cassie. 'Maybe he never got the Beamer back. Either that or no one's home.'

I drove on and pulled up behind a Bentley.

'I don't like this,' Sparks said. 'Can ya take me back to St Kilda? Think I've done enough.'

'Relax,' Cassie said. 'If he's home, we'll just make something up, tell him there's been a few burgs in the street. Besides, he can't exactly see you from here, can he?'

Sparks slumped against the seat, resigned, hugging his dog. I followed Cassie along the footpath to a paved driveway. The

Sunday newspaper had yet to be retrieved and all the blinds were drawn. Our feet creaked on the porch as we stepped up to a towering front door.

'Recognise the door?' Cassie murmured.

'Yeah, the school kids movie with Dallas and Tammy,' I whispered back, then pressed a brass buzzer on the wall and waited. After a moment I pressed it again but again no one answered.

Cassie checked the letterbox; it was empty. I pulled out my phone and called Mark Finetti on his mobile. More than one way to skin a cat.

'What's up, Bad Boy?' I said when he answered. 'You still on two legs?'

'Nope, we're on a split rotation. I'm in the tank till eleven, babysitting the drunks.'

Good, right where I wanted him.

'Listen, I need one more favour.'

'Oh man.'

'Then we're even.'

'Whatever.'

'I just need a name to match an address and any vehicle registrations that go with it.'

Finetti groaned and I pictured him in the watch-house, his feet up on the bench, watching the CCTV screens with a bowl of pasta, a napkin over his shirt.

'Look, we're on the wave here. Sparks gave us a good one, could go all the way. Just run an address then we're square.'

'Yeah, square as a peg. What is it?'

I doubled-checked the letterbox and gave him the address, then told him to check for the registration of a late-model BMW, or any other vehicles that might be listed at the address. I also told him how Sparks had broken into the house, stolen the car keys and returned later to steal the car.

'Yeah, righto,' Finetti said. 'I'll go with the car first. Let me call you back.'

Cassie and I went back to the car while Finetti went to work.

Sparks had unwound the window for his dog, which had slobbered all over the back pillar. I was annoyed but didn't let on.

'Where'd you get him?' I asked instead, nodding at the dog.

'Found him on the beach,' Sparks said. 'About three months ago. No lead or collar, nobody around, just another runaway. Like me, I s'pose. I could tell he was just a pup, so I played with him a bit, even gave him some chips, and he followed me back to the squat. I tried to make him go away, but he wouldn't leave me alone. Anyhow, I knew he wasn't gonna survive on his own in the streets, and I don't really like bein' on me own either, so I started lookin' after him. Even in summer it gets cold sometimes in the squat, especially at night.' He gave the dog a vigorous pat and it licked his face. 'We keep each other warm, don't we, mate?'

'More loyalty and faithfulness in one dog than in a hundred men,' Cassie said, stepping in beside me to pat the dog.

'Shit yeah,' said Sparks. 'Hooch doesn't care about what I look like or whether I've got any money. He just cares if I'm around.'

I smiled, unsure whether the story was a happy or sad one, then stepped away from the car to call Ella and cancel dinner. Finetti called back as I was dialling her number.

'Not gonna believe this, mate,' he said. 'I ran the address and got a hit.'

'Right, and?'

'Cop this. Comes up with a 2006 M5 Beamer, navy blue in colour, registered to a Karl Vitazul,' he said, then waited for me to place the name.

It took a moment, but then the familiarity hit me like a jab in the nose.

'You're shittin' me,' I said out loud, looking at Cassie. 'It's Vitazul, the café owner who found the body.'

'Still there, man?' Finetti said after a second.

'I want a full set on this guy, Mark. Get on LEAP and check all variations to his name. Also, get on to the Feds and see what —'

'Done all that, McCauley. When the name came up, I recognised it as the guy who found Dallas Boyd in the first place. And since he specifically said he didn't know the kid, I'm thinking he's got something major to hide. Like, whoever smelt it dealt it.'

'What's his sheet say?'

'I've got it up on the screen right now and that's the thing. Nada.'

'Nothing at all?'

'Well, according to his driver's licence, Vitazul was born in 1915, which doesn't gel with the guy we saw at the café. So I checked his licence photo through VicRoads and guess what, it's not our guy. The guy on the licence is older than dirt.'

I tried to think it through. Either we were talking about two different people with the same name who just happened to be connected to the same murder, or the name Vitazul was bullshit.

'What about the address?' I asked. 'Any crime reports, maybe a burg or stolen car?'

'Sweet bugger all. This Vitazul character, or whoever the hell he is, didn't report his car stolen or the break-in. Maybe your kid's telling porkies about where he got the laptop.'

I looked at Sparks sitting hunched up in the back seat. 'He's telling the truth.'

'All right, man. Want me to put a KALOF out on this guy?'

'No, I know where to find him,' I said. I hung up before Finetti said anything else, then filled Cassie in on the details.

'Whoever Vitazul is, he's hiding something,' she said. 'Maybe we should call Homicide, give them the news and get a posse going?'

I didn't need to think about a response. 'No, I want to talk to this guy myself. And anyway, all I'm going to do is bring this prick in on the kiddie porn and see what shakes out. No need to mention anything about Dallas Boyd or the Talbot Reserve job last night.'

'And therefore no need to call Homicide?' she finished.

I smiled at her across the roof of the Falcon. 'Now you're with me.'

'You're as shifty as a shithouse rat, you know that?'

'One of Victoria's finest.'

# 26

I DROPPED SPARKS BACK AT the squat, we swapped mobile phone numbers and I said I'd be in touch. Then I parked in a clearway and Cassie and I walked the two blocks to Acland Street. The crowd seemed to move at an agonisingly slow pace and I ended up pushing my way through. As we passed a black BMW roadster a thought occurred to me.

'What colour did Sparks say Vitazul's Beamer was?'

'Dark blue,' Cassie said. 'And Finetti confirmed that, right?'

I nodded, a sudden realisation dawning on me. Tammy York had been strangled by an overweight man in a navy blue BMW. She'd even said he'd spoken with a European accent. *He kept patting my head and telling me I'd been a good girl but now I was bad.*

'Son of a bitch,' I said. 'He was trying to kill her too.'

'What?' said Cassie.

I told her about Tammy York and how her attacker might very well have been Vitazul.

'Maybe she was in on the scam too. Like Dallas and Justin,' she said. 'All three of them are on that disk. That would explain

why she never mentioned anything about it when you questioned her.'

I was thinking the same thing and was about to suggest we
question her again when my mobile rang. The caller ID read
private number.

'McCauley.'

'Rubes, is that you?'

'Andy?' I said, unsure because of all the noise of the crowd.

Covering my other ear, I heard my brother mention something about a gym membership, so I turned down an alley to
hear him better.

'Say again?'

'I said, you wanted me to check the names on our client list
at the gym, see if those kids you were looking for had membership, right?'

Cassie came around the corner, her face curious, and I
mouthed the word 'Anthony'.

'No Derek Jardine on our current client list,' Anthony said.
'His membership expired last June. No continuance. As I
said, not surprising. Not many stick with it.'

'Never mind him. I think he's in Queensland anyhow.'

'This other bloke, Dallas Boyd, his membership's still current,
though we haven't seen him for a while either. Maybe he's in
Queensland too. Wish I was. Maybe if I start using heroin every
day the government'll pay for me to go on a holiday. That how
it works?'

'Something like that. Listen, I'm on to something here. Gotta
fly. Thanks, Andy.'

'No worries. Thanks for going to see Mum this morning, by
the way. I've just got back myself.'

I winced and turned away from Cassie. 'Ah, how is she?'

'Still knocked out on painkillers. Dad's going to stay overnight and take her back to the nursing home tomorrow, if the
fires don't get too close.'

'Anything I can do?'

'Just speak to Chloe. I'll deal with Mum and Dad for now.'

'All right, mate. You take care.'

'Thanks. Ciao.'

'Everything okay?' Cassie asked when I hung up.

'Family politics,' I said, brushing her off. 'Let's go do this.'

I filled her in on the YMCA dead end as we walked into Café Vit. Like everywhere else in St Kilda that day, it was crowded, hot and loud.

'I don't know a Karl Vitazul,' a waiter named Nigel said in answer to my question. 'Nobody by that name works here.'

'Think!' Cassie said. 'He told us he was the owner.'

'He's overweight,' I added. 'Maybe five ten, thin hair, round face. Speaks with a European accent.'

The waiter frowned. 'You must mean Gervas.'

'Who's Gervas?'

'Gervas Kirzek. *He's* the owner.'

I frowned, confused. Why had the owner given me a different name, one that matched the registration plate and home address of a ninety-three year old?

'Where is he?' I asked.

'I don't know.'

Cassie stepped closer, lowering her voice. 'Don't lie to us, Nigel. We've got a job to do, just like you. Just tell us where he is and we'll be out of here.' She nodded towards the seating area. 'If not, we'll make a real scene.'

Nigel ran a hand through oily hair. 'Look, I don't know where he is. He hasn't been in since that dead kid was found out back. Freaked him out.'

'Did you know Dallas Boyd?' Cassie prodded.

'Who?'

'The kid your boss found outside.'

'Just some junkie, wasn't he? Shame they can't all go that way, I reckon. You should see what some of them do around here. Just last week we had one guy –'

'Your boss,' I interrupted. 'Where can we find him?'

'At home, I suppose. I hope he hasn't done something stupid.'

'Like what?'

'Shit, I don't know. As I said, he was pretty freaked out after finding that kid. And they say it's victimless to use drugs. Tell that to Gervas. He had to wait outside with the body. He was a mess afterwards. People feel sorry for junkies, but I don't. They come in here all the time, thieving and harassing everyone. Last week one of them even vomited in the —'

'Save it,' I hissed.

'Kitchen,' he finished.

'Just tell us where he lives.'

'All right! I'll get you the address. I'm just saying that thing last week had him real wired, man. Maybe you could check on him, make sure he's all right,' he said, leading us past the kitchen to an office at the rear.

At the back door, I looked out at the loading bay where Dallas Boyd had died and thought about how far we'd come in just a few days. There were cops who said that all cases had a rush point: the moment you knew you were face to face with evil, when all your instincts and gut feelings were proven. With it came an immense rush of adrenaline that surpassed anything else on the planet. Before Nigel even wrote down the address, I knew it would be the same house we'd just been to in Elwood, and I felt that familiar sensation build in my stomach. I looked at Cassie and knew she felt it too. Rush point. We were closing in.

# 27

IT TOOK SOME PERSUADING, but Cassie agreed to keep the Dallas Boyd murder and the laptop separate, even though we knew the two were linked. My rationale was that it would be premature to inform the Homicide Squad of our suspicions since we didn't know yet who Gervas Kirzek or Karl Vitazul were.

I left her at the station to run record checks and she soon rang back to confirm that the name Vitazul matched the BMW Sparks had stolen, which in turn matched the address the waiter had said Gervas Kirzek, the owner of the café, lived at.

Meantime, I drove north towards the city, trying to fit it all together. Why had Kirzek, or whoever the hell he was, given me a false name when I first spoke to him at the crime scene? It wasn't unusual for crooks to adopt an alias, especially when questioned by police. Usually they did it to protect a past they didn't want exposed. That would fit with having a driver's licence and the BMW's rego being under a bogus identity. The more I thought about it, the more I agreed with Finetti that Kirzek had killed Boyd, staged the scene and called police with a concocted story and phoney name.

The traffic freed up as I got onto Punt Road and passed by the Nylex clock in Richmond, but it was past eight by the time I pulled into the visitors lot outside Ella's apartment building in Carlton. I hurried to the intercom, pressed her apartment number, grinned at the camera and listened to her voice crackle through the speaker.

'Hey there, hunksta. You're a little late. Our booking's for eight.'

'Right, ah, that's why I'm here. I've got a problem. Can I come up?'

The door clicked and I stepped into the elevator. Ella greeted me at her door with a cautious peck on the cheek. I followed her to the kitchen where a bag of groceries was on the bench, waiting to be put away.

'You're here to cancel, aren't you?' she said, swigging from a Powerade bottle.

'Not cancel. Reschedule.'

'You've had a better offer from a twenty-year-old bikini model?'

I smiled even though the cynicism was obvious. 'No, something's come up with the Boyd case. A lead.'

She waited, silent.

'We may have ID'd the killer. I've left Cassie at the watch-house to do some backgrounding on the guy. If it looks good, we'll probably make a move tonight.'

'Hang on, aren't you supposed to be on carer's leave?' she said, frowning.

'Well, sort of. I'm just . . . I just don't want to let this go, that's all. A lot has happened today and I've made good progress.'

'What do you mean, sort of? Are you on leave or not?'

'Well, technically I still am.'

'Okay, so . . . ?'

'So I'm moonlighting.'

'Fine. Why did you bother coming over?' she said, carrying the groceries to the fridge.

'I just wanted to see you. And I wanted to tell you about Mum. She had a fall today, landed on her hip.'

'Oh.'

She put the bag back on the bench as I explained my trip this morning, the ambulance and the hospital.

'Just bruising they say, this time anyway,' I concluded.

'Why didn't you say you were going to visit today? I would've come with you.'

'I know, just something I wanted to do on my own.'

'Like talking to Chloe,' she said. 'Seems there are a lot of things you want to do on your own.'

I put a hand on her arm but she stepped around me and walked to the window by the balcony.

'I know what I want, Ella,' I said, walking up behind her.

She didn't react.

'After this is all finished, I want family time. Real time. With you. With everyone. I just need to finish this. I mean, everybody keeps calling this kid a junkie, but it's just like Jacko. Nobody looked out for him. Now he's dead. Somebody has to answer for that.'

'You can't blame yourself for what happened to your friend. You were just a kid and so was he. If anyone's to blame, it's his father.'

'I'm not talking about him. I mean Dallas. I pegged it as an accidental overdose even though I knew things didn't add up. I let my own shit stop me seeing what I should've seen.'

She looked at me a long moment, conflicting emotions running across her face.

'Ella, you said you wanted me to find whoever did this,' I said.

'Not if it means ruining everything we've worked to rebuild. Shit, I don't want you messed up, like you were when we were together. I want a normal, stable relationship.'

I was silent, surprised. It was the first time she'd defined what she wanted and her reference to a relationship confused me. Was she giving me an ultimatum?

She walked to the front door, opened it and I followed her out into the hall.

'Just do what you have to, Rubens. Get it out of your system. And afterwards, have a good think about what you want. About what you *really* want.'

'I know what I want. I just told you. I want to be *us* again. I want what we had last night. It was special, you know. It was real.'

She nodded quickly, looked away. 'I hope so.'

I went to kiss her but my mobile phone rang.

'I have to take this,' I said, seeing Cassie's name on the screen.

'Just remember what I said.' Ella stepped back over the threshold. 'You need to work out what you really want.'

I winced as the door closed, then let out a long breath and answered the phone.

'Gervas Kirzek is a real pearler,' Cassie said excitedly. 'Wait till you get a load of this guy.'

'Got form, I take it?' I asked.

'Form isn't the word. Kirzek's docket reads like a paedophile's guide to the galaxy. We could probably add his name to the Three Misters,' she said, referring to the titles the media had given three of Australia's most notorious paedophiles: Mr Baldy, Mr Stinky and Mr Cruel.

I shared the elevator with a young couple and told Cassie to wait a minute before continuing. As the door opened, I let the couple walk ahead and listened as she explained how Kirzek had no priors in Victoria, but numerous offences in New South Wales.

'Goes back almost ten years,' she said. 'Six separate hits on indecent exposure, a few more trespass and misconduct. All in Sydney. He even got done on a child porn racket in 2004. After that, seems he moved to Melbourne and bought the café.'

Outside, I stared at the park across the street. It was filled with families, parents watching their children playing on the swings.

'What about Vitazul?' I asked.

'Well, this is where it gets tricky. We're working on this with the Feds. Apparently Vitazul and Kirzek are related. Both are Romanian nationals who emigrated after some government dictatorship collapsed.'

Puzzled, I headed back to my car.

'But anyway, that's not the only reason I rang,' Cassie said. 'You need to get back here. Eckles has the Homicide Squad running with it. They know about Dallas Boyd.'

'What? We agreed to keep the laptop separate.'

'I'm not talking about the laptop. Homicide rechecked all your footsteps, so they tried to contact this Karl Vitazul character, since he'd supposedly found the body. But they hit a brick wall, just like we did. You know why?'

'He's dead, isn't he?'

'How'd you know?' she said, surprised.

'Just makes sense. If you want to adopt a bogus ID, why not find someone who's not around to challenge it. Even better if it's someone you're related to.'

'Right, well, they checked the registry. Like most ninety-three-year-old smokers, his lungs gave out. That was in 2004, right about the time Gervas Kirzek moved to Melbourne.'

I got in the car and unwound the windows. It made no difference to the heat.

'So based on all that, plus his form as a rock spider, the hommies have set up an operations room around the conference table,' Cassie continued. 'A KALOF has been broadcast across the air. They're even lining up an SOG raid team. You need to get your arse back here.'

'I'm on leave, remember?'

'Eckles wants you back in.'

'What?'

'Probably wants to keep an eye on you. Told me to get you back here.'

'Cassie, I'm not some monkey he can make jump through

hoops. Either he wants me on the team or he doesn't. Either way, he can ring me himself, otherwise he can go and get –'

'You want to get this guy, don't you?' she said.

'Of course.'

'Then stop being so bloody precious. This is your only chance. You can sit at home and let us do it, or forget your pride for a minute and get back here. Either way, we're gonna get this guy, *tonight*.'

I started the engine, drove out of the car park and headed back to St Kilda.

# 28

I SNEAKED INTO THE watch-house via the back and sent a text to Cassie asking her to meet me in the mess room.

'Where's the disk?' I said when she came in.

'On your desk, why?'

I nodded, relieved, then thanked her.

'Why?' she said again.

'Because I thought you might've given it to them.'

'That's your guilty conscience, Rubens. The disk *should* be with them,' she said, checking over her shoulder and stepping closer. 'If you want my advice, and you want to keep your job, you'll take it in to Eckles right now.'

'Look, let's just put in a request to have the techs take a look at the laptop,' I said. 'That way we're not holding out on anything and we're not making judgements based on a few pictures.'

'A few *pictures*?' she hissed. 'I saw that boy this morning. Some sicko cut his throat so deep it damn near severed his head. Don't tell me all we're talking about is kiddie porn, okay?'

'Okay, okay!' I said, raising my hands. 'But either way, Computer Crime will have to analyse the laptop. If I give it to

Eckles, they'll do it for him and report back to him. But if we give it to them, we'll stay in the loop. I mean, don't pretend after seeing that kid this morning you don't want to get this guy?'

'Of course I do.'

'Then trust me. Put in a request for Computer Crime to check out the laptop. Do you know anyone who works over there?'

'Yeah, I know someone,' she finally said.

'So give them a call and tell them it's a hot one. Give them a few details, but not too many. Just enough to get them interested. I'm sure they won't mind working a Sunday for this.'

I stepped around her and crossed to the conference room adjoining Eckles' office. Through the window, I recognised most of the people in there, except a woman in a beige suit pointing to a whiteboard. I opened the door and the woman stopped talking.

'Ah, sorry,' I said as everyone turned to look at me.

Two large colour photographs hung on the whiteboard. One was the man I'd spoken to at Café Vit on the day of Dallas Boyd's murder. Gervas Kirzek. The other was an elderly man I didn't recognise. Beneath him was the name 'Karl Vitazul'.

'Sit down, McCauley,' said Eckles, pointing to a seat opposite him. 'This is Fiona Johns. She's a forensic psychologist on loan from the Feds and is bringing us up to speed on the man we're after.'

Nik Stello sat across the table, flanked by three other detectives from the Homicide Squad. I nodded but none of them nodded back. To my left were an SOG sergeant, the divisional superintendent and two inspectors. I didn't acknowledge any of them. Instead I looked at the woman in front of the whiteboard, who cleared her throat and used a pen to point to the elderly man on the right.

'Karl Vitazul arrived in Australia in 1987, just prior to the collapse of the Ceauşescu government in Romania,' she explained. 'The name Vitazul, by the way, means "brave man". Not sure whether that's relevant, but from what the Immigration Department records show, he was granted refugee status under the claim he was fleeing the Romanian dictatorship. We believe Karl Vitazul married a Romanian woman and subsequently moved to Brashov in Transylvania, where he worked for the Communist government. In effect, he lied to gain entry and residence in Australia.'

There were groans at the table as everyone feigned surprise.

'We believe they were unable to have children of their own and so fostered a child from one of the notorious orphanages in Romania, known as *leaganes*,' she continued, pointing to the other photograph on the whiteboard. 'Gervas Kirzek.'

I began taking notes, as was everyone at the table except the SOG sergeant. He didn't need to know any of this for his mission. All he needed was an address.

'According to intel,' Johns went on, 'and this comes straight from the spooks in Canberra, Kirzek was born in 1960 in a village outside Brashov. We don't know who his biological parents were, but ASIO believe he was fostered out of the orphanage at age four, after which he lived with the Vitazuls until he was eighteen. He joined the Securiate where he remained until the age of thirty when —'

'The security what?' the superintendent asked.

'The Sec-u-ri-ate,' Johns said, writing it on the whiteboard. 'The Communist Party's secret political police. They were responsible for guarding the internal security of the Ceauşescu regime and suppressing any dissident groups that criticised or challenged it.' She crossed her arms and turned to the photo of Kirzek. 'I've seen pictures and read personal accounts of the tactics they used to achieve this. They trained their recruits in slaughterhouses and used live pigs as practice. Trust me, they were barbarians.'

I thought about the boy who'd been murdered in Talbot Reserve and Cassie's words reverberated in my mind. *Some sicko cut his throat so deep it damn near severed his head.* I wanted to tell them about the laptop, the disk and the connection with Justin Quinn, but decided to wait until the end of the meeting.

'In 1990, the Ceauşescu dictatorship collapsed and the Securiate scattered,' Johns went on. 'Some fled to the US or Britain, others left for more remote and accepting countries in West Africa or South America. Kirzek disappeared for seven years, then guess where he turned up?'

Several people answered at once. 'Australia.'

'Right, but not Melbourne,' Johns replied, pointing at the picture of the elderly man. 'The foster father, Karl Vitazul, sponsored him and Kirzek was granted residency. This is where it gets interesting. Kirzek spent seven years in Sydney and clocked up a decent docket, mostly for sex offences and assault. Then in 2004 the stepfather died and Kirzek saw an opportunity to start afresh and pick up some inheritance, so he moved into the Elwood residence and took over the café, then buys himself a BMW, under the old man's name, of course.'

'What about the foster mother?' I asked, writing it all down. 'Is she accounted for?'

Stello glanced at Eckles, who glared across the table at me. Eckles had probably told Stello I wouldn't be involved any further in the investigation. Cassie was right. The only reason Eckles had called me back was to keep an eye on me. The Federal Police, on the other hand, obviously weren't privy to this.

'Good question,' said Johns. 'Immigration records show Vitazul entered Australia with his wife. But we checked with death registrations. She died in 1997, just before Kirzek arrived in Australia.'

I made a note about this as Johns elaborated.

'So you have an elderly man running a café in Melbourne. His wife dies and suddenly he's alone. He contacts his foster son in Europe, tells him he'll sponsor his immigration to Australia. They set it up, and Kirzek moves out here. Now let's think about the psychopathology. He's been part of an institution for the greater part of his life.' She pointed at the picture of Kirzek then began counting fingers. 'First, the orphanage. Second, the foster care system. Then, when he's eighteen, he

246

joins the Securiate, where for ten years he learns how to disembowel pigs – and probably humans – with a filleting knife. Then, all these years later, he shows up in St Kilda as your suspect. Isn't really surprising, is it?'

Everybody stared at the photo of Kirzek and for a while nobody said anything. Then, finally, Eckles spoke up. 'Well, thanks for that, Fiona. If it turns out this prick is our guy, we'll make sure he spends the rest of his life in another kind of institution.' Getting up, he turned to Stello. 'I want to wrap this up. How are you placed?'

'All set. We've put this photo out through all media networks and got extra staff at Crime Stoppers to take the calls.'

Eckles nodded. 'So what now?'

'We're heading back to the Elwood house. They're still down there and last I heard the guy's a keeper. No BMW in the garage, but a fair stack of movie magic. Lights, cameras and all sorts of action.'

Eckles looked across at the SOG sergeant. The man's black T-shirt was stretched tight over thick slabs of muscle and across his chest was an imprint of the SOG helmet and a machine gun. Beneath it were the words: *Always Bet on Black*.

'Good as gold,' the sergeant said. 'Just give me an address and we'll take him down.'

'Right then, that's it.'

Everyone else stood up, ready to roll. Eckles leant across the table and put a hand on my shoulder.

'Not you, sunshine. We're not done yet,' he said, nodding towards his office.

He closed the door and drew the blinds so no one could see in. 'I don't know why you're doing this,' he said.

'Doing what?' I asked.

'Shut up!' he cut in. 'I didn't ask you to speak. When I want to hear your voice, I'll ask you to speak. Now sit down.'

'I know why you're angry, but we don't have time for it now.'

'What?'

'We don't have time for this. I think we need to –'

'I don't care what you think!' he hissed. 'You don't seem to understand that. And you don't seem to get that *I'm* the boss. I'm in charge. I make the rules. I decide what's important and what we have time for. Now sit your arse in that chair or I'll make sure you never work here again.'

'I know why you're pissed off, and I'm sorry,' I said, easing into the chair.

'*Sorry?*' he sneered, leaning over his desk. 'Sorry won't cut it. You have no idea how much shit you are in, pal. I personally signed an agreement with ESD to have you on carer's leave, basically gave you a get-out-of-strife pass, for *free*.'

'Oh, turn it up. You made that deal to cover your own arse because you couldn't accept we missed a curve ball on the overdose.'

Eckles snorted. '*You* missed the curve ball. Not me, not anyone else. *You*! That's why I sent you packing. Only you couldn't cop it. You went after the stepfather, manhandled him like a schoolyard bully. That'll cost you big time when ESD come around.'

I crossed my arms, silent, fuming.

'But that's not all. I know you questioned the kid's girlfriend. Jesus Christ, McCauley. You took the bloody social worker along for the ride. Mate, I've even got you questioning the clerk at the 7-Eleven.' Eckles let his knowledge hang in the air like a bad smell, then added, 'If ESD get a hold of all that, it's strike number three for you.'

'What do you want, Ben?' I asked calmly.

'Tell me what else you know.'

'What do you mean?'

'You know exactly what I mean,' he said, his face the colour of ripe beetroot, two veins protruding from his neck. 'What kind of fucking *idiot* do you think I am? Either give me what else you've got on this, or I make a call to ESD and tell them about you gallivanting all over the joint while you're supposed to be at home on the couch.

'I have a witness,' I said, accepting defeat.

'What?'

'Well, sort of,' I started, then explained my contact with Stuart Parks and how he'd pointed me in the direction of Kirzek before the Homicide Squad had officially identified him as a suspect. I also told him about the disk and the pornography of both Dallas Boyd and Justin Quinn, the boy who'd been murdered the previous night, and how Sparks had stolen the laptop from Kirzek's house in Elwood.

When I was done, Eckles sat wide-eyed and silent. I could almost see the political cogs in his brain turning.

'Kirzek murdered that kid last night, as well as Boyd?' he said.

'I think so.'

'So where's the laptop?'

'In transit,' I lied. 'There's a request for the Computer Crime Squad to check it out as we speak.'

'Not good enough. This is a murder investigation, McCauley. It needs to be with Homicide. I want you to call Computer Crime and have them contact Stello ASAP. Is that clear?'

'Fine.'

'I've given you too much slack, McCauley. That's your problem. You're like a dog off a lead, pissing all over the place. Now it's time to put you on a choker-chain. Make the call to Computer Crime, then stay the hell away from this case.'

I was about to respond when the SOG sergeant opened the door, now dressed in a black jumpsuit, Kevlar helmet in his hands.

'Sorry, sir,' he said to Eckles. 'Thought you'd want to know. Somebody called Crime Stoppers and made an ID on Kirzek. Said he'd just seen him. We've got an address.'

Eckles raised his eyebrows. 'Where?'

'Apartment in South Yarra. We're ready to crash and bash. You wanna roll?'

'Sure.' Eckles followed the sergeant out then turned back to me. 'Don't fuck this up, McCauley. You get that laptop to Homicide and piss off home.'

# 29

I MADE NO EFFORT WITH my information report for the Homicide Squad, indicating only that the laptop had allegedly belonged to Gervas Kirzek and had been seized from a local crook. After burning a copy of the disk for my own reference, I attached the original to the report, but didn't state that there were images of Dallas Boyd or Justin Quinn on it. It wouldn't make any difference to the homicide investigation anyway. Stello would still require Computer Crime experts to run through it, and this wouldn't be a priority. Not when SOG was about to arrest the prime suspect.

After printing and proofing the report, I taped it to the laptop and sealed it all in a courier's box. My connection to the case was over and I felt flat and dejected. At the same time I felt shallow for being so self-centred.

'Hey, Ruby,' Cassie called from the mess room. 'Check this out. Our guy's on the TV.'

An ABC news anchor stood outside the St Kilda Road police complex describing how detectives hunting a man over a series of murders in the St Kilda area were about to bring in a suspect for questioning.

'A series?' Cassie said. 'He kills two people and all of a sudden he's a serial killer.'

'Two that we know of,' I muttered as a picture of Kirzek appeared on the screen. It was the same photo that had been released to Crime Stoppers. Beneath it was the label 'Mr Fatty'.

'I was right,' Cassie said. 'They are adding him to the Three Misters.'

'Mr Fatty.' I snorted. 'Who the hell gave them that?'

'A witness,' Cassie said.

'What witness?'

'Apparently a hooker told Homicide she saw an overweight man running away from Talbot Reserve after Justin Quinn was killed. She obviously leaked it to the media. Probably copped a quid for it too.'

I shook my head in disgust. A media title gave killers clout and status, and often impeded the investigation. It annoyed me that Dallas Boyd's actual murder hadn't received any media coverage, yet a flock of journalists and cameramen were camped outside headquarters waiting for his killer's arrival. Kirzek was a celebrity now. No doubt somebody would get a six-figure advance for writing a book about him.

Cassie turned up the volume as, onscreen, an unmarked police cruiser slowed to turn into the car park at the police complex. A man was huddled between two detectives in the back seat. I stepped up to the screen as the news anchor explained that a suspect had been taken into custody by the Homicide Squad. But when the news cameras pressed a light against the side window of the car, I was staring at a man I'd never seen before.

'That's not him,' I said to Cassie. 'It's not Kirzek.'

'Huh?'

'Look!' I said, pointing to the figure in the back seat. 'It's not him.'

'Then who the hell have they got?'

I was dialling Eckles' number when there was a sound of running footsteps and Mark Finetti entered the room, a startled look across his face.

'You guys need to haul arse,' he spluttered. 'That kid from today, your informant, we just found him outside the squat off Acland Street. Looks like he had a fight with Freddy Krueger.'

'Sparks?' I said, my mouth dry.

'Yeah, stabbed to death.'

The narrow street was blocked at the entrance, blue and red police lights pulsing against the darkening night sky. Hundreds of festival goers were packed against the crime scene tape, like fans queuing for a grand final. Finetti wound down his window and began yelling at the crowd to move, but it made no difference, so Cassie flicked the siren on. When that didn't work I got out of the car and physically ushered the rubber-neckers to the sides, giving us just enough space to get the car through. We signed the attendance log and stepped under the plastic tape. Already the forensic process was in full swing. A team of crime scene officers had their cameras and toolboxes ready, while another team had assembled floodlights to illuminate the driveway where Sparks had been killed.

Kim Pendlebury came over to us. 'Look at this place,' she said, nodding to the surging crowd and the lone constable who stood guarding the crime scene. 'We need as many bodies as we can get down here. Cassie, you help out Powers over there, keep these people in line. Mark, I want you on media watch. We don't want any shifty journos breaking through, got it?'

They both nodded and walked off towards the crowd.

'So you knew this kid?' Kim asked me.

'An informant,' I said, looking over her shoulder to the crumpled and bloodied body. The sight sickened me and I had to look away.

'Well, you know how it goes. You can't go in. I gotta keep it clear.'

'What can you tell me?'

'We think the killer staked out the house from over there,' she said, pointing to a palm tree. A crime scene examiner crawled around on the ground beneath it, examining the road and nature strip. I could see an old syringe and a used condom that the CSO had highlighted with numbered evidence tags, even though they probably weren't related to the murder. For a second I wondered what sort of photo the image would make. A used condom, a dirty needle and a crime scene cop crawling around a palm tree. Very St Kilda. Maybe they could make a postcard out of it and sell it to the tourists.

'Why over there?'

'Well, we got witnesses.'

'No way!'

'A couple walked by here just before the kid got sliced. They saw an overweight transvestite on the other side of the street, leaning against the tree, looking like he was waiting for something.'

An image of the trannie I'd seen earlier flashed in my mind and I suddenly felt weak at the knees.

'That prick, I saw him,' I said. 'I was here about five this arvo, looking for Sparks. There was a fat trannie in a red dress right here. I didn't recognise him, thought he was just another newcomer.'

I closed my eyes and tried to remember the face, a telling detail, maybe a tattoo, anything, but all I could see was the dress. There'd been a blonde wig too, but the dress had been all-consuming. Bright red and bursting at the seams. That had probably been his intention. Make yourself look disgusting, that way no one looks at your face. Perfect disguise.

'The hommies might want to speak to you,' Kim said.

'Yeah. How much did the witnesses see?'

'Not a lot. They live around here, a married couple. They see trannies all the time, so this was no biggie, except when they got back from their evening stroll us cops were here with the body.

Anyway, we didn't want them skipping the scene so we got Homicide on to them real quick.'

That ruled out any option of me being able to talk to them.

'What do you make of the transvestite angle? Real or staged?'

Kim chuckled. 'All you heteros are the same, if you ask me. Wouldn't know shit from shine when it comes to our side of the fence. My guess is your guy, Mr Fatty or whatever the hell they've called him, put on a bit of lippy and a wig, slipped into a dress and there you go: an overweight transvestite.'

I nodded slowly. 'Yeah, like you say, not out of place in St Kilda.'

'Nothing's out of place in St Kilda. Come with me,' she said, leading me across the street to a white panel van with a cage on the back, a Port Phillip Council emblem on the doors.

'Dog catchers,' she explained, pointing to the dog in the rear cabin. 'The kid had a mutt. Some kind of pit bull by the look of it. It wouldn't let us or the ambos near the body so we had to get a dog catcher out. Poor bastard had to ignore the body while trying to catch the dog. In the end he caught the dog then puked his guts up.' Kim laughed. 'Bloody ambos had to treat him for shock. Guess he's still not well enough to drive.'

I didn't find the story amusing. The dog was asleep on a blanket, probably in shock too. Sparks had had little to offer the dog but he was still loyal enough to defend his master.

'Hooch,' I said, easing away from the window.

'What's that?'

'The dog's name's Hooch. He's a bull mastiff. Not a pit bull.'

'Not going to be anything for long. Not once they get him in the pound.'

I looked around for Cassie and saw Eckles step under the tape and stride towards me.

'What the hell are you doing here, McCauley?' he snarled. 'Are you trying to give me a fucking heart attack?'

'Don't even start,' I said. 'This is Kirzek's handiwork, which to me is one hell of a mystery since you were supposed to arrest him. They even had his face plastered all over the news. What the *hell* happened?'

'It's not your concern, McCauley. Go home before I –'

'Not *my* concern? Mate, my informant's dead. Killed by the same prick you and Stello took off to arrest an *hour* ago. What happened?'

When Eckles didn't reply I knew there'd been a screw-up.

'Let me guess,' I said. 'Somebody tipped off the media that an arrest was imminent, then when you realised Kirzek wasn't where he was supposed to be, you decided to cover your arse. Who was in the back seat of the arrest car?'

He didn't answer.

'I wouldn't be surprised if you put one of our guys in there just for show.'

'Hey, we got a righteous bust,' Eckles blustered. 'The guy was driving Kirzek's Beamer. He even has photos of him in his apartment. From what I can see, they're mates or something and this guy just played the red herring so Kirzek could take a walk.'

'So who is he then?'

Eckles looked away but I wasn't having it.

'Don't ignore me, Ben. Sparks was helping me . . . helping *us*. Kirzek killed him and he's still out there, making us look like idiots. Who the hell have you got?'

'Some priest named Miles Jorgensen, works for Back Outside. You know, the kiddie prison program.'

I didn't recognise either the name or the program, and thought about ringing Will Novak to ask what he knew about it, but there wasn't time.

'We tried to sweat this guy right off the top but he flexed his silent rights,' Eckles said. 'The cheeky son of a bitch even started praying in the interrogation room. Asked the Lord to forgive *us*, can you believe that shit?'

I looked up at the sky. It was a dark and murky red with no stars and no moon, the city still encased in smoke. The priest under arrest only served to twist the knot in my gut even tighter. Kirzek was playing with us, stalling us. There could be only one reason for that. I studied the strain in my boss's eyes and realised he'd reached the same conclusion.

'You want my help or not?' I said.

He kicked at rubble on the ground and said, 'Just do what you have to do to catch this prick.'

I left him with his head bowed and walked to the edge of the crime scene where Cassie was telling a reporter to back up and keep the camera out of her face.

'It's a setup,' I said quietly, pulling her out of earshot. 'Kirzek had one of his cronies bait the hommies and SOG so he could slip away. That means he's not finished.'

'Tammy York,' she said, a look of fear suffusing her face. 'She can tie Kirzek to the laptop. He's going back for seconds.'

We ran back to my car and I fired the engine while Cassie ordered the crowd back. When we pulled onto Acland Street, my mobile phone chirped. With one hand on the wheel, I checked the screen.

'Ella,' I said, wondering why she would be calling me.

When I answered my heart skipped a beat. The voice coming back at me wasn't Ella's. It was male, with a thick European accent. Gervas Kirzek.

# 30

I SWUNG THE CAR OVER TO the sidewalk and shrieked to a halt.

'You steal my life,' Kirzek said. 'I want it back.'

'Your life? I don't understand,' I said, trying to keep the panic out of my voice.

'You have something of mine. I have something of yours.'

'Ella?'

'Yes, your wife.'

I rested a hand on the dash to steady myself. 'What do you want?'

'I want the laptop back. Give it back or I flay your bitch wife like filthy pig.'

I blinked away an image of Kirzek cutting Ella like he had Sparks and Justin Quinn. Cassie held up her radio to ask if I wanted her to call it in. I shook my head and she put a hand on my shoulder, a silent message that she was onside.

'I don't have the laptop with me, but I can get it. How do I know Ella is okay?'

'One thing at one time, Mr Rubens. Be very slow and very

careful, you understand? Do not tell pig friends, and bitch won't get knife.'

'What do you want me to do?'

'Get laptop, no pigs, and I call one hour.'

I started to reply but the line went dead. When I tried to call Ella's mobile phone it was switched off.

'Motherfucker!' I roared, punching the dash and getting out of the car. I paced back and forth, trying to control my panic.

'You need to stay calm,' Cassie said, getting out too. 'What did he say?'

'He wants the laptop back, but he'll kill her if I bring in other cops.'

I couldn't risk involving anyone else. Not Eckles or Stello. Not Kim Pendlebury or Mark Finetti. Not even the tactical response units specially trained for this type of thing. But what about Cassie? If she hadn't been in the car when the call came through, I probably wouldn't involve her either, but she was my partner and I had to trust her.

'We need to get the laptop somewhere safe,' I said. 'I don't give a shit what's on the hard drive. I'm not letting Eckles or any other fuckwit bargain with Ella's life.'

Cassie looked back at me, silent. Finally she walked over to the driver's side door and pointed at the passenger seat.

'Get in,' she said. 'I'm driving. We'll go to my place. If he's planning anything shifty, he'll go to your place first. He won't know about mine.'

Back at the watch-house, I ran upstairs, collected the laptop and a knapsack from the property room that contained a two-way mike set and earpiece. Cassie made a U-turn and spun the car hard and fast onto Brighton Road. She swung onto the tram tracks down to the junction into South Melbourne and eventually screeched to a halt outside her two-bedroom cottage. I followed her through the front gate and into the house, checking the street for anything out of place.

I waited in the lounge while Cassie brought in her own laptop and set it up on the coffee table next to Kirzek's.

'I'm going to call him,' I said.

'Wait.' Cassie grabbed my wrist. 'He said *he* would ring.'

'I don't care. Let's get it over with.'

I dialled the number but the phone was still switched off. Thoughts of Kirzek lying to me, trying to trick me, exploded in my mind. I pressed my fingers into my temples, reminding myself that I had the one thing Kirzek wanted. The laptop. It was my only chance.

Unable to stay still, I headed outside onto the front porch, adrenaline racing as I tried to work out what to do. My hands began to tremble and I had to grip the balustrade. How the fuck did Kirzek even *know* about Ella? I closed my eyes and tried to control my breathing. One of Anthony's relaxation mantras played in my mind. *One-one thousand, two-one thousand, three-one thousand. Reee-laaaax.* I counted with the slow rhythm and imagined swimming in the baths at Brighton Beach, each breath a new stroke, closer and closer to the shore.

It was a while before I realised Cassie was talking to me.

'What's that?' I said.

'I think I've found something on the internet. Come take a look.'

I followed her back into the lounge and sat next to her on the sofa.

'I started with a simple Google search on the name Gervas Kirzek,' she said, facing the screen. 'Got nothing on that so I ran another on the priest the Soggies just arrested.'

'Miles Jorgensen?'

'Right. Again nothing came up, but when I added the words "children" and "charges" to the search, I found an article in the *Bulletin* about a group they call The Holy Brethren. Have a look.'

**BRETHREN BROTHERS SPIN WEB OF PERVERSION**
Australian Federal Police believe The Holy Brethren is a loosely connected group of paedophiles banded together by the internet and

a now-defunct travel agency in Sydney allegedly responsible for organising hundreds of sex tours to countries such as the Philippines, Thailand and Cambodia.

According to sources close to the AFP's Locust Taskforce, an anti-child-pornography operation, The Holy Brethren has an estimated membership of at least 300 individuals across the nation, with affiliations to the Catholic Church, various community groups, some elements of the education system and the welfare sector.

'Members of The Holy Brethren often take part in various bonding rituals,' said Fiona Johns, a Federal Agent attached to the Locust Taskforce. 'These include prayer groups and camping trips where new members are sworn in, promoted and, if necessary, disciplined.'

The AFP believes The Holy Brethren, like many organisations, is structured according to hierarchy. However, when asked about leadership, officials remained tight-lipped, but according to documents obtained under Freedom of Information legislation, a number of AFP agents assigned to the Locust Taskforce have recently visited countries in the European Eastern Bloc, namely Poland and Romania.

'There are other commonalities between members both in their personal lives and in business,' Agent Johns added. 'For instance, they might all arrange their holidays through the same travel agent, whom they know to be a fellow member. Even purchasing cars or having them serviced might be done through fellow members. It's a very secular way of life.'

When asked how members could be identified, Agent Johns explained that it wasn't that simple. 'They don't wear uniforms or advertise their membership in any particular way,' she said. 'They don't have tattoos or a club emblem, for instance. However, they can sometimes be identified by a small silver crucifix, either worn on a necklace or as an earring.'

'It goes on to mention they have cells in all major Australian cities, and that child pornography and the sex tours are its main forms of connection and economy,' Cassie explained.

I knew then that we were nudging an iceberg.

'Romania,' I said, recalling Agent Johns' briefing on Kirzek and his role in the Romanian secret police. 'How does the priest fit into it?'

'That's where it gets interesting. His name's in the middle of the article. Here,' she said, pointing to the screen.

Among the dozens of organisations mentioned in a concluding report filed by the Locust Taskforce are some of the nation's leading charity and welfare groups, including the former prison release service Breaking the Wall, which has been staunchly defended by its founder, Father Miles Jorgensen.

'Breaking the Wall absolutely refutes these accusations,' Jorgensen said. 'We are a charity organisation and have been helping incarcerated young people form better connections with the community for more than ten years. The AFP's comments have only served to worsen the lives of thousands of at-risk young people who depend on us for a better future.'

Breaking the Wall was a name I did remember. I hadn't heard it referred to for a long time though and was surprised it was still operating. It was a post-prison release service whose primary function was to assist kids re-entering the community after a period of incarceration. It helped them find employment, accommodation and other essential services.

'What else have you got?' I asked Cassie, remembering something Will Novak had said to me at the crisis centre. 'Anything about a group called Back Outside?'

She tapped at the keyboard, then said, 'I ran a name search on Breaking the Wall and got redirected to the Back Outside website. Guess whose name comes up in the annual report?'

'Miles Jorgensen?'

'Right. Looks like he started up a new service under a different name. So typical, isn't it – just move your problem elsewhere and hope it goes away.'

I nodded, thinking it through.

'There's something else,' Cassie said. 'This is an old press release from early last year on their "what's news" page. Check it out.'

I leant into the screen and read the text she'd highlighted.

### FUNDING BOOST FOR KIDS IN CRISIS

The Hon Brooke Porter MP, Victorian Minister for Health, is pleased to announce a $2.5m funding package to boost the Back Outside program, a move that will improve juvenile offender access to post-release support services.

'Much of this funding will go straight towards improving coal-face services such as accommodation and employment,' Minister Porter said. 'Because Back Outside already has established relation-ships with primary welfare providers, we are able to cut down on the administration costs normally associated with this type of funding package. And since many of these kids are homeless and extremely marginalised after a period of incarceration, these funds are a victory for both the offenders and the community.'

'Are you thinking what I'm thinking?' Cassie said, easing back on the sofa.

'Yeah, established relationships,' I said, staring blankly at the words on the screen. 'CARS get a lot of referrals from Back Outside. Dallas Boyd, for one.'

'And Sparks too,' Cassie added. 'Maybe even Justin Quinn. Who knows how many others.'

I tapped my leg, agitated, unsure what to make of it. 'Okay, what about Kirzek?'

'Nothing yet. Can't find any obvious connection, but he has to be in it somewhere. Jorgensen wouldn't cop an arrest just for the sake of it. They're helping each other.' She looked at me. 'I figure that's how they all met, through this program. I mean, we know Dallas Boyd did time for armed robbery. And remember Sparks said Boyd was always talking about making money, acting cocky before he got out, as though he knew he was going to earn a whole pile of it?'

'Yeah, Dallas had a plan but kept it secret. Helping these guys make porn and then blackmailing them was his plan. Obviously it backfired.'

My mind spun with how this information could help find Ella. Somehow Kirzek and Jorgensen knew each other and were in partnership, possibly with CARS somewhere in the picture, but none of this helped me now. Before I could suggest anything more, my phone rang. It was Kirzek.

'You have laptop, yes?'

'Yes,' I said, heart pumping.

'Very good. Do not lie, McCauley.'

'I'm not.'

'I have your wife, remember.'

I swallowed. 'Let's get on with it.'

'You have email?' he said. 'You can send email to wife, yes?'

'Send her an email? But what –'

'What is problem?' Kirzek snapped. 'You have your own computer, yes?'

'Yes!'

'Then send email to wife. Do it now. Then we talk more. If not, I give her my favourite trick.'

He hung up, leaving me with an empty phone line. Cassie took the phone from me gently.

'He wants you to send an email somewhere?' she asked.

'Yeah, to Ella. I don't understand.'

'I do,' she said. 'He's at Ella's apartment, waiting by her computer. He's probably checked her emails and seen some from your hotmail account, so he knows he can communicate with you this way. Remember, this guy's a rock spider. They *live* on the internet. He feels comfortable with computers.'

'I don't want to lose her, Cass. I love her.'

'I know,' she said, squeezing my hand. 'Maybe we should try to set up a trace, either on the emails or phone calls. How long would that take?'

I shrugged, despondent. 'Too long. By the time they get it up and running he'll know we're stalling him. I can't risk it.'

She nodded in agreement, then shuffled closer to her laptop and opened Hotmail. I logged on to my account and she typed a message to Ella's email address: *I'm here . . . now what?*

Shortly after, an email arrived back: *Look closely. U can see wife.*

'What the hell does that mean?' I asked.

'Attachments,' Cassie explained, pointing at two orange icons beneath the address tabs. 'These are jpeg files. Photos.'

I leant closer, saw that the files were named simply 1 and 2. Fear surged through my body as Cassie opened the first one.

'Oh Jesus,' I gasped, staring at a picture of Ella bound and gagged on her bed, eyes wide with fear. By the bed was a television, the screen depicting a scene from the movie *Titanic*.

'It's a proof-of-life shot,' Cassie said, reaching for the remote control and turning her television on. She scrolled through the channels until *Titanic* came on. 'He's telling us she's still alive.'

'What about the other photo?'

It was an almost exact copy of the previous picture, but this time Kirzek had positioned his knife on top of the television.

'That bastard,' I snarled. 'I'm gonna take that knife and gouge out his fucking heart.'

I paced the room and felt a surge of rage so pure and clear it scared me. In nearly twenty years as a cop, I'd never taken a human life, not even in self-defence. But in that moment I knew I'd have no problem killing Kirzek.

'He has to know you understand his message,' said Cassie, typing another email. *Loud and clear. What now?*

Almost immediately Kirzek responded: *Take laptop to souvlaki bar on Lygon Street. Go alone, wait inside. Someone will come for laptop.*

*What about Ella?* Cassie typed.

*When laptop secure, wife go free,* came the reply.

Cassie went to type a response but I stopped her. I wasn't

happy with Kirzek's instructions. 'Tell him I want a straight swap,' I said. 'Out in the open.'

She nodded and typed: *Bring Ella to the souvlaki store. We'll do a direct swap.*

Kirzek replied immediately: *No. She stay here. When laptop secure, I set her free. Leave now. Twenty minutes. Remember, I see everything.*

I pictured Kirzek in Ella's bedroom, staring out the window towards Lygon Street, watching the souvlaki bar. It was an amateur and desperate plan but that didn't matter. Kirzek had us stumped. We'd seen what he'd done to Sparks and Justin Quinn. By comparison, Dallas Boyd got it easy.

'He won't hesitate to take her out if we screw him over,' I said tersely. 'I don't have a choice, Cass. I have to play ball. I have to get her back myself.'

# 31

CASSIE REVERSE-PARKED behind a bus stop on Lygon Street. From there we had a clear view of the top floors of Ella's apartment building and the souvlaki bar further up. Even at this hour, the street was abuzz with people on the sidewalks and a steady stream of cars gliding back and forth along the road.

Through the park, I could see some of the lights on in Ella's apartment, but little else. At one point I thought I saw a silhouette in the window but wasn't sure.

'I don't like this,' Cassie said. 'I've got a bad feeling, big time. There's another building opposite Ella's. Maybe we could get SOG to put a sniper on him.'

'There's no time.' I checked my watch and realised I had about five minutes before I had to be in the souvlaki store. 'I have to move.'

'We could be playing right into his hands and doing everything he wants.'

'We *are* doing what he wants,' I said. 'That's the *point*. It's the safest way to stop him killing her.'

'But how do you know he . . .' Her voice faltered and she looked away.

'How do I know he's not going to kill her anyway? Is that what you mean?' I grabbed her by the wrist and made her face me.

When she didn't answer I let go of her wrist and clenched my fists, forcing my anger and frustration into two hard balls.

'Look, we made a decision and we're here now. So why don't you stop questioning me and just fucking *help* me?'

'I *am* fucking helping, you bloody twat. Jesus, all I'm saying is that something like this needs to be surgical, not emotional. No attachment. I mean, what if it all goes wrong? You'll never forgive yourself.'

'I don't want to think about that.'

'Well, you should.'

I slid out of the car and stood in the shadows of the bus stop, Cassie's reasoning clouding me like the smoke covering the city.

'All right,' I said, taking the laptop off the back seat. 'I'm not waiting any longer. Let's do it.'

She got out of the car and followed me into a nearby alley, carrying the knapsack with the two-way radio and mike I'd borrowed from the watch-house.

'Unbutton your shirt,' she said, a little too loudly. 'Put this on.'

A couple strolling past heard her comment and looked into the alley. I stared back until they kept walking, then undid my shirt and tried to tape the mike lead to my chest. It was awkward because I hadn't shaved my chest hair but it would have to do. I clipped the transponder to my belt and Cassie ran the receiver lead up my back, leaving it disguised under my collar.

'Put it in your ear now in case there's someone in there watching you,' she said, straightening my shirt. 'I know we have to do this. I just wish there was another way.'

I switched on the transponder. 'Well, there isn't. So just keep watch, and remember he'll probably sneak out the back so be ready. I'll let you know when Kirzek rings me.'

She nodded, looking concerned.

'This is my show, Cass,' I said. 'You're not responsible for anything that happens. It's all me, okay?'

Finally she nodded, wished me luck and went back to the car. I walked out of the alley and crossed Lygon Street towards the souvlaki bar. Standing on the centre median strip, waiting to cross, I used the time to survey the interior of the store and its surrounds. A man with sweat stains under his arms and a white apron carved lamb off a rotisserie. About a dozen punters queued for souvlaki inside the store. Others lingered outside, eating, drinking, smoking. None looked familiar.

I crossed the street and entered the store. The smell of grilled lamb, garlic sauce and alcohol filled the hot air. I lingered in line for a moment, pretending to read the menu board while I scrutinised everyone in the store.

'No Kirzek,' I whispered into the chest mike.

'Received,' I heard Cassie reply. 'Nothing here either,' she added.

I sat at a bench by the window next to a couple of young bucks either winding up a long day on the piss or about to start a Sunday-night bender. They paused for a second while I arranged the laptop at my feet, then continued their discussion about a new nightclub on Chapel Street. I watched the street outside intently, looking around methodically. Predatory.

'A couple just turned out of the apartment foyer,' Cassie said. A moment later she added, 'All clear. It's not him.'

I tapped my chest twice to indicate I'd heard her. Minutes passed and nothing changed except the beating of my heart, which seemed so loud that I wondered if everyone in the shop could hear it. I checked my watch. Five past midnight. Where the hell was he?

Suddenly my phone rang. I scooped up the laptop, stepped out onto the sidewalk. 'I'm here. What now?'

'Go back in shop,' Kirzek ordered. 'Put laptop back on bench.'

I scanned the restaurants and bars for a familiar face but found nothing. I looked up at the second-storey terraces above the shops but still nothing. There was movement behind the curtain in one of the motel rooms down the street, but that could have been anything.

'All right, I'm going back in the shop,' I said, knowing Cassie would receive the message. 'I'll put the laptop under the window bench. Then what?'

'Buy souvlaki.'

'What?'

'Buy souvlaki and do not turn around.'

'Okay. I'll buy a souvlaki, but then —'

'Why do you repeat me?'

'Huh, I just wanted to make sure I had your instructions correct.'

'Don't fuck with me, Mr Rubens. I have your bitch wife, remember?'

'Okay, I'm in line. What now?'

'Nothing. Do not turn around. You stay in shop ten more minutes, then collect wife.'

The line went dead. I used the reflection in the glass of the bain-marie to watch the laptop. This was it. Rush point. When the queue cleared I stepped to the counter and ordered a lamb souvlaki.

'You want the king special?' the man asked.

'Huh?'

'The king special. Souvlaki with the lot.'

Suddenly Cassie's voice shrieked in my ear. 'Kirzek just scooped up the laptop. Red dress, blonde wig.'

Pushing away from the counter, I caught a glimpse of someone in a red dress fleeing across Lygon Street, heading away from the store. I waited a safe length of time then rushed outside, almost diving between the two young bucks finishing their souvlaki. Kirzek broke into a jog and disappeared down a side street.

'He's on the run,' I said into the mike. 'Where are you?'

'Outside the apartment building. Get back here. Forget about Kirzek.'

I sprinted across Lygon Street, through the playground, meeting Cassie outside the foyer to Ella's building.

'How do we get in?' she asked. 'It's all locked up. I've tried buzzing her apartment but she's not answering.'

I cupped a hand to my mouth, sick with fear and adrenaline.

'Don't start freaking,' Cassie said. 'It could mean anything. Remember the photo? He tied her up, so she probably can't get to the intercom.'

I looked at the glass entrance and thought about smashing the window but that wouldn't get us up the lift. There was only one way to get in, and it occurred to me that Kirzek must have somehow bluffed his way up to the apartment.

'There are four apartments on Ella's floor,' I said, typing in one of her neighbour's numbers.

Nobody answered, so I pressed again. Still nothing. I was about to try another number when a croaky voice rasped through the speaker.

'Yes, who is it?'

I opened my badge case and looked at the camera next to the speaker.

'This is the police, sir. We have an emergency and need you to buzz us up.'

I couldn't see the man or his reaction but guessed he was staring at me on the tiny black and white screen, half-asleep, trying to work out whether I was serious.

'I don't need access to your apartment,' I added. 'Just your floor.'

'Ah, I don't know about this,' the man said. 'Where's your uniform?'

'We're detectives, sir. There's a woman in the apartment next door to you who needs us. Please, let us in. We may also need an ambulance.'

'The woman next door? You mean Ella?'

'Yes, please let us in.'

The door clicked open and I heard the man tell us he would unlock the lift as we ran through the foyer. In the elevator, Cassie worked the slide on her gun and chambered a round.

'I don't have mine,' I said when she looked at me. 'Eckles took it.'

The elevator stopped and we eased out into the hall. I stayed behind Cassie as she took the corner with smooth and practised sweeps of her weapon. Halfway along the hall a door opened and an old man I figured was Ella's neighbour poked his head out. Cassie trained the weapon on him and the door closed immediately without the need for us to speak. Further down, Ella's apartment door was ajar.

'Take this,' Cassie whispered, handing me the gun. 'You know the layout.'

I nodded, took the Glock and stood in front of her. The entranceway light was off and so was the lounge room's. The bedrooms were separated by a bathroom and laundry, which we checked and found to be empty. I wasn't really expecting anyone else to be in the apartment, but my heart was pounding like a kick drum. Just the thought of Kirzek having been here was enough to make me sick.

Finally we came to the master bedroom, where Ella lay bound and gagged on the bed. Cassie rushed forward while I kept cover, the gun shaking in my hands.

'She's alive,' Cassie said as she removed the mouth gag.

'Oh sweet Jesus.'

Ella moaned and rolled her head from side to side. I put the gun down and tore the tape away from her ankles.

'It's okay, babe,' I said. 'I'm here. You're safe now.'

I said it over and over, hugging her like I never had before.

Tears poured out of me and I was unable to stop shaking. Cassie called for an ambulance. Somewhere in the relief and confusion I overheard her tell the dispatcher that Ella might have been drugged.

'We have to keep her in the recovery position,' Cassie said after ending the call. 'Roll her on her side with one arm back. Keep the airway open.'

I rolled Ella into position while Cassie went outside to call Eckles. I heard her arranging a search team to track down Kirzek. I sat on the bed, stroking Ella's face and waiting for what seemed like an eternity before Cassie led the medics into the room. I stood back as they went to work, checking her vitals.

'Is she gonna be okay?' I said, panicked.

'Not sure, sir. She has a low pulse and low blood pressure. We'll put her on a ventilator and take her into the Royal Melbourne.'

They injected her with something, then lifted her onto a stretcher and carried her out into the hall. Cassie said she'd meet me at the hospital and went back to the car. I insisted on climbing into the back of the ambulance and sat in a corner while they loaded Ella in.

'I think she'll be fine, sir,' one of the medics said as we raced towards the hospital. 'It's basically an overdose of some sort, but we got there early enough by the look of it.'

I nodded. Ella looked so vulnerable and yet also strangely at peace.

'Your colleague told me she's a nurse, right?' he said, nodding to Ella.

'Right.'

'Don't worry, she's one of our own, so she'll get the best we can offer.'

I found some comfort in this and thanked him, then went back to watching Ella. My relief quickly turned to furious anger. Kirzek would suffer for this. I'd make sure he felt the pain of everything he'd done.

When we pulled into the hospital, I followed the medics in and met Cassie by the triage desk.

'Both birds are in the air,' she said. 'Three German shepherds sniffing the backstreets and every single blue shirt on duty is on four wheels. They'll find him.'

'They have to,' I said angrily. 'We need to send a message, or every single shithead out there will think they can screw with a cop's family and get away with it.'

She nodded.

'There are two rules, Cass. Never fuck with the cops and never hurt a child. This guy broke both, and he needs to pay.'

Cassie looked over her shoulder nervously and I realised my voice had become shrill. People in the triage area were looking at me but I didn't care. I wanted to shout at everyone.

'So what do you want to do?' Cassie said.

'I want to find him.'

# 32

'I NEED A GUN,' I SAID AS we drove out of the hospital. 'Let's head back to my place. I've got one under my bed.'

My private gun was a Colt .45 that I sometimes used on the firing range. Although it was fully registered, I wasn't supposed to carry it around with me, but I didn't care about that.

Cassie turned the car onto Kings Way. She appeared to be considering my request.

'You don't want to get one from the watch-house?' she said.

'No. Eckles won't sign one out to me, so I need my own.'

'You're going to kill him, aren't you?' she said, edgy.

I didn't answer her.

'I can't talk you out of it?'

'Nope.'

'Shit.'

When we pulled up outside my building, I unclipped the microphone, earpiece and transponder and packed them into the glove compartment. Cassie waited in the car while I ran up the internal staircase. The sensor light outside my apartment lit up the hallway as I fumbled with the front door key. Inside,

I only had time to register that Prince wasn't there to greet me when a shadow floated in behind me and a blade pressed against my throat.

'Do not reach for gun,' Kirzek whispered in my ear. 'Put hands on chest.'

I gritted my teeth and did as he ordered, kicking myself for not expecting this. After giving the laptop back I'd assumed he'd go on the defence, disappear into the night. In hindsight, I should've realised Kirzek was not a man to run and leave unfinished business. Foolishly, I'd let my guard down and fallen into his trap.

'Filthy pig. Pity you come home so soon, huh?' said Kirzek. 'I figure you would eventually, but not so soon. I am still not caught yet. So what is the matter? Are you weak, McCauley?'

I could smell his body odour, feel his breath on the back of my neck.

'Perhaps if you had listened to me it could be okay,' he said.

'Hey, I did listen. I did everything you asked. I played by your rules.'

'Ah, you think I am stupid immigrant?'

'I never said that.'

'You don't have to. See, you think you are smarter than me. You think I have no brain. Let me tell you, I have been in police too. In Romania, I am police, like you, but we do things differently. Do you know what my expertise was?'

'No.'

'Torture,' he said, patting down my chest and waist, looking for a gun. 'And counter-surveillance. You didn't listen to me. I told you: no pigs.'

'I came alone for the swap. You saw me. I was on my own.'

'Then why are helicopters and filthy dogs out there looking for me?'

'That wasn't my fault. I kept you out of this until after the swap. That was the deal as far as –'

'Shut up, shut up! Just walk backwards, slowly.'

The blade pressed against my throat as Kirzek led me into the lounge. Glass lay on the floor and the curtain flapped against the balcony door. He must have scaled the outside of the building to break in. Not bad for a man his size. In the reflection of the television screen I saw that he'd changed into a dark T-shirt and pants. I also caught a glimpse of a bruise on his forehead and a tiny silver crucifix hanging from his left ear. As he pushed me into the sofa, I scanned the coffee table, searching for a pair of scissors, a steak knife, anything to defend myself with. But there was nothing.

'You don't have to do this,' I said. 'You turn me loose, maybe you'll get some leniency.'

He laughed. 'I don't want leniency.'

'What do you want?'

'I want you to scream,' he hissed, pressing the blade harder against my throat.

Instinctively, I spun away from it, scrambled around the coffee table then kicked it over as Kirzek lurched around the sofa. He stumbled at first then charged across the room towards me. I raced to the front door but stopped to avoid having my back to him. Swivelling, I ducked low as he swung the knife in a broad arc. It hit off-centre, slashing the side of my neck, and I was able to sidestep and run down the hall towards my bedroom. My knee crunched against the skirting board as Kirzek brought me down with a crash tackle.

'Now I will hear it,' he wheezed in my ear. 'You will scream like pig.'

My whole body felt like it was squashed in a vice and my knee throbbed in pain. Kirzek twisted my head and forced me to look him in the eye.

'I gave you plenty chance. Now look what happens,' he said, a smile spread across his meaty face.

'You're a filthy cockroach,' I snapped back. 'You won't be safe anywhere. Even in protective custody they'll make you eat your own shit.'

He chuckled, wiped at sweat on his forehead.

'You think I will go to prison? Let me tell you something, I will never go back. Never.'

'Right.'

'It is shame about your bitch wife, huh. Pity we not have more time. Pity for her. Maybe I spend some time with her after I finish here.'

'She's a grown woman, Kirzek. Don't you like them younger?'

A look of alarm passed over his face.

'We know what's on the laptop. We know about everything. The Holy Brethren's going down. No one walks away from this.'

Somewhere outside I heard Cassie yelling, but I couldn't focus on the words. I couldn't focus on anything any more. All I saw was the knife, smeared with my own blood, striking towards me, then three loud cracks splintered the blackness, jolting Kirzek like a fit. His eyes fixed to mine as the knife fell to the floor. I looked back up the hall and saw Cassie in silhouette, gun trained on Kirzek's body.

# 33

AS SOON AS I'D BEEN CLEANED up and had my neck stitched, I checked on Ella, who'd been treated and was under observation in an emergency department cubicle. After that, the questioning lasted three hours. Ben Eckles, Ian Gurt of ESD, Nik Stello, Cassie and I all squeezed into a tiny visitors room at the Royal Melbourne Hospital. I leant forward on my plastic chair and let out a long sigh. I was stiff and rigid and the stitches in my neck pulled tight every time I turned my head. The local anaesthetic had worn off and fatigue left me parched and moody.

'It's ironic,' Eckles said. 'We send out half the friggin' force looking for this prick, and he heads straight for your place. How'd he even know where you live?'

I had no idea. 'Maybe he rang your office and asked for an address,' I said, not wanting to talk any more.

Apparently Kirzek had used a rope to gain access to my balcony, three storeys above street level. I often didn't bother to lock those doors, assuming no burglar would ever attempt the climb. I was still amazed that a man his size could manage it.

Guess it wasn't all fat after all. I'd have to make up a story of some sort for Edgar so he didn't freak out on me.

'Is that it?' Cassie said to Gurt, who'd scribbled everything we said in his daybook.

The fact they'd allowed Cassie and me to be quizzed informally, and in the same room, indicated that they weren't interested in using the shooting against us. Just as well. We'd effectively captured and shot a suspected serial killer who'd evaded both the Homicide Squad and the Special Operations Group. To go after Cassie for the shooting would mean bringing about their own undoing for the foiled arrest.

'That's it for now,' Gurt said, closing his book. 'There'll be more to come though. We'll need it on record, from both of you.'

Stello stood, stretched his legs. 'Hope we can contain it, keep the media off it.'

'You will,' Cassie said. 'What's happening with the priest, by the way? Miles Jorgensen?'

'Ah, we're holding on to him,' said Stello, looking at Eckles, then back at me. 'Thanks for your help on that too. Kirzek's car was around the corner from your place. Had the laptop in it. It's a real doozy. We've got the techs on it as we speak. They've struck a list of what looks like coded phone numbers and email addresses. It'll probably take all night to break it, but from what they're saying it looks like the genuine article. A real spider web. Teachers, prison workers, clergymen, all sorts of fruitcakes.'

I nodded, relieved.

Cassie asked Gurt if they wanted to do the formal interview tonight or if it could wait.

'You're the shooter, Withers. We can knock it off now, then we can all go home. Or we can come back another time. It's up to you.'

'Do I get a rep?'

'Sure,' said Gurt. 'A Police Association rep has been contacted and is waiting at the Crime Department.'

'All right, just give us a minute,' she said.

I followed Cassie out of the room. Once we were out of earshot, I put a hand on her shoulder and squeezed it gently.

'You'll be fine. They're not gunning for you or else we would've been grilled in the furnace to start with. That was all about getting our stories straight, making sure what goes on the news is palatable. Like a rehearsal.'

'I know. What about you?'

'I'm good.'

'Sure?'

'Yeah, I just . . . I just wanted to thank you. I mean, when Kirzek had me on the floor . . .'

'It's okay,' Cassie said. 'You don't need to say it.'

'Yes, I do. You got there just in time, Cass. He had me down and if you hadn't shown up . . .'

Again I choked, and this time I gave up trying to say what we both already knew: that she'd saved my life.

'Thank you,' I said, hugging her gently. 'For Ella too.'

Cassie held my embrace. 'Wish me luck,' she said when she pulled away.

'You won't need it.'

I watched her follow the others down the hall. At the exit she looked back at me, like a child on the first day of school, and a terrible feeling that I'd never see her again washed over me. I contemplated going after them but knew I was being irrational. Instead I limped through to Ella's cubicle in the emergency room, favouring my sprained right knee. Ella was still asleep, but looked peaceful and calm, her face no longer as pale as when she'd been brought in.

A nurse was standing by the bed, writing notes on a clipboard.

'How's she doing?' I asked.

'Better,' she replied. 'Blood pressure and heart rate are both normal. She's breathing on her own and the saline drip's keeping her hydrated. But she'll be out of it for a few more hours, at least. Depends how long it takes to wear off.'

'It?'

'Tests aren't back yet, but we're thinking a benzodiazepine of some sort. Temazepam or something like it.'

I frowned in confusion. 'Sleeping tablets? Wasn't GHB?'

'What makes you say that?'

'Never mind.'

When the nurse was gone I sat down beside the bed and watched Ella sleep. Her chest rose and fell in a slow rhythm, arms laid at each side. *To get what you want, you have to know what you want.* I took one of her thin, pale hands and stroked it gently. One of her nails had snapped and it reminded me how fragile the human body was, how life could change in the blink of an eye. I touched the stitches on my neck and my hand traced its way down to the scar beneath my left collar where the bullet had torn into me a year before, leaving me lying in a hospital bed for three weeks. Then there were the emotional scars, the marriage separation and the effort we'd both made over the past twelve months to rebuild our relationship. In that moment I knew I would never go back to St Kilda.

'Wake up, baby,' I whispered, leaning over the bed and kissing her forehead. 'It's over. Let's go home.'

Over the next couple of hours, I wondered how men like Gervas Kirzek could exist without notice for so long, then suddenly unleash such brutal rage. I also thought about how the laptop housed details of the entire network of paedophiles known as The Holy Brethren. With any luck, the priest – Father Miles Jorgensen – would go down for something. With a little more luck, maybe they'd put him in the general prison population, see how he liked it.

'Excuse me,' said a nurse from behind me. 'I have a woman from DHS here to see you – Sarah Harrigan. She's at the front counter asking for you. Something about a file you requested.'

I was about to say I didn't want to see her when I realised she'd probably gone out of her way to get the information I'd asked for about Dallas Boyd. I made my way to the emergency room foyer where a woman in a khaki suit waited in one of the moulded plastic chairs.

'Detective McCauley,' she said, extending a hand. 'I was up early this morning, saw the news on television and decided to come straight over. Is everything okay?'

'I'm a tad banged up but I'll live,' I said, shaking her hand.

'I tried your mobile but it didn't answer,' she said, holding up a manila file. 'Figured I'd take the chance and drop this off on my way to work. Feel like a coffee?'

I stared at the file as if it could answer something for me.

'I don't know that there's anything left to discuss. If you watched the news, you would've seen that the guy responsible for Dallas Boyd's murder is dead.'

'That's not what I wanted to talk about,' she said, lowering her voice so the other people in the waiting room didn't hear. 'When I saw the news report on Stuart Parks, I couldn't believe it. That makes three of them.'

'Three what?'

'Three kids, all dead. I mean, they all grew up in foster care together, they were all incarcerated together, then within a few years all three of them are dead. It's a tragedy.'

I studied the sadness in her face. It was the same look I'd seen on Will Novak when he'd learnt Dallas Boyd was involved in the child sex trade. She believed in her mission the same way Novak believed in his.

'Okay, there's a cafeteria around the corner,' I said.

We small-talked about my injuries on the way to the cafeteria, but the whole time a question nagged me. It was something she'd said about all three kids being dead. Dallas Boyd, given a hot shot and left to die in the loading bay behind Café Vit. Justin Quinn, his throat slit in Talbot Reserve. And Sparks, stabbed to death outside the squat. Why was Dallas Boyd's murder so different from the others?

The hospital cafeteria smelt of coffee and frying bacon. The seating area was sprinkled with family members and visitors waiting for news of loved ones, and the odd patient who'd slipped out for an early breakfast or a cheeky cigarette.

'I pulled a lot of strings for this, detective,' Sarah said after we'd ordered and sat down. 'I made copies of everything we have on the three boys you asked about. It's all here.'

She opened the file, which contained three neat piles, each held in place by a bulldog clip. I fanned through the first few pages, trying to think of a polite way to tell her I didn't need them any more.

'Thank you,' I said finally. 'Hopefully I'll have a chance to go through it later today.'

'I hope so too, even if the killer is dead.'

She sipped her coffee and we both watched as an elderly lady on a walking frame hobbled through the cafeteria to a table in the back. I took a bite of my croissant and absently thumbed through pages of case notes, psychological assessments and progress reports, most of which I knew would be heavy on detail and overly repetitious. Halfway through the croissant, I recognised a name highlighted on the jacket of the folder that triggered a memory, a loose end.

'Derek Jardine,' I said, reading the name. 'He went to Queensland, didn't he?'

'That's right. After they all got out of Malmsbury, they lived at the CARS shelter for a short time then went their separate ways. Dallas Boyd moved into the flat, Stuart Parks lived the street life and Derek Jardine went to live on the Gold Coast. In the end I guess none of their choices mattered: they all led to the same place.'

And just then it hit me.

'You're saying Derek Jardine is dead as well?'

'Well, yeah.' She took the file back and opened it to a page of case notes. 'My last contact with Dallas Boyd was in November last year. He'd just come back from Queensland. Dallas went up to find Jardine and came back after he learnt he was dead. Needless to say he was distraught.'

284

'Right. How'd he die?'

'Bashed in a hotel room,' she said. 'No one was ever charged, but the police up there were thinking it might've been a client.'

'A client?' I said, blinking away fatigue. 'Was he hooking?'

'Not just hooking,' she said, lowering her voice. 'He was *deep* into the skin trade. That's probably why he went to live on the Gold Coast. It's sin city up there.'

I sipped my coffee, thinking.

'Between you and me,' Sarah added, flipping through the file, 'I wasn't that surprised when I heard he was dead. Derek was always a bit wild. He used to rip off clients, beat them up and take their money. That was his scam. Of course, I doubt many of his victims ever reported it to the police. If they did, they probably made something up.'

Nodding, I wondered whether Derek Jardine's murder might have been connected to Dallas Boyd's and the others in St Kilda. It seemed unlikely, given the time difference, the varying circumstances and the distance between locations. But there was one thing it might explain: Dallas Boyd's motive. First his friend was bashed to death in a hotel room, possibly by a paedophile client, then his little sister was infected with chlamydia by the stepfather. It just might've been enough to make him turn against them. Like a blind man with a cane, I could sense the path ahead even though I couldn't see it. I packed up the file, thanked her and asked if I could hold on to it.

'Sure, just don't burn me on this.'

'You have my word, I won't. Thank you.'

Walking with her to the door, I asked for an update on Rachel Boyd.

'See, now you're asking about an active case,' she said. 'A *live* one, which I can't go into.'

'Have you seen the place they live in?' I replied, following her outside. 'It's a disgrace. They shouldn't even be allowed to keep her there.'

'You're entitled to your opinion, but like I said, I can't talk about it.'

'Well, if you want my opinion, she needs to be removed from there. Her stepfather's a genuine scumbag. Surely you know about the chlamydia?'

She stopped and stared at the traffic whizzing by on Royal Parade, unsure how far to commit.

'Come on,' I said. 'We're both on the same side, right?'

'Of course we are, but it's complicated. Leaving kids in an abusive environment isn't right, but shunting them in and out of foster care doesn't help either. Children need security and routine as much as they need safety.'

I shook my head, unconvinced.

'All I can tell you is that wheels are in motion and a decision on Rachel's welfare will be made soon,' she said.

'Better not wait too long or she'll end up in this file too,' I said.

'Look, I know what you think, that we should just march in there and take her away, but removing a child from their legal guardian isn't always the best solution.'

'What is the best solution? Waiting until they're hooked on drugs or infected with HIV? Jesus, you should read the coroner's report on Dallas Boyd, count how many broken bones he suffered at the hands of his so-called guardian. Seriously, at what point do we say enough is enough?'

Sarah let out a long sigh, as though she was tired of having the debate.

'It depends what research you accept,' she said. 'If you accept the research that the government accepts, then you take the view that children are best off remaining with their family unless they're in immediate physical danger. Removing a child from the family home, however dysfunctional the household might be, causes undue stress on all members of the family, including the child, and should be the absolute last resort.'

'Sounds like some rehearsed bureau-speak straight out of a manual,' I said.

'It is,' she said, deadpan.

'And you believe that shit?'

'Detective, I've been doing this for over ten years now. Quite frankly, I don't know what to believe any more.'

We stopped at a government sedan parked outside the hospital. Two crates were on the back seat, full of files just like the one I was carrying.

'I'm sorry, I know it's not your call,' I said. 'Just keep me in the loop as much as you can.'

'I will,' she said, opening the door and getting in the car. 'I'll call you as soon as I can let you know what the plan is. That's the best I can do.'

I spent the next hour in Ella's cubicle reading the file cover to cover. Between the three boys I counted over ninety separate reports from police, Juvenile Justice, Child Protection, hospitals, drug and alcohol workers and psychologists. Each was a depressingly dismal story of neglect, rebellion and child abuse. Parents like Dallas Boyd's were the norm and I again wondered why it took so long before the system intervened. Why did a child's life have to be in immediate physical danger before somebody stepped in?

As I packed the file into my briefcase, I noticed the mug shot and intel report on Sparks had slipped out of the side pocket. Still clipped to the back of the report was the call charge record on Dallas Boyd's mobile phone that I'd yet to examine. The CCR provided a basic list of phone numbers for all the calls made to and from Boyd's mobile in the hours either side of his murder. There were nine in total, the last being at 12.17 a.m., not long after he was dead. I cast my eyes over the list of numbers and noted that six of the calls were from the same number, five before midnight and the final one after the murder. Flipping back to the intel report, I confirmed that the number belonged to Sparks, which tallied with his report of trying to contact Boyd several times after he'd failed to show up at the rendezvous.

The remaining three calls were from another number, the most recent at 11.25 p.m. By this stage, Boyd would've left Tammy and Fletch at McDonald's and headed off to meet Sparks to exchange the laptop. Just then it occurred to me that the timeline didn't quite gel. McDonald's was less than a hundred metres from Luna Park where Boyd and Sparks were to meet at *midnight*. So why did Boyd leave Tammy and Fletch so early, given it would've only taken him a few minutes to walk to Luna Park?

Maybe he planned to meet somebody en route, possibly a rock spider, perhaps make a quick sale. Or maybe he had another partner involved in the scam, somebody he needed to see before he met Sparks. Whatever the reason, there was one thing I was sure of: not long after receiving that last phone call he was murdered. Remembering Dr Wong's belief that Boyd had shared a beer with his killer in the hour prior to his death, it seemed plausible that whoever this number belonged to had at least some involvement in the murder.

I stared at the number, reciting the combination in my mind, and suddenly a jolt of recognition sparked in me.

'Son of a bitch,' I said, fumbling with my wallet.

I found the business card I was looking for and my heart started pounding. The numbers matched.

# 34

ELLA STIRRED A LITTLE when I kissed her goodbye, but the nurse had assured me she wouldn't wake properly for another few hours. Much as I wanted to be there when she did, I couldn't ignore what was now in my possession. The system had failed Dallas Boyd, and so had we – the police. I couldn't allow that to happen again.

I took a taxi home. Once inside, I opened my briefcase again, took out my daybook and located the DVD I'd copied from the 7-Eleven security camera. I put the disk in the player, sat back on the couch and opened my daybook, reviewing my case notes. According to my timeline, Dallas Boyd had been in the 7-Eleven with Tammy York at about 10 p.m. That I could confirm. From there they had hung around McDonald's for around an hour, before Boyd had left to meet Sparks and en route had met up with his killer, whom I now suspected had called him and arranged to meet.

My thoughts kept circling back to Dallas Boyd's mobile phone, a phone that had yet to surface, most likely because the killer had removed it from him. But why? The only logical explanation was that the killer had been worried about the calls made to and from Boyd's phone raising the suspicion of the investigators. Were it not for Boyd purchasing the recharge card and having the receipt in his wallet at the time of death, I probably never would've regarded the missing phone as a potential lead. This led me to believe the killer didn't know about the receipt or else they would have removed that also, which in effect ruled out Tammy York and Fletch as suspects, since they were with Dallas when he bought the recharge card.

I flipped through my daybook until I found the notes I'd made while questioning Tammy. She couldn't remember the exact type of phone Boyd had, but she'd described the ringtone as annoying. I ran my finger down the page and located the notation *Hi Ho Silver ringtone*.

I turned on the DVD player and let the security footage play. When I'd watched the disk in the store, the sound on the computer had been muted. At the time sound hadn't seemed necessary, but something about what I'd seen on the tape didn't add up. If what I was now thinking was true, I'd made possibly the biggest oversight in my career as a detective, one I wasn't sure I'd recover from.

I turned up the volume and immediately the traffic on Fitzroy Street and the echoing sound of the convenience store filled my lounge room. I skipped past Dallas Boyd and Tammy York entering the store, knowing what I wanted was further on. I watched the clock on screen tick quickly over and let it play until just after midnight, when Will Novak entered the store to purchase the cigarettes he'd told me about.

I leant forward on the couch as Novak walked through the doors and approached the counter. Just as the clock on the screen read 12.17 a.m., the exact time Sparks had called Dallas Boyd to ask where he was, a phone started ringing. Novak took a mobile out of his shirt pocket, pressed a button and the ringing stopped.

'You bastard,' I said.

My hands trembled as I burnt a copy of the DVD, retrieved the Colt .45 from under my bed, then gathered up the documents I needed and headed down to the car park. By the time I arrived at the Carlisle Accommodation & Recovery Service, it was just on 9 a.m. and my eyes were stinging with fatigue as the painkillers the nurses had given me wore off.

I parked across the road and hobbled towards the hostel's porch, noticing the blue glow of a computer screen through the last window on the left. Will Novak's office. The front door creaked as I entered the foyer. A young girl sat behind the reception desk.

'Will in?' I asked.

'Yeah, sure,' said the girl, picking up the phone. 'Your name, please?'

Holding open my badge case, I said there was no need to call him. Before she could protest, I made my way down the hall. Novak's door was half-open, as if to invite entry, but I still knocked.

He swivelled on his chair. 'Jesus,' he said, eyes widening at the sight of me. Then, nodding to his computer, he added, 'I've just been reading the news reports online. You okay? How's Ella?'

'She's still under, but she'll be fine.'

'Thank God.'

The headline COP TANGLED IN SPIDER WEB spread across the top of the screen, an article underneath.

'Didn't realise it was in the news so soon.'

'That's the internet for you,' said Novak, gesturing to a chair by his desk. 'Come in, please. Sit down.'

I eased into the chair.

'You want a coffee?' he asked.

'No, I just wanted to stop by and let you know how it all panned out, like I said I would. That was the deal.'

'Yes, of course. Thank you.'

I read from my daybook even though I knew it all ad lib.

'As you've probably read in the press, a man named Gervas

Kirzek was shot and killed early this morning by one of our members. Off the record, we believe Kirzek was responsible for at least two of the recent murders.'

'Two?'

'We think he killed Justin Quinn in the Talbot Reserve and Stuart Parks outside the squat behind Acland Street. As to why he killed them, my view is that he learnt they were all involved in a scam to blackmail him.'

'Blackmail?'

I gave him a quick rundown on how Dallas had hired Sparks to burgle the house and steal the laptop.

'I think he also hired Justin Quinn to star in a porn movie so they could use it as leverage,' I said. 'That's why Justin had to go. Same with Tammy York, only she got lucky and Fletch came to her rescue just as Kirzek was about to kill her.'

Novak nodded thoughtfully. 'So Kirzek was the guy who attacked her, the rich prick she told us about?'

'Looks that way.'

'But hang on,' Novak said, 'Tammy said Dallas wasn't into making porn, just selling it.'

'She said he didn't do kiddie porn. What he did do was . . . I don't know, in the middle somewhere, I suppose.'

Novak looked confused.

'Anyway, as for Sparks, well, somehow Kirzek must've known he was either helping me with the case or in on the scam,' I said. 'I didn't recognise him at the time, but I saw Kirzek outside the squat before the killing, dressed like a trannie. He was staking it out, waiting for Sparks.'

'So anyone connected with the scam had to go?' Novak said.

'Basically, yes.'

'Including Dallas Boyd?'

I flipped to the back of my daybook, removed one of the documents I'd pulled from the DHS file Sarah Harrigan had given me and slid it across the desk.

'Actually, I don't think Kirzek killed him,' I said. 'This is a post-release report on Dallas Boyd, dated the year before last, just after he was released from Malmsbury. The clinician's name is at the bottom – you recognise it?'

Novak frowned. 'Where did you get this?'

'Doesn't matter where I got it. Do you recognise the name of the clinician who wrote the report?'

'Yes. Josh Graham. He used to work here. Left about six months ago.'

'Now works for the Back Outside program, correct?'

'Ah, I don't . . . what are you getting at? We have a lot of links with Back Outside. We receive at least half of our clients through that program.'

'I know. Can you read the text I've highlighted?'

> . . . *while the client's substance abuse issues appear to have stabilised, his current involvement in the sex industry, particularly in and around the St Kilda environs, gives rise for concern. This is especially concerning given the link between sex work, physical abuse and substance misuse* . . .

Novak folded the page in half, looked up.

'You told me you had no idea he was in the sex game,' I said.

'That's right, I didn't.'

'But this report says otherwise.'

'I didn't write that report. Josh Graham did.'

'Come on, Will. You're the boss here. Don't tell me these reports don't cross your desk.'

Novak opened the page again and stared at the text, as if it were a cue card prompting an answer.

'I see hundreds of these reports every month. I have to skim through the details.'

'Dallas Boyd was a star client here, a success story,' I countered. 'You said yourself, it's not every day you get kids like him come along. Surely you would've noticed a report raising concerns about your star client working the sex game.'

'What are you implying? I'm not sure I like the tone of these questions.'

'You lied to me, Will. In my experience there are only two reasons why people lie to police. They're either scared or they're involved.'

'I completely resent that. I've been nothing but open and frank with you. Any other worker would have made you jump through a whole bunch of legal hoops before they even agreed to open the door. But not me, I gave you full cooperation. Jesus, I even gave you keys to Dallas Boyd's apartment. Did you actually have a warrant before you looked through it?'

I didn't answer.

'I got you addresses. I even went with you to visit –'

Novak was cut off by the phone ringing on his desk. At first he ignored it then snatched it up, turning away to face the window and speaking in a low voice. Outside, Tammy York and Fletch walked through the gate and approached the front porch, stopping halfway up the path to speak to another client. I wondered what they were doing here and got my answer when Fletch shook hands and exchanged something with the other client.

Novak put down the phone, swivelled back around on his chair. 'That was our sister agency in Footscray,' he said. 'We've got a kid holed up in his room threatening to slash up, off his face on meth. A Critical Assessment Team's on the way. Who knows if they'll get there in time.'

I waited.

'Meanwhile, three kids from our detox unit over there have decided to go AWOL and two clinicians have called in sick,' he continued. 'As you can see, it's a typical Monday morning and I've got all the time in the world.'

'Want to hear the rest or not?'

'Sure. I like being accused of impropriety, especially by someone I've bent over backwards for.'

From my daybook I produced a list I'd pulled from within the files Sarah Harrigan had given me. It comprised almost fifty names, one of which I'd highlighted.

'Justin Quinn,' I said, putting the page on the desk in front of him. 'You said you didn't know him.'

'I don't.'

'Then why is his name on this list?'

Novak snatched up the page and read over it.

'That's your current client list,' I explained. 'Says right there that Justin Quinn had his first assessment last week, referred to CARS by Back Outside. So why did you tell me you didn't know him?'

'This is a total breach of privacy,' Novak blurted. 'These kids deserve more respect. Did Sarah Harrigan give you this?'

'Like I said, it doesn't matter who gave it to me. Just answer my question about –'

I stopped talking as the receptionist appeared in the doorway, a worried look across her face.

'Is everything okay in here?' she asked.

'Everything's fine,' Novak said. 'The officer was just leaving.'

'I'm not going anywhere,' I said firmly.

The girl stood awkwardly in the doorway before finally getting the hint and scurrying back to her desk in the foyer.

'You still haven't answered my question about Justin Quinn,' I said when she was gone. 'When we drove past the murder scene, you said you didn't know him. By itself that little fib means nothing, except that Justin happened to be the second client of yours who was murdered in a week, something you obviously didn't think was worth sharing with me.'

'Justin was only recently referred to us,' Novak said in a cool voice, rocking back in his chair. 'So at the time of his death I didn't realise he was a client of ours. It wasn't a lie.'

I realised then Novak wasn't going to crack that easily. I would have to take him all the way to the edge. I removed the 7-Eleven DVD from my briefcase and handed it across the desk.

'Put this in your computer,' I said. 'Mute the volume and let it play.'

'What the fuck is this? Kiddie porn? I don't wanna see that shit.'

'Just play it. It's not porn, but it is something you need to explain.'

Guardedly, Novak slid the disk into the PC and soon the inside of the 7-Eleven appeared on the screen. We both watched in silence as a series of customers walked in and out of the store. I watched Novak's eyes as they dropped to the clock in the corner of the screen.

'You told me you purchased cigarettes at around midnight the night Dallas Boyd was killed,' I said.

'Like I told you, I was manning the soup kitchen. I always give smokes to the clients. Stops the need for begging. You know how many homeless people get bashed for trying to bum a smoke?'

'I don't care about the smokes, Will. I care about all the lies I keep uncovering. When I first spoke to you, you told me you hadn't seen or spoken to Dallas for a couple of days, right?'

'That's right. We had lunch and spent the time planning a way to get his sister out of the flat. What's the problem with that?'

I nodded to the screen. 'Just watch.'

We turned back to the PC as a grainy image of Novak appeared on the screen. The clock counter read 12.17 a.m.

'There!' Novak said, watching himself approach the counter. 'Just after midnight. Exactly like I told you.'

He went to eject the disk but I told him to let it play.

'Will, I want you to explain something to me.'

'What's there to explain? I bought the bloody smokes and left.'

'No, you didn't. So rewind it, and let it play again. This time with the sound up.'

Tiny beads of sweat dotted Novak's forehead. Finally he clicked the sound icon and turned the volume up. The small speakers on his desk vibrated with distortion as the disk played again.

'Happy now?'

As Novak approached the counter on screen, Dallas Boyd's mobile phone started ringing through the speakers. Novak could be seen removing the phone from his pocket to cancel the call. But it wasn't fast enough. I watched his face pale now as the tune to 'Hi Ho Silver' sounded through the office. It was loud and high-pitched. The kids outside seemed to look towards the window and for a second I wondered if they could hear it ringing.

'This is a call charge record for Dallas Boyd's phone from the night he died,' I said, placing the CCR on the desk. 'It tells me that Sparks tried to call Dallas at exactly 12.17 a.m. The call was cancelled, but it still showed up on this report because Sparks left a message through the phone company's missed call service.'

Running my finger down the list, I pointed out the recurring number I knew belonged to Novak and which confirmed he'd lied to me about the last time he'd spoken to Dallas Boyd.

'Sparks and Dallas were supposed to meet at midnight to exchange the laptop, but Dallas never showed up because he was dead by then,' I continued. 'The killer took his phone, most likely because he was worried about us checking it and linking him to these three calls.'

When Novak didn't respond, I leant forward and said, 'That's Dallas Boyd's phone right there on the screen. I can tell because of the ringtone. "Hi Ho Silver".'

Novak got out of his chair and moved away from his desk until he was against the window. His eyes darted about the room and I knew it was true. As he backed along the window to the east wall, his arm disappeared behind a filing cabinet. By the time I realised what was happening and went to draw my own weapon, it was too late. When his arm came back in sight, he was pointing a handgun directly at me.

# 35

'DON'T MAKE THIS ANY WORSE than it has to be,' I said. 'We don't want it to turn into a situ–'

'Just shut up!' Novak snapped. 'There is no "we" here. We're not a team. We're not the same, never have been. You're a cop and I'm a social worker, get it?'

'You're wrong, Will. We *are* the same. We've got different angles, but we work the same streets. We both want the same things.'

'Oh, get your hand off it. Cheap psychology tricks won't work on me,' he sneered, the gun waving fiercely, his eyes wild with emotion.

My instinct was to bolt through the door behind me and draw my weapon, but I didn't want to frighten him with any sudden moves. Over his shoulder, I saw Tammy and Fletch still outside under the tree looking in our direction. I hoped they could see what was going on.

'Put your gun on the floor and kick it over to me,' he ordered. 'Then empty your pockets. Get everything out!'

I put my gun on the floor and kicked it over.

'Now give me your second gun,' he said, scooping up the Colt and stuffing it into his waist. 'Your spare, give it to me.'

'I don't have a second gun.'

'Bullshit! You're lying. You're a cop. You always lie.' Novak braced one trembling hand with the other then crossed the room and locked the office door. 'Get down on your knees and put your hands behind your head.'

I had a sudden terrible image of the gun going off and the bullet tearing again into my shoulder, just as it had done over twelve months ago.

'You can't get away with this, Will,' I said. 'There are kids outside. The receptionist knows I'm in here.'

'I don't care! Just get on your knees, now!'

I sank to the floor, hands shaking.

'Let's talk about this, Will. It doesn't have to end like this.'

'Stop using my first name! We're no longer on a first-name basis.'

My impression was that Novak didn't *want* to shoot me, but he seemed unhinged, unstable, and I'd end up just as dead whether I was killed intentionally or by accident.

Keeping his gun trained on me, he snatched the DVD out of the tray and fed it into a shredder next to his desk. The machine screamed in protest, but chewed up the DVD nonetheless. He then gathered up the documents I'd shown him and fed them into the machine as well.

'Are there copies?' he snarled.

I shook my head.

'I don't believe you!' He pressed the gun hard into the top of my head. 'On the floor, lie forward and put your hands behind your back.'

When I didn't move, he smashed me over the head with the butt of the gun. Carpet grazed my face as I fell forward, the pain in my head excruciating. My vision blurred as I struggled to find a way to save myself. Novak paced the office, opening and closing drawers, tossing items around on the desk, muttering to himself. It seemed he was yet to formulate a plan of action, though I suspected he was looking for something to tie me up with. My only hope was to play on his frustration and uncertainty, keep him talking while I figured out a plan of my own.

'You knew about the scam, didn't you?' I said.

No response.

'That's why you called Dallas on the night he died. You knew he had the laptop and was planning to blackmail The Holy Brethren. Did you try and talk him out of it?'

'The Holy Brethren?' he repeated. 'Never heard of them.'

'Sure you haven't. What about all those referrals you get from Back Outside, all that money you get by being in bed with them?'

He located something in a drawer and then slammed it shut.

'I know about the priest, Miles Jorgensen,' I said. 'He used to run Breaking the Wall until it got exposed by the Feds in Operation Locust. So he packed his bags, changed the program name to Back Outside and moved to Melbourne. Tell me, how'd you secure such a sweet funding deal with him? You have the minister in your pocket, maybe a member of The Holy Brethren in the health department?'

Novak gripped my left arm and yanked it back. 'If you try to fight me, I won't shoot you,' he said. 'Instead, I'll tear out every last stitch in your neck. Got it, partner?'

I almost vomited with the pain as he pinched my neck wound hard. I lay limp on the floor, taking long breaths until the nausea passed. He took advantage of my helplessness to tie my wrists together with string.

'What happened, Will?' I wheezed. 'Did Dallas tell you he wanted to run a scam on them and you freaked because so much of your funding here depends on them? Did he want your help to do it? Is that why you did it?'

The shredder whined and groaned as Novak filled it with documents from a box under his desk. Blinking away sweat, I noticed the box was an old beer carton, the label *Amstel* on the side.

'I have to admit, you're slick,' I said. 'You fooled me; fooled everyone. You knew Dallas was involved in the sex game. I bet he even told you he was selling porn for Kirzek. That's why you chose to dump the body at the café, isn't it? It was a safeguard in case us cops realised it wasn't an overdose. You knew if we worked out it wasn't an OD, we'd eventually look at the owner of the café.'

'That's it, just keep talking,' he said. 'Get it all out. No one else is going to hear it anyway.'

I used my right leg to push a few inches along the carpet until I was able to peer up out of the window. No one was out there. I briefly contemplated screaming for help, but it was too risky. Novak might panic and shoot me or one of the staff. Or we might end up in a full-blown hostage situation. Better to keep him distracted.

'I know how it went down,' I said. 'You rang Dallas on the night to arrange a meeting, didn't you? I'll bet you told him you'd help him, maybe over a beer or two. What he didn't know, of course, was that good old Uncle Will had no intention of helping him and that you'd dosed the beer with GHB. I wouldn't have picked you for a Dutch beer man, though. Amstel, a nice drop. Thought you'd be more the VB type.'

Novak pulled a file from the cabinet, the name 'Jardine' written in the top corner, and fed its contents through the shredder. I gritted my teeth, knowing vital evidence was being destroyed.

'What happened next, Will? After you did the deed, you raced up to the soup kitchen and started work, knowing everyone there would vouch for you and no one would remember exactly what time you arrived. That how it went?'

Novak seemed almost frenzied now. He had both guns tucked down his pants and kept feeding more papers into the machine.

'But that wasn't good enough, was it? No, you wanted a fool-proof alibi, so you bought a pack of smokes and got yourself on camera, just in case you needed to prove you were somewhere else at the time of death. Just brilliant, Will. Fucking perfect.'

He ignored me, raced back to his desk and punched a series of commands into his keyboard, no doubt to erase any incriminating electronic documents he had stored.

'Don't you think it's ironic? It was the 7-Eleven alibi that nailed you. You hung on to Dallas's phone because you wanted to get rid of it, because you were worried it would come back to haunt you, and guess what . . . it has.'

When he started emptying another filing cabinet, I noticed the top buttons of his shirt had come loose. Underneath I could see he wore a silver necklace with a tiny silver crucifix attached to it.

'You slimy bastard,' I sneered. 'You're not just in bed with The Holy Brethren. You're one of them.'

'Say what you like, McCauley. It's all just theory. When all's said and done, who do you think they're going to believe – me or some fruitcake from Romania, who you guys touted as the next big paedophile? What did you call him again – Mr Fatty?' He came around the desk and stood over me. 'I really like that name. Did *you* make that one up?'

I ignored the jibe.

'Gervas Kirzek killed Dallas just like he did the others,' Novak went on. 'That's the way it'll play out once I'm done. No one's going to believe you, McCauley. You're just as washed up as Kirzek, only you're too stupid to realise it. I know you're on leave. All I had to do was ring your boss and he just told me. So I knew all along you weren't on the team. Don't you get it, I exploited that. I exploited *you*. And you thought I was trying to help. Who do you think gave Kirzek your address?' He squatted down next to me. 'How's the rehab coming along, Ruby? Still swimming every week?'

Anger clouded my thoughts. The son of a bitch had betrayed me.

'I suppose you gave up Sparks as well?' I said. 'Where's the client care in that, Will?'

302

'The greater good, McCauley. You know how it is. Speaking of which, who do you think gave him Ella?'

'You motherfucker!' I roared, a surge of rage bursting through me. Novak looked pleased. This was exactly what he wanted. Somehow I had to ignore the agitation, not let it affect my judgement. Somehow I had to turn the tables.

'You know what I don't get,' I said. 'How you can look yourself in the mirror and pretend you're actually helping these kids.'

'We are helping them.'

'What, by putting them in porn movies, getting them to fuck each other so you sickos can jerk off over it? You're no better than scrotes like Vincent Rowe. You're just better at hiding what you do.'

'I *was* helping them!' Novak said. 'Those kids come in here more fucked up than you could ever imagine. They're hooked on all sorts of drugs, living on the streets with absolutely nothing. But we turn their lives around. We buy them clothes, find them a place to live and we have a sixty per cent success rate at getting them off drugs. Jesus, some of them even get jobs or go back to school. Who else does that? Nobody has a track record like ours.'

'And after everything you'd worked for, Dallas was going to bring it all down,' I said, finally realising why he'd done it. 'You couldn't let that happen, so you killed him. Just like that, huh?'

Novak pushed my face into the carpet, opening the wound in my neck even further. 'Don't you get it?' he hissed. 'I didn't *want* to do it, but I had no choice. Dallas knew I was in business with them. He knew CARS depended on them, but he wanted to bring them down anyway. I tried to talk him out of it, but he wouldn't listen. He said either I could jump on board or go down with them.'

'Them?' I said. 'You mean The Holy Brethren?'

'Yes!' Novak snapped, tearing off his necklace and throwing it across the room. 'When the laptop went missing I told them I'd get it back and talk Dallas out of whatever he had planned.

303

But he wouldn't budge. He wouldn't even tell me who had the bloody thing. That's when I knew *I* had to do it.'

I looked up gingerly and saw a broken and beaten man.

'Because if *you* didn't do it, someone else would've?' I said.

Novak sniffed and his lower lip trembled. 'They would've sent Gervas Kirzek to do it and he would've cut him up like he did Sparks and Justin Quinn. I couldn't let that happen. I just couldn't.'

'So you made sure he went peacefully?' I prodded.

'Yes! There was no way I was going to let Kirzek near him. He's a fucking monster.'

'You're all monsters, Will. Dallas trusted you and chose to tell you about the scam, but you betrayed him and killed him anyway. What makes you so bloody different?'

Suddenly Novak began to cry. I tried to wriggle my hands free but they were bound tight.

'Because I loved him, you know?' he spluttered. 'I really *loved* him.'

I closed my eyes, wincing at his use of the word.

'I know what you're thinking,' he said, wiping his face. 'But you're wrong. Years ago society didn't accept that a man could love another man. Homosexuality was shunned as immoral and wrong, but now everyone's starting to accept it. Some day it will be the same for us and you people will see that we're no different. There's nothing wrong with us. Nothing wrong with what we do.'

'*Nothing wrong?* You can't be serious.'

'I know you don't understand,' he said, leaning over me, 'but let me tell you something. There's nothing more beautiful and pure than to be in love with a child.'

It was a line I'd heard before and it sickened me. I wanted to tell him that he had no right comparing what he did to consenting homosexual adults. I also wanted to ask how he figured a young child was supposed to understand the real meaning of love when many adults couldn't. But it wouldn't change a damned thing. Instead I just waited while he stood up, an emotional wreck. This was the end. He was either going to shoot me or kill himself. Or both.

'You're going to let me go, McCauley,' he said slowly. 'You let me walk out of here and we all live happily ever after. Kirzek killed Dallas and I get to keep helping the kids. That's the way it's gonna work.'

'I can't do that, Will. It's over.'

'Then we both die,' he said quietly, pulling one of the guns from his waistband and pressing the muzzle hard against my head. 'You first, then me. We go together, the cop and the social worker, on opposite sides of the street but heading in the same direction. Isn't that how it goes?'

'You don't need to do this,' I pleaded, my words muffled against the carpet. 'You did it to protect Dallas from Kirzek because you loved him. The courts will understand that.'

'Nice try,' he snorted. 'See you on the other side.'

I used every bit of strength and adrenaline to break free. Then, suddenly, the window exploded with a loud crash, glass spraying over us, a chair landing beside me. Another chair flew through the window, smashing against the wall, then somebody jumped through the broken pane.

Rolling over, I saw Fletch leap across the desk. As Novak raised his gun to fire, I kicked his ankles, throwing him off balance. Fletch dived on top of him and they wrestled on the floor, Fletch punching Novak and grappling for the gun.

I clambered to my feet, pressed my back against the door and unlocked it. Novak scrambled across the floor after the gun and I kicked out at him but the kick didn't stop him. He grabbed the gun and swung it towards me just as the door burst open and Tammy York charged in.

'You sick bastard,' she screamed. 'It was you! We heard you talking through the –' The gun went off, the bullet clipping her left arm and catapulting her body backwards. Her shriek filled the room.

Fletch hurled himself at Novak and the gun went sliding

across the carpet. Novak swung his elbow, catching Fletch across the jaw, before making another grab for the gun. I leapt into the air, bringing my good knee down on the back of Novak's neck. There was a loud crunch and I fell sideways. Fletch raced over and kicked Novak in the face, knocking him out.

'Shit, look at your neck, man,' he said to me. 'You're hit.'

I looked down. My wound had split completely and blood covered my shirt, but I couldn't feel any pain. Adrenaline.

'I'm okay, just cut me loose,' I said.

Fletch found a pair of scissors and cut the string, which I then used to bind Novak's wrists. A groan sounded from Tammy – she was crumpled on the floor, blood running from her arm. Fletch staggered towards her as several residents and staff appeared at the door. Panicked screams began to sound from the hallway and I heard the receptionist yelling for an ambulance.

I stumbled outside and slumped on the front porch, waiting for the circus to arrive.

# 36

BY LUNCHTIME I WAS BACK in hospital, the Alfred this time. Tammy York had been lucky; the bullet had only clipped her arm. They didn't even need to put her into surgery; simply stitched and bandaged the wound, then pumped her full of painkillers and antibiotics.

'So this is round two?' Ella's friend Jenny said as she restitched my neck wound. She'd jabbed me with a hit of local anaesthetic so the whole area was numb, but I could feel her pulling and tugging. 'Stuff like this happens in threes, you know?' she added.

'Then we might as well just leave them undone,' I said, trying to joke with her but wincing at the same time. 'How many more stitches are there?'

'This is the last one. Have you heard from Ella?'

'I saw her this morning,' I said, knowing they were all probably blaming me for her being in hospital.

It was no secret that Ella wanted me to transfer out of detective duties and many of her colleagues and friends agreed with her. Some of them were in the same boat, also having boyfriends or husbands in high-risk jobs. Knowing Ella had suffered because of my work would only cement their views.

'I'm going to quit,' I said as she snipped off the last stitch. 'I've made a decision. I'll tell Ella as soon as she's out.'

'Really?' Jenny said. 'My hubby says that after every bush-fire. He'll probably say it this time too. Never makes any difference.'

'Well, this *is* different. *I'm* different.'

'Okay,' she said, wiping down my neck with something. 'Just tell her I said hi, will you?'

'Sure.'

On my way out of the emergency department I stopped by Tammy York's cubicle, where Fletch was waiting with her.

'Sarge,' he said when I opened the curtain. 'How's the neck?'

'Bit stiff. I'll be right though. How's she doing?'

'Not bad, by the look of her,' he said, a cheeky grin on his face. 'She looks pretty happy to me, all that pethidine they got her on. I tried to get 'em to give me some, but they wouldn't cop it.'

Tammy opened her eyes halfway and her lips stretched to a smirk. 'Hey there,' she drawled. 'Can't believe I got shot.'

'You're very lucky,' I said, nodding at her bandaged arm. 'Could've been a lot worse, but they say you'll be fine. You should be able to go home tomorrow.'

'I don't think she wants to go home at all,' Fletch said, tapping the drip stand next to her. 'Not with all the good gear they've got her on. It's like a free ride, hey babe?'

I tried to think of something polite to say but couldn't.

'So what's gonna happen to Will?' Tammy asked as I was about to say goodbye. 'He's gonna go down, right?'

'Depends if he makes a confession,' I said. 'He's with the Homicide Squad now and they're usually pretty good at talking you into a confession. So we'll see.'

'And what about The Holy Brethren?'

'Well, that depends on how much cooperation Will is prepared to give, but the laptop should go a long way towards ensuring we get a good result.'

Tammy's hand slid out of the sheets and Fletch took it. 'Least it wasn't all for nothin',' he said to her. Then, looking at me, he added, 'Dall tried to do the right thing and he died for it. So did Sparks and Jussie. Fuck, maybe even Derek. But at least if some of them go down, then Dall would've been happy.'

'What do you mean?' I said in disbelief. 'Dallas was trying to *blackmail* them. You *all* were. How is that the right thing?'

'What blackmail?' said Fletch, frowning.

'We weren't trying to blackmail no one,' Tammy added.

'Hang on,' I said. 'Dallas hired Justin Quinn to star in the kiddie porn movie, then he recruited Sparks to steal the laptop once the movie was made so he could force The Holy Brethren to pay up. It was a scam. No point trying to hide it now.'

'That's bullshit,' Fletch said. 'Dall wanted to give the laptop to the coppers. He wanted The Holy Brethren to go down. He wanted them *busted*. That was his plan.'

I shook my head, confused.

'That's why me and Dall made that movie,' Tammy said. 'Because we wanted as much dirt on them as possible. Getting Jussie on board for the blow job wasn't easy, but he went along in the end.'

A nurse I didn't recognise pulled back the curtain and checked Tammy's blood pressure and drip bag.

'But Sparks never mentioned anything about that,' I said when she was gone.

'Sparks wasn't in on it,' Fletch said. 'Dall just hired him to steal the laptop.'

I nodded, remembering Sparks saying he was just a ring-in. From that I'd assumed the laptop was part of a scam. It had never entered my mind that Dallas Boyd had justice in his sights.

'Is this about his sister?' I said.

'Yeah, her and Derek Jardine,' said Tammy. 'Derek and Dall were best mates. Both of them got recruited by The Holy Brethren when they came out of Malmsbury. Derek went to the Gold Coast and started working as a scout up there and Dallas came to St Kilda. They used to keep in contact on the phone and through email, but then all of a sudden Derek stopped returning calls and emails. So Dallas went up to Queensland to look for him and found out he'd been bashed to death.'

Suddenly it all fell into place. I remembered Will Novak saying that Dallas had given him an ultimatum: either jump on board or go down with them. He never said anything about blackmail.

'Go on,' I said. 'What happened when he came back?'

'He was furious,' she said. 'Said they were to blame, that they'd killed him.'

'Who, The Holy Brethren?'

'Yes! Either them or some lowlife paedophile. It didn't matter to Dallas. Far as he was concerned it was all the same thing. So not long after that, when Rachel got sick and we found out she had chlamydia, he went right off. Said he was gonna get her back and take down the whole lot of them.'

She waved a shaky hand towards a water bottle next to her bed. Fletch passed it to her and helped her take a sip.

'I thought it was just hot air,' he said, screwing the cap back on the bottle. 'But a few weeks later he started working on his plan. That was Dall, for ya. No bullshit artist.'

I nodded respectfully.

'So why did you need the laptop?' I asked. 'Why not just keep copies of the movies?'

'Simple,' Fletch said. 'The copies are edited. Ya can't see people's faces, only the kids. But Dall knew that the laptop had the master copies on it, plus who knows what else.'

'Why didn't you tell me any of this when I came to see you?' I asked, frowning at Tammy.

'Because you were with Will Novak,' she said, her voice croaky. 'And we were suss on him since it happened. See, Dall went to meet him after he left us at Macca's. Will was supposed to go with Dall to meet Sparks and do the exchange, then take the laptop to the cops. That was his part in the whole thing. At least, that's what Dall thought he was gonna do. Obviously Will had other ideas.'

Shaking her head, she blinked away tears.

'So he was playin' both sides,' Fletch said. 'When you showed up on our doorstep, we figured youse was workin' together. That's when we put it all together and realised it had to be Novak, since he was askin' questions as though he knew nothin' when all along he knew exactly what was goin' on.'

'That's right,' Tammy said. 'That's why I kept my mouth shut, because I knew Will was there to see how much I knew and how much I told ya. So I only told ya what I knew was safe. Sneaky fuckin' dog.'

Letting out a long breath of fatigue, I thought about how cunning Will Novak had been to trick everyone, even his own people.

'Well, you can trust *me*,' I said, giving them both a business card. I pulled back the curtain then looked at Fletch. 'Look after her, mate. Dall would've wanted that.'

'I will,' he said, sliding the card in his pocket. 'See ya round, hey.'

I caught a cab back to St Kilda and picked up my car, which was still parked opposite the CARS hostel. Crime scene tape was strung up across the front of the building, three police cars in the car park. I hoped Novak's involvement in the killing and his links with The Holy Brethren didn't ruin the hostel for good, but I wasn't optimistic.

Just as I started the engine, my phone rang. It was Sarah Harrigan from Child Protection.

'Thought you'd want to know,' she said. 'We've got a warrant to remove Rachel Boyd from the flat.'

'When?'

'Next week,' she said. 'We'll be assembling in the car park at six next Friday morning. Fridays are always better because it means we can get them into foster care over the weekend.'

'Shit,' I said, unsure how to feel.

'I couldn't tell you before because it wasn't signed off,' she said. 'But with everything that happened down there at CARS this morning, we were able to light a match under the director's arse and get a decision made. Anyway, we got the request order signed and I'm just leaving the magistrates court now with the warrant. You're the first person I've called.'

'Thank you,' I said. 'I'll be there.'

# 37

PHYSICALLY THE DOG ALREADY looked much healthier than when I'd last seen him. It had only been a few days but a good bath and decent food had done wonders. I stood outside the cage, staring at the bull mastiff, the only witness to Sparks' murder. Right now he was asleep, curled up on a blanket like a prisoner in his tiny cell. I watched for a long moment, wondering if this was the right thing to do.

The woman in reception had volunteered to show me the range of dogs on offer, but I'd declined, preferring to be alone. I tapped the cage and Hooch opened his eyes, then tilted his head, as if trying to recognise a familiar face.

'Hooch,' I said. 'Remember me?'

He trotted over to the cage door and I squatted eye to eye with him, speaking in a cheerful voice. 'Who's a good boy? Want some tucker?'

I pulled out a packet of Smacko strips and slipped one through the wire mesh. He sniffed at it suspiciously, then took it from my grasp. After a few more strips, I put my fingers through the wire and he licked at them.

I called out to the woman on reception and told her I wanted to take him home.

'He'll be hard work,' she said, sliding a key in the lock. 'You'll need to train him, walk him every day.'

'I know.'

'Hope you've got a big backyard.'

I pictured Hooch in my tiny apartment, curled up on the rug, fighting Prince for space. It was better than a cell. The door opened and he bounded out, leapt up at me, paws pressed against my chest, tongue lashing my cheek.

The drive back from the dog shelter took me through the bayside suburbs along the Nepean Highway. It was late afternoon and a cool change was on the way. Grey clouds plumed in the west and I could almost smell the rain. It was about time. The relentless heat had left the city scorched and drained. More than a million hectares of bushland had burnt in some of the worst fires on record. Even in the city, everywhere I looked front lawns were dry, nature strips a patchwork of dead grass and dust. Trees appeared limp and thirsty, and some had died completely. In the rear-view mirror, I watched Hooch in the back seat, head out the window, lips flapping in the breeze. Already slobber lacquered the window but I didn't care. A new life was on the horizon and I felt a level of freedom that I hadn't felt in years.

When Cold Chisel's 'Khe Sanh' came on the radio I cranked the volume, not caring what the young girls in the Alfa convertible next to me thought. No matter how many times I heard Barnesy's earthy vocals in the opening verse I never tired of it, never found it clichéd. To me it was a timeless piece of musical storytelling, as powerful now as it had been to the Vietnam vets thirty years beforehand. If only kids like Johnno had any idea. Driving through Mordialloc, about twenty-five kilometres from home, I thought about Dad and my brother and how the song symbolised an era and a generation.

When the last plane had finally left Sydney, I killed the radio, inserted my earpiece and dialled the number.

'Hello, Dad,' I said when he answered.

'Anthony, is that you?'

'No, it's me. Rubens.'

'Oh,' he said, sounding disappointed. He had every right to be.

'I just wanted to call, in case you see anything on the news. I've been working a case down here and, um, it's Ella, she's been in hospital.'

'Hospital? Is she okay?'

'Yeah, she's all right. She was discharged yesterday. She's at home resting.'

Outside the Sandringham Hotel traffic slowed to a crawl as a parade of high school students stepped off a bus and scattered across the road. I waited for a break in the pack before I continued.

'I know I haven't been around much lately, Dad. I'd like to visit soon, spend a bit more time together.'

'Okay.'

'Maybe on the weekend. I could tell you all about it then, if you like?'

'Sure.'

We were silent then and I knew what he was thinking.

'I'll have more time now. I want to help out a bit with Mum. We'll get her out of there, one day.'

'That'd be nice, you helping more.'

'I mean it.'

'Hope so.'

Silence again.

'What about Ella? How're things with you two? I didn't speak to her that much at the birthday.'

'I know. Things are getting better, I think. I'm meeting her for dinner tonight.'

'Ah, that's the way,' he said, a sense of excitement in his tone.

I felt an internal warmth. 'Dad?'

'Yes, son.'

'There's something else I want to ask you about. Remember Jacko, my old mate from Benalla?'

There was a long silence. I pictured my father with his eyes closed, trying to push away the images and the memories.

'The camping trip,' he finally said.

'Yeah. You remember it?' I asked, knowing the answer.

'Of course. Why?'

'Because I need you to explain some things to me. Things I don't understand.'

'Like what?'

'Well, best we do it over a beer or two, huh?'

Again he was silent and I was about to tell him to forget it when he said, 'Sure, I'd like that.'

I ended the call then, pleased with myself. Dad and I would be fine, and so would Anthony. We were a team, a family. And we would prevail. Of this I was sure.

A few minutes after two I arrived in Brighton and parked opposite a service station. Hooch was feeling the heat, panting, drooling. We crossed the street and found a bucket of water. The pumps were full and I watched my niece work the till through the window. Chloe's part-time place of employment was an old-fashioned service station and still provided driveway assistance. Wouldn't take the sting out of fuel prices though.

Hooch emptied half the bucket in no time, lapping the water loudly, then belched. We walked to a garden bed and stood by Chloe's car, waiting for her to finish work. Hooch sniffed at a bush then cocked his leg and I wondered whether dogs learnt to do this or if it was a natural instinct. There would be a lot of learning, I decided. Getting to know my new friend. Training him, walking, bonding.

Chloe wandered out, then stopped when she saw me standing by her car.

'Uncle Ruby, what are you doing here?' Her eyes dropped to my neck. 'What happened to you? Dad said you got hurt.'

'It's nothing. Just a cut, a few stitches.'

'Ouch. What about Ella?'

'She's okay now. They kept her overnight but she's home.'

I wondered how much Anthony had told the kids, or what they'd read in the papers. I tugged Hooch's lead and he stepped out from behind the car.

'Got a new buddy,' I said. 'Thought I'd introduce you. S'pose you'll be cousins, in a way.'

Chloe's eyes widened and a smile stretched her face as Hooch jumped around and lapped at her as she greeted him. Chloe was a looker, even in the uniform. Sporty, full of energy. No wonder the boys loved her.

'He's gorgeous,' she said as I brought him back with the lead. 'What breed?'

'Bull mastiff. Pure, I think.'

She opened the car, threw a plastic bag of clothes on the back seat.

'What's his name?'

'Hooch. Like the movie.'

'What movie?'

'Never mind. Before your time maybe.'

She patted him again, then looked at me, realising I wasn't just there to show her the dog.

'So, you were just in the area?'

'Yeah, I parked over there.' I nodded to my car across the street. 'Want to take a walk? Down the beach.'

Her head tilted, curious, lines creasing her brow. 'A walk?'

'Sure. Just down the beach. I want to tell you something,' I said, uncomfortable, feeling like a deviant.

'Okay. A walk on the beach. Sure.'

We walked past rows of ten-foot fences and huge box hedges hiding million-dollar-plus homes, crossed Beach Road and cut through the foreshore towards the water. Wind gusted and sand spiralled around. It wasn't particularly pleasant, but neither was what I had to say.

'Your dad's worried,' I said. 'Says you're going out a lot. Night-clubs and parties.'

'Yeah, so? I'm twenty years old. Is that what this is about? Dad can't talk to me himself so he sends his cop brother?'

'He just doesn't want anything to happen to you, that's all.'

'Like what, having fun? God forbid I actually enjoy myself.'

Hooch was tugging at the lead towards a flock of seagulls. I wasn't sure what the rules were but decided to let him off. He bounded playfully at the birds, ran towards the water, stopped at the edge, then ran away when it moved up the sand.

Chloe stared out at the bay, wind whipping her hair around. 'What's this really about, Uncle Ruby?' she said. 'I don't see you in . . . well, hardly ever, and all of a sudden you show up at work wanting to talk.'

I removed a parcel from my pocket, handed it to her. 'I brought you something.'

She unwrapped the brown paper bag to reveal a white canister with fluorescent labelling on it.

'Is this what I think it is?' she said, reading the label with a deep frown.

'It's not a pregnancy test.'

'Very funny. I can see that.'

'It's a reagent test kit. They're not totally reliable, but they're a good guide. At the very least, it sends a message that you care about what you –'

'Wait a second,' she said, stuffing the canister back in the bag. 'Let me get this right. This is a *pill* tester.'

'That's right. Tells you what the dominant ingredient is.'

Hooch bounded back, barked at us. It was more of a yelp than anything. He barked again and I remembered Sparks throwing the stick for him in the park. I found a stick, threw it along the sand, and we started walking again.

'This is bullshit,' Chloe said. 'My dad thinks I'm using drugs, just because I go to nightclubs. God, everyone goes to night-clubs. I mean, hello, that's what you do when you're twenty. What does he want me to do on the weekend, stay at home and read the *Age* like a sixty-year-old?' She handed the parcel back and kept walking. 'I can't believe he sent you. He's such a wanker.'

I jogged to catch up. 'It's not him, Chloe. Your dad doesn't think you're using drugs.'

She stopped and shook her head. 'Then what is it?'

'I do.'

'You –?' She frowned at me. 'Uncle Ruby, what the –'

'Your dad doesn't know I'm here,' I said, giving the parcel back. 'Please take it, Chloe. Keep it and use it.'

She went to reply but I stopped her. 'Look, you can't bullshit me. I know how it is. I know what the dance clubs are like for a pretty girl like you. They're probably safer and more enjoyable than your average drinking swill. You don't have guys groping you, sleazing onto your friends. No fights. Everyone's there to party and hear the music. Isn't that what you say? It's all about the tunes?'

'Sounds like you've been a few times,' she said.

'More than a few, Chloe. St Kilda's my patch. Most people have no idea how big this thing is unless they're in it. I've been doing this job almost twenty years now, and I've brought down some of the biggest gangsters in the country. It hasn't always been easy,' I said, tapping my left shoulder. 'I nearly died for it, and you know what, it's taken me this long to realise it doesn't matter what we do, we'll never stop it. We'll probably never even be able to slow it. It's too big.'

She waited, unsure how far to commit.

'Am I right?'

'Wouldn't be a problem if they were legal,' she said.

'Maybe not, but until then they are illegal and no one can guarantee what's in them. Think you're taking ecstasy and all of a sudden you end up seeing monsters. Could be anything in pills these days. Ketamine. LSD. Worse.' I nodded to the test kit in her hands. 'There's a dark side to it, Chloe. People overdose. Have strokes. Heart attacks. Some even die.'

She looked away then and I knew there was no point in lecturing her any further.

'So anyway, I figure if you're going to do it, you might as well have some idea about what you're taking.'

She unwrapped the parcel again and studied the canister label with a smirk.

'This is such a trip. I thought you'd bloody arrest me.'

'Could've told you horror stories, shown you pictures. Tried to scare you.'

'Why didn't you?'

'Wouldn't have worked. Never does.'

'So instead you're giving me this?' she said.

'I'm not giving you anything. You bought that yourself, from a bong shop. Understand?'

'Ah, right. A bong shop.'

I whistled for Hooch, clipped him to the lead and we headed up the beach, back towards the car.

'Find a hiding spot for that, Chloe. A good one. Not your drawer.'

'Okay.'

'You don't want your parents finding it. Or your drugs. They'll freak. Send you to Tasmania.'

'What's in Tasmania?'

'Nothing.'

She laughed.

'And don't score in clubs. Only buy from people you know.'

'I know.'

'And don't ever sell them.'

She scoffed. 'Oh, so now I'm a dealer? What next, the first female Don?'

'I'm just telling you. We send our undercover guys into the clubs every weekend. It's like shooting fish in a barrel.'

She laughed again, louder this time, and pointed at Hooch's backside. 'Yeah right, you cops stand out like dogs' balls.'

Now I laughed. She was right. It wasn't something you could fake.

'You're a good kid, Chloe. Smart. Don't fuck that up.'

'I won't. Study's important to me. I'm halfway to an Honours in Commerce. After that I'll count beans for a living. For now, weekends are my playtime. That's it.'

We crossed Beach Road and walked slowly by the millionaires' village. I felt a connection with her, a bridge. I knew she'd be fine.

'Guess what,' I said, removing an envelope from my pocket. 'I got two tickets to Wolfmother.'

'Really?'

'Yeah, I was going to take Ella, but we can't make it and I thought you might want to go. They're playing at the Espy next week. You should take your dad,' I said, handing her the envelope.

'Thanks,' she said, smiling awkwardly, 'but Dad doesn't like Wolfmother. He likes, I don't know, stuff like . . . God, I don't even know what he likes.'

'Exactly.'

After Chloe had stuffed the envelope away there was a moment of silence. She probably wanted to take her boyfriend but that wasn't the deal.

'Look, I don't have a daughter,' I said. 'If I did, I'd want one just like you.'

'Yeah, *right*.'

'I would. And you know what? I'd want her to take me out from time to time. It wouldn't matter where we went. I'd just want to spend some time with her. I know your dad feels the same way about you.'

'You think so?'

'I know so. So take him out and have a good time.'

When we reached the service station I gave her my mobile number and she keyed it into her phone.

'If ever anything goes wrong for you when you're out with your friends, call me,' I said. 'Anything at all, okay?'

'Thank you.'

I tugged Hooch's lead and said, 'I'll be walking him a bit from now on. Might need a buddy. Interested?'

'Sure. What about Ella? Hear you're getting back together?'

'Yeah, we'll see.'

She got in the car, started the engine and wound down the window. 'Thanks again.'

'We never had this conversation, Chloe.'

'What conversation?'

She smiled cheekily, winked at me and drove out of the forecourt.

# 38

ST KILDA FELT DIFFERENT that Saturday, everything still. Traffic on the Esplanade was light, the beach near empty. Even Luna Park was unusually silent. No music, no screams. After months of almost relentless heat there was a crisp breeze in the air, reminding me that everything came to an end.

Hooch tugged at the lead, pulling me towards the water. Already I knew he would grow into a powerful dog, and a sense of pride filled my gait as we crossed the grassy foreshore together. Funny how life dealt its cards, I mused. Working the Dallas Boyd case had been a lesson in irony. Through the loss of life came the saving of life, and the clarification of my own. Hooch was the perfect reminder of this. I no longer had certainty in my career, but I didn't mind.

When that call came through over the radio and I found Dallas Boyd's body in the loading bay at the rear of Café Vit, everything changed. I'd been back on deck only a month and thought I was ready for anything, but I was wrong. The case had cost me dearly. I'd fallen out with my boss, made vital mistakes in the investigation, and for the second time in my career I'd almost lost my life.

But seeing Ella in hospital was the final straw. From then on the direction of my life would change forever.

*To get what you want, you have to know what you want. Think carefully about what you want, for knowing what you want is often harder than getting it.* As I guided Hooch around to the Stokehouse courtyard, I finally understood my mother's wisdom.

'Easy boy,' I said, tying Hooch to a palm tree and heading inside.

As usual, Logan was there, loading a dishwasher and wiping down the bar. He smiled as I approached, then noticed the bandage on my neck. 'Hey big fella, I heard you copped a bit of a flogging. Didn't think I'd see you for a while.'

'It's been a big week,' I said. 'And I'm rooted.'

'You look it, man. Maybe you need a break.'

'Yeah, but give me a beer first.'

Logan filled a pot and handed it over, nodding quickly, no payment needed. My hand trembled as I lifted the glass to my lips and I had to rest it back on the bar.

While Logan served some other customers, I watched a television news report about the web of paedophiles netted over the past few days. The sound was muted but it wasn't hard to read what was happening. Will Novak had been charged with murder and was on remand. Together with his cooperation, the laptop had provided enough evidence to arrest the priest, Miles Jorgensen, along with several other staff at Back Outside, all members of The Holy Brethren. Perhaps more significantly, a senior bureaucrat from the health minister's office had also been implicated. No charges had been laid as yet, but the bureaucrat's face had been all over the news and the wheels were in motion to bring him down for receiving kickbacks after advising the minister to approve the joint-funding package to Back Outside and CARS the previous year. In response to this, as well as the revelations about the physical abuse Dallas Boyd had suffered, the state government had promised a full-scale inquiry into the Child Protection system in Victoria. To top it off,

324

Vincent Rowe had been charged with molestation and Rachel Boyd was in foster care, out of harm's way. For now, at least.

It wasn't an ideal outcome but one I thought Dallas would still have been proud of. Perhaps I would've been pleased too had I not been so badly duped by Novak. It was a betrayal of trust I didn't think I'd ever recover from.

'Cool change is finally coming,' Logan said, leaning on the bar, watching the horizon. 'They say it might even snow on the Alps tonight, help put all the fires out. Can you imagine that, snow in February?'

'A miracle,' I said. 'It's probably all that could've done it.'

He gestured towards the water in the bay, which was sloshing in chaotic swirls as a cold southerly swept in. Clouds gathered in the distance, thunder rumbling somewhere beyond. There would be no more blood sunsets for a while, hopefully not for the rest of the year. Autumn and winter were on the way, and the city was ready for it.

'People say it's ugly when it's like that,' Logan said. 'But I like it. It's mysterious and brooding at the same time. The water actually looks dangerous, like the mask has been removed.'

I'd never thought about it like that before, but I had to agree.

'Supposed to be meeting Ella again,' I said. 'Reckon you could make her a drink?'

'Sure, the usual?'

'Nah, probably just a soda to start with, then we'll see what she —' I stopped when I saw her walking along the path towards the courtyard. 'Here she comes.'

Logan made the drink and slid it across the bar but didn't offer me one.

'You don't need another glass just yet,' he said with a wink. 'Yours is still half full.'

'Thanks. You're a good man, Logan,' I said.

I carried the drinks out to Ella, who peeled off her sunglasses and kissed me gently on the cheek.

'How're the stitches?' she asked, eyeing my neck.

'Itchy.'

'Jenny said you had to have them redone.'

I nodded and a long silence followed. I'd figured it would be awkward like this until she knew I was serious about my decision. She'd said she didn't blame me for what had happened, but I suspected she was just being polite. What she'd really meant was that our relationship would remain in limbo until I could prove I was ready for a change. That wasn't a problem any more. I knew *exactly* what I wanted.

Sipping my beer, I slid a copy of the *Police Gazette* across the table, open to the job opportunities section, where I'd high-lighted a position on offer at headquarters.

'What's this?' she asked.

'There's a job going at Prisoner Movements. I've put in for it.'

She looked at me, unsure what I was telling her.

'It's a desk job,' I said. 'All I'd have to do is keep records on the prisoners and liaise with government and the brass. No street action.'

'So no more investigations?'

'Maybe a bit of assistance to the Prison Squad, but no hands-on work.'

She read the page again, as if it could confirm or dispute my answer.

'So you're leaving St Kilda?'

'If I get the job.'

'What if you don't?'

'Then I'm still done, Ella. I'll stay on carer's leave for as long as I can. Either way, I'm out. Finished. I'm not going back to St Kilda.'

'But . . .' She put the page down and stared out over the bay, the wind blowing strands of hair across her face. I followed her line of sight and saw an ocean liner coming into port.

'Are you doing this for me?' she asked.

'No. For us.'

Hooch startled me by barking from behind the palm tree. When no one responded Ella lowered her voice and asked if I knew whose dog it was.

'Ah, that's the other thing I wanted to talk to you about,' I said. I explained how Hooch fitted into the case, how Sparks had been murdered and how the dog would most likely be destroyed if he didn't find a home. I ended the story with my visit to the animal shelter and my decision to adopt him. I didn't tell her about my talk with Chloe or my phone call to Dad because I figured – or at least hoped – there would be time for that later.

'He's still a puppy,' I said, not sensing support. 'And now I've got time to train him, get him socialised.'

'What about Prince?'

'It's not Prince I'm worried about. Lots of people own dogs and cats.'

'Well, what about your apartment? It's barely big enough for you.'

I nodded. 'That's the only issue. I mean, I've got the beach and the park nearby, but it's not the same. Dogs need space, a piece of dirt to call their own.'

'So what are you going to do?'

'I'll just have to make do, see how it goes. If it doesn't work out, at least I've tried.'

Ella stared at Hooch for a long moment. A cold wind blew leaves about in mini whirlwinds. Specks of rain dotted the path. The water in the bay was now a deep charcoal and looked like a giant pool of oil sloshing about. People scurried for shelter as the cool change rolled in. St Kilda's mask had finally been lifted and the blood sunset extinguished, but Ella made no attempt to move.

Nor did Hooch. He sat at the base of the palm tree, head bowed, eyes on the ground, sensing her judgement. Finally she smiled at me and said, 'Who says we have to live in an apartment?'

# ACKNOWLEDGEMENTS

*Blood Sunset* is the culmination of a lot of hard work and commitment from many people, without whom publication would not have been possible.

Firstly, to Louise Thurtell, Clara Finlay, Nicola O'Shea and the whole crew at Allen & Unwin, you are true professionals and I thank you for your support and enthusiasm throughout the development of this book.

To the judges and sponsors of *The Australian/*Vogel Award, my sincere thanks for your support of emerging writers.

To Vikki Petraitis, true-crime writer and bona fide expert on paedophiles and forensic procedure, I am very grateful for your mentoring during the early stages of writing. Likewise, thanks to Dr Shelley Robertson at the Victorian Institute of Forensic Medicine, for your advice and the guided tour of the institute.

To Meera Govil at the Eltham Bookshop: you show real interest in all the writers you meet, and we appreciate it.

To Joel Becker, Mary Napier and the team at the Victorian Writers Centre: keep up the great work.

To the handful of close friends who read the manuscript in its early stages and provided valuable feedback, I hope you enjoy the finished product!

To my immediate and extended family, your support is invaluable.

To all the readers who have written to me or spoken to me at festivals, thanks for your comments and praise. I hope you like *Blood Sunset* as much as *Head Shot*.

And finally, to my editor in chief, Liz, you are the first and last words on every page.